RUINWASTER'S
BANE

THE ANNALS OF THE LAST EMISSARY

BOOK ONE

RUINWASTER'S
BANE

THE ANNALS OF THE LAST EMISSARY

BOOK ONE

J. JASON HICKS

DASMURWIL PROPERTIES LLC

Eden Prairie, Minnesota
Tucson, Arizona

For information about this title or to order other books and/or electronic media, contact the publisher:

Dasmurwil Properties LLC
Tucson, Arizona USA
www.jjasonhicks.com

Cover art by Jeff Brown
Cover design by Jeff Brown

Book interior design by Open Book Design LLC

Original map design by J. Jason Hicks

Digital map design by Ryan Thompson

Digital/Leather map design by Sarah Edwards

Names: Hicks, J. Jason, Author
Title: Ruinwaster's Bane / J. Jason Hicks
Identifiers: LCCN 2023902146 | ISBN 978-1-960481-08-5 (hardback) |
ISBN 978-1-960481-07-8 (paperback) | ISBN 978-1-960481-06-1 (ebook)
Series: The Annals of the Last Emissary
Subjects: | BISAC: FICTION / Fantasy / Epic | GSAFD: Fantasy Fiction.
LC Record available at https://lccn.loc.gov/2023902146

Library of Congress Control Number: 2023902146

978-1-960481-08-5 Hardcover
978-1-960481-07-8 Paperback
978-1-960481-06-1 eBook
978-1-960481-05-4 Audiobook

FIRST EDITION
SEPTEMBER, 2023

For
Jennifer Rebekah

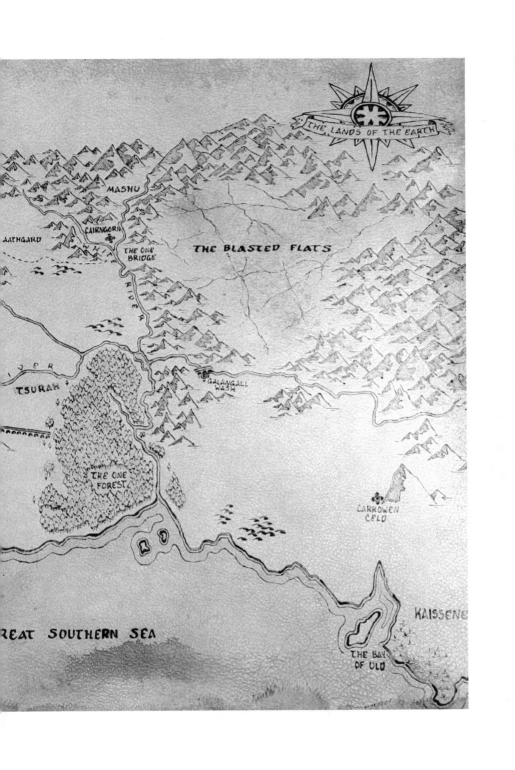

CONTENTS

PART I
PASSAGE

1

〜〜

AN INTERRUPTED WAKE

In an instant, his world contracted. The broad chambers that defined his existence were collapsing in. It was as if an essential support had been suddenly knocked away. And with its strength gone, a series of sudden and unexpected ruptures flooded whole segments of his life. Possibilities and expectations he had for his future were lost in the deluge. The seams that held the remaining spaces together creaked and groaned. Aenguz struggled for any answer to reclaim what remained of his life.

His father's sudden death on their last hunt was the first chamber that was lost. Aenguz tried to imagine that he hadn't insisted on one final adventure with his father before his mating to Selene. Both men seemed to sense that their relationship was shifting into a new season. Time alone with the Ruler of the Akkeidii and the Lord of the Sidor Clan was rare, even for Aenguz. That was all he craved. Time alone with his father.

But that was why the walls of Mashuan Limestone in his father's childhood bedroom were so familiar. Aenguz had stayed here with his grandparents as a boy when Sairik was pulled away by clan or Akkeidii duties. It had been years since he had slept here but the memories of his times here were familiar and sound.

Twenty-two winters had come and gone for Aenguz. The responsibilities of lordship should have become his full-time learning. He could mate Selene and try for children if the blight cast on creation passed over them. He could plumb the lore of his people. He could learn to defend the Two Lands from without and within.

Now, those possibilities were submerging.

He shouldered the blame of his father's loss, felt its weight, and readied his frame to add it to the other. The loss of his mother when he was barely two. It was a childlike reasoning that formed the logic of that guilt, an assumption of culpability. Even though it wasn't true, it felt true to him. It was as familiar as the walls.

Aenguz's head pulled down like a stone, like a simple anchor that threatened to draw him down instead of holding him steady and secure against the current. There seemed to be no bottom to his pool of losses. The unrelenting pain and denuding exhaustion intensified the pressure in his skull. His neck bent under the weight. He rested his head in the heel of his right hand. His elbow bore into his knee. He leaned his weight to the right toward the foot of the pallet. In the rapidly shrinking world, the small, spartan bedroom felt like the smallest corner in all the Lands of the Earth.

The thrum of his pulse and his short panting breaths tinged his abraded nerves. They traced every nook and cranny of his wound. The beating anguish reminded him each moment of his fault, his failure at the forge.

His left arm was an exposed sleeve of crimson, purple, and black. Red lines traced over muscle. Charred remnants of flesh peeled away like burned parchment. It looked as if he had reached into a narrow gullet of hell. As if he was trying to reach for some periapt that might save his father or reclaim the world. But it lay just out of reach and taunted Aenguz beyond his fingertips. His arm was bent, burned, and fused to his side. His fist was curled shut, and it clutched emptiness into a fused mute claw. His shield arm was stripped and useless.

It left him hopelessly vulnerable. With Sairik gone, a Challenge would be called for the right to rule. If Aenguz was whole, it would have likely been no more than a formality. Sairik was beloved. Aenguz was the hope of the future though largely unproven. He had passed the Rites of Passage and had been proclaimed a Warrior. Aenguz's succession ceremony would have been brief. And he would not have been alone. He would have been surrounded by others to help him. His grandparents, his clan, his friends, the Honored Guard, the Warriors. Stability and security for the clans and the Akkeidii would have been fait accompli.

But his grief allowed in an arrogance that threatened it all. All his father had built in smoothing the divisions between the clans. Aenguz endangered it all by attempting a rite that was forbidden to him.

Between the pyres and the internment, he had sought to preserve the memory of his father. Sought to immortalize him with the sacred metal of the Mashu. He meant to craft a death mask for Sairik. A permanent totem for his father.

But the arcane art was beyond him. It was beyond the loremasters who had taught him. In a way, he had tried to expiate his supposed guilt by immortalizing his father's memory. The lore was known to be lost, but he thought he had seen an answer in the Lay of *Montmorillionite*. But the metal objected to the attempt. The mystical steel had refused him. It had rejected him in a fundamental way. Could he still be a Warrior if the metal had responded so? His scoured arm told him no.

Aenguz raised his head and delicately pulled away the remaining soiled bandages from his arm. He let them drop like discarded ribbons. Suppurations glistened and left a sickening sheen. Without his arm, without the ability to hold a shield or fight, never mind the indictment of the metal, he would never survive a Challenge. Even if he lost the Challenge but somehow survived, he would most certainly relinquish his warriorhood. And he could not lead the clan if he was no longer a Warrior. The places his life turned, in the wake of the flooding chambers, were filled with self-revulsion and shame.

He needed more and better healing than the bandages and the knotted herbs could provide. He plucked the green burrs out from the creases. Sweat sluiced into his eyes and made the edges of everything bleary. It blended with the tears he held for the inevitable loss of Selene.

Even if he found a way to save his wounded arm, that piece of the plan was nascent and uncertain, he still had to survive the Challenge. And if he lost the Challenge but preserved his life, she could not be his. She would be claimed, along with the other marriageable maids of the Sidor Clan, by the Challenger and his clan. He did not know how he could weather the loss of rule or reconcile the repudiation of the metal. It would be too much. Even if she wasn't claimed, he couldn't expect her to love him. Too much of his promised life would be lost. Staying alive would not be enough. There was no solution where Selene remained a part of his world.

"No, no, you must leave those, Aeng." His grandmother, Hertha, rushed into the room and dropped the tray down onto the narrow table beneath the high transept window. The stone pitcher rocked. The empty mug tipped over. She hurried down to his feet and gathered up the discarded bandages and bloodied herbs.

The table was stacked with other medicated wraps and a confusion of stalks and buds. Aenguz had heard the desperate pleading of Sidor mothers and their betrothed daughters. In the slurry of days after his accident, they came to appeal to Hertha to protect them, and heal Aenguz, to forestall the Challenge. They bore whatever unguents and healing flora they had in supplication to help the son of their fallen lord. Their daughters' betrothals would be nullified if Aenguz failed in the Challenge. His actions were radiating outward into the Sidor Clan like a miasma of doom. But those bandages and herbs were for lesser wounds.

"I need *morillion*," Aenguz's voice scraped like dry rock.

Hertha braced on the edge of the pallet and climbed up as if she was ascending from her own private well of sorrow. She set the collected remains on the table beside a bowl and a mortar and poured Aenguz some water. She handed him the cup as if it took the last of her strength.

His grandmother had aged, it seemed, a score of years in the last span of days. For years, she had always looked the same to him as if time had passed over her in a measure of grace. A kind of gift to her for bearing Sairik the eventual Ruler of the Akkeidii. Being the mate of his grandfather, the Lord of the Deerherds, added to her soulful power. Love and beneficence radiated from her. She was quick to smile, familiar with joy. Her heart glowed.

But now, her tightly-bound iron-gray hair was fraying. Jagged strands of white erupted from the usual smooth dome into a kind of frail headdress. The lines around her dark eyes looked as if they were carved by something inconceivably sharp and precise. Grief and worry had carved those lines more than age. The Clan Mother of the Akkeidii looked like a scattered servant.

Aenguz wished the cool water would flow directly into his arm and mitigate the heat. He would have to get past the pain until enough *morillion* could be brought to him.

Dahlward, Aenguz's grandfather and the Lord of the Deerherds, entered his son's old room.

"Aenguz, lay down. You must rest." The timbre of his voice resonated with authority. His pronouncement chased the gravid silence from the room.

His simple ochre robe was cinched tight at his waist. The several cords marked his rank. Strands of dull colors were woven in with the pale beige rope. The cords looked like they might cut him in two. He looked more like an ascetic who glimpsed indescribable things beyond the edges of sanity. The white goatee and unkempt eyebrows could not obscure his scowl.

"Call for the Deerherds. I need their *morillion*," Aenguz demanded gently. He passed the stone mug back to his grandmother. He did not ask why the Deerherds hadn't been called sooner. He knew that such a large amount of the rare loam would be difficult to cull from their ranks. And using so much of the healing loam, even for the son of the Ruler of the Akkeidii, would be extravagant for just one person, one wound. And too, there was a risk of madness in using so large an amount. The medicinal effects might be rendered moot by the insanity induced. That risk was tertiary. There was another matter. His failure at the forge endeavoring to craft his father's death mask, and the moral repercussion of attempting such a rite - without his father's assent or that of the loremasters, seemed to affirm that the sacred metal had passed a harsh judgment on him that could not or should not be ignored. Too much risked the mind. And using any amount of *morillion* on such a large wound would be considered an unconscionable waste.

Dahlward's concern brought his goatee and his eyebrows together near enough to touch. He moved to Hertha and placed an arm around her. Her pleading eyes filled as she looked up at him. Dahlward tugged at a small pouch between the folds in his robe. What little *morillion* he had left could not cover Aenguz's arm.

"The Deerherds are gone. The last of our herd has left already for the Valley of Gathering," Dahlward said.

"Already left?" Aenguz processed thickly, trying to count the past days. "What day is it?"

"The Rites of Passage will take place in two days. The first full moon of spring arrives in five days. The Sidor's caravan leaves on the morrow for the Gathering."

Time had contracted on Aenguz. More of the world was shrinking away. The Rites of Passage. If he did not fulfill his father's responsibility, he would cede the Challenge automatically. Waves of desecration were congregating, readying to roll out from him. He needed to turn the surge.

"Then I must make for the Valley of Gathering right away. Where are my boots?" He searched the floor and tested the strength in his legs from the edge of the bed.

The couple stared at Aenguz as if he had just said that he would scale the tallest peak in the Mashu barefoot. Hertha's tears flowed easily now. Tremors shook her lips and rippled her eyes. Dahlward's eyes, hardened by grief, welled.

"You are in no condition to go," his grandfather said with a mixture of compassion and futility. "Rest. Heal."

But Aenguz could do neither of those things. Time was running short. He had to stem the losses and right his mistakes.

"It is the only option." What life would be left for him if he stayed here? How could he live with the shame? With his guilt?

Aenguz strained to reach the foot of the bed. The raw, taut wound burned and wailed. His boots were there. He dragged himself over with his elbow. Aenguz reached down and swung them one at a time to his feet.

"The roads are closed now at night until the Gathering," Dahlward said flatly. "Only Deerherds shepherding the roe deer may pass on them. The watch is set."

Aenguz fumbled with the doe skin boot. The sheer pain depleted his reserves and brought him up from the task panting and drenched again with sweat. He might have been able to pull the boot on with one hand if he was otherwise whole if his left arm was merely incapacitated. But with his hand wretched as it was, lacing them would be impossible. They limped over beside his feet.

His head drooped. He was only swaddled in a loose white cloth. He needed clothes.

"I need leggings and a shirt."

When the pair did not budge, Aenguz leaned forward and pressed to stand. His legs were stiff, but he was not so far removed from the trials of his own Rites of Passage, and warrior training for them to have forgotten all their strength. The floor seemed to pitch as if on a storm-churned sea.

They stepped toward him, ready to catch him. Hertha warded his warped arm. Dahlward reached to Aenguz's right, ready to steady him. He offered his thin and sturdy frame to support or catch him if he fell. Poised as they were they looked like they had stepped onto the deck of the storm-doomed ship with their grandson.

"Aeng, you cannot go. You cannot-" Die too.

Aenguz guessed the end of her sentence by the devastated contortion of her face. The fruition of her life was being truncated right before her eyes.

He took slow, deliberate steps to the table, took the pitcher, and drank in measured gulps. Then he emptied the bowl onto the spent bandages and poured some water in the bowl and splashed water on his face. The droplets that rained down on his left arm were a scorching stream of molten lead. He pivoted quickly to his right as he sluiced the sweat away.

When he turned back to his grandparents, they had found no way to move.

———— ◆ ————

"I NEED CLOTHES, AND I need help with my boots. And where is my weapon?" He walked to the door. His grandparents may have exchanged glances.

Aenguz walked out of the room and to the head of the stairs. He braced his right hand against the wall and started navigating down the stone steps.

Hertha hovered at his left side. Dahlward slid past ahead of them. He disappeared into the first of three doorways at the base of the stair. Aenguz reached the hall and shrugged his grandmother back. She turned back up the stair.

Vague hints of dusk came in from the clotted rooms. The spring day was receding and shrinking the world further. Racks of barrels were stacked within. Hocks of cured and smoked meats dangled here and there. Their piquant salty flavor mixed with the wood and filled the hall. There were baskets and sacks of rough milled grains. Sturdy fabrics and leathers were piled in the last room. This food and the aged ales would have been the most prized items that his father would have assembled for the son of the Ruler of the Akkeidii and his bride. Sairik must have been assembling these things here for weeks and preparing the ales for months. The joy they all must have shared hiding such a rich hoard for the wedding feast.

He felt the essence of his father here, and his grief only dilated. The constant reminder for his grandparents of their loss and also Aenguz's failure. He had to get clear of it.

In the familiar dining room, everything seemed to lean to the right. The long, wooden table was pressed up against the wall. High-backed chairs were lined alongside it. The room seemed like a captain's mess canted by a fatal wave. On the table was a dark wooden box bound in black iron. His father's coffin. A box for his bones. A bolt of rich black cloth, limned in purple, was folded meticulously beside it. Before it lay a tooled mahogany leather sheath. It was empty and awkward. The *montmorillionite* weapon was long gone beneath the glacier and the earth.

This was one of the last stops for Sairik's remains on his final journey to the Cairngorm. There to be interred with the clan lords of old and the heroes of the Last Battle. A trek that Aenguz might not now get to see through. Another chamber filled.

Dahlward came up beside Aenguz and steadied his grandson with the sturdy pillar of his own denuding grief. He bore a bundle under his arm. He placed a hand on Aenguz's neck, careful of the edges of the wound, and squeezed.

"Has it been returned? Is it intact? Did any of the metal take?" Aenguz's words were labored but reverent as he touched on the fringes of his sacrilege.

"Some. A splash. Most lies splayed on the floor and walls of the smithy. Yes, his skull is at rest."

"What of the loremasters? What punishment do they consider?"

Dahlward took long breaths before answering. "They are still trying to unravel what you have done. They believe the *montmorillionite* is exacting its toll. And with Sairik's death and your pain... Some feel that it is punishment enough. Others are considering other penalties."

The question Aenguz really asked himself was what his father would think about what he was planning. The choices left to him led Aenguz into the face of every rule and tenet of the Akkeidii, of Warriorhood, of the Sidors, and of their former leader. In the narrow space left to him, it was the only place where he could find answers, in things forbidden. In order to save what he lost, what he was losing, Aenguz had to adopt an utter rejection of everything Sairik had tried to build for the Akkeidii and had tried to teach him. Always, his father asked, "How would your choice impact the Akkeidii? How would it impact the Sidor Clan? Your family? And now with Selene – your mate?" Only after all of those considerations, and answered in that order, could Aenguz think about his own needs and wants. What would his father say about the plan he was formulating in the maelstrom of his bereavement?

Aenguz looked to the bundle at Dahlward's side. The Lord of the Deerherds unfurled a docent's robe. A single pale cord dangled from the fabric.

At first Aenguz thought this was an out, Dahlward's answer to the question of Aenguz's survival. Aenguz could have been a Deerherd. He knew the lore from his grandfather. He'd learned about their responsibilities as a child before he'd chosen the Way of the Warrior. Tending and herding the roe deer. Birthing, healing, caring, and culling them. Commanding the herd hounds to manage them. He knew how to see the earliest signs in the turning of the seasons and the ways of the moon. He could even discern between viable and dead seeds. A way to see around the curse of the blight. He could have passed the Deerherd's Rites of Passage with ease.

But Aenguz's course was set at birth. The only son of a clan lord would be a Warrior.

But then he understood Dahlward's gaze. This was a disguise. And more than that, the sharp look told Aenguz that his grandfather meant to help beyond the robe. "Your clothes were ruined."

Hertha came up with Aenguz's boots. She set them down and helped Dahlward get the robe over Aenguz's shoulders. The fabric scored and burned. Aenguz groaned and gritted his teeth. There was no way to straighten the burned arm. In the end, they just draped the robe over his left side.

Dahlward's brow worked. And after a moment, he sent Hertha back for some bandages.

When she returned, Dahlward took the bandages and tucked them in carefully around Aenguz's mottled limb. Then he drew the robe around the arm and cinched the single cord. The red glistening wrist looked like a birthed fawn head poking out from the robe.

He stepped back and said, "Deerherds often bear newborn fawns in their arms when the mother dies. Sometimes the mother dies." A forlorn regret bent Dahlward's tone toward the memory of Aenguz's mother. But he quickly returned to his purpose. "It is out of season but not unheard of. And all the roe deer must be counted."

The strain sapped Aenguz. He staggered to a chair in the corner and lowered himself down carefully. "Where is my weapon? It must be here." Hertha and Dahlward went back to the packed rooms and rooted around for Aenguz's weapon.

Donning the robe was like a repudiation of Warriorhood for Aenguz, and a repudiation of his father. While the possibility of changing course and adopting the Way of the Deerherd would technically be possible for a Warrior with nothing to lose, nothing at stake but his own personal shame, too much rode on Aenguz's succession. Too many depended on him ascending to his prescribed role. He might one day be respected as a

Deerherd, but the legacy of the Sidors would be irrevocably altered. The face of the Akkeidii would be changed completely. He would be alienated, his presence a reminder of all the desecrations his actions had wrought. He had to move forward with his plan. He had to heal his arm. And to do that, he had to make it to the Valley of Gathering.

Where could his weapon be? Aenguz leaned to his right, away from his pain, his failure, from his grandparent's search, and his father's coffin. As he pivoted on the chair, his knuckles brushed something half-hidden behind him. There, perched in the corner, was the unmistakable tooled mahogany scabbard. His weapon. It looked ready to go as if it had been placed there for a long journey ahead. How did it get there?

"I found it. It is here," he called back to his grandparents.

He flipped up the leather flap. The sharp spike poked out. The top of the curved hook bowed at the base of the spike. The keen outer edge and tip of the hook were tucked safely inside. His *montmorillionite* was as clean and perfect as the day it was formed and drawn from the forge.

His grandparents came back. A timid shock clouded their eyes as they came to him. Hertha knelt and slid on Aenguz's boots and tied them. When they were done, Aenguz stood and shouldered his weapon easily. Dahlward pulled the hood up over Aenguz's head. He stepped back and inspected his grandson.

"That will not do," Dahlward said. "They will know a Warrior's weapon instantly."

Dahlward gestured for Aenguz to let his weapon down. Aenguz knew it would be too heavy for Dahlward to handle. He did not possess the necessary lore. Aenguz balanced it upright at his hip. The Lord of the Deerherds uncinched one of his own cords and threaded it under the hook and through the scabbard's flap and then under Aenguz's robe at his waist. He tied it tight and closed his grandson's robe again. The bottom dragged at Aenguz's feet, but it would have to do. The disguise was complete. Or as complete as it would get.

Hertha nodded reluctantly. She was caught between competing exigencies and, like Aenguz, was left with few options. She met Dahlward's, eyes and then realization drained the life out of her.

"No, no," she uttered.

"My light, my dawn, he will need my help. He cannot go alone." His tenderness reached through her grief.

Hertha's head shook side to side but not in a wordless "no." She seemed to be searching for another answer, another hand to help. She looked at all the men who were closest to her, living and dead, and the prospect of losing all three undid her. Tears came in a flood. Her head dropped, and her shoulders collapsed.

Dahlward drew her into his arms. Aenguz placed his right hand on her shoulder. He had no words to add to his grandfather's. Going alone touched on a fear that he could scarcely name. He could not bring himself to even feign dissuading his grandfather. Dahlward was right. Aenguz needed his help.

Hertha gathered a measure of composure and went for a last time to the nearest room with the stagnant wedding gifts. When she returned, she pressed a small, embroidered pouch into Dahlward's hand.

A confused gaze fluttered across his face.

"For the Deerherds, to barter," she said.

Dahlward held the pouch of rare, viable seeds.

"You will need them."

Dahlward nodded and tucked it into a safe place under his robe.

Hertha restrained her sobs. She reached for Aenguz and hugged him not caring about the scald. The bright pain jolted Aenguz. He touched his forehead to the top of her head and hugged her with his right arm.

"You are my grandson. You are the son of the Ruler of the Akkeidii. You are the grandson of the Lord of the Deerherds. Until you are challenged you are the Ruler of the Akkeidii and the Lord of the Sidor Clan. Do not forget that."

He nodded and pulled away from her. Dahlward led the way out of the house. Hertha stood at the door and looked at the two men as if she had just sent them off in an unsound boat into a fatal storm.

2

〰〰

A DESPERATE FLIGHT

The distance from the door of his grandparent's home to the gate across the small high-walled courtyard seemed implausible. With each tenuous step, a new drumbeat added to the rhythm of his pain, and the Valley of Gathering seemed to move further and further away.

Dahlward blocked the crack in the stone doors. He searched the quieting streets. When Aenguz reached him, Dahlward said, "Remember, you are a docent." He pulled the hood closer over Aenguz. "Keep your head down. Whisper as if you are speaking Words of Lore to the newborn." He positioned Aenguz's arm underneath the faux bundle. "Bend your shoulders more if you can. You still look like a Warrior." Aenguz curled his shoulders as much as he could. "Do not speak. If you are addressed, I will speak for you."

Aenguz nodded in between labored breaths.

With that, Dahlward led Aenguz out onto the darkening street.

It was not just his voice or his frame that would give Aenguz away. Anyone who passed close enough would recognize Sairik's son. The amber flecks in his deep brown eyes were a dead giveaway. Empathy and curiosity radiated from them and made him receptive and welcoming. But shades of his grandfather's eccentricity, though his face was thinner due to the recent days of privation, made him pensive as if he bore an obscure dread. As if he had glimpsed the doom at the end of the world and struggled with how to articulate it. Had he been able to choose the path of a Deerherd or a Stonemage that countenance may well have taken over his whole aspect. But Warrior training had hardened him and added a grim confidence. His hair was matted and damp and that hid the fired bronze that flowed within the black. Were he not trying to disguise himself as he was, had he not broken the rules of the *montmorillionite* loremasters, he would have been easily noticeable as his father's son even in the cool twilight.

But Dahlward turned off the main street in front of his home and led Aenguz down a narrow, cobbled road. Raw *montmorillionite* ore lamps flickered behind the shuttered windows. He led Aenguz away from the center ville where the caravan preparations would be finalized. Away from the main boulevard that led out of the city.

The seat of the Sidor Clan sat atop a round promontory at the center of their Hearth Valley. Mashuan Limestone buildings clustered tightly at the top and spilled over the sides and clung to them down to the valley floor. Steep, angled pathways channeled water off the mound and cut a maze of steps and access paths down off the stone hill. Dahlward led Aenguz down an obscure course away from the main boulevards of the city.

But the streets were quiet, and the Sidors withdrew into their homes to their own private dreads. The pall that hung over the city had layers. It was a sullen fog that revealed itself through absences. The normal ebullience, especially before a Gathering and the expected weddings, was simply gone.

Mourning permeated as the most immediate layer. Although its sharpest edges had dulled with time, the loss of Sairik was still keen. The men who did speak in the dark used low uncertain tones. They seemed to be commiserating in their loss and wrestling with the unknowns that lay before the clan.

Aenguz's failure and injury at the forge brought a fresh layer to the trepidation in the city. The future had suddenly become uncertain. Security and stability had been chased out as if by the appearance of a sudden curse.

And then there were the tears. The daughters who wept in their rooms. There should have been excitement and anticipation. The final preparations for the clothing and plans for dressing their hair to join with their loves would have consumed them. Their excitement would have been palpable. Now, their anxious sleeplessness was replaced with a denuding worry and sobs. Down a steep descent, as the combined rhythm of his pain counted out the steps, he heard a maid's desperate, panting gasps. He heard others as he plopped down the steps. Their pain stabbed his heart with its own discordant beat.

Aenguz stepped down onto the valley floor just outside of an orchard. Stumps were as prevalent as the mixed stand of trees. Finding trees that bore fruit and then seeds that carried life was long and tedious work in the hampered earth. The outcome of the Last Battle, the final blow from the defeated Flayer. His interruption of the course of creation was a basic fact of the world. Finding and tending life in trees and crops with seeds that held the spark of life was difficult. It made the tenders work laborious and defeating.

Dahlward led Aenguz along a hedgerow to the southeast away from the main zig-zagged ramp that led up to the city. And away from the road that led out of their Hearth Valley. There would be more people there and likely a watch. Any encounter might foil their flight.

Sharp, snow-meshed peaks ringed the Sidor Hearth Valley. Stone pines skirted the peaks and draped on the foothills. Spring had come but winter was always slow to recede in the north. Swaths of snow remained in places aided by shadows and creases. The stripes of white fed the streams and flowed out of the southern end of the valley next to the road.

All of the Stonemage paved roads of the Upper Mashu led to the Valley of Gathering. Stonemage lore would have kept the smooth cobble free of snow at this time of year. If Aenguz and Dahlward could have taken those roads their flight would have been swift. But passage on the roads was forbidden, especially to Warriors the nights before a Gathering. It was an edict his father had set. Divisions among the clans had given rise to feuds and piqued grievances that sometimes would lead to fights or in the worst cases, clan wars. Sairik sought to strip the divisions that had arisen and take away at least one cause for the Akkeidii's internal strife. Here was another disobedience Aenguz had taken on in the wake of his shrinking life.

Dahlward led Aenguz up into the foothills in the southeast corner of the valley. He had left the old rough cobbled lanes and even the dirt paths behind. The Lord of the Deerherds pressed up into the forest. Aenguz took a deep breath and followed behind.

Walking down off the promontory on clear and narrow streets was one thing. But climbing up into the brush and brambles was another. Navigating branches was difficult. Needled limbs scratched and whacked at his arm. Fiery wails of pain drowned out the other thrumming. Aenguz led with his right shoulder. Out of sight from prying eyes, he could swipe at branches and bushes. The pain became a kind of load of its own.

Up and up, they climbed. Dahlward weaved among the trees and paused long enough to make certain Aenguz was still tracking behind him. Aenguz began to question how much pain he could endure. He began to blame all of his choices again even back to becoming a Warrior. If he had been a Deerherd or a Stonemage he probably could not have endured this trek. But the point was irrelevant. If he was a Deerherd or a Stonemage he wouldn't even be in this situation. He had to heal his arm. He forced the pain to remind him of that one fact. He had to heal his arm.

Finally, Aenguz broke through the trees. Sweat and tears poured down his face and neck. The front of the docent's robe was soaked. The coarse fabric was spotted with needles and burrs and pointed brown leaves. His panting was weak and automatic.

He stood at the edge of a teardrop pool. A wild deer path ran alongside the oblong pond. The growing moon smoothed the surface and silvered all of the leaves in the quiet meadow. Furtive clouds blocked stars here and there.

Dahlward stared up at the peaks. He seemed to be reading them gauging their aspect and distance. A trick of their size made them seem close enough to touch.

The Lord of the Deerherds followed the complex network of deer paths. He chose forks without hesitating. Found openings in copses where none could be seen.

After a time of more gradual climbing, the paths led downward. Dahlward made one last check of the peaks above, confirmed that Aenguz could see him, and then he descended into the body of the forest.

After a distance, Aenguz walked down to his grandfather. He stood at a steep drop-off. The bushy tops of the stone pines met the pair. Their trunks were rooted far below. A thick bed of brown needles clung to the steep slope. Climbing looked impossible.

As if to answer Aenguz's consternation, Dahlward sat on the edge, gathered up the cuffs of his robe, inched over the lip, and slid down to the nearest trunk. He caught himself with his feet and hugged the tree.

Aenguz balked. There wasn't enough air in the whole world for him. There were no options, no choices left to him. The world was shrinking and dropping into a hole.

Dahlward 'hissed' up to Aenguz and pointed to a trunk near his position.

Aenguz sat down and slid his scabbard underneath him like a kind of saddle. He inched forward. His arm pulsed with hammers of pain. He targeted the tree, tipped forward, and dropped off the ledge.

There was no controlled descent as Dahlward had done. The brown needles were slick, the slope too steep. Aenguz buried his right elbow into the ground to try and break the slide. His elbow raked across buried teeth of rock. His leaning and digging steered him away from his target. He careened off the side of the trunk and rolled into a full tumble. The first blow to his left side was white fury. It brought all the pain from the forge back to him. With each turn, it was like he was stoking the hot embers of a blast furnace with his naked arm. He bounced off trees unable to stop.

Suddenly, he slammed headlong into a trunk. His torso took the worst of the blow. His lungs gave up all their air. His arm drowned his mind in pain. It was the sole definition of his existence.

Somehow, after a time, Aenguz drew himself up into the crook of the tree and the slope. He looked beyond the edge of the tree and there, below him, was the Valley of Gathering.

Even from the aerie, the edict barring entry in the Valley of Gathering was palpable. The restriction preceded his father. In extending the prohibition to the roads, Sairik drew a direct line unintentionally back to the clan lords of old linking himself to them. Aenguz's violations were multiplying. If he was caught, the shame and punishment would be severe. His father, the Sidors, his grandparents, even Selene would all bear the shame. What would happen to Dahlward for helping him? Stripped of his role? Punished along with Aenguz? Deerherds were allowed, with their herds, to enter the Valley of Gathering. But apart from the herd, there would be no excuse for him. Aenguz was pulling everything and everyone down with him.

The irony of the situation was that, as Ruler of the Akkeidii, albeit in name only, he would be responsible to mete out his own punishment. Of course, the other clan lords would strip that responsibility from him. But there would be a fierce argument and debate.

Aenguz would, however, have to survive the Challenge first. Losing there in front of all the Akkeidii would make any punishment from entering into the valley moot. He would be dead. The clan lords would be spared the conundrum.

————◆————

AENGUZ LOOKED DOWN ON the Valley of Gathering as the thrum and pulse of his pain steadied into a higher level of agony. The wind that tore at the scraps of cloud made his head bob and weave as if he were navigating chop in a growing squall.

Grieg's Gate dominated the Valley of Gathering. The smooth stone-metal wall spun on itself like a thick nautilus at the elbow of the valley. Dark water filled the spaces in between, seemed to coalesce the essence of shadow and night into an impenetrable black. The moonlight that did show on the gate disappeared into those spaces between. This was the man-made headwater that secured access to the Upper Mashu and the clan's Hearth Valleys. And the Stonemages governed its opening and closing with their own inscrutable lore.

The stone-metal wall, whose construction none knew nor could they replicate, unwound from the coil, dropped, and ran alongside a channel that traced a vaguely straight path northward out of the valley. In the waxing moonlight, the line looked like a languid ribbon, a trimming from the tailoring of creation. Pale light glinted here and there like diamonds in the narrow channel.

Aenguz had never had such a perspective on Grieg's Gate. From the ground, it was just a curved wall, more like a stone cistern than the perfect coil below. But his eyes were soon drawn to the watch-fires at the fronts of the half a dozen or so main clan shelters. Ponderous Mashuan Stone Pine timbers supported sharp curved roofs. Smaller similar buildings surrounded the main ones. They looked like inverted ships sailing out from the tidal wave of rock and earth. The stacked stone bases were sails that captured the massive plume of the mountain's surge.

Novitiates stood watch at the fires before the main shelters. They would be pronounced Warriors if they had completed all their Rites of Passage. A small group, chosen for the honor, maintained and ensured the edict. Aenguz had stood watch there at the Sidor shelter the night before his rite of passage two years prior. That sleepless expectant night seemed as far away as the Novitiates did now. The shelter and watch nearest to Grieg's Gate were Sidors. To be caught by Novitiates, that he probably knew, was difficult to digest. They would not cover for him.

The Valley of Gathering constricted at the joint. Directly across from Aenguz and adjacent to the gate and the Sidor's clan shelter was the spur. A massive buttress of exposed limestone ran from the floor of the valley and up into the forest. It bifurcated the arms of the valley. The longer arm held the shelters and ran north. The shorter ran east from Grieg's Gate and held the clans Deerherd Shelters and the pastures where the roe deer were gathered. Aenguz could make out the stirring of the roe deer. They extended the wave of the long grasses and circled the oval pool in the distance.

Squat siloed Deerherd Shelters lined the internal edge of the valley. A mirror to the more extravagant shelters on the other arm. They were half rounds of stone built into the slope with timbered steepled peaks that leaned against the mountain. Wisps of smoke trailed up from where their tips met the slope in the trees.

In the crook of the arm of the Valley of Gathering, opposite Grieg's Gate, on the back side of the spur was the amphitheater. The Warrior's amphitheater. The spur obscured the narrow wedge of seats cut into the mountainside, but he could see most of the facade that ringed the blocked stage. Two curved walls with a space in between and a third curved wall behind. Aenguz felt more than saw the carvings on those walls.

His goal was the Sidor Deerherd shelter but how could he cross and not be seen? *Morillion* lay beyond the spur with the Deerherds gathered in the shelter. Sidors, Kriels, and Baierls would be gathered there. Perhaps even a few Finits. Hopefully, there would be enough to give him what he needed to heal his arm and save his clan and the Sidors legacy. Save his constricting world.

Dahlward slid down to Aenguz's side. His grandfather inspected the wound. The bandages were gone. The arm was bleeding and suppurating. Dahlward's concern was just another grief for Aenguz's failing faculties. He voiced the only question that mattered now. "How do I cross?" There was no indictment for bringing him to a seemingly impossible point. His grandfather had already risked too much. They would have not been able to fool their way here on the Stonemage roads. Now, the docent's disguise was functionally useless. There seemed to be no way to cross without being caught.

Two bands stretched down the steep slope from their perch to the neck of Grieg's Gate where the wall unspooled from the coil. One was grass, the other was a swathe of snow.

"Follow the snowline down," Dahlward pointed to the edge. "The snow piles over the water onto the wall. Cross carefully and not too near the waters at the neck.

There wasn't much space. From this distance, Aenguz wasn't certain there would be enough room between him and the watch. Their fire was not far from the convergence.

Dahlward peered down the valley. He perked up as if a new vision had enlivened his ascetic's heart. "The Sidor's herd! Do you see it?" He cut the air with his hand as he pointed northward. The Sidor's roe deer herd was entering the Valley of Gathering. They were just coming up to the Finit Clan's shelter. The Finit watch let the Deerherds pass after a brief inspection. Herd hounds ran at the edges.

"I have an idea. I will go and disrupt the herd and create a distraction for you to cross. Meet me on the other side of the spur."

The Lord of the Deerherds locked eyes with Aenguz. The tenor of his concern attenuated his eyes. He tried to draw the discipline out of Aenguz to make this leap before the pain and exhaustion overwhelmed him.

Dahlward looked one last time down the strips of grass and snow. Then, he cursed through his goatee. "A Stonemage. You will have to mind the Stonemage."

A solitary figure stood on the outer wall of the coil. The Stonemage stared up the valley at the incoming herd. After a moment, the shadowy gatekeeper meandered pensively back around the outer ring toward the center of the coil.

The body of the herd was passing the Finit shelter. Dahlward pierced Aenguz with a gaze one last time and darted off along the tree line.

Breaking the invisible barrier of the valley was a criminal act. Crossing the physical barrier below would manifest all of his violations and transgressions. There were no choices left to him. There was no space left in his world.

Aenguz examined the distance. He sat on his scabbard once again and scooted to the edge of the snowfield. After confirming that the Stonemage was out of sight, he leaned back and slid down the green.

At the midway point, the slope lessened enough to where the possibility of falling uncontrollably faded. He was able to move faster on the lesser grade. The edge of the snow field grew. There was no way to gauge his grandfather's efforts or to determine the focus and position of the Sidor watch. What kind of distraction was he intending? The Stonemage's frame grew as Aenguz descended and the wall rose. He waited for the shadowy sentinel to disappear. Then he darted down the last distance to the neck where the wall dipped to the stream, and the snow field met the water and the wall.

A calamity of waters enveloped the shoreline. Sheets of water gushed from under the snowpack and cut under the surface. A concave edge was cut along the wall-facing edge of white. The lip of snow that hung over did not reach the wall. There was no way to cross over.

Another sound rode on top of the chattering waters. It was a chaos of roe deer and herd hounds beyond the wall. Whatever was happening, whatever his grandfather intended was happening now.

He would have to wade through to the other side with only the robe for protection. During Warrior training, he and his friends would wade into a cold mountain lake in the winter and see who could stay the longest. But there was always a waiting fire on the shore. And there were others around to help those who faded to the cold, in spite of their will.

But the icy water was not the main problem. To his left nearer Grieg's Gate was a terse slurping waterfall. The viscous black swallowed the minor falls whole. Whirling fractures on the surface promised profound depths.

Aenguz waded into the gelid stream with an ill-fitting robe and little else. Freezing water stung his legs and ignored his boots. Chunks of ice drifted by and battered his knees. His feet and calves grew cold, then numb. He could barely feel the contour of the stream bed. All of his limbs burned except his right arm. His right steered in the air to balance himself as he stepped across the distance. The water came up to his waist.

Suddenly, his numb feet lost their purchase and he fell sideways into the frigid channel. Both arms shot out instinctively to catch his fall. The seams at his fused arm tore and ripped free. The icy water was like magma against his exposed arm. The water masked his agony and reduced his scream to a bubbly gurgle.

The current pulled him toward the falls. He spun underwater and clawed at the channel bed. The knuckles of his knotted hand scraped on brook stone. His robe was a sea anchor dragging him inexorably to the falls almost in league with the current. His weapon conspired with them.

Aenguz worked to right himself, to gain any kind of purchase. Death and disgrace were close. That is if the waters of Grieg's Gate even gave him up. In that moment, the waters seemed ready to take him down to subterranean depths.

Hot adrenaline burned his heart. His lungs were strangled. In a moment, he would breathe water. With one last wild effort, Aenguz dove down and grabbed on the rocks, and threw himself upstream. The fierce pain in his arm and fist and the numbing water decoupled him from himself. He sprang two more times. The first to go upstream, the second to reach the surface. His lungs could hold on no longer.

He took in water with his mad gasp for air. Numbness, exhaustion, and pain stripped all of his strength. He would be aware of his drowning in the black. The will of the current and the short falls were winning.

Suddenly, Aenguz was drawn like a piece of iron to a magnet. He was drawn at his waist and slammed against the wall. He was locked in place. His weapon moored him at the hip to the low wall at the base of the neck.

He raised up out of the water coughing and gagging. The cold air blew fire onto his exposed arm. His legs were lost to numbness.

As Aenguz cleared the water from his lungs and caught his breath, a hand touched his head.

The Sidors of the watch had found him. The ruin of his life would now be complete. His world had shrunk to the size of a thimble.

"Aenguz! Aenguz!" Dahlward's hoarse whisper called down.

Aenguz looked up and gave his grandfather his right arm.

Dahlward hauled his grandson over the wall to the paved culvert on the other side.

Roe deer were all around them. Their hooves clattered on the stone tiers, kicked at the water. Herd hounds raced to bring the edges in line. A roan bitch and a golden male came up and began to bark at the pair. Dahlward hissed at the dogs. They came up and nosed Aenguz.

Aenguz reached out to them, let them sniff him. "Good boy, good girl." They licked at him and nosed his hand. Aenguz scratched their heads limply.

"Now, Hold!" His words were drenched and garbled. He held his fist up, heel out, to them.

The two hounds understood. They held perfectly still. They waited on his next command. Their legs quivered with expectation.

"Ready."

Their training defined them. Their eyes locked on him.

"Round!" Aenguz snapped his hand open and pointed outward. The herd hounds bolted out of the water and worked around the roe deer chasing them out of the culvert back up to the path and to the pasture.

Dahlward brought Aenguz up and the two moved on with the herd. The Lord of the Deerherds called back to the watch and waved them off. He warned them to be careful of the slick pavers at the water. The Sidors waved a thanks to the Lord of the Deerherds and the drenched docent. Then he hauled Aenguz out of sight around the spur.

3

MORILLION

Aenguz drifted beside his grandfather. He wondered blithely why he struggled so. The gnawing pain was a weight that dragged at his side. But the rest of him was light. He thought the shivering might shake the arm loose and take the pain away. But the pain reminded him of his purpose.

He gazed at the facade. The names of the Champions, the reliefs of the Heroes of the Venture, and the rectangle memorials for the fallen chieftains. The past rushed by under the stratocumulus of the seats that ran up into the sky against the spur.

He felt a nudge. His head knocked against stone. But it seemed distant, like a chime from an early morning bell. Dahlward looked crushed against the stone of the Deerherd shelter. His own robe was drenched in places. His ascetic's gaze was all focus and intensity. He could turn his will against the exhaustion and strain. The imperative that drove his grandfather was unknown to Aenguz. His grandfather adjusted the hood again. He closed the sleeve to keep the blood from dripping. He shifted his grip around Aenguz and continued around the shelter.

The Lord of the Deerherds carried Aenguz around to the front of the Sidor Deerherd shelter. Inside, to the left and the right, half-walls ran into the darkness. The stables for the roe deer. Manure and straw. Aenguz receded into memories of his childhood. His grandfather had brought him here as a boy. That smaller, simple world was close. As the memories flooded in, Aenguz maintained a tenuous grasp on his purpose. The trespass was complete, but the goal was not yet achieved.

Dahlward pushed through a tarp into the refectory. He turned to the left and followed the inner wall past door after door. Long wooden tables with benches were arranged in half-circles facing the kitchen at the front. A stone counter ran through the diameter of the space. The kitchen beyond filled the rest of the back. A fire blazed in the wide hearth. A pair of smaller cook fires burned in the darker corners of the hearth. The chimney was made of stacked river stone. It ran up the wall to the peak where the timbers met. It slumped like a witch's hat and looked like it could fall with a slight jostle. But Stonemage work was strong.

Deerherds were crowded near the front. Sidor, Kriel, and Baierl Deerherds were taking a late meal of meaty stew and drinking roasted dark ale. A few heads turned to the Lord of the Deerherds. Aenguz recalled how welcomed he felt among the Deerherds. The esoteric strands that bound them in their lore created a brotherhood that was not wholly unfamiliar to him. Memories of those feelings surged in with the other memories.

Dahlward turned into a bunkroom near the kitchen wall. A pair of triple-tiered bunks rested on each side of the room. A narrow table stood against the wall between them. A conical lamp sat on the center of the table. A small nugget of raw *montmorillionite* blinked and flickered like a captured star.

Aenguz drifted down to the pallet. He seemed heavy and light at the same time. He oscillated between being a boy and a man. His world shrank and expanded with each pulse.

Dahlward peeled away the sopping docent's robe and dropped it at the foot of the bed. Aenguz's weapon was knotted to his side. Dahlward gave up on the cord after a few moments. And Aenguz floated back down onto the bed. His legs swung up as if they rose onto the pallet of their own accord.

Dahlward pulled out the small pouch Hertha had given him. He said something to Aenguz, spun around, and left. The wheels turned and the door slid shut.

The smell of the stew and ale, the slow warmth of a familiar place lessened his shivering. The fiery pain was finding its way back. It rose gradually and steadily like a siren louder and louder. Soon he would come to understand that the siren was in his head.

He swung on the end of a line like a pendulum. Gradually the swinging increased from his past to his present. From boyhood to manhood. From a wide world he knew to another smaller chamber. From a hard run to a drowsy repose, he didn't think he could rise from. One moment he was on a familiar pallet. And in the next, he was out over the abyss.

The flickering light cast shadows on the walls and timbered ceiling. Aenguz receded to his boyhood and the stories and adventures he imagined in the animated lines. Visions of the Venture as his childlike mind imagined. Battles and treks in the wild wilderness of the Lands of the Earth. All the conflicts against the hordes of the Flayer played out against stone and timber. All of it converged in the climax of the Last Battle. The story looped and culminated over and over as his grandfather came and went with supplies. The opening and closing door revealed the firelight beyond and roared in like an apocalypse.

Heaviness and lightness were unreconciled. The pat on his cheek chased away the lightness for the moment.

Dahlward was seated beside Aenguz. He loved his grandfather. An old friend, resolute and unflagging in his devotion. Aenguz had asked him to sacrifice so much. He swung back to his purpose and his violations. What had he become? What was he doing to those around him?

Bowls and pitchers were stacked on the table. Dahlward was scooping lumps into a larger bowl. The silver-flecked mud disappeared beneath the rim. Dahlward worked the small round knife in the tiny crocks drawing out every bit of *morillion.*

The scene appeared to loop in Aenguz's mind. He needed a lot of *morillion* but to see so much gathered in one place seemed impossible to his failing perception.

When Dahlward was done, he poured water into the bowl. He looked down into it as if he could divine only horrors in the cloudy pool.

He turned to Aenguz after a moment and said, "I do not know what this will do to you. I do not know if I can guide the loam clearly. I am not sure what will happen."

Aenguz had swung back to his pain and his present moment. The needs that pressed on him were galvanized by the shrieks of fire and heat. The seams at his joints were flayed away.

Aenguz could see that his grandfather wrestled with fears of inadequacy against the dire task. And his grandson's life hung on a fragile ledge.

"Perhaps you could turn your life to the Deerherds. You would not need your whole arm to tend the roe deer. You could have a life. Maybe not the life you envisioned for yourself but still a life."

Aenguz could tell that his grandfather struggled. Dahlward's goatee trembled. He wound a bundle of *roona* and *gingrass* together slowly. The analeptic herbs were for the roe deer. For humans, the healing herbs acted as a stimulant. Dahlward was unsure his grandson would survive. New crags of grief were scrawled across his face. Like Hertha, the primal meaning and purpose of his life were slipping away.

The Oath of Life, the tenant that guided all he did as a Deerherd, was being threatened. Until this moment, his actions did not directly jeopardize his grandson's life. The next step could strip his grandfather of a cardinal belief.

It was a stab of that realization. Only he could decide to take the *morillion.* But he could not apply it himself. His grip on consciousness was nearly lost. And the fatigue left by all the pain and cold made him too weak.

Aenguz looked at the large stone bowl and shivered at the *morillion* that must lie within. His heart galloped into a fretful tempo. He could tend the roe deer, but he could not live with the shame. The ire and disdain of the Sidors would be too much. Selene would be gone. Who would he become if he abandoned his path now? Too much would be lost.

Aenguz took the bundle of herbs from his grandfather's tremoring hands. "Apply the *morillion*. I can endure it." Aenguz cleared his mouth and licked his lips. He was thirsty but any water now might cause him to convulse. "I want to do what I was supposed to do. I want to be what I was supposed to be." Then he took the bit into his mouth, clamped down on it, and presented his ruined arm to his grandfather.

Dahlward shouldered out of his robe and rolled up his sleeves. He reached into the bowl and coated his hands with the silver-flecked mud. The *morillion* responded to the lamplight and glinted in turn. Dahlward held up Aenguz's arm by the knotted fist with a delicate precision. Aenguz clamped down on the herbs in agony. Then Dahlward took a scoop and slathered it under Aenguz's arm and around the shoulder. He did the same at the elbow and the wrist. He pulled the arm straight so as not to leave any seam uncovered.

Open nerves raged like a wildfire. Aenguz's jaw cramped. The cords of his neck strained so hard it felt like his neck might rip.

Dahlward covered the upper arm and the forearm. He made sure to cover the raw places at his neck and any exposed places on the arm.

Then he turned to the fist. Aenguz was panting through the bit. Tears and spittle drained off his face and mixed with the sweat.

Then Dahlward reached for the small round knife he used to scrape out the *morillion*. He grabbed Aenguz's arm by the wrist.

"I have to free the fingers."

Aenguz may have managed an assent. But truthfully, the storm of pain had already subsumed him.

Dahlward dug in and pealed the fingers away one at a time from one another. He cut under and freed them from the palm. Aenguz did not recognize his own strangled shrieks. His gasps were wails of horror. The bundle of herbs filtered the worst of it.

Dahlward slopped handfuls in between the fingers and around the thumb until a thick glove of *morillion* covered the hand.

Then, mercifully, the pendulum took him. He swung from his ledge out over the void. The line snapped and Aenguz plunged headlong into the black.

4

~~

A DOLOROUS CHARGE

The animated shadows overwhelmed the light and rushed toward Aenguz. They carried him over the brink and plummeted with him into the black hole of the abyss. The darknesses coalesced and strangled him. They both hid and hinted at the boundless expanse of the void. Vertigo ripped at him and threatened to pull him apart.

The whirling storm of fire and pain affirmed a connection, albeit tenuous to his former life. But it was distant, like a beacon far away on the ocean of the abyss. The sanative stupor of the *morillion* cordoned the fierce hurt off and gave Aenguz some relief. But the maddening descent made that succor meaningless. Death in the Black Earth, it seemed, would catch him.

Then Aenguz spun on the void. Like a needle on a hastily unpacked compass, he wobbled and righted. And in a way, the void oriented as the *morillion* set a kind of north star for him in the deep black. For the moment, the madness of the abyss was held at bay.

But this sacred expression of the mystical metal could not prevent its own inscrutable nature from impinging on Aenguz's mortal mind.

The sentient and enigmatic elemental metal oriented and affirmed itself. It located its place in the dark universe and established its link, its unbreakable link to all *montmorillionite*.

Aenguz's grasp on the structure of reality shifted. His mind spun like a dervish and stretched beyond its bounds in another kind of vertigo. Walls of sound crashed like a tsunami and tore at the pillars of reason.

All of the minuscule flecks of silver in his arm were distinct. He felt capable of numbering and inventorying each one as if they were needles on a stone pine. Distance became irrelevant. Connections reached out in a fine chiaroscuro map of silken tracery.

Aenguz listened at hidden gurgling pools in the Mashu where undiscovered *morillion* gathered and waited like grains of sand. He rested on a bed of pulverized rocks at the base of towering glaciers where blue ice ground out bits of the precious metal throughout the edges of the White Deeps. He was in the pouches of Makan and Gambl Deerherds who did not offer up their stores to Dahlward. He was also within solid rock, beneath the mountains of the Mashu, with all the glowing veins of *montmorillionite* - mined and unmined everywhere.

Aenguz saw all the silent armories in all the Hearth Valleys in the Upper Mashu. Spears, shields, myriads of weapons beside common Akkeidii steel. He recognized the Sidor armory in his home Hearth Valley. It chimed a note to his old life. It was a melancholic chord in the din.

His mind was fraying. Seeing, being with, cataloging, inventorying all the *montmorillionite* stretched and strained his mind in a wholly unfamiliar way. He may have been wrong to believe he could endure the effects.

He looked out on flickering streams of light from innumerable lanterns and braziers in each room in every Akkeidii home throughout the Mashu. He glimpsed unfamiliar stone in sparely peopled corridors in some unknown fortress.

He pressed against the leathers of the scabbards of every Warrior from old to unascended. Each curve and haft and wild flourish of each weapon was present and poignant to him. He could see them all and could count them all. Even his own weapon tied to his hip on the pallet in the Deerherd shelter was there.

The pace was beyond him. His mind attenuated as if forced through a thin tube and stretched beyond reckoning.

All the tools of all the Stonemages. Chisels, hammers, stone saws, *duranns*, pry bars, levers. He was loaded onto a wagon. He was carefully organized and counted.

Aenguz gazed up from a forge at a Kriel Loremaster, a novitiate Warrior, a curious daughter, and loving Warrior father.

He even touched the pensive liquid flow of his father's weapon as it descended through the Earth to settle again into a quiet vein of rock.

In the maelstrom of connectivity and vastness, as quantities and inventories mounted beyond anything Aenguz could categorize or conceptualize, as his wit and reason faltered, the metal only tallied One. In all its myriad forms, from the flecks in his arm to the deepest vein in the Mashu, *montmorillionite* counted itself as One.

It imparted to Aenguz a single impression, seemed to articulate one idea to him in the void.

You are not alone.

The assurance seemed to address a nascent fear in him. It could not halt the presentation and representation of all of its forms and expressions. He would need to cling to what strictures he could grasp in his own mind to maintain himself.

The metal said to him again, *you are not alone*. But this time he sensed the different meaning, a warning. *You are not alone.*

A focal point in the void emerged and took notice of Aenguz. From the whirl of grays and blacks a shape converged. Eyes emerged into clusters in the vague shape of a skull. Varying pupils darted like a close gulp of cormorants. Different sizes and groupings of eyes all pressed in on a single larger off-centered eye. As Aenguz sought to define the contour and shape of the face he was caught gazing fully into a bunch of eyes here, a clutch there, a line of five along the main off-kilter eye. There was no respite or relief from eye contact.

Most of the eyes were bloodshot as if sleep had been abandoned for malice. Some were jaundiced by gall. They had yellowed over eons. A sickening discoloration like plague had colored the others.

The eyes raked over Aenguz like a sieve. Razor screens separated and sorted him down to smaller and smaller pieces. The eyes searched him hungrily and pierced into every secret corner of his heart. The pieces of Aenguz's spirit calcified. Then in an instant, they dropped like a sudden rain from a heavily leaden cloud.

The void dissipated and the dark face of the Earth appeared. He dropped down over a scarred plain. Fine dust and stale ash left a vast field of despite. The spine of a crescent-shaped ridge breached the surface like a slain behemoth. Its back warded the east and the shunning mountains in the distance. The tips opened toward the west and the barren plain. In the center was an adit, a bleak entrance to a hallowed tomb. Symbols like sharpened runes marked the plain opening. Aenguz rained down and flowed in.

His heart would have ruptured if he was in the flesh. He rushed past bone-lined corridors. Walls framed in femurs and ulnas. Long chambers and passageways of stacked skulls stared out. Empty sockets looked at him and through him like the eyes that cast him down.

Aenguz poured and swirled down a wide drain. He spilled over, caught onto a jagged ledge. The thin substance of his form coalesced. And the flint-like edges cut into his ephemeral knees and palms. Although Aenguz's eyes were cast downward he recalled the depth and the blackness of the hole in the wide cylindrical chamber. The vacant sockets in the walls were desiccated by unrelieved horror.

Below he seemed to be looking on the bowels of hell. A titan's gorgon writhed below. Its lower half was a gordian confusion of knotted scaled coils. Squeezing, tightening, struggling to release but confounding in on themselves. They churned on their own vice in a darkness like the womb of night.

Aenguz strived against the terror that seemed to drop his heart over and over again. He worked to orient himself. His mind wobbled like a compass unable to locate true north. Everything in his senses pointed down.

"So, this is what the Earth sends against me." The voice grated like megalithic boulders. It surrounded and submerged him. Each eye seemed to speak. A ghastly chorus pierced through him. "Beware, it sends its servants to dooms that exceed death. Curse the One."

Aenguz averred his eyes to the horror of the skulls and broken bones. He prayed to the Mashu to not be the focus of the voice or the eyes.

"I see that you are of the same line as the failed hero of the Last Battle." Derision roiled the voice when it said, *failed hero*. "Creation has learned no lessons from its pyrrhic victory." Some of the eyes held on Aenguz. Others drew away. Aenguz drew his head up.

"My designs have escaped notice for an adequate time. The Earth must be aware of my assaults. It is time for my plans to come to fruition."

Aenguz searched the chamber. He followed the curved edge of the ledge into darkness. His heart continued to tip into the black below. He sensed there was heat. He knew the depths of the earth were molten. But the atmosphere was gelid. It made the waters of the Neck seem lukewarm.

On the ledge, four or five creatures circled the scleritic eyes. Their withered feet dangled uselessly above the ledge. The tattered ends of vestments trailed down alongside their decaying feet. Their bulbous heads bore lappets of what looked to be barely tamed asps. Their chins tapered to a point giving their heads the look of a cruel stout awl. Their cicatriced torso was all gray tendons and exposed ribs. Their thin arms were wrapped tightly in shredded bands. They traced lines and shapes in the air, like conductors. Short jerrids or scepters added a joint to the arms that made them look spider-like. They chanted as they worked the offal-laden air. The coils below responded to them. They appeared oblivious to Aenguz's presence.

He looked for doors, for any way out. "Where am I?" His own dread astounded him.

When the grating voice spoke, Aenguz was confronted with a nightmare of unpitied murder. His own insides twisted like the writhing coils below.

"You are in Carrowen Celd. The Deepest Hole. My eminence way on low. You see my Urnings labor against the fraught work of your progenitor.

"I was diminished for an age. But my foe learned that I cannot be destroyed. I have gnashed on my wounds and toiled against these knots. They have not prevented me from enacting my divisions."

The twin impossibilities of the void and the pit of Carrowen Celd pressed in on Aenguz. Even in his strange form, his breath was short. His teetering heart beat through constrictions. In a continued effort to orient himself and halt the threat of a whirling fall, he asked, "Who are you?"

"I see ignorance, disbelief, and confusion in you. So that you may know who to pray to, I have had many names. To you, and the 'failed hero' and your remnant I am known as the Flayer. To the blinded Counsel Lords, I am Lord Morgrom the Divider. The Moresi name me First Treacher. To the rebellious Hyrrokkin, I am called Reaver. In the shallow introspection of their one gift, the Azari whisper my name as Oblivion. But to the people of the Lands of the Earth, I am known as Woe Sower. I am to command the Law of Creation."

The anchor of *morillion* held him firm against utter dissolution. The Flayer was defeated. The lore stated it. Grieg Sidor's sacrifice was undisputed. The Earth was left wounded and blighted. Crops floundered. Litters were left incomplete. But the evil that had brought that was gone. His present and ages past collided in him. The wide chamber grew smaller and smaller.

Aenguz wanted to get free of Carrowen Celd and free of the denuding gaze. He searched the darkness again for any opening, any way out. He climbed to his feet. The sharp ledge poked at his vaporous feet.

"Why does my enemy send you so unprepared and so ignorant against me? And so disfigured. No doubt my foe has felt my rise, my works. But the mind of creation is not without guile." The eyes pondered. Blood lines and sickness devoured the whites. Vile malice and long contemplated revenge squeezed the clustered eyes.

"My long-delayed victory cannot be averted. I will give you the opportunity for repentance that my Enemy never offered you. I will give you mighty purpose."

Aenguz wanted to run, wanted to escape. The Urnings on the ledge held a barrier against him. The bilious air was stilled on either side of him.

"My Emissaries are shunned among the Remnant. They are no longer heard or received. So, I will set you as the Last Emissary from among their number so that they will receive my words and know that my victory is nigh."

Anger found a way through the stripping fears. Aenguz blurted out, "I would never serve the Flayer."

Morgrom roared. The skulls rattled in the walls. The Urnings drifted back from the ledge. Their arms stilled.

"You dare to reject my beneficence! My words *are* law! You can only serve me. If you reject me, my victory will come that much sooner. But I wish for my enemies to dine on the full measure of the vengeance I have prepared for them. I wish my enemy to taste the full depth of failure. The Last Battle will be enjoined again. And I mean to exact the uttermost despair and woe from the Remnant and the peoples of the Earth. I will rend the Earth to be free."

He was trapped as if he stood in a coffin too small for his frame. Rejection and acceptance of Morgrom's charge both led to the same point, the same doom. He needed to live. Had needed to be healed. But death here, or worse, and failure stretched beyond the borders of his life and the Akkeidii. Beyond the walls of the Mashu. The needs of the world overshadowed the needs of his people. The demands of the Earth, of Morgrom, of the *montmorillionite* dwarfed him.

He needed time to process. Time for the *morillion* to heal or help. Time to see if *Montmorillion* lore held an answer. If he could forestall Morgrom's doom, he might stand before it until he could find a way out of it. Find a way for some aid. Mustering the courage and fortitude Warrior training had taught him he said quietly and surely, "What do you task me with?"

The eyes acknowledged Aenguz's assent. The shuddering walls quieted. The Urnings resumed their labor.

"You will bear a message to the Counsel Lords and the Mono Lord in Corundum. Say to them that the limit of their days upon the Lands of the Earth are before them. Five quinquennia will not pass before my will is sown in every corner of the Earth. The Remnant and the peoples of the Lands squat on lands I have granted to my servants. Your time on the earth is at an end.

"To the Urnings, I have granted the air. They are masters of it. I have sent them forth to find the portals and free all five Ruinwasters. With the aid of my wisdom, they have divined the means of their escape. Before twenty-five moons grow full all five will be freed. Four will wreak havoc on all the hope and beauty in the Earth you hold so dear. Hear me, when Tycho Ruinwaster is found and his shackle removed, the Blasted Flats, the Shattered Lands, and even the Ganzir will seem like a garden.

"I have given the land to the Erebim. It is now theirs to take. The warrens in Galangall teem. They only await Shivic Ruinwaster to lead their number against you. When Shivic is found, the Last Battle will be enjoined again. Hear me, my victory will come in a new form of war. Its ways and movements will be beyond your ken. Five seasons will not pass before Earthmight is under siege and the One King's army is lost. You will know the grieving of the Lower Lands. But war is not the worst thing you should fear. Nadirs of despair will unwind the fabric of your souls. All will be divided against all.

"I have given the waters to the Sallow. Even now, with knowledge I have granted them, they navigate the rivers of the east. In time they will master them all.

"To the Tsurah I have given dominion over animal-kind. With the prepotency I have granted them, their husbandry will draw loathsome beasts from new quinary lines. The Wester now groans under their labors.

"Mark me! Before this very year is divided, the Dagba Stone will be lost to this age. You will not be able to use it against me as before. Even if you were able to locate it no mortal hand may wield it. Its power is for my hand alone. When my Ruinwasters have done their work. When you are gone from the Earth, I will locate it and become unfettered from the Earth. And then the universe and Time itself will bow to my dominion."

Aenguz was overwhelmed. The force of Morgom's voice, his spite crushed him.

"For you, Last Emissary, do not fail in your task. My desires are without end. I crave for my enemies to savor a full measure of despair. If you fail to deliver my message, death will be your raiment. And I will only require one Ruinwaster to bring about the ruin of the Earth. One Ruinwaster alone would be enough to rend the Vaults of Corundum. Hear me now. Five days will not pass before the first Ruinwaster is freed from the Black Earth.

"Be warned, the lands south of the Wester are already mine. Only the One Forest stands against me, but it is beset. This generation will not pass before it is felled utterly. My servants are abroad in the Lands finding egress for my Ruinwasters and enacting my will. Keep to the north. Avoid the south. Do not hazard the *verrandulum*. You cannot hope to navigate them.

Deliver my message before the year is divided thus the loss of all hope for the Remnant may be savored and filled with my vengeance."

"Vengeance," hung on the suffocating air.

Aenguz's arm torqued and pulled at him. He drew up from the bottom as if he was a weight at the end of a plumb line. The dark hole faded away and the barren plain dissolved beneath mists and blacks. The adit was a mote beneath the moon.

Then, walls of the Valley of Gathering and the familiar lumps of the pallet with the damp pillow assured him of his weight and mass. But it was short-lived. Aenguz was taken off into a dream-filled sleep deep as the grave.

5

WARRIOR AND SQUIRE

Aenguz rose out of the gossamer of dreams. Impressions of gloom caressed him. Solitary and untimely funerals, attar-laden pyres, hollowing griefs brushed through him. But those impressions did not hold the firmness and solidity of Carrowen Celd. Morgrom's voice and the craven eyes were physical, real. The chants of the floating Urnings and their conducting arms were visible to him. The twisting knots of Morgrom's coils were unwholesome and utterly tangible. Those images set themselves apart from the fading viscera of his sorrow-filled dreams. And they established themselves as memories.

The message was inscribed on the walls of his mind. Already it was charting a new warped purpose for his life. Its doom advanced toward him like a lamed golem. Closer and closer the slow steps came with a long drag and a heavy stomp. It came to wreak havoc with a murderous single-mindedness. Its slow advance prodded him further out of his heavy slumber.

The discomfort of his damp pillow also brought him up through his medicated sleep. The aches at his hips and joints affirmed his body and drew his roaming spirit firmly back into place. His eyes were caked shut.

Aenguz reached up with his left hand to claw away the crust. Hard matter seemed to multiply in his socket before he realized his mistake.

He snatched his arm back and let it rest on his chest while he waited for the wave of fiery pain to rush over him. He counted the pulses as his heart oriented itself. He readied himself for the agony. But only muted aches and a dulled heat came from his arm. He was unsure of his state. Had it worked? He held his breath until the promise of the pain faded away.

Morillion.

Had that part of his plan succeeded? He maneuvered himself with his right arm to the edge of the bed and swung his legs over. He had to see what the mystical healing loam had done. His memory of the connections to all of the metal was a fading echo. In a way, that communion was more terrifying than Carrowen Celd. He did not focus on it.

He scratched away the crust and blinked through to see his new arm. The ambient light up in the rafters alluded to day but left the bunkroom dim. He wondered briefly what time of day it was and even what day it was. Had he missed the Rites of Passage? Had he forfeited himself in the Challenge? Had he traded a healed arm for the purposes that his healed arm was meant to enable? Was Selene already gone?

He picked and pulled away the skin of dried, inert mud. Pieces dropped from his arm like thin bits of unfired clay. Shards of fragile gray porcelain fell from between his fingers. His hand was still bent. And his arm still drawn up in a palsy. The joints still held the memory of their long stiffness.

He brushed the spent loam away from his arm. He plucked and pealed hunks away from his shoulder and his neck. The silver flecks were gone from the pale, dry mud.

His eyes had not yet come back to him, and the light was too slim. A fine gray powder coated his hairless arm. The contour of the flesh seemed off. He reached over to the pewter lamp and slid the door open.

His skin was translucent and paper-thin. The pale veneer revealed the fine tracings of veins and tendons. Muscle masses looked like smooth red coals just beneath the surface.

His heart found a different gear of panic and dread. The room crushed in. Air was scarce. He reached for the bowl, cupped some water, and tried to wipe the ghoulish skin away. He picked at it and tried to believe it was just another layer of spent *morillion*. That whole and hale flesh lay just beneath. But this was no residual layer.

Suddenly, the door slid open and stopped with a thump. The sound wasn't a lasting thread from his dream. It wasn't a golem coming to pound him. Jorgen, his Squire peeked into the room. Jorgen looked more like a beast than a man. The young Sidor Squire gasped at the sight of Aenguz.

"Thank the Mashu!" the Squire said.

Aenguz turned on the pallet and hid his arm. After the initial shock passed, Aenguz wondered where his grandfather was. He had to find out if this was how his arm was going to be forever.

His Squire navigated his way through the door. Two spears poked out like straight legs. Satchels and packs rounded out his shoulders and back. A course white, fur cloak made a hump of his back. A *montmorillionite* shield also hung at his back. He looked like a miserly tortoise carrying more than his shell could contain.

He leaned the bundles down onto the pallet opposite Aenguz. He arranged the piles and organized them hurriedly. He pulled out a small pouch and then turned to Aenguz. His black hair was greasy with sweat, and his face was slick. A single dimple hinted at a permanent grin. Even through his heaving an alacrity shown through. His eyes were bright and attentive.

Jorgen cleared a space on the table. All of the bandages were gone. All evidence of *morillion* was removed. Two wide bowls and a pair of pitchers of water were there. He moved a platter to the side. It held hearty brown bread, wedges of dry white and yellow cheeses. And there was a pile of tan and brown nuts next to a heap of dried berries that looked like gobs of coagulated blood.

Aenguz's stomach rumbled. Aenguz realized that he had no clothes. Just the sweat-soaked swaddle at his groin. The docent's robe still lay in a heap at the foot of the bunks.

Jorgen unrolled the pouch and revealed, herbs, unguents, and salves. He dabbed some water on his hands, took some of the salve and, turned to Aenguz.

Aenguz tried to turn but there was no hiding his ghastly arm. Jorgen was as familiar with Aenguz as a younger brother. But he was also respectful.

He paused when he saw the arm.

Aenguz turned to him.

"By Grieg!" he breathed. "My master. What happened?"

Shame and self-revulsion tore at Aenguz. He scrambled to organize his thoughts. "Forget about the salve. Get me some clothes. And pass over that tray." And as a last most important thought, "What time is it? What day is it? Have I missed the Rites?"

Jorgen returned the white gel to the pouch and brought the platter over. He stole another look at the arm.

Aenguz tore a hunk of bread, held it up the left and to the right. "To the Two Lands and the Twin Rivers." Then he bit into the bread and began shoveling nuts and cheese into his mouth.

Jorgen spoke as he pulled out clothes from the packs. "The Rites of Passage for the Stonemages and the Deerherds are complete. They wait on the Warriors. The Lord of the Deerherds, your grandfather seems bent on every delay. He defers to his dual responsibilities. He insisted on performing the Rites for the Deerherds. Now he leads the assembly for the Warriors. Before I left it seemed that he meant to tell the old version, the long version of the tale of Grieg Sidor the Venturer. He started with the time of the One Race before the Division. Before Grieg Sidor was even born. The clan lords must be restless. He must be at the Last Battle by now. I tried every Deerherd shelter on my way here. He told me to search the shelters. I went to the furthest point in the valley first. I checked every room looking for you."

Dahlward was buying Aenguz time. It was not too late. But only barely.

"Get my clothes. We have to hurry."

Jorgen turned to the bunk and dug through packs for Aenguz ceremonial clothes. He bore fine leggings, undergarments, and a quill-embroidered leather shirt. The pattern showed the White and Millin Rivers running against the green of the Mashuan Stone Pines. The design ran over his shoulders and converged at the V just over his heart. This was a fine ceremonial garment.

His mother would have made this for him. But the responsibility fell to Hertha. He wondered how his grandmother was faring. Had his grandfather had a chance to talk with her or had his responsibilities kept him from updating her on the outcome of their flight?

The table was crowded. Jorgen set the clothes down on the bed next to Aenguz.

"How did you get to the Valley of Gathering?"

Aenguz pointed to the wet robe. Too much information might be detrimental to his Squire. If Aenguz was found out, Jorgen could share in the punishment.

Jorgen wrestled with Aenguz's indication. His dimpled cheek winced as he thought. Then he turned back to the packs for his other gear.

"Everyone wonders where you are. The Sidors are nervous. They think you would not or could not come to the Valley of Gathering. The unbetrothed women worry like I have never seen before. Sister-friends and mother-aunts try to console them. Father-uncles and brother-friends whisper and promise blood."

He had to get to the amphitheater. His fears were coming to pass. The condition of his arm would have to be hidden for now. His presence was more important. Perhaps it would be enough to avoid the Challenge. Aenguz had to hold the clans together. He had to preserve his father's life's work.

Aenguz stood and filled the stone bowl and lowered his face into the water. Jorgen poured water over Aenguz's hair. He splashed water on his chest and bent arm. Then he stripped out of his cloth and went to the corner to squat and relieve himself.

Jorgen had staged the rest of his gear on the opposite bunk. The *montmorillionite* tipped spear and coated shield with the three distinctive peaks of the Upper Mashu emblazoned on the face. The course white-furred cloak lay draped beside them.

Aenguz took the unused blanket from the bunk above and dried himself. He continued to chomp on the cheese and bread in between his movements. He set the shirt carefully back and tried to slide on his shorts. But his bent arm was too stiff and the knotted pain too sharp. He could not stand and dress. Aenguz's frustration grew.

He sat on the edge of the bed and struggled to slide on the shorts. Jorgen waited but he teetered so far forward he looked about to fall onto Aenguz. Then Aenguz tried with his leggings but after getting one foot then the other he couldn't pull them up. He gritted at his infirmity. If he couldn't dress, how could he fight? Why had the *morillion's* effects been so incomplete? He hoped it was purely a matter of time or of more *morillion*. Only his grandfather could answer that.

After struggling and fuming, the process was too slow, Aenguz called to Jorgen. His Squire flew to his master and helped him on with his leggings. Then he helped Aenguz on with his boots. Aenguz could not pull them on. And lacing the fine boots that Jorgen brought would be impossible. He let his Squire do the work.

While he laced his boots, Jorgen asked, "What happened to your arm, my master?"

"This is the work of *morillion*."

Jorgen stole a few solicitous glances. He worked amid the spent tailings at Aenguz's feet. "Your grandmother instructed me in the use of those medicines. Are you sure you want to forego them?"

Aenguz was grateful for Jorgen. But those medicines were useless against such a fierce burn. If anything further was going to be done with his arm it would take someone with more knowledge, more *morillion*, and more time than he had, if there was anything to be done at all. The workings of the metal was a mystery. The tendrils that reached out to the other *montmorillionite* from his vision were receding. But that too had happened to his mind and revealed what kind of power and potency lay beneath the silver sheen.

"I need more than those, Jorgen."

Aenguz stood and took the shirt. The two worked to try and get the ceremonial shirt over his head and onto his arm. He was losing time and his patience was nearly gone.

Exasperated with his arm he shoved the shirt at Jorgen and commanded him to cut the arm off.

The Squire hesitated but then he took it to his packs produced a knife and cut the sleeve off. Then, with help, they were able to slide it over his head.

Aenguz took the severed sleeve and pushed it onto his forearm to cover the burn. It was not perfect. It would have to do.

Jorgen went back to the bunk and came back with a white fur cloak but Aenguz waved it off.

"But this is from the beast you slew who slew your father. Your grandmother bade me to bring it."

He couldn't bear to look at it never mind wear it. Another truth was that it outsized him. His grandmother would have made it larger to fit the man he was still yet to become. But Aenguz withheld that thought from Jorgen.

"No, I will have all eyes on me as it is. I will feel more myself in my own Warrior's cloak. Do you have it?"

"Of course."

Jorgen unfolded the cloak from the packs and draped the slate blue cloak over Aenguz's shoulders. Snow Leopard fur lined the neck like a mane. The Sidor insignia was embroidered over his left breast.

Aenguz relished the familiar cloak and then he went to his bunk. He took his scabbard strap and swung the metal up to his shoulder. The last vestiges of the vision gave him a glimpse as if he was looking out from within his weapon to the dark interior of the scabbard. He tried to shake the image loose.

He felt like himself, or at least a version of himself. He strode out of the room. Jorgen gathered up his spear and shield and followed behind him. The door slid closed behind Aenguz with a thump.

6

RITES OF PASSAGE

Heavy gray clouds capped the Valley of Gathering. Flourishes curved like the undersides of waves. Aenguz's memories of this time had always been of a bright blue sky. Even with the sharp teeth of the protective mountain walls of the Upper Mashu closing in, the sky would have felt vast. Perhaps it was the instinctive anticipation of spring. Or perhaps it was the shared relief and release of the Akkeidii from the fastness of their winter hardened hearth valleys. Everything added to the openness of the first Gathering of the Spring.

He had felt that excitement each year. Now there was trepidation. A fear that he would be found out. That his trespass would be discovered. That his wounded arm would be revealed. The waste of the *morillion* uncovered.

The cold breath from the White Deeps also inverted the day. It felt more like an autumn day than spring. The smoke from the Deerherd shelter hearth fires and the thick roe deer musk contributed to the upending sensation of the season.

With each step toward the amphitheater, the contrary nature of the world oriented itself and established its inverse reality. Approaching the facade from the Deerherd Shelters, ostensibly slinking to the Warriors

Rites of Passage, out of sight, or at least avoiding most prying eyes, was wholly different from every other approach to the amphitheater. Even as a young boy, Aenguz never came to the pasture valley until after the Rites had concluded. He processed with his father, with the Sidors at the head of the clan as they paraded past the line of clan shelters in the main arm of the valley. Laden wagons rumbled behind them. Pennons ripped the air with the Sidor sigil. All eyes of the clans, of the Akkeidii would be on them, on him. The promise of the future.

And when the Rites completed the celebrations could begin. The roe deer herd would be counted and released down into the Lower Mashu to roam and appease the untamed part of their nature. But now, herd hounds traced the near edges of the herd and kept them back toward the pond. Kept them from marching toward Grieg's Gate. The Deerherds clumped together in groups in the open area between the hound managed edge of the herd and the rippling pool at the edge of Grieg's Gate. A stasis held the Deerherds and the roe deer.

Aenguz saw that their Rites had completed. Fathers beamed with pride at their ascended sons. Some were artisans and brewers and a few Stonemage fathers hovered near their sons with pride even though they had chosen a different path.

Atop Grieg's Gate, Stonemages milled in groups on the outer wall. They waited too for the command to open the gate. Aenguz wondered if the Stonemage sentinel from the night before witnessed his crossing. They were not spaced out evenly as they usually were to call open the gate. Everything was in a holding pattern. They were all waiting on him. In place of laughter and cheers the air was cold and morose. And he walked alone, without his father, with only Jorgen in tow.

Aenguz looked more like the Sidor Warrior who stood at the entrance of the rear wall of the facade than the leader he was meant to be. Trying to be.

Deerherd lords from the clans were gathered at the edge of the rear wall. They were held back by the Sidor Warrior. Were they waiting to reveal what they knew about Aenguz and the *morillion*?

The Warrior straightened when he recognized Aenguz. His eyes fluttered as if he had failed in tracking the Sidor Clan Lord somehow. He sharpened his attentiveness. Held a crisp gaze. He nodded and greeted Aenguz, his dead lord's son, with a terse and respectful tone. He did not appear to notice the bulge under Aenguz's cloak.

The Deerherd lords greeted Aenguz as well. If they meant to reveal him, they didn't show it. They were waiting on Dahlward to fulfill his responsibilities in place of Sairik so that he could fulfill his primary obligations as Lord of the Deerherds. Dahlward was delaying and waiting on Aenguz. Everything was on hold.

Aenguz responded with a distracted familiarity. He was not his father. He had not learned how to comport himself in the role as Ruler of the Akkeidii. Watching his father was easier than assuming his role.

The three curved walls of the skene looked like sections pulled from Grieg's Gate. But unlike the inscrutable and smooth stone-metal of the Water Gate, the facade was made of perfectly fitted polygonal joined limestone blocks. The concave face held sculptures and friezes that shown toward the audience. The rear side held lists of names. Neither side was completely covered. Blank spaces filled the edges waiting on further Stonemage skill to record future Akkeidii accomplishments or notable events. The sculptures were set in the stone like shallow dioramas. Within the carven rectangles were stories in miniature of Akkeidii acts and myths. All of the vignettes in one way or another contributed to the overall story of Grieg Sidor the Venturer. The smaller scenes fit into the largest block that held a living statue of Grieg Sidor himself. He moved out of the bounds of the scene and the inset depth of the stone. His determined gaze tested the strength of the Mashuan Limestone. His frame extended out from the skene in a lurch or a stride as if the stone could not hold him.

Aenguz knew the stories of the Venturer. But he could not draw any courage or assurance from the stern visage. Grieg Sidor was struggling with his own battles. At least the Akkeidii had rallied around him at that time.

A group of Stonemages were gathered at the opposite end of the outer wall. A master scrawled with chalk in a blank space at the edge of two other sculpted rectangles. His smock was dusty and weathered. Three younger Stonemages stood in closely and listened to every word. Another Sidor Warrior stood between them and the entrance to the inner walls. The unfinished business of the Gathering was bursting at the seams.

Aenguz crept to the opening of the inner two walls. The lists of names read back at him and questioned his worthiness. Dahlward's voice reverberated off the stone with sagacious authority. The stone carved faces seemed to hold still in respect and reverence to the Lord of the Deerherds. Or in amazement that a Deerherd and not the Warrior Ruler of the Akkeidii was presiding over the Assembly.

"Who here can guess the measure of his sacrifice? Who can say that he would, if presented with the choice, would grasp the Dagba Stone and loose himself to its creative destruction for the sake of others? For the sake of the Mashu? For the sake of the Lands of the Earth? All we can know is what he faced and what he saved. We live in what he preserved for all Akkeidii, for all peoples."

Dahlward caught Aenguz out of the corner of his eye. The slightest inflection of relief escaped from his lined face. He stepped back and raised his arms to the assembled host.

"Clan Lords and Warriors. Novitiates and Squires. Sons and Fathers. I present you, Lord Aenguz. Son of Sairik, Ruler of the Akkeidii, Lord of the Sidor Clan, Master of the Two Lands, and the Twin Rivers. Polemarch of the Warriors."

Jorgen stepped up and proffered the spear. Aenguz took it. Then he checked the grip he kept on his cloak around the ruined arm. He wished his hand was stronger. The feel of the spear didn't stanch the hammering in his heart. A few deep breaths only intensified the knots. He wasn't ready to take his father's place.

He walked out from the security of the wall onto the stage before the Assembly of the Warriors. Dahlward stepped back and deferred to his grandson.

The host shifted and straightened like a forest surprised by a sudden gale. All eyes fixed on him. For a moment, Aenguz was back before Morgrom the Flayer. The tapered wedge of Warriors and male Akkeidii mimicked the vague shape of the eye-filled skull in the pit of Carrowen Celd. But these eyes could not pierce him the way Morgrom's eyes had.

The amphitheater was cordoned into sections governed by hierarchies. The clan lords sat on the lowest tier. Their Honored Guards clustered tightly around them. Then decreasing ranks of Warriors filled the seats roughly halfway up the tiers. Warriors who held their own renown in strength, contests of speed, extreme endurance, or in lore wisdom. Above them were Squires. Then the Novitiates sat, spears in hand across the breadth of the arena. There were no clan designations in their seating. They were one graduating army.

Behind them, filling up to the uppermost tiers, were the rest of the Akkeidii. Young boys who would swear an Oath of Fealty to become Squires and eventually Warriors. Their fathers or father-uncles were with them. Artisans, Stonemages, Deerherds, brewers, farmers. Akkeidii from all walks of life.

Clans sat in their own wedges. The Finits sat furthest to the left from Aenguz. They were the smallest clan in terms of numbers. They were isolated, removed from the others. The Gambls sat beside them but kept a space from them. They flanked the Makans and deferred to them, the second most powerful clan. The Makans enmity with the Sidors stretched back to the Challenge that saw Sairik win rulership of the Akkeidii.

An invisible line divided the arena down the middle. On the right, the Kriels and the Baierls flanked the Sidors wedge. Loyal to the Sidors, only the different cowls of animal fur distinguished the different clans. And their own distinct clan sigils. All the Warriors wore the same slate blue cloaks. The Sidors wore, like Aenguz's cloak, cowls of snow leopard fur. The Baierls wore a course black fur over their shoulders from the fierce bears that dwelled in the Mashu. It made their own black hair seem doubly long. The Kriels cloaks were adorned with smooth tan Mashu lion fur. It made their shoulders look like stone. The Makans wore gray ram pelts. The Gambls wore finely tailored gray fur cowls flecked with black that looked more like fine fabric than fur. And the Finits caparisoned their cloaks with large spotted feathers. And their black hair was slicked back with a firm white paste.

The clans and spectators had their own perceptions and agendas. Curiosity had the appearance of anger in the stern Akkeidii complexion. Despite their different concerns they were still intimidating and over-whelming as a crowd. Aenguz looked over them, without actually looking at them. But he could still feel their fierce gaze.

He had always been a spectator during the Rites of Passage. Even when he passed the Rites two years earlier, he was not alone. He was with his own class of matriculating Warriors. Now he was completely alone before them all. And the assignment of Last Emissary, which he tried to ignore, isolated him in a more fundamental way from the Warriors, and the Akkeidii. He was convinced they all saw the grievous role as if it was branded on him.

His father had made the ritual seem easy. But now with all eyes on him the pieces of the ceremony fled. The stone floor might have been vapor. His eyes went back to the Sidors, to his clan. He hoped the familiar faces of brother-friends and father-uncles would steady him. But as his eyes focused on the wedge between the Kriels and the Baierls a hand wrenched his stomach out from his gut.

In the front row, where his father would have been, was the iron-bound box. It was covered with the heavy black cloth. The cerement draped over the box and spilled onto the stage. It looked like a fountain of concentrated grief pouring onto the stone. Deep lines of purple filled the creases. All the tears of the Sidor Clan were distilled there.

Aenguz's eyes locked on the coffin and the thought of his father's bones within. Thought of his failed attempt to honor him, immortalize him. The Honored Guard looked lost around the small coffin. Their eyes were as vacant as those of the long-dead heroes on the friezes behind him. Long black mourning scarves hung over their cloaks and covered the black blotches of snow leopard fur. The Sidor sigil was buried in the black. Their purpose stripped suddenly from them. The meaning of the Honored Guards' lives was scattered like ash.

There was no help there for Aenguz. Only an emptying hollowness. Without thinking, Aenguz said, "Let the Rites of Passage commence." There was no certainty or authority in his tone. His voice broke as if he was at the front edge of adolescence.

The wisps of the gale turned heads and brushed consternation across the faces of Akkeidii. No one moved.

His breath quickened and shallowed. Even in the cool air sweat pushed out through his entire face. The lump in his throat could not be freed. The eyes bored deeper.

Then he saw Ragbald. First of the Honored Guard to Sairik. Aenguz's father-uncle whom he had squired for. He stood over the small, draped coffin. He pumped his fist slightly up and down as he stared hard at Aenguz.

Aenguz shook out of his grim reverie. He grabbed the spear and gaveled the stage with the heel.

The clan lords then gaveled in unison.

Then Aenguz said, "Let the Rites of Passage commence," this time with a loud unbroken voice.

The Novitiates filed down past the Squires and Warriors and Honored Guard. They lined the oval stage in tight rows. Aenguz thought their nerves seemed heightened by the pervasive uncertainty of his absence and sudden presence - and the threat of Challenge. A threat he meant to head off by completing this ceremony.

Still, they stood like Warriors at the first bloom of manhood. Shoulders square and strong. Their various weapons strung across their chest or over their shoulders or slung at their sides. They looked up into the sculptures behind Aenguz and waited at attention.

Once they were set, Aenguz continued. The words came back to him.

"Let the Mashu listen. Let the White Deeps hear. Let the White and Millen know as these Warrior Akkeidii recite the Lay of *Montmorillionite*."

As one the young Warriors started reciting.

> *Montmorillionite, silver bone*
> *Of the Mashu, leather and stone*
>
> *Light of the Earth burnished and true*
> *Warrior forger silver hue*
>
> *Forged in the mind, crafted in soul*
> *Singular kind for one alone*
>
> *Ev'r keen, ever new, ever bright*
> *Earth's first star to dispel the night*
>
> *Born of the mind bound to the life*
> *Down to Earth with death's final strife*
>
> *Light in the dark and in the hands*
> *Pow'r concentrated from the Lands*
>
> *The final darkness to the foe*
> *Blood to the Earth, red seeds to sow*
>
> *Montmorillionite truest blade*
> *To its mysteries, we are bade*
>
> *Manifold mysteries unknown*
> *'Til all of life's metal is grown*

Aenguz's lips shadowed the words with the matriculating Warriors. He felt closer to them than to the role he sought to insinuate himself into in the absence of his father. The Lay was woven into the discipline of his Warrior's mind. This recitation was a precursor to the revealing of each Warrior's own newly forged unique *montmorillionite* weapon. And then Aenguz would pronounce them ascended with all the rights and privileges of Warriorhood.

As the Warriors chanted on, Aenguz sought to recall the particulars of the final Rites he would perform. But his mind drifted. A tinnitus sounded from a deep distant place within him. The note, like a solitary chime, grew gradually louder. It rose and grew closer to the nearer part of his mind.

The sound grew louder. It rose from a clean chime into a sustained distortion. It drowned out his own searching thoughts and eradicated the Warriors words. Their lips moved in unison but only the ever-loudening wail filled his ears and his mind.

Aenguz gripped the spear and leaned into it to counter the listing sensation caused by the wave of sound. Formication reeled in his wounded arm. The *morillion* worked like angry ants. The ring rose to a loud chorus. A thousand tuning forks vibrating at the extent of their upper range. His own weapon rang and pierced through the base of his neck.

The Warriors silent lips stopped. They moved to unshoulder or unholster their tooled leather scabbards to reveal their weapons to the Warrior host for the first time.

The holdover from the *morillion's* ecstasy lingered in Aenguz. He saw the edges of each of these newly formed weapons from within the darkness of each scabbard as the first light of the ceremony day reached them. Each edge on triple-headed axes. Every inch on the long edges of swords or curved cutlasses. Fanciful fans and branches of oddly esoteric weapons. Every sharp point or curved tooth of metal. The sheen of hafts and hilts and knurled handles were all vivid and present and immediate.

The spears and weapons of the Warriors in the tiers were vaguely visible to Aenguz, too, but their hum and keenness resided behind a fog. The residual potency of the vision was fading. The newness and proximity of this freshly forged metal commanded the entirety of his perception.

Again, an uncomfortable stillness and awkwardness gripped the assembled Warriors. The last piece that Aenguz held before the wave took him was the ritual of the procession through the Warriors. He should walk amid the rows and inspect each weapon. He recalled that piece of the responsibility that would have him process among the Warriors. It was the last thing he recalled from his memory before his perceptions were hijacked. But his experience with the effects of the *morillion* made each weapon known to him. His knowledge of each was intimate as if he had contemplated each one along with each Warrior before it was even formed. He didn't need to look at them. He knew them all in an instant. He leaned with all his strength into his spear and warded against a fall.

He recalled the words his father would have said. A brief pronouncement proclaiming the Warriors as ascended. This was the last step. His action a final act to complete his plan, his decision to preserve the Sidors, his father's legacy, the course of the Akkeidii. Selene.

He hadn't accepted the path his grandfather had proffered. The life of a Deerherd. That option was cutoff the moment he stepped onto the stage after his grandfather had announced his arrival.

Here in front of the assembled Warrior host he could call out the message the Flayer had given him. He could warn them, rally them. But then, he would eschew his role, his inheritance, his privilege. Aenguz would become the Flayer's messenger. He would become the Last Emissary. That decision would make him more an outcast than choosing to revert to being a Deerherd. The concept of being so alone, touched on a fear he could only look away from and avoid acknowledging.

His lips moved. His throat worked. But he could neither hear, nor confirm the order of the words he said. The scream of the revealed metal was too much for him. His balance shifted and the heel of the spear skipped across the stone. The procession was missed altogether.

The clan lords gaveled the stone after Aenguz as if the sound was intentional. Then the *montmorillionite* siren halted. The Warriors sheathed their weapons. And the cheers in the amphitheater confirmed that his ears were his own again. His life was a different matter.

He wanted to right things. To return things to normal. To how they were supposed to be.

In completing the Rites of Passage and assuming the role of Ruler of the Akkeidii, he had taken on a responsibility he scarcely understood. War was coming. He had condemned these new Warriors to death. He had slipped into a role with even more difficult challenges. One he didn't know how to broach.

Morgrom's words remained in him. *"The Last Battle will be enjoined again. My victory will come in a new form of war. Its ways and movements will be beyond your ken. But war is not the worst thing you should fear."*

7

~~~

THE CALL FOR CHALLENGE

The cheers rode on the heels of the clan lords' gavel. Warriors poured down onto the stage to congratulate their peers. Aenguz's heart pulled toward them. He would have been the first to jump up and clap the shoulders of the matriculated Sidor Warriors. He would have complimented them on their skill in crafting their weapons. He would have joked with them about the trials. But his father had remained removed and reserved. A proud smile would have brightened his whole face but his role as Ruler of the Akkeidii kept him separate and stern.

Aenguz worked to recall and emulate the things his father would have done. Staying apart from the Warriors was the one outward thing. Inside, his mind raced through the many decisions that he would be asked to preside over. The Deerherd lords would have questions about the herd that would need to be mediated. The labor of the Stonemages would have to be meted out and likely argued over.

The squire assignments and promotions could take place now. Referrals and acceptance into the Honored Guard would be determined. And matings could commence. He could wed Selene. But who would perform the ceremony? The Kriel Clan Lord would do it or the Baierl. Aenguz had to figure out how to navigate that discussion so as not to offend either of the Sidor allies.

For the first time, clear light cast shadows in the amphitheater. Though the clouds still hid the sun a distinct patch of blue countered the wave-like clouds. The stasis that had held the Valley of Gathering was released. All of the proceedings, decisions, and ceremonies could continue or begin. His plan had worked. The arm was still excoriating and the knots at the joints still held it bent and awkward beneath his cloak. But now at least it would have time to heal. He could see his father interred without fear of the Challenge. He could begin to take on the role with the help of the Honored Guard and the Sidor's allies. His daring ploy had worked.

With everything falling into place toward normal, albeit a new normal, the void where his uncertain future lay was fading away. Aenguz's mind returned to the Flayer and the message. He started back to the curved walls to find his grandfather.

Behind him, the Deerherd lords had converged on the Stonemages and on Dahlward at the blank space on the rear wall. Grieg Sidor loomed over them all. His enigmatic stone gaze warning the Akkeidii from the past.

A slight change emerged in him as he slipped behind the inner wall. A timid bloom unsure of the light. Instead of a boy running to his grandfather to ask what to do, what the message might mean, he thought about all the Akkeidii now, the hearth valleys, their homes. How would he tell them and prepare them for the incursions that would be coming from the east? He would be the one to make decisions and the call to arms. He was the Polemarch of the Warriors now. He would be expected to command the force that would respond to whatever the Flayer intended for the Akkeidii. He would be an integral part of the Akkeidii response whatever it was and not just a solitary messenger. Could he eschew the edicts and responsibilities of the Flayer's charge by handing off the message? Who would he command to deliver the message to Corundum in his stead? He could not leave the Akkeidii now.

With each step, Aenguz increased his pace. Time seemed to accelerate and contract. The cacophony of cheers and release filled the concave walls like the waves of a post-storm surge. He nudged past the Deerherd lords and to the backs of the Stonemages crowded around the chalk-filled rectangle at the wall. The Deerherds were annoyed when Aenguz bumped into them, but their complexions shifted to respect when they realized who was forcing his way through. With a spear in one hand and his left arm buried in his cloak and severed sleeve covering his effectively useless left arm, he had to shoulder his way past. His arm still piqued with pain and rigor. Even though he was taller than those around him, he felt like a child trying to muscle his way past adults. Urgency gathered momentum in Aenguz.

Dahlward was listening and nodding to the white-haired Stonemage master. He did not turn to Aenguz or his calls. When Aenguz broke through the line and called out for the Lord of the Deerherds Dahlward reached for his grandson and raised his arm as if he needed the pillar of his grandson for strength.

"Lord, you know Cuzzuol, the son of Curufin," Dahlward held Aenguz's eyes and silently commanded him to be still.

Aenguz knew the Stonemage master. Every Akkeidii knew Cuzzuol. His skill rivaled the masters of old. Much of the newer sculptures and dioramas on the facade were fashioned by Cuzzuol's delicate hand.

The master stopped. He looked perturbed as if his chain of thought had been unnecessarily disrupted. He considered Aenguz and his eyes sharpened and intensified. He might have been assessing Aenguz the way he sized up a carefully chosen slab of limestone. His leather smock was smudged with chalk and stone dust. His hair was a cap of white nearly covering the old coal beneath.

The pocket of novice sculptors and Deerherds stilled. They were already silent, and they hung on every word of their teacher. A wave of shame flushed Aenguz's cheeks. The master's eyes moved over Aenguz's cloak, stopped on the bulge on his left side. Then they dropped down to his legs and to his feet. He turned back to the smooth wall and raised the hunk of chalk.

An image was already emerging in the white strokes. The borders of a rough rectangle were already measured out. A silhouette of a figure was already distinct in the center. Arms reached from the shoulders and the nascent face gazed down. On the right, rough renditions of the Hearth Valleys with their distinct terrains and capitals were arranged. The Valley of Gathering was nestled in between. The swirl of Grieg's Gate was unmistakable. On the left, was a wider contoured map of the Upper and the Lower Mashu. The White Deeps were set to merge with the sculptures above. And the Twin Rivers ran down to the tip of the Cairngorm. The southernmost point of Akkeidii Lands. The figure at the center seemed to emerge from a mound there and raise up over all of the Mashu.

Then the figure, albeit rough, snapped into sudden focus for Aenguz. This was Sairik's memorial. The Stonemage master had crafted a benevolent Ruler who considered everything in the Mashu and all of the Akkeidii. This was a stark departure from the heroic and war like friezes elsewhere on the wall.

Aenguz froze. First the covered coffin behind him, now the memorial. He leaned into Dahlward. Aenguz had witnessed his father being torn to shreds in the icy crevasse. He had stood at the pyre for two days. He had removed his father's skull from the iron box on his grandparent's table. He had handled it in order to perform the failed ritual to set a permanent *montmorillionite* helm on it. But even with all of that, there was still a part of him that couldn't believe he was gone. A place below the sediment of his life had not accepted or internalized that fact. Somehow it was all an intractable dream. But now here in front of the image, albeit abstract, was a rendition that was definitely him. Sairik was moving to join the figures of stone. There was no more denial left in Aenguz. All of it had accumulated and then vanished in the deft skill of the Stonemage master. His grandfather's damp eyes told him in a new way that his father was gone. A way that he could finally understand. Aenguz felt alone and rudderless. Now one of his first acts, perhaps his most important act, would be to see his father interred on the Cairngorm with the chieftains of old and the heroes of the Last Battle.

"What do you think?" Dahlward's voice gulped out the question.

Dahlward and Aenguz steadied one another. The third leg of their triumvirate was gone. Their tenuous balance left them vulnerable.

Then metal gaveled stone. Confusion flashed across the eyes of the Stonemages and Deerherds.

Aenguz looked to his spear in disbelief to confirm that it had not moved on its own. Then he waved out his left hand, still beneath his cloak, assuring the others that he had not hammered the floor. He needed the spear to keep his feet. And he was not done taking in the chalky image. He was still processing his final responsibility and duty to his father's bones.

Metal gaveled again. The cheers and elated timber of the host shifted to sternness and the hard observance of discipline.

Aenguz walked through the parting Deerherd lords back to the opening to the stage. Warriors were clearing the oval floor. Some climbed up into the stairs. Most poured out to the sides and closed off the arena between the tiers and the facade.

Aenguz and Dahlward staggard as if they walked on broken glass.

As the last of the Warriors cleared, Aenguz saw the Makan Clan Lord standing out from the wedge of the Makans. He was a rotund man. The various ram pelts dressed over his cloak made him look as if he had slain a mob of rams. His black beard held bolts of white like thin streaks of lightning that reached down onto the shelf of his chest. His eyes were hard and determined. This was a clan lord used to getting his way and wholly unfamiliar with being thwarted or denied.

He gaveled one final time and the other clan lords acquiesced.

The Makan Clan Lord passed his spear back to his first and strode forward inured to the pain in his severe limp.

The Gambl leader stepped in beside him. The Kriel Clan Lord and the Baierl Clan Lord passed off their spears and walked to the center side by side. The Kriel lord waved Ragbald down to join them and represent the Sidors for Sairik. The two lords flanked Ragbald.

The Finit Clan Lord passed off his spear, adjusted his feathered cloak, exchanged a few words with the Finit Warriors behind him, and then walked alone to the closing circle.

Aenguz's heart jumped from a mournful sorrow to a hare's race. He was not ready for a conclave of clan lords.

Jorgen was at his side. He grasped the spear and said something that helped Aenguz release it. He looked to his grandfather, but the imposing force of the gathering clan lords pushed him back to the edge of the opening. The patch of blue in the cloud deck was gone. The bright light turned back to a milky gray.

As they came to a stop in a tight circle the clan lords said, "Grieg's will. Grieg's will," to one another as a kind of greeting or commencement.

Ragbald, Aenguz's father-uncle, said the words directly to Aenguz, then nodded and turned his head slightly, intimating that Aenguz do the same.

Aenguz mouthed the words, but he could not look into the eyes of the other clan lords. The Kriel and Baierl lords were reassuring. They greeted Ragbald and Aenguz with a certainty and confidence. The Makan Clan Lord looked like he was about to berate Aenguz. The Gambl lord at his side held a calm sly smile. He gazed at Aenguz as if he was wounded prey.

The Finit Clan Lord seemed removed, almost ignored by the Gambl and the Makan lords. But the Finit Clan Lord looked aloof, beyond their subtle disdain.

Murmurs, whispers, and rumblings fluttered throughout the tiers. The Warriors had not stilled completely. Their voices sounded like a confused surf on a sharp rocked shore.

Ragbald nodded nearly imperceptibly to Aenguz. Aenguz understood his uncle-father.

His face was still slick. His eyes were damp. He was utterly transparent before the Akkeidii clan lords. He steeled his face. A Warrior's imperturbable mien.

"Why have you called us together?" Aenguz asked of the Makan lord.

"There are matters that require our attention," The Makan chieftain replied.

Aenguz tensed. What did he know? What did he intend to call out?

"What matters require this hasty conclave?" the Kriel Clan Lord asked.

"Our lord is dead. We are without a leader."

"Did you mean for us to discuss facts?" The Baierl lord interjected.

The Makan lord puffed. His beard was a growing plume of black smoke. He mastered his suppressed anger and continued. "There are many matters before us, but all those needs wait behind this matter."

The Gambl lord spoke up. His words were oily. "The roe deer are held back. Stone lies still. Ceremonies and matings wait. Lord Warrum seeks only to restore order to our peoples."

"And what of Sairik's ceremony?" Ragbald asked. "Perhaps you forgot about that matter." Ragbald's voice was salted with anger and grief.

"Surely not," the Gambl lord continued. He reached out gesturing to include all the clan lords. "This matter pertains to all of us."

"And all other matters needs wait behind it," the Makan lord interrupted. "I will see it resolved first off."

Aenguz's plan was slipping from his gnarled fingers. The Makan lord saw his opening and he was going to take it. The normal course he had pushed the world toward was falling back. The order that he hoped to restore or maintain was collapsing.

The gallery quieted. The curved walls carried the clan lords' words easily up into the tiers. As their dispute deepened, the volume of their replies lowered. Their words hovered above a growled whisper as the intensity increased.

Ragbald and the Kriel and Baierl cut back at the Makan and the Gambl. The Finit lord remained silent. The two factions were arguing about whether to bury Sairik first or resolve the absence of his leadership first.

Aenguz's heart pitched. His head whirled. The clan lord's voices raised and roared. Soon their arguments hung just below a shout. To Aenguz they appeared to be fighting over his father's body right before his eyes.

It was more than he could handle. His frangible emotions left no room for organized thoughts or reason. The back and forth tore at him as it seemed to tear at his father's Rites. He had no idea how to quell them. His father had not taught him enough.

He wanted to interject, to calm them. The Warriors in the gallery seemed to all be looking at him. He couldn't find an opening. His breathing quickened but air didn't reach him.

The Makan lord's rage was expansive. He rebuffed the Kriel and the Baierl. He questioned Ragbald's presence at all in the conclave.

The Gambl danced around and affirmed the Makan lords' assertions and demands.

"You lap at the heels of the Sidors."

"You would raise your arm against them? Against Sairik and Aenguz?"

"The law in this matter is clear," the Gambl iterated.

"What are you saying, Warrum?" The Baierl lord called to the Makan.

Aenguz wanted to quell them and still the arguing. His heart beat like he was sprinting. His father would have been able to negotiate and manage these lords of men. Aenguz was not ready. His plan was beginning to topple. These lords seemed on the verge of blows.

He reached out his hands and patted the air to quiet them. His left arm came out from under the cloak. The severed sleeve slid off his forearm and dropped to the stage as if his skin had detached.

The crucible of clan lords gasped. The Finit lord may have squawked. The Gambl lowered his arms. A slight smile crossed his mouth. The closest Warriors in the gallery heaved a sigh laden with shock. Other heads craned to look around the clan lords. Sought to glimpse the horror of Aenguz's arm.

Aenguz snatched back his mottled and gruesome limb. He fumbled with his cloak, but he couldn't get his bent arm under it. His face grew red and hot. He pulled the snow leopard cowl over the gnarled hand with his right.

"There is only one matter before us," the Makan lord resumed. "I call for Challenge."

The Kriel lord's complexion sagged but then firm resolved returned to his sharp eyes. "The Kriel's call for Challenge as well."

The Gambl lord said with a flourish as if he had practiced his response. "The Gambls Challenge for the right to rule the Akkeidii."

The Baierl huffed. "We Challenge the challengers." It was clear he not only spoke for the Baierls but in one phrase, aligned himself with the Kriels and the Sidors.

Aenguz might have been grateful for their unquestioning support, even after witnessing the state of his arm. But the chambers he had sought to save were flooding around him. The message and the charge seemed far away. There was no way he could bring it up here. It would seem like a ruse, a false distraction. In the face of the Challenge, it seemed to barely matter.

The eyes in the circle turned to the Finit lord who maintained a composure that startled Aenguz. He looked as if he deliberated for an eon before he spoke. "The Finits will join in the Challenge."

The Gambl and Makan were vaguely surprised as if the Finit lord had suddenly appeared or if a statue had come to life. But both lords had achieved their aim. And they looked self-satisfied with the result.

Then the Finit lord turned his white-matted head to Aenguz. "Where will you meet the Challenge son of Sairik?"

The question tumbled around him with the fall of everything he knew. Conflicting thoughts whirled in the maelstrom of his mind. His throat was clenched in a vice. His breathing was so shallow it was nearly non-existent. All eyes bored into him, pierced like a thousand spears.

Dual shames warred for prominence in the negative side of his nature. The self-defeating part of himself that sought to sabotage him from within. Fighting and dying here in front of this host. Losing everything knowing what would happen to the Sidors, the maids, Selene, his father's lifelong work redounded on him with a lonely prospect of failure more profound than he could fully contemplate in the moment.

Not seeing his father interred on the Cairngorm. Not setting his own stones on the cairn or planting the seed for the cairn tree at the head of the mound hollowed him in a way that competed for a deeper low than the shame of his other failures. He had not born his coffin to the Valley of Gathering. Had desecrated his skull. Had not offered any word of praise or assent to Cuzzoul for his father's memorial. And now he would not see his remains to their final resting place.

When he spoke, he responded to the competing shames. "The Cairngorm."

The Makan lord shouted, "Here, the Challenge will happen right here! Right now!"

"You are not the one being challenged, Lord Warrum," the Finit lord replied.

Ragbald chimed in, "It is Aenguz's right and the word of the law."

The Makan and Gambl were flummoxed. For the moment, their plan was thwarted or at least delayed.

Ragbald was within his role to speak. He turned to face the gallery of enrapt Warriors.

"The Challenge is called by Lord Warrum. And accepted by the Sidors, Kriels, Gambls, Baierls, and Finits." He turned his head back to the circle of clan lords. "Go and choose your Champions from among Aenguz's contemporaries." Then back to the audience. "The Challenge will take place on the Cairngorm. The Champions will depart and determine the outcome for the right to rule the Akkeidii. We will await their return. All proceedings in the valley will wait until by force or wisdom the Ruler of the Akkeidii returns to us. By Grieg's will."

In a final shot at Warrum, Ragbald looked at Aenguz and asked, "My Lord?"

Aenguz heard his father's words and not his own. He knew what Ragbald was asking. He answered with a finality that outstripped him. "Let it be so," Aenguz said as if he was pronouncing his own execution.

"Stonemages," Ragbald turned over his other shoulder to the Stonemages gathered behind the wall. "Prepare to open Grieg's Gate."

The host roiled as if a massive wave had crashed up into the seats. Even the stone pines beyond the last row quaked. The clan lords spun and returned to their wedges to select their Champions and check their strategies as their men gathered around them.

Amid the rising chaos of Akkeidii Warriors, Aenguz stood as alone and isolated as if he had already been drawn back into the memory of stone behind him.

8

CHAMPIONS

The nearest Warriors poured down onto the stage around the clan chieftains. The stairs were suddenly clotted. Warriors took staggered strides to climb down the tiers. Squires tried to squeeze in between one another and past the wall of Warriors to get to their masters.

The top tiers where the fathers and hopeful sons sat were blocked by the commotion below. Worried fathers who had not chosen the path of Warriorhood wanted to escape with their sons. The eyes of the young boys were wide and enthralled. Aenguz could see their curiosity and excitement. They drank in all of the movements and protestations of honor beneath them as if they saw themselves, saw their future.

Their fathers were worried for their sons and concerned for the Akkeidii. Some clung to their boys while they waited against the downward press. Others admonished their sons, tried to break the enrapt attention they threw down onto the stage. These young Warriors below with their broad shoulders and enigmatic weapons piqued the boys' adventurous hearts. They would have sworn fealty to the Squire's path right then and there if there was anyone to administer the Rites.

Ragbald was the last of the circle of clan lords to depart. He may have said 'Do not worry,' to Aenguz over the din. Kriel and Baierl Warriors held their sheathed weapons out offering themselves and their weapons to the Challenge in support of Aenguz. Many were beyond the acceptable age range, but the point of honor compelled them. The two clan lords wrangled with that firm fealty with their men. This group of Champions would be the youngest on record.

Ragbald waved to Jorgen. Aenguz's squire ran across his face and handed his uncle-father the spear. The scepter of authority was no longer his. Ragbald said something to Jorgen and the Squire shot off through the crowd. Ragbald met the wave of Sidors who swore and insisted that they be the ones to join Aenguz. Sairik's coffin was effaced in the crush.

His plan to restore and retain everything was collapsing. The flood he fought against was stronger than him. The decisions he worried about making a moment earlier as a clan lord evaporated like a subsiding spray.

Aenguz was back in his original dilemma. The consequence of his attempt with *montmorillionite* and the wreckage it left of his arm. As Ragbald and Jorgen disappeared, Aenguz was left isolated on the stage. He was removed from the Warriors. From the clan lords. From everyone.

Then a hand took Aenguz's shoulder and drew him back behind the wall like the only valuable bit of flotsam left from a lost wreck. The last piece capable of keeping the final survivor afloat.

Dahlward pulled back the cloak and examined Aenguz's ruined limb. The Stonemages and Deerherd lords were gone. Semi-transparent gray and jagged lines of purple covered the limb. It was still crooked as if he had just completed some harsh shield exercise. His hand still curled in an open clutch as if he held the wide shaft of an invisible spear. The color and translucence had shifted and changed some since Aenguz had first examined it.

Dahlward inspected the hand and the joints with a curious and clinical eye. Rather than a healer's gaze, there was a disturbing and discomfiting realization. It was similar to the shock the clan lords had. It was the impression that his arm had lost its skin in some horrific, unknown, and revealing act of theurgy. That beneath the gruesome flesh and contorted arm was the sheen of some newly exposed flesh. It looked ghoulish like he was becoming something less than human.

"I need more *morillion*. Can you heal this?"

Dahlward looked up from his inspection and met his grandson's eyes. "There was not much skin left for the *morillion* to work with."

"Look at this. How can I fight?" But the thought in his head was, *how will Selena have me like this?*

"The loam needs more time to work. Is that not why you chose to go to the Cairngorm?"

Aenguz couldn't revisit the shames. And the benefit in the delay played no role in his calculations. Perhaps it was a hidden boon. But his joints were still too stiff. The gray sheen was too taut. He did not believe three days would be enough time to get his arm fully back.

He flexed his claw. Turned and twisted the wrist. Attempted to straighten the ugly limb.

"Stretch it. Work the joints. There may be enough time," Dahlward trailed off. The hope in his voice was incipient. He wrestled with his inadequacy and his supposed failure with the *morillion*. His eyes held unnamed tremors.

Too much was happening around Aenguz. He put his consternation and exacerbation about his arm to the side for a moment. Time was slipping from him.

"Grappa, I had a dream."

Just then, a Sidor Warrior came around the edge of the wall at the opening.

"You may want to practice the ritual beforehand a little more next time." His smile was a combination of mock seriousness and emerging laughter. He greeted Dahlward respectfully.

"Ridder," Dahlward replied. He gestured to Aenguz's arm.

Aenguz was reluctant to show his arm to his best friend.

"What do you keep doing to this arm? Perhaps choose some other part of your body to flog? At least it looks a little better than the last time I saw it."

"It will heal further," Aenguz said.

"Yes, he just needs time," Dahlward confirmed.

Ridder wore the same cloak, the same Sidor sigil, and a similar ceremonial embroidered shirt. His weapon hung at his back. He was chiseled and handsome. His sharp features and sculpted cheeks echoed those of his father – Ragbald. An easy confidence radiated from him. He mostly ignored the chaos in the arena behind them. When a louder commotion erupted and died down his eyes shifted to the side and another different laugh crossed his face.

"The Kriels and Baierls are picking their Champions. My father is helping them. The Makans and Gambls will have more to consider in a moment." He stepped closer, looked over the arm again. Then he sniffed and snorted with an exaggerated release. "Well, at least we can be grateful for one thing."

Aenguz was too buried to bring himself to laugh. He was thankful for his friend. He wished he could have met him where he was at. Aenguz was too withered and overwhelmed to respond in kind.

Looking at both of them, "I have to tell you something," Aenguz continued.

Ragbald returned with Sairik's *montmorillionite* tipped spear in hand from the outer edge of the facade. He was focused and stern. His black scarf trailed at his sides.

"The Kriel and Baierl Champions are chosen. Lord," he spoke to Dahlward. "They will need guides. But choose only one Sidor. Two may roil Warrum. Pick a Kriel if you can."

Dahlward and Ragbald nodded at one another as understanding passed between them. The Lord of the Deerherds pulled the slate cloak back over Aenguz's arm and walked out of the wing.

Aenguz opened his mouth to stop him, but he was already fast away.

Ragbald motioned Aenguz and Ridder to the opening. He spoke in a low tone as the young men looked on.

The line that had divided the amphitheater in half earlier was more distinct. The fathers and sons who were trapped above now flowed down the middle like a waterfall. They emptied out past the Sidors, Kriels, and Baierls to the right out of the amphitheater to the spur and the waiting tremulous Akkeidii.

Squires ran back in, against the grain with packs and satchels. They wormed their way into the crowd of Warriors on the left side of the stage.

The Finits overflowed to the left out of the arena. The Finit Warriors still in the tiers were pushed to the edge of the amphitheater by the Gambl Warriors. Their clan lord's back was to the arena. His cloak was a cascade of large brown feathers with white bands down the length. His cloak and white matted hair kept their deliberations secret.

The Makans and Gambls on the oval floor were ebullient. They clustered around their four Champions like they were at a celebration. Like they were already celebrating a victory. As Squires broke through, Aenguz could see into the center they were all gathered around.

In flashes, he saw Warrum holding the silvered spear. A meaty arm clutched the spear above his father's hand. Bodies shuffled again. The eye of the storm closed and then opened. Another Champion stood at Warrum's right. The clan lord reached up to the shoulder of the second Warrior. He was self-assured. He looked around the circle as if he was searching out anyone who would dare challenge the source of his father's pride. He nodded and flashed a terse smile to the adulation from the other Warriors. His eyes were alert. He looked past the praise and welcomed his father's affirming grasp. Warrum's pride radiated with a broad smile out from his bulbous beard.

"Warrum sees his opening. He sends his two sons Mandavu and Kachota on the Challenge."

Aenguz caught glimpses of Mandavu's face. He stood taller than all the Makan Warriors around him. Taller than anyone in the amphitheater. Although he held a reserved grin, almost self-satisfied, he still possessed the same bent toward anger in the shelf of his brow that his father had. The scruff on his face was short but tightly groomed. His shoulders were mountains. His cloak was unnecessary in accentuating his size. It seemed like a contrivance. His chest bulged from his Makan ceremonial shirt.

"Word has moved through the ranks. Mandavu and Kachota intend to kill you," Ragbald uttered.

"The Kriels and Baierls will have something to say about that," Ridder spat.

"I mean to say that they will likely not negotiate. Be wary of their words. The Gambls they have chosen were selected for their cunning, not their size."

Aenguz could not make out the Gambl Champions in their wolf-cut cloaks beside the Makans. The circle was too dense. He could just make out the Gambl Clan lord's spear poking up from the Warriors heads.

A pair of Squires ran past the Sidors through the wings to the Finits. They carried packs and water skins. The feathers in their hair flapped as they passed.

"Byrgir has chosen the brothers Roberge and Strey to counter Warrum."

Ridder nodded heartily. "Roberge is big. He is not intimidated by size. He is not intimidated by anyone."

"Strey is younger," Aenguz offered.

"Roberge dotes on his brother. He intimated that he might withdraw if his brother could not share in the victory."

"Strey is a good fighter. He is quick. And he has learned much from his brother. He has more experience than his age belies." Ridder was pleased with the choice.

"Tavinahl has chosen Lokah for his wisdom. He is already on the path of being a Loremaster. One wise in the ways of *Montmorillion* lore may be helpful. And Slocum will join him."

"He is the Kriel that-" Ridder started.

"Yes, that is him," Ragbald finished.

"Good," Ridder answered.

As nervous as Aenguz was about the news of the Makan brothers, he was grateful for the choices of the Kriels and the Baierls. Their loyalty was a boon to him. He wondered how they might feel if they got a closer look at his arm. If he was doomed to fail how might that change their calculations. He knew of their Champions, but he did not know them well. All of the Champions except for Strey were older than him by two or three years. The Finits deliberations were still going on behind the slope to the pasture. But they would likely be the oldest and most experienced they could choose.

"What about the Sidors?" Aenguz asked. "Who did you choose to join me?"

"What am I to you, deer guts?" Ridder said sideways. Then in a genuine tone, "We are brother-friends."

He was so close to Aenguz that they were experiencing this together. Ragbald, his uncle-father had sent his son straight away to be at Aenguz's side. He had rebuffed the Sidors with the only choice that suited Aenguz and his own protective nature.

Aenguz gratitude pillowed his heart. Tears moistened his eyes. His throat shuddered. He reached across with his right hand and rested it on Ridder's shoulder. "We are brothers."

The Finits parted to reveal their Champions. Aenguz glimpsed the feather cloaked Warriors.

"Shudaak and Ondolfur," Ragbald said. He nodded at the Finit choice and then turned to his son and Aenguz.

Ragald leaned the spear against his chest, grabbed his son, and touched his forehead to Ridder's. He whispered to his son. Then he grasped Aenguz the same way and touched his forehead to Aenguz's. "Be wary. Negotiate as you must. There may be a course that does not force them to kill. But Warrum expects a victor. Even in the face of greater odds, they will still be expected to defeat you. Be strong."

Ragbald then gathered both boys by the shoulders in a wide reach. Smiled at them both. "For the Song of the Sidors."

"For the Song of the Sidors," they both repeated.

Then he took the spear, said, "My Lord," he again deferred to Aenguz and then departed around the wall onto the stage.

Ragbald gaveled Sairik's spear. The clans shuffled and came to order. Squires darted clear.

"Lord Warrum of the Makan Clan has called a Challenge against Aenguz son of Sairik. Who does Lord Warrum offer to the Challenge?"

Warrum rocked on his bad knee. "The Makans offer Mandavu and Kachota, sons of Warrum." The brothers walked out from the Makans and took a place several paces from Ragbald.

"Who do the Gambls offer for the Challenge?"

The Gambl Clan lord smoothed his cloak and waved his arm out in a grand sweep. "The Gambls offer Hallock and Remille."

The Gambl Champions strode to Mandavu's side. They did not hide their allegiance with the Makans.

"Who do the Finits offer?"

The feather cloaked clan lord dispassionately offered Shudaak and Ondolfur. The two walked forward and stood apart from the Gambls. They bore packs and looked ready to live in the wild for days.

Byrgir chortled when he presented Roberge and Strey. He said, 'I present these two,' and then deferred to their father to offer them up by name. "My sons will honor the Baierls. Roberge and Strey. And I am their father Lakaadon."

The Kriel lord held himself formally and deliberately, respecting the strictures of the ceremony. "The Kriels, Sidor-Friends, offer Lokah son of Ruel and Slocum son of Shurn."

The Kriel Warriors marched into step and filled the gap between Kachota and Roberge.

"The Challenged is Aenguz son of Sairik and with him is offered Ridder son of Ragbald."

Aenguz's heart set to motion again.

"Ready?" Ridder asked.

Aenguz nodded. He gripped his cloak again and walked out to the stage. With Ridder at his side, there was a steadiness and confidence. And the pair walked out to join and complete the wide circle.

Ragbald commanded silence in the theater and spoke.

"The Challenge is called. The place is chosen. These Champions of the Akkeidii Clans will descend through the Lower Mashu to the Cairngorm. Their names will be entered on the wall. May they, through wisdom or force, decide who has the right to rule the Akkeidii and be the Polemarch for the Warriors. We will await your return and your final decision. No Akkeidii may raise the sacred metal against one another in force. May all the Champions return. By Grieg's will."

"By Grieg's will!" the Champions echoed.

The Makans and Gambls may have snorted.

The Assembly echoed, "By Grieg's will!"

Ragbald hit the stone with the heel of the spear. The clan lords echoed in kind and the circle broke.

Mandavu and his brother strode off the stage with the Gambls close behind as if they were already incensed and inconvenienced. The Makan and Gambl Clan Warriors stood in disorganized clumps. They were silent. Warrum beamed.

Roberge chuckled. He acknowledged Aenguz and addressed him as "My Lord" and then turned after the Makan and Gambl Champions. He threw a wave at the Baierls and a warm gesture to his father as he hugged Strey around the neck.

Slocum and Lokah nodded and deferred to Aenguz. Then they followed the Baierls out of the arena to the outer wall to leave their names as their clan's chosen Champions. And then to say their farewells to their clans and their mates. The Kriels in the tiers stood at attention and watched the pair exit.

The Finit pair looked suspicious of the other Champions. They floated past Aenguz and Ridder with little more than a glance. The wind fluttered their feathers and those of the Finits left behind.

9

FAREWELLS

As the Assembly frayed, Ridder's squire ran up to the lone Sidor Champions and began handing packs to Ridder. He was panting and drenched in sweat.

"Where is Jorgen?" Aenguz asked. He was woefully unprepared. All the other Champions had packs and waterskins.

"My lord, our Clan Mother fainted. When word reached her of the Challenge she fell. Jorgen is with her."

"Is she awake? Is she well?"

"She seems to be unharmed. She commanded Jorgen to gather all you need. The Sidors all want to help."

"Where is my grandfather?"

"I do not know, my lord."

This dissolution of his world was happening before his eyes. He wanted to check on his grandmother, but his choices were calving off from him and disappearing into the sea. His harrowing course to the valley narrowed toward the mouth of Grieg's Gate.

Aenguz's eyes drifted back to his father's coffin and the black-sashed

Honored Guard around it. The Sidor Warriors snapped to attention as one. And they shouted out together 'Rhet.' It was one of the abbreviated shorthand words the Warriors used to communicate quickly and effectively. 'Rhet' was 'Ready to'. It meant they were ready to take any orders their leader might give them. Even unto death. They honored both their lord and his son with that call. The Kriels and Baierls straightened to attention with them.

Tears blurred his eyes further. His heart closed his throat. He couldn't speak. And he didn't know what to say. Aenguz reached out with his hand open toward them and then brought it closed to a fist over his heart. And then back again to them all. It was a small gesture that a squad leader used to communicate with his cadre. It was an intimate signal. *You are with me, and I am with you.* It was not a more elevated signal a Polemarch might use. He couldn't recall one in any event.

Ridder nudged Aenguz out of the amphitheater. Beyond, the scene was so foreign as to be unrecognizable.

Akkeidii crowded the graveled slope between the spur and the neck. The Finit Champions had made their farewells and were heading to the wall to leave their names. Aenguz heard the remnants of a chant, 'Ondo, Ondo,' from the Finits gathered there. The Makan and Gambl Akkeidii had already pulled back from the others who were waiting to say goodbye.

To his right, the herd hounds were frantic. The roe deer herd had pushed closer to the pool at the mouth of Grieg's Gate. Their instinct to roam the Lower Mashu was almost greater than the sharp training of the hounds. Deerherds set a cordon behind them. He did not see his grandfather. He must have gone to his grandmother's side. He thought he might have even just a few moments to share the briefest account of the message with his grandfather but that opportunity fell when his grandmother toppled.

Two Deerherds stood apart from the line. They acknowledged Aenguz with a curt salute. Aenguz recognized Selvin, Selene's brother. The younger one he didn't know but he could see from his emblem that he was a Kriel. Lokah and Slocum spoke to the younger one as they walked toward the pool.

Stonemages stood evenly spaced atop the outer wall of Grieg's Gate. Their backs were turned to Aenguz as if they were shunning him. Their chant thrummed like a distant steady thunder. He imagined that Stonemages must ring the entire coil. And at the center, the Lord of the Stonemages.

A subterranean tremor shook the ground. The stone under his feet vibrated as if gigantic horns had been sounded deep within the Mashu. He was running out of time.

He should have been climbing over the slope with Selene to the Sidor shelter at the center of attention. He would have joined in the celebrations that were already underway. The ceremony would have commenced. They would have been mated. The cheers would have been deafening. His father would have been full of life, filled with smiles and enormous pride. He would greet everyone, welcome anyone. No one would have ever forgotten about the Ruler of the Akkeidii. Instead, Aenguz was drawn to the edge of a watery abyss, on the verge of expulsion from the Valley of Gathering.

Jorgen broke through the line of Sidors and ran down the slope. He looked more laden than when he found Aenguz in the Deerherd shelter that morning. Breathy apologies slipped out between his haggard pants. He began looping straps up over his neck. He draped one on his wounded shoulder and had to pull it off. The Sidors on the slope may have groaned. Soon the mass of packs and satchels were piled on his right side. His back was a hump.

"What am I to do with all of this?"

"All of the Sidors wanted to help. Once your grandmother's word went out, they all insisted on helping."

"Is she well?"

"Yes, my lord. The Lord of the Deerherds is with her now. He told me to tell you to stretch the arm and the joints. The *morillon* is still working."

"Jorgen," Aenguz held his squires' gaze.

"You will be a great Warrior one day. I know this. You have been a great squire to me. I leave you with one last charge. Serve my grandparents while I am gone. Ward them and ward Selene as you are able until I return."

Jorgen sensed the gravity of Aenguz's charge. His eyes turned glassy. He pressed his wrist into his eyes. His dimple deepened. His voice quaked as he answered, "I will my lord." He stepped back and floated away as if he was saying goodbye for the last time.

Then Aenguz saw Selene. Mother-aunts hovered behind her. Akkeidii women who had cared for Aenguz as a child ached to run to him and protect their adopted nephew-son.

Selene stood apart from the tearful and disheveled Sidor maids. The betrothed clawed out their braids and undid the ribbons from their carefully coifed buns. Tears streaked their cheeks. Mother-aunts wrapped them in their shawls to cover their exposed midriffs. Mated sister-friends and protective mother-aunts set a cordon around mother and expectant daughter. They tried to soothe them, protect them from the victor clan Warriors that would come to claim them if Aenguz failed. Already, Makan eyes were caressing the Sidor maids.

Ridder tensed at their gloom. He said to Aenguz, "Go to her. I'll make sure they get our names right on the wall."

She was higher on the slope than Aenguz. The shawl could not hide the comely shape of her curves. Her finery for the ceremony was blotted by the gray and brown cloth. She held a shawl wrapped around her arms but her white belly button was exposed to him. Her hair turned in braids and whirls. Only one band with a pale blue ribbon dangled out of place.

She had wiped most of the tears from her face but dampness blotched her soft cheeks. She was a Sidor woman and strong-willed. She held back her tears for Aenguz's sake and her chin flexed and rippled against the strain.

As Aenguz came up to her, she looked at the packs and asked, "How long were you planning on being gone? You have an appointment with me."

He marveled at her fortitude and gathered strength from her effort to lighten his load.

Aenguz moved up to hug her. His right arm was too laden in packs and straps. His weapon pressed against his back. He couldn't grab her as he wanted. He reached up with his bent wing and hugged her shoulder. The packs shifted and jostled the pair.

It reminded them both of their first hug. They had been on uneven ground at that time, too. Aenguz had meant to prove himself with a trial of endurance with a training shield. His arm had floated up in front of him bent like it was now. He had tried to hug her then with the tired arm and between that and the uneven footing they had stumbled into a kind of a short rocking dance.

They laughed as they swayed. They shared a timid intimate laugh as they both recalled that hug.

Selene's eyes moved from the briefest joy to worry as she looked under the cloak at Aenguz's arm.

"My grandfather says it will heal further. He applied *morillion* to it." He wasn't sure if it was helping or hurting her. "The Kriels and Baierls are with us. Ridder is with me. I will find a way to..."

The tremors in the earth were growing louder. Grieg's Gate was about to open.

She gathered her firmness and looked at him with an intensity that made him love her more.

"You come back to me. You come back here," she said with a sternness and sweetness that he could not refute, could not assuage.

She reached up and unspooled a pale blue ribbon from her dangling braid. On the ends, impressions and colors from delicate mountain flowers accented the tips. They were a reminder of the frangible flowers that drank from the ponds high up in the Mashu. A reminder of the first flowers he had given her. She wound the ribbon into his fingers on his left hand and squeezed it tight. The wound meant nothing to her. Her love was broader than that, broader than his expected role in the Akkeidii.

"I will," he answered. But in the plinth of his soul, he wasn't certain it was a promise he could keep.

She moved in and hugged him again. This time she pressed into him hard. He felt her breasts and her hips. He wanted to hold her more to reciprocate her squeeze in return. They kissed deeply, their tongues caressed and longed. Her hand ran up to his neck and strained his hair. Aenguz gripped her shoulder and wished for both his arms to be free, to give her the full breadth of his love.

He pulled back from her sooner than he wanted and turned for the gate. The tremors were reaching their peak. The packs swung awkwardly on him.

Behind her, the Sidors hopes, and dreads followed him down the slope.

10

~~~

HEARTHLESS

Aenguz followed the lapping gutter that ran along the base of the curved wall to the submerged exit of the Valley of Gathering. He joined Ridder and completed the company of the twelve Champions and two Deerherds at the arced edge of the pool. Ridder reached over without a word and took some of the packs from Aenguz's shoulder. It freed his hand enough to unwind Selene's ribbon and slide it into his pocket. He was glad the Sidors and other Akkeidii were out of view though he wished to look on her one last time before the gate opened. Only the anxious roe deer roiled at his back.

The sound rose and Aenguz's bones reverberated. The low rumble enveloped him from within and shut out all other noise. A seismic tremor thrummed beneath the roots of the mountains. He had trained here, had witnessed this as a boy when he played at being a Deerherd. The power was immense. It was as if avalanches originated below the earth and migrated through stone upward to the frosted peaks. It left him with the sensation that he might be crushed by an indiscriminate power. Only the sure lore of the Stonemages gave certainty of control to the elemental force.

The waves that radiated from the emptying gutter were overruled by a sheen of ripples that covered the face of the pool. Then, the surface dropped. The water receded as if it presaged a tsunami.

One by one, wide terraced steps emerged as the water drained. To his left, the gutter continued further down around the wall beside the wide wet stair.

On the right, the damp rough-hewn anthracite gleamed here and there like exposed gems. The rough wall was a counterpoint to the inscrutable skin of the Water Gate and the precision of the wet limestone stair.

The rapid draining drew a roaring wind at his back. Hair blew over the Champions faces. Cloaks pressed against their bodies and flapped between and around their legs.

The two Makan brothers followed the edge of the descending water as if it wasn't draining fast enough for their liking. Their hair whipped in a fury. The Gambl Champions followed right behind them, flanked their rear.

The Kriels and Baierls stepped down after a moment as if they had walked through Grieg's Gate a thousand times. They held a reverent awe for the power of the gate. But their eyes were fixed on the Makans and the Gambls. Selvin led Moodley and the pair followed behind them. The young Deerherd drank in the maw with wide eyes. Selvin's steadiness was the life preserver Moodley clung to. The Finits stuck to the rough-hewn wall as if it provided some kind of cover. The two feathered Champions searched the groups as if they expected betrayal at any moment.

Ridder stepped down and followed behind the line of Champions down into the narrowing throat of Grieg's Gate. The curved outer wall appeared to close behind him as he descended around it, like a cylindrical door. It shut out the Valley of Gathering and separated Aenguz from everything that he knew and loved in the world. He was heading down and out to the Lower Mashu, but it seemed as if he was descending into the swallowing hole of the Black Earth.

All of his options were now closed off. He was left with just one. Survive the Challenge - somehow and relay the message. The Akkeidii had to be readied for what the Flayer intended. They needed to know that Morgrom was still alive and that his ill volition was still intact. Perhaps warning them, once they could believe that he was telling the truth and not trying to avoid the Challenge, would remove the mark of being the Flayer's Last Emissary. If he lived but lost the Challenge, he might retain some honor and not wholly become a pariah. Selene might even see past the stain of being the Last Emissary if it meant he had preserved the Akkeidii. He had to find a way to defuse the Challenge and the Makan's intent.

A rippling sheen of water poured down the stone-metal wall. The clinging waves reflected the torrent of wind and spray in the new chasm. It held the promise of sealing in the howl and mist. Greig's Gate was as inscrutable as Earth's first stone. And it was the surest door, a devouring Water Gate. No enemy had ever crossed its threshold.

A violent whirlpool formed at the bottom of the stair. A vicious spray spouted up as if a long-gathered wave was crashing into a narrow cove.

But just as quickly as it came it drained away into some hidden ocean. A primitive Gothic portal emerged opposite the smooth wall in the coal black rock face. It was big enough for giants to pass.

The waterline dropped and dropped until it revealed a knotted spine of black wet boulders. They ran out through the center of the portal at the base and under the mountain wall. Rusted and broken weapons were wedged in the rocks. The brittle metal was being gnashed between the grinding boulders. Water sluiced away between the rocks and revealed a causeway. An angry froth of white rushed out on the opposite side of the boulder wall.

The Makans had turned first and disappeared onto the shadowed causeway. The groups of Champions observed their spacing and slowed as they turned onto the narrowing portal even though they could have walked ten across on the damp path.

The exigency of the Challenge pulled Aenguz down, but his feet were leaden. The demands of the law drew him inexorably out of the Valley of Gathering and the hearths of the Upper Mashu. He turned onto the path, well after Ridder, far to the rear.

The light was all but shut out. Only a shard of day remained out of reach beyond in the coal black. The sucking gasp of the portal stilled. Heavy droplets splatted down on the pathway like water that dripped from leaves after a storm in the forest. The roar from the channel echoed off the rough walls and swallowed the damp footfalls.

For a moment, it was as if night and chaos were within a sliver of overcoming day forever. A glimpse into the morning of creation when the lines between day and night, chaos and order, life and death were shocking, new - and tenuous.

Aenguz could make out a few gray bones here and there in the crevices amid the corroded weapons. It drew his mind to Carrowen Celd and the raw materials that made up the walls of the deepening hole.

These weapons and bones were more recent than those ancient, stacked bones. The result and reminder of the failed siege from Straathgard when avarice drew an army to the threshold of Grieg's Gate. The memory of it, generations old, after the Venture but before the Last Battle, fueled the harshness and intensity of Akkeidii Warrior training. The Drill Captains often referred to the siege as if it had just happened, as if the siege was still being prosecuted. But those stories and memories were just passed down as a reminder of what kind of battle they might encounter – and the potential failure if they did not train hard enough. The Warriors in training were made to feel like they were being readied just in time to join the war. But the younger generations saw it as an old story that teetered on legend. Here now, in the channel, the tales roared to life.

Aenguz pondered the nameless invader's weapons in their newly ex-posed grave. Would new weapons and fresh bones join these corroded ones? Without warning would the Akkeidii be ready for what the Flayer had in store? Would Grieg's Gate hold against the power of the Flayer or the might of the Ruinwasters?

These bones looked as if they were rising out of the rock and spray to fight again or flee now that the Water Gate was open. What could have made the Straathgardians believe they could overcome the rushing waters of Grieg's Gate?

One by one the Champions dissolved into the pinprick of light at the end of the tunnel. The promise of light beyond could do nothing to clear away his growing dread. Aenguz lingered on the causeway as if the old bones were somehow holding him back or trying to teach him some essential lesson about war.

Clattering echoed in the tunnel as if the roof suddenly rained stone. Roe deer trotted in behind him anxious for the light. They quickly caught up to him. They surrounded him and carried him forward. When he emerged from the portal, he was enveloped by the herd. He looked like an ascetic forgotten by myth and time who bore all he possessed in the world on his back. Shunned by man but welcomed and accepted by the deer.

The roe deer were comfortable with him. Perhaps their collective memory recalled the boy who played at being a Deerherd among them. Their wild imperative drove them out to roam the mountains and forests of the Lower Mashu. Aenguz normally would have watched their hindquarters as they processed out. Now he was pushed out with them at the heart of the herd. They had both seen him in to and out of the Valley of Gathering.

Aenguz climbed the wet ramp up out of the channel toward Selvin and Moodley. Ridder stood apart from them. His eyes were trained on the receding line of Champions. Selene's brother stood with Moodley in a crude pulpit of rock. He pointed over Moodley's shoulder at the gate like a prophet.

Aenguz walked up and past the waterline onto dry rock. Roe deer poured anxiously past him. He joined the pair of Deerherds in the cup of gray stone and looked back. A solitary Stonemage stood at the head of the smooth wall. The tip of the tunnel framed him perfectly. Stonemages had carved a perfect but subtle line of sight straight from the pulpit to the gate. Two feet to the right or the left and one could see nothing. Moodley nodded and acknowledged Selvin. Selvin showed Moodley the hand signals to send in order to open the gate. There was no other way past the warding wall of water.

He left the Deerherds and took in the raw earth that contrasted with the green valley behind. Stark granite formed into a lopsided horseshoe that opened away from the Water Gate. Bitter snow clung to the pointed peaks and fashioned a kind of natural crenellation. There was only one way in. And if Grieg's Gate wasn't opened, it was the only way out. The all-white peaks of the White Deeps rose above far beyond to the north and east. They ringed another barrier beyond capable of keeping giants out. They fortified and surrounded the cusp of granite and basalt. It was a remorseless hollow to lay siege. Glaciers had warred here, and fans of scree and detritus followed the ridges of moraines that were left in their wake at the knees of the mountains. Beyond this cul-de-sac, the ways in the mountains branched off and became difficult to follow. It was those first mountainous land markers that Selvin then shared with Moodley.

Aenguz joined Ridder. Roe deer fanned out and trotted after the southward departing Champions. Ridder looked out after the Makans and Gambls. They were nearly out of sight. They followed the shallow rapids out of the hollow. Their slate cloaks blended in with the surrounding rock. Their black hair stood out among the lesser shadows that tucked in between the crevices of stone. Kachota and the Gambls flanked Mandavu. They walked at a quick pace. Even from a distance, they looked angry.

The Kriels and Baierls marched on at a more relaxed pace. Roberge talked with the Kriel Champions. His brother was near to his side. Aenguz thought he could hear laughter echoing off the mountains. He wished he could absorb Roberge's confidence.

"Where are the Finits?" Aenguz asked.

Ridder pointed to the opposite side of the shallow watercourse. Grieg's Gate was open, and this river was reduced to a shallow stream. "They crossed right away."

"I was hoping we could learn where they stand."

"As long as they are not with Makans we will be well."

But neither of them could be sure where the Finits saw their allegiance or opportunity. If they sided with the Makans and Gambls, and if it came to it, the number would be six against six. The Deerherds could not interfere. Even if Selvin wanted to, he could not aid Aenguz. Their numbers looked greater with the Deerherds, but the actual numbers would be even.

Ridder gestured to Aenguz to let down his packs. The cords of his shoulder ached. He was glad to let the load down. Then they divided the largesse from the Sidors among all of them. With their ceremonial clothes, they appeared ill-prepared for the journey to the Cairngorm.

Selvin took his leave to catch and lead the Makans through the maze of scrag and crevasses beyond the hollow. They would have to camp in the open. Their late departure meant that they would not reach any Deerherd camps before nightfall. They would sleep in the open among the mountains he said.

Moodley walked ahead of Aenguz and Ridder to keep his eyes trained on Selvin if he could. The young Kriel Deerherd did not smile. His eyes darted at the scenery as if the mountains might come alive and snatch him up without warning.

After an hour or so, the shallow stream filled into a white river.

"Grieg's Gate is closed," Ridder said.

Aenguz thought he might have heard a finality in his friend's tone.

After a time, the clouds lost their light and the dim ambient dusk ushered in nightfall. Scraps of winter clung to the air. At a wide bend in the river, before it turned east toward the Millin, the Champions made their disparate camps. A hand signal had come from Roberge, but it had originated from the lead, from Mandavu. The decision and order was to stagger their camps. There was too much uncertainty and too little trust to have them camp near one another. And Selvin was to remain with the Makans.

Ridder was riled at Mandavu's assumption and subtle abrogation of leadership, but Aenguz was tired. The day had been long, and his arm still hurt. He was drained from his meeting and parting with Selene. And the stress of the Assembly and the conclave with the clan lords left him sapped of strength. Besides, camping apart was preferable at the moment. He had thought that maybe with all the food they bore that they could share a meal provided by Sidors and perhaps begin to cool the tension. But he still did not want to reveal the state of his arm to the others. If they saw it as it was now, they might rethink their positions. They would see clearly, that Aenguz could not fight with his wrecked shield arm. Well, he could fight, he just couldn't win against Mandavu. Aenguz needed as much time as possible to let the *morillion* do its work.

The three found a spot about fifty yards or so from the Kriels and Baierls. The sheer ravine captured the cold. The recollection of ice radiated from the stone. There was no wood, no fuel for a fire.

Aenguz flung the packs down and unslung his weapon. He drew out his *montmorillionite* and wedged the daggered hilt in between the rocks and angled the edged hook toward the river. Ridder drew out his glaive. The tip tapered to a fine deadly point. The whole weapon was a heavy blade.

Aenguz closed his eyes, pressed his tongue between his teeth. He exhaled through his nose and stilled his mind. Then he opened his mouth and the Words of Lore flowed out of him on his breath.

"Light in the dark and in the hands,
Pow'r concentrated from the Lands.

Bring your heat from Earth's fiery forge,
Dispel all cold, winnowing form."

The *montmorillionite* may have chimed. White light brightened from deep within the haft. Soon it grew to the tip of the spike and the curved hook. It looked like the thin sliver of the moon. Heat radiated out as the light grew. After a brief meditation, Aenguz opened his eyes, sat down, and held out his hands to warm them even though his left only registered dull pain.

Moodley's eyes were as wide and white as the light coming from the Warrior's weapons. They warmed themselves for a moment before they searched for some food from what the Sidors had given them.

Aenguz found some dried deer loin. He held it up to his right and his left. An offering of thanks to the Millin and the White. And to the Upper and Lower Mashu. Then he passed a strip to Ridder and one to Moodley.

Ridder tore hunks of bread, raised them up to his left and right, and then handed Aenguz and Moodley a piece.

Moodley foraged in the bags and pulled out a ball of cloth that held some cheese. He held up the ball of white cheese as the others had done but breaking it apart with his hands was crude. He set it down and found some nuts and passed those to the Warriors instead. In this way, they started their meal in the Akkeidii tradition. Serving others first with their first food.

They ate in silence until Ridder said, after a draught from a waterskin, "This is not how I expected this day to end. We would be looped by now. I guess there is no ale hidden in these bags."

Aenguz managed a strained snort. He was spent from the day's events and the effects of the *morillion* and the *montmorillionite* apotheosis. It felt like he had left his strength back in the Deerherd's shelter.

He nestled the packs in and around the scree and turned away from the bright light. The deeper knitting of the *morillion* took him back into sleep and away from Ridder and Moodley.

In the morning, new aches drew Aenguz out of sleep. He rolled out of his nest of rocks and searched for his waterskin. He drank deep. If the *morillion* had done any work overnight he couldn't tell. His wing was bent and stiff, the skin was still ghoulish and taut. As he looked at his arm, he began to internalize that more *morillion* would likely not remedy the appearance of his arm. But if he didn't find a way to halt the Challenge, he would never know for sure.

When he rolled over, he thought he had been abandoned. Moodley was gone and Ridder was nowhere to be seen.

But then he saw Ridder down by the rapids edge. He was practicing *salaage* with his weapon. He swung the two-handed glaive through the five forms. Basic thrusting moves and parries that all Warriors mastered with a spear. Then they incorporated those forms into their own style with their own weapon. Then the moves branched off from five forms into a unique fighting style based on the shape of their own unique weapon. He turned and pirouetted on the rocky shore jabbing and swinging. He swung wide arcs to the sky as if he was conducting a threnody only he and the mountains could hear.

Aenguz was hungry, but he needed to test his arm. He needed to perform his own *salaage*. He pulled his inert weapon from the rocks with the intent to swing the stiffness out of his joints. He walked a handful of paces away from Ridder.

Aenguz swung wide circles with his right arm. Then, he brought the shaft up to his left hand and tried the grip. His fingers barely closed on the haft. He tried to raise the weapon up over his head. Tried to pull it and his wounded arm away from his body to stretch the stiff joints. He tried to grip it with his left hand, but the blade slipped from his fingers and clattered on the ground. He couldn't use his weapon against another

Akkeidii. And this hardened *montmorillionite* couldn't heal him faster. Aenguz walked back to the camp. He sheathed the blade and rummaged for something to eat.

Ridder ignored the clattering ring of *montmorillionite*. When his practice was done, he came back to their meager camp and took up both waterskins to fill at the stream. Then he sat back down beside Aenguz.

"More time?"

"Yes." Aenguz couldn't bring himself to look at Ridder. "Where are the others?"

"They left right at dawn."

"Where is Moodley?"

Ridder looked down the shore. "There. See him?"

Aenguz made out the young Deerherd. He half-danced and paced at the further edge of the defile.

"Selvin gave him some guidance on how to follow but-"

"What time is it?" The overcast sky gave no hint to Aenguz.

"You might want to have a big morn meal."

"Why did you not wake me?" Aenguz was harsher than he intended.

"They cannot have the Challenge without you," Ridder said. Laughter hung just under the surface. "If anything, we should get going to settle him down. He looks like he is about to wet himself."

The pair readied to leave. Aenguz took his weapon back out and down to the water's edge. He spoke the Words of Lore and plunged the reddening metal into a pocket of icy water. Steam rose as the metal and water screamed. He splashed the hot water on his face as best he could and picked away a few more pieces of spent *morillion* from his left arm.

When he came back, Ridder had slung Aenguz's packs.

"I can take those," Aenguz said.

"I have them. Work on that arm. Do not worry. I am only carrying them as far as the Deerherd."

Moodley might have bolted on ahead but for the packs Ridder had handed to him. There was a shame at having them help him in such a way. Aenguz was more grateful for their presence than their help.

He took the time to press and stretch his arm and fingers as they walked. He found a stone he could clutch, and let it pull his arm down to stretch it out.

Moodley led them away from the watercourse and around the knees of the mountains to the south. He paused at possible branches and at one point led them to a sudden dead end.

After they had doubled back Ridder said, "I am not sure this is what your grandfather intended."

"Anyone's guess is as good as any in the dark."

They descended into a forest a short while later. They paused for a mid-meal rest at the Deerherd coverts where they might have camped the night before if they had left earlier. The stone and timber shelters were crude by Stonemage standards. But they would provide ample shelter from the weather. A small hearth rested within, and an abundance of chopped wood was stacked around it in walls in a fractured maze.

Aenguz's arm ached from the stone. He dropped it with a groan.

Moodley had glimpsed the arm the night before but said nothing. In the daylight, he stole more looks but still said nothing.

Ridder and Moodley pulled out new prizes from other Sidor families. Food was raised and passed. Waterskins were raised.

Then a rustling in the trees ahead. The Warriors stilled. Their eyes trained on the sound.

Selvin appeared through the trees.

"Are they so certain they know the way through the Lower Mashu?" Ridder asked.

Selvin shook his head. "I am bidden to deliver a message from Lord Mandavu." His words were wooden, almost official. "He grows weary of this trek. He finds your delays unseemly. He wishes to end the Challenge with an offer."

Aenguz's heart leaped in a mixture of trepidation and hope.

Ridder was guarded. He swelled on the outskirts of rage.

"He seeks to honor our fallen Ruler, your father, and lessen the grief of the Sidors and the Lord of the Deerherds and the Clan Mother.

"Therefore, in his benevolence, he would grant you release from the Challenge."

Aenguz and Ridder scanned one another's eyes.

"Maybe he fears our numbers more than I thought," Ridder said.

Perhaps his grandfather was right.

Selvin chewed on the words.

"He grants you the path of the Hearthless. You may live out the rest of your days in the Lower Mashu, but you may never again cross Grieg's Gate."

The floor of Aenguz's heart dropped out.

"One final condition," Selvin continued, "You must surrender your weapon to him. He will deliver it back so the Sidors will know the day of your death."

Ridder froze and then erupted in a flurry of curses and threats.

Aenguz was gaunt as if he might fade out of existence in that moment.

"Or," Selvin said finally, "'if you eschew my offer then you can try your hand against me in the Challenge. You may accept before the Champions on the morning of the Challenge.'"

Aenguz's lungs worked but no air came. His last chamber, his final chamber was filling up. The waterline was at his neck.

Ridder stomped in the circle and kicked stones. He reached for his weapon but checked himself and garbled curses.

Questions drifted across Aenguz's mind.

"Have the Kriels and Baierls aligned with Mandavu and the Gambls?" he asked.

"The Kriels and the Baierls have not spoken with them."

"What of the Finits? Have they sided with anyone?"

"I do not believe so, my lord. They keep apart from the other Champions."

"Do the Kriels and Baierls know about Mandavu's message?"

"They know that I bear a message to you, but they do not know what it is. They are wary of Mandavu."

They were still in packs.

There was still separation and suspicion.

Mandavu might be bluffing.

"Thank you, Selvin. You can tell Mandavu he will have his answer."

Ridder stopped, "You cannot!"

"How far do we have to go?" Aenguz asked.

"The Champions make their way down to Haags Lake. We rest there for the night. And on the morrow by nightfall, we will camp just outside the Cairngorm."

"The day after tomorrow," Aenguz said more to himself. Time was accelerating. And he had no plan to alter the Challenge other than Mandavu's offer.

Selvin led the stunned group from the Deerherd coverts.

Aenguz trailed behind Selvin, Moodley, and Ridder. He needed time to think. It seemed like they were rushing him toward his doom.

Hearthless or Dead?

If Lord Warrum wasn't so bitter. If Mandavu wasn't here, if he was a little older, none of this might even be a concern. The Gambls would not be so bold. And the Kriels and Baierls would not be worried. They would align with the Sidors. And the Finits would likely add their number to his own.

The compassion of the clan lords would have forestalled the Challenge for Sairik's burial.

Except for his ruined arm. His foolish grieving attempt had tipped the scales.

He stretched and flexed his arm as Selvin led the party through the pathless woods.

11

~~~

A SIDOR BETRAYAL

Selvin pointed out markers to Moodley. The serene Deerherd pointed to clearings. The blight, the result of dead seeds, left openings to the mountains. He traced the shapes of peaks, described distant ridges filled with snow. At other points, massive boulders amid the trees acted as signposts. He would pause to explain bends in the land that led up or downward and how to tell which way to go southward.

Aenguz half listened as he ruminated on the two deaths that were before him. Weaponless and excommunicated from his people or dead and interred with his father. Either way, the Sidors were forsaken. His grandmother's fears for their women would be realized either way. He imagined bethrotheds being torn away from the embrace of their lovers. He tried to burn out the thought of Selene being taken away by Mandavu. The thought, the intimate thoughts of what he might do to her seared his heart.

The Honored Guard would be dispelled. In all likelihood, Kachota would hold that place of honor in guarding his brother. The best of the Akkeidii Warriors and many hand-picked Makans would serve under his command. Dahlward's mantel would be removed and a Makan Deerherd set in his place. The Sidors would be ejected from their shelters in the Valley of Gathering immediately. They would be relegated to the furthest shelters. The mourning and debasement would be profound for his clan.

What would be better? To be alive while all this transpired or to be dead?

Living like a wild animal. Searching in the Lower Mashu for food and shelter. Waiting and hoping for any procession from Grieg's Gate. Deerherds would be prohibited from talking with him or providing any aid. He would be alone until his death. How long would that be? Could that be?

He would be exiled, alone. Counting the days till his death. His message would die with him. Even in Mandavu's offer, there was no redemption for him.

Wrong turns and dead ends dotted the way to the Cairngorm.

Selvin led them over a pass into an oval valley that held a large opal lake. Haags Lake.

Three streams of smoke trailed up into the dimming sky along the western shore. They were still spaced far apart. There was a relief in that. But there was also a grim acknowledgment of failure in not having found a way to bring the Champions together as Ragbald had counseled. It didn't matter. It didn't change anything. Weakened as he was there would be no way to talk Mandavu out of his offer or halt the Challenge.

The thin plumes trailed out of sight as Selvin led the party into the forest and finally to a clearing at the north end of the lake.

Moodley and Ridder unshouldered their loads and pulled together wood and tinder.

Ridder pulled out his long sword, spoke Words of Lore, and set the tip into the base of the kindling. The metal grew hot instantly and soon tiny wisps of smoke escaped, and then incipient flames appeared.

They raised their food, shared it, and shared the first bites together in a quiet meal.

Selvin talked about the earth signs that Moodley should look for the next day."Once you hit the edge of the ruin in the Lower Mashu there is only one path. It will lead you to the Cairngorm."

Moodley filled the waterskins at dusk.

Selvin excused himself and departed for the Makan and Gambl camp. He didn't need to explain the command he was under. Aenguz was too lost in a morose gloom to say farewell. The riddles in the fire mingled with his dead end thoughts.

Moodley asked Selvin something that Aenguz couldn't make out.

"We shall see," was all he said. Then he wended his way to the southern shore.

Ridder questioned Moodley about the Kriels and Baierls. What did he know about the Champions? Where did their hearts lie?

He sent Moodley off to learn more about them and report back the next day. As a Kriel, the Deerherd would be welcomed.

Ridder fed the fire.

"How is it?"

Aenguz stretched his mottled arm out into the light and turned it at the joints, opened and closed his fingers as much as he was able.

"I think I am beginning to see the wisdom of your grandfather," he started. "With these Deerherds, we have more of an advantage than just as guides or to add to our number. They are message bearers, too." There was a lilt of derision in his tone when he said 'Deerherds.' "I just wish we could use them to fight. I think the Finits could be persuaded to join us."

"I am not sure." Aenguz pulled his eyes out of the fire.

"You will not survive the Challenge. And you cannot surrender your weapon."

"I need to talk to Mandavu - alone."

"What do propose?"

"If I can get him alone and talk with him, away from his brother or the Gambls, he might listen to me."

Ridder set the metal of his consternation in the fire for a moment before he spoke.

"What can you say that will dissuade him?"

"That we must stay united. We are weak, divided as we are."

"My brother-friend, that was your father's dream. If he had lived it might have come to pass. But the Akkeidii have too much fire in them. Without an enemy and with the paucity of the Mashu, I fear we are doomed to turn our ferocity on one another."

What would his father do? What would he choose in this situation? His father's dreams did not even touch the horizon.

"I must make him hear me."

"How do you plan to get him alone?"

"I can send Moodley to summon him. Tell him that I wish to discuss the terms of his offer. That would not be untoward."

"What if he does not treat with you?"

"You will be there, in hiding, with our weapons."

"What are you proposing?" he asked again. Trepidation clenched his face.

"If I cannot get him to listen to me, then I," his throat tightened, "we," he gulped a knot, "will have to kill him."

Ridder pulled back from his friend as if he had transformed into a monster. As if the ghoulish arm had taken him over completely.

"Murder? Ambush? Ahead of the Challenge? We would be reviled. Think of the Song of the Sidors. The Sidors would bear a stain forever. We would replace the Dormund Treachery in the eyes of the Akkeidii.

"What about the Deerherds? What do you think they will do?"

"If Moodley will not help, he will not hinder. Once it is done, I can swear him to silence."

"What about Mandavu's brother if we succeed? He is devoted to his brother. He will bring the Makans down on us?"

"He is only one in the Lower Mashu. He can contemplate a choice similar to the one Mandavu gives me."

Ridder's jaw dropped but his lips remained sealed. His eyes darted from Aenguz to the dark as if he was contemplating evil for the first time in his life.

Aenguz writhed inside. "Listen, if he hears me, we will not have to kill him. This will all make sense, I promise you."

"If."

The embers shifted in the dying fire.

"You are my friend and my lord. I cannot see you become Hearthless nor surrender your weapon. I would be remiss to watch you die in the Challenge even though it is the law. I do not know that I can watch him beat you to death and do nothing.

"I do not like this plan," he gathered himself. "But I will honor it, and you. And hope that the Makan giant can be reasoned with. For the sake of the Akkeidii."

Aenguz welled up, overwhelmed by his brother-friend's fealty, and racked by the treachery he was asking him to undertake.

"My thanks, my friend. This will all make sense." He did not want to burden Ridder with the message. It might change the course of what he intended to try to do with Mandavu. Like the Warriors in the amphitheater, the Champions would not believe him. They would see it as a ruse. This was the only option Aenguz could conceive.

The nearly full moon gazed at its imperfect reflection in the mirror black lake. The stars were perturbed by the affront but remained silent.

Aenguz rolled down to sleep after a few moments.

Ridder did not budge.

Aenguz did not hear him settle down to sleep before he drifted off. He sensed his friend contemplating the impending dark.

Aenguz was jolted from his sleep. Ridder was bent over him.

"It is time to go."

He looked ashen. His eyes hardened into a veiled brutality. He may not have slept at all.

Aenguz gathered himself by the lake's edge. Moodley was further up the shore staring at a family of roe deer that were wading through the forest. They were making their way instinctively to the summer pastures. A pair of bucks and a half a dozen or so does. He may have been speaking to them.

The time Aenguz needed for his arm to heal was up. He circled his bent wing and pulled his fingers into a loose fist. It was not enough. He had no other choice. He would have to convince Mandavu of the greater threat to the Akkeidii. Perhaps alone and as a Lord of the Sidors he might be able to persuade him.

Ridder waved off Aenguz from grabbing his gear.

They walked past the dead fires at the other three camps along the shore.

Moodley sprinted down and took some of the load from Ridder. Then the two Champions let him drift ahead as they exited the southern end of the valley.

Ridder said in a low voice, "When do you want to do this?"

"Keep your eyes open for a dead end."

After they had left the lake, the signs were difficult for Moodley to read.

The Deerherd would pause and scan the sky and the ground. In places, he found a score in the needle bed that helped guide him. At other times, a collapsed rockfall left a clear edge for the three to follow.

Their path was always generally downward and southward. But occasionally they would have to climb to navigate between mountain roots.

At one of those points, Moodley stopped, apologized, and doubled back the way they had come. The path ended into a short, sealed ravine. A patch of stubborn white snow marked the V.

This was it.

As they walked back to the trail Aenguz halted the Deerherd.

"Moodley. I want you to go and summon Mandavu and bring him here. I wish to discuss his terms. Tell him to come alone. I will send Ridder away. Just he and I. And you. A Sidor, a Makan, and a Kriel. Go now, I will wait."

Tremors fluttered across his face. Whether it was confusion or being caught up in matters that were beyond him Aenguz couldn't be sure. Moodley looked back to Ridder. But his face was as implacable as stone.

He turned to go but Aenguz stopped him.

"Lighten your load. There is no point in carrying your burden thrice."

Moodley nodded as if he was chastising himself.

Once he was out of sight Aenguz turned to Ridder.

"Here?"

"Yes. I will go and wait up there. Take my weapon. Go back around there. Once he comes in, I will send Moodley out so that we can talk. Then come in behind him."

"With our weapons?"

"I hope we will not need them."

Ridder's familiar light-hearted demeanor was effaced by a gravity that Aenguz barely recognized. He took Aenguz's scabbard mechanically. His eyes were cold and hollow. He acknowledged Aenguz without a word and walked back the way they had come.

Aenguz walked up into the closed gullet of the ravine. The ground was littered with leaves and broken branches and patches of wet firm snow.

He worked his arm violently as he walked up. The dull pain and soreness distracted him from what he meant to do.

Convincing Mandavu might be impossible. But he would try for the sake of the Akkeidii. Morgrom was returning to the Lands, was nearly free. He had already returned from some bleak hell Aenguz shuddered to imagine. The giant Makan would have to understand.

And if he didn't?

Aenguz would explain it to the Champions. This was bigger than the Challenge. He needed to make them ready. His father would want that.

But would they believe me? He would have to make them believe. Aenguz didn't want to contemplate the fact that he would cease being what he was, and he would become if he indeed convinced them of the message's verity.

The chill in the dark alcove was sharp. He hugged his cloak and stamped his feet on the square boulders.

After a time, he sat. He turned over different arguments in his head to convince Mandavu but then they gave way to modes of attack. Should he move on him before Ridder arrived? Mandavu might be more dangerous if he knew he was trapped and betrayed. If he could get him to the ground and not worry about landing a blow perhaps it might go quickly. Denial cozied up into his line of thought as he cursed Moodley for taking so long.

Aenguz started to wonder if the Deerherd had gotten lost again. Just as he was about to head out,

"My lord!" Moodley shouted.

He was back! What was he doing? Just lead him up here.

"My lord!" Moodley called again.

Bring him up. Aenguz set his feet and squared his shoulders.

"I am here," Aenguz called back.

"My lord, come out."

What was he doing? Just bring him up here.

"Sidor snakes! Come out!" a different voice called.

He was confused and unsure.

"Come out, now!" the voice snapped.

Aenguz walked down out of the ravine. He left the cold shadows behind. At the mouth, in the trees, stood Moodley, and beside him was Kachota,

Mandavu's younger brother. He held the young Deerherd by the neck as if he had caught a thief.

He was not gifted with the same size as Mandavu but he was still powerfully built. His black hair was pulled into a ponytail and loose strands framed his face. He was a lesser approximation of his brother but an Akkeidii Warrior through and through. Thick across the shoulders. Large strong hands nicked with scars. His Warrior's cloak was collared with ram's pelt. He seemed uncomfortable in the Makan ceremonial shirt. His short, tooled scabbard hung at his hip as if he was ready to draw it at any moment.

"Where is the other snake?" he called back with a practiced disdain.

"Where is Mandavu?" Aenguz called on his authority and tried to dispel the tenor of his shame.

"Safe. He would just as soon trust an Emissary." He said the words like a curse.

"Come out of there snake!" he shouted past Aenguz

"I wish to speak with him about his terms," his grip on his position was slipping.

Kachota smacked his lips as if he was perturbed and impatient as if he was delayed from another engagement.

"You have two choices before you Sidor. I counseled none. You can become Hearthless and live here," he looked around at the ravine and nearly laughed. "Or you can try your hand in the Challenge on the Cairngorm as you chose." He released Moodley with a shove. Kachota had nothing to fear here.

"At first, I was incensed at having to come all the way down here. But now I see you wish to save your clan the trouble of having to come to the Cairngorm twice." He spoke as if it was a sudden realization.

"My brother has been kinder than I would have been. As I understand it, leaders must be so. I do not understand the mercy myself. The time of the Sidors is over. The Makans will rule the Akkeidii. And your women will help to serve our lines." As he leered at Aenguz, he rolled his lips as if he was sucking on a piece of fruit.

"Tomorrow morning. On the Cairngorm. Hearthless or Challenge. Leave your weapon with my brother to return to the Sidors or leave it to the earth. I do not care which."

Kachota spun on his heels and strode away.

Moodley pleaded for forgiveness. But his words passed through Aenguz.

Ridder climbed down from hiding. The two Warriors could only glance at one another. Their shame and embarrassment reflected back and forth in their brief looks. He handed Aenguz his scabbard.

Aenguz took the weapon. He ignored Moodley's apologies and waved and barked at the Deerherd to lead on.

Aenguz growled a "No" at the pile of gear. He took up all of his belongings and the satchels of hastily prepared food.

He wanted to punish himself for being so stupid. And for forcing Ridder into complicity.

Ridder gave Aenguz his space. And the three continued on through the forest.

His burdens slowed him. Soon he was drifting behind.

12

A MEMORY OF RUIN

Moodley trotted past Ridder and called out to Aenguz that this was the path. "I found it!" His excitement at navigating the final distance provided a small joy. Aenguz had asked much of the young Deerherd.

A definite path opened up in the forest.

Aenguz smiled at Moodley, but he was too lost in his own thoughts to say anything.

"This is the path, just as my master described it. There is only one path through the ruined lands to the Cairngorm."

Ridder drank from his waterskin and then held it out to Aenguz.

Aenguz took it and softened his gaze. His mouth was dry. His stomach growled for food, but the turns of his narrowing path choked down his appetite. He let his packs down and gave his shoulder a rest.

Moodley was anxious to finish the trek as if he was anxious to see the hallowed burial ground.

Thankfully, Ridder sent him on to meet with Selvin. They would join him after a time.

The Deerherd accepted the command, bid farewell to both Champions, and headed off alone.

"Are you well?" Ridder asked.

His gentleness allowed Aenguz to raise his eyes to his friend.

"I am sorry, my friend. It was a foolish idea. I should never have asked you to do that."

Ridder dismissed it with a terse shake of his head.

"What is the plan now?" he said instead.

"I do not know," Aenguz wiped his mouth and handed the skin back.

The pair continued down the path. Aenguz rambled about his choices and the fallout with their clan.

Ridder just listened patiently. He acknowledged Aenguz's conclusions.

The sun had sunk below the western peaks. The stark shadows turned into a preternatural gloom. The ocean of the sky opened up as the line of pines and firs abruptly ended.

The sullen Champions stood on the threshold between two lands. The difference was as sheer as the difference between both sides of Grieg's Gate.

The path continued out into a desecrated land. Rounded hills looked like giant swells on an antediluvian ocean. Stripped and blighted trunks lay flat on the ground. The surging waves looked like an abstract sea. The clear sky was discordant. Miserable thunderheads should have clotted the sky. Peals of lightning should have ripped across the black. It was like they were witnessing something that should be hidden from human eyes.

They walked out into the middle of the wooden ocean. The wide road cut a level path midway between the swell and the valley below. It snaked in and out between the stilled waves.

They walked together in a tacit need for courage.

Solitary trunks, shorn of bark and limb, dotted the devastated landscape. They looked like the masts of a doomed fleet. As if they were caught all at once in a catastrophic moment of sinking. Only the masts were left as a tombstone to mark their inevitable plunge.

This was Ruinwaster's work. And it led to the epicenter of desecration. It led to the Cairngorm.

The ruin jolted Aenguz. The exigencies of the Sidors and the women, his friends, and his grandparents shrank suddenly as if all those cares and concerns were drawn into the distance.

Even the value and meaning of his life. His wants and dreams seemed to capsize in the silent storm.

"My friend, I am going to fight Mandavu tomorrow."

The words startled Ridder after so much silence.

He swung out at Aenguz's chest.

Aenguz brought his left arm up to block the blow. But his wing crumpled against his chest. He stumbled and nearly fell.

Ridder stood still and resisted helping Aenguz.

Aenguz hiked up his packs and faced his friend.

"Let us see where the other Champions lie. If we can overmatch them-"

"No," Aenguz said sharply.

Ridder clamped his mouth shut.

"I do not want any of the Champions to die for my sake." He looked Ridder dead in the eye. "I should never have asked you to do what I asked."

"What about living in the Lower Mashu? I can find a way to- Maybe they will-"

Aenguz shook his head slowly holding Ridder's eyes. "I risked your honor once. Let me redeem it now for both of us."

Ridder broke his stare. His eyes searched around as if there was an answer, a way out he just couldn't see.

"You must do me a favor,"

"Anything. What is it?"

"After the Challenge tomorrow you must deliver a message to the Akkeidii for me." He paused and swallowed. "I will not be able to deliver it."

"You may yet win. You can deliver it yourself."

"You must do this for me, for our people." Aenguz's eyes demanded his friend swear it.

The words were slow but finally, he said, "I will."

"Remember when I told you about the *morillion*?"

"Yes."

"When the power of the healing loam took, I thought it had killed me. I was already near to the mid-road. I was drifting off. Then something happened."

Ridder's brow furrowed. His eyes squeezed to understand.

"I was *seen* and taken to a Hole. I was met by the Flayer.

"It was real, I was there." Aenguz held Ridder's eyes grave and plain.

Ridder peered at Aenguz as if he was gauging his brother-friend's sanity.

"It was a lot of *morillion*. Who can say what that might have done to your mind? The Flayer is defeated. The Last Battle is over; he is gone. This is just a side effect of the *morillion*."

"Listen, it was as real to me then as my standing before you is now."

Ridder's head swung back and forth from Aenguz to the ruined land. He tried to process Aenguz's words.

"And... I was charged with a message.

"You must take this message back to the clan lords for me. They will know what to do. The Akkeidii must be made ready.

"The Last Battle is not over," Aenguz recited Morgrom's message.

"'*The Last Battle will be enjoined again. Hear me, my victory will come in a new form of war. Its ways and movements will be beyond your ken.*'"

Desperation crept into his voice. He could not maintain his calm.

"You must warn the Akkeidii.

"You must do this. If the clan lords do not deliver the message to Corundum, he said his plans would come to pass in five seasons."

"Let us go and tell the others," Ridder implored.

A wry frown crept across Aenguz's face.

"What do you think will happen if I tell them this now?" Ridder's complexion changed as he reasoned out the problem. Aenguz watched as resignation settled over his friend's face.

"They will call you a liar, a coward. They will say you dreamed up this story to avoid the Challenge in a final desperate-"

"And cowardly-" Aenguz interjected.

"-ploy."

"Still the same, they must be warned. And I am placing it on you to warn them. Tomorrow. After the Challenge."

"But-" his objection stalled. "They will not believe me."

"You must wait until the Challenge is done. With me gone, there is no reason to lie. You must make them believe you. I will share everything I heard with you. Do this for our people. Do this for my father. Do this for me."

For a second time, Aenguz was putting his friend in a box with no way out. He understood Ridder's pressed eyes and crunched brow now.

The sun had long set behind the western swell on the troubled ocean. A bone-yellow pall seeped into the edges of the sky. The moon popped into the dusk. A perfect skeletal orb announcing a kind of pale day on the face of the Earth.

Aenguz urged Ridder into motion.

They staggered down the desolate road as the day turned cold and dim.

Aenguz recounted the details of his nightmarish sojourn in the depths of Carrowen Celd.

Ridder shook his head constantly as if he was trying to shake the thoughts and images free.

They continued on and Aenguz shared the warning Morgrom gave him if he failed.

"I have already failed. In you there is hope."

"I, I-" was all he could muster.

"I have put so much on you. I would have seen you at the head of the Honored Guard. You and I leading together like our fathers. Now you must prepare the Akkeidii. Whatever the Makans might do does not matter now. War has come to the Lands of the Earth again. War will come to the Mashu."

The road led to the final timber carpeted hills. Night opened beyond three swells as the first stars ventured out. They might have been on the edge of the world.

A forsaken lake lay down below between the rounded hills. The water was ashen. Part of the surface was covered with clustered dead trunks. They looked like discarded matchsticks in a filthy puddle. Ruin was distilled and concentrated there.

The faint rush of the White and the Millin washed the clear night. Their convergence sounded like a remnant echo, a sustain from a final epic concussion. Those waters could not redeem this land.

As the last light surrendered, Aenguz and Ridder approached the shelter built into the hillside. A glacier-carved furrow left a scallop in the body of the hill.

Bone-gray timbers were stacked into the space. A sad city of mourning. A place made for grieving. Where tears could run down to the gray lake. The space looked like a wide frown of broken teeth. Ill-fitted bridges joined across the spaces and jutted out here and there.

"The stone is not suitable here for building," Ridder said.

The road led along the front of the rickety facades up over the saddle. Beyond was the Cairngorm and the end of his life's journey.

Aenguz could make out firelight peeking out here and there, spread out as they had been at the lake the day prior. Their allegiances or lack of them didn't matter anymore.

Selvin stood at the furthest edge of the line of buildings. Moodley's shadow flickered between the trunks.

Low walls at the front marked small courtyards. The fires of the other Champions burned bright from rooms within. The light gave off a gangrenous hue.

They passed the Makans and Gambls first. Aenguz thought he heard surety in their tones. A kind of certainty mixed with affirmations. The jots of laughter were vaguely maniacal. Or so he thought.

The Finits were quiet around their fire. As he peered through to the light, he saw eyes on him. He looked away suddenly, ashamed.

The Baierls and Kriels were subdued. There was laughter and good nature between them. But none of the boisterousness took hold. It would die down until another Champion tried to distract with a story or a quip.

Aenguz's flawed heart strained, and his feet dragged through sludge the final steps to Selvin.

Selvin greeted Aenguz and Ridder with deference and respect. He ushered them through the courtyard to the drafty chamber within.

A fresh fire was cracking in a simple hearth at the back of the room. It cast light between the stacked timbers to the darker chambers beyond.

Moodley was muscling a stump against the wall to line up with the others he had presumably moved. He bolted up and welcomed the Champions in between his heaving breaths.

A long table was angled off-center in the room. It was a halved trunk set atop two thick stump posts. Four stumps were positioned around the furthest end near the bowl-shaped hearth.

Aenguz dropped his packs and gear on the stumps against the wall in a heap. He laid his scabbard apart and took up his waterskin to drink and splash the yellow dust and grime he wore from the long hike through the wasted land.

Ridder mirrored him on the opposite side of the room.

Moodley returned to the stump, but Aenguz stopped him. He left to join Selvin in the darkened courtyard while the Warriors refreshed themselves.

Aenguz wrestled the stump near to the hearth. He went over and unsheathed his weapon. He planted the tip into the center and drove it down deep into the hardwood as if it was firm clay.

Then he uttered, *"Earth's first star to dispel the night"*

An argent light bloomed from his *montmorillionite* weapon. Light gleamed across the table and rarefied the room. Shafts of white poured through the walls.

After a time, Ridder thrust a pack onto the table and dropped to a stump near Aenguz. He pulled out the first food he meant to share.

Selvin and Moodley returned and sat opposite the Warriors. Moodley faced Ridder and Selvin faced Aenguz. They set down their packs as the fire gave off reluctant pops.

Aenguz stalled them. He instead set the food bags on the table from the Sidors. There were questioning looks from Ridder and the Deerherds but he did not acknowledge them.

Then he sat and drew a deep breath.

The three reached out tentatively with bread or meat, or cheese for Aenguz.

"Thank you, my friends," Aenguz forced a tattered smile to his lips. He raised his palm gently and gave a reserved nod.

"You have given me much on this long journey. Our mother-aunts and sister-friends have provided a great meal for us."

Their eyes were still locked in consternation. Moodley looked around as if he had missed something. Ridder was racked but confused. Selvin seemed concerned for Aenguz.

One by one, Aenguz pulled out every delicately wrapped piece of food. He mostly spoke to himself. But occasionally he uttered the type of cheese or the kind of bread within with a pleasant surprise. The deer jerky he held up with an approving grunt.

Then, as if he was gifting all of his possessions, he doled out all of the food. He passed each bit deliberately, reverently as if he was performing a sacred rite. He elected to not struggle with his left hand. He rested his warped claw on the table as he bent toward the others with the offerings.

Once he was done, he gathered himself. His dislocated reverie dissolved and then he said, "We have come a long way on my account. Eat, please. Enjoy these viands tonight and on your journey home tomorrow. Thank the Sidors for these gifts when you return."

Ridder and the Deerherds began to eat. They sat up straight and ate as if they were sitting at a ceremonial dinner. Each raised the bits up to the left and right before taking small bites. They ate with careful chewing and delicate hands to mouth.

Aenguz left a small amount, enough for himself to enjoy the generous gift from his clan.

After a time, before they finished eating, he said again.

"I will enter into the Challenge tomorrow. I will face Mandavu alone." His implication was clear. Do not interfere.

"If I do not prevail, heed Ridder. I have left words with him for the Akkeidii."

Ridder nodded firmly as if he was swearing an oath.

Moodley looked terrified and helpless. Some other regret tugged at his eyes.

"Also," Aenguz started breathing heavily as if he was about to hyper-ventilate. "Find a good place on the Cairngorm for my father among the fallen chieftains and heroes," breathing heavily, "and for me."

Their chewing stopped.

Aenguz set down the half-eaten piece of deer loin. His appetite had evaporated. There was nothing left.

Ridder was as sullen as the gray wood. Selvin's eyes dropped. Moodley mumbled an apology. He stood and left the table and rushed out of the room.

"What is it?" Aenguz asked Selvin.

"He feels that he has failed you, my lord. And-" Selvin stopped.

"What?"

"It is nothing, my lord. He has never looked on the One Bridge. He fears there will not be an opportunity tomorrow. He feels shame at thinking about his wants ahead of your needs. But there will be other opportunities."

"The spans are barely a mist in the night," Ridder muttered to no one in particular.

"True. But they are most easily viewed when the moon is full," Selvin answered.

Now Aenguz pieced together Moodley's behavior.

"Tell him to go and look on it," Aenguz said. What difference could it make?

13

~~~

TERRA DI OMBRA

The sands of night siphoned away. Aenguz grew fey. The possibilities for his life had been reduced to one. The minor rituals he performed for his final meal and his final words were his last. This night was his last. This full moon his last. Moodley's desire held for Aenguz the last things he might do for his father and his grandfather. With his last hours, he could select a spot on the burial ground for his father and himself. He wouldn't be able to see his father's bones to the Cairngorm, but he could choose their place. And looking on the One Bridge with a pair of Deerherds would be a nod to his grandfather and the Lord of the Deerherds. A kind of gratitude for all that he had done for him. And a kind of apology. In the end, he would choose the only option available to a Warrior. A fight to the death. A courage in the face of futility for the sake of honor. The message had been passed to Ridder. He would see that the Champions heard it and that the Akkeidii listened. In the end, Aenguz had done as much as he could with the little time he had left.

He rested his hand on Selvin's shoulder. The vague similarities of Selene's face were more torturous than soothing. Selvin looked at his sister's intended with a hard sadness. A dual sadness for the both of them. They leaned into motion to meet Moodley and cross onto the sacred ground.

The dead lake swallowed the moonlight. Dead logs clustered to the southern shore and fractured the surface.

Moodley was forlorn but understanding and hope softened his eyes. Without a word, they walked together the short distance up over the saddle.

On the edge of the Cairngorm, the nature of the ground changed. Aenguz could feel the difference under his boots. It was like crystal, like vanadinite. The ground was discolored. Shades of yellow and brown accentuated by the moonlight. The color of gangrene and mustard.

The land and the path sloped downward into the bottomless night. Rigid mountains converged in the near distance beyond the southernmost tip of the Lower Mashu.

The churn of the Millin and the White echoed white noise over the prow of land. Oblong stone cairns dotted the triangle of land. They looked like a haphazard scattering of giant overturned lifeboats.

War graves.

Chieftain cairns.

A single tree jutted out at the head of each cairn like a kind of rudder designed to navigate the underworld.

Dead leaves clung to the tips of solitary trees like a memory of autumn eons ago. They pointed in unison like a shout toward the tip of the burial ground. Bowls of boulders were held together by obdurate roots. They clung to the stone and splayed at the base of the cairn.

The three descended down the slope in a timid procession.

Aenguz led the way through the maze of cairns and shadows. He forgot for a moment his desire to find a good place for his father - and himself.

The ancient tombs would be Aenguz's home and his father's.

He zig-zagged downward past the towering piles of rock amid the sparse forest. Aenguz lingered at a cairn and let the Deerherds pass him. He ran through the catalog of Deerherd lore to recall if there was some homage or veneration they made ahead of viewing the One Bridge.

The air seemed preternaturally still as if the moon was distilling light onto the hallowed ground.

The stillness pulled the skin of his face taut. There was no resistance in the wind or the cold. The odd feeling seemed to hold him in place like a sacred ritual. It was as if a force was holding him and bidding him to take note of the fallen Akkeidii chieftains.

He leaned forward to move out of the fugue. The prayer or rite had gone on for too long. He edged forward but the spell was firm. He leaned to move out of it and realized that he was frozen in place. The signals that fired movement were suddenly mute.

Then out of the dark, the night fluttered and personified in front of Moodley. It drifted toward him, gliding effortlessly as if it was floating through the abyss. The roiling lappets, the desiccated toes, jerrids flicked at the ends of the bony arms.

Urning! Aenguz thought. A shout was forbidden to him. The instinct to spring backward as if he had uncovered a poisonous snake was suppressed completely. The magnified horror reverberated off his immured mind.

The Urning tricked the jerrid flat and Moodley fell slowly backward. The Deerherd was vulnerable and immobile to the unrestricted power.

The Urning floated past.

Selvin drifted back too as if he was sinking. He met the ground like he was being lowered into a coffin.

The black horror drifted over him. Ratty vestments dragged over his face.

Aenguz's heart was pierced. The cords of his neck threatened to wrench his head from his body. He fought against the loss of balance. He drifted backward, downward. The full moon swung into view.

Panic gripped his already shallow breath and quickened it as if he was being lowered into a pool of ice. Hyperventilation unmoored him utterly. His eyes rolled back into his head as he fell into an unfathomable void.

---◆---

NIGHT TERRORS CLAWED AT him, threatened the tenuous fabric of his soul. The shapes of floating Urnings and craven Erebim gave contours to the nightmare. It was a blackness as replete as entombment.

Narcosis held him, swallowed him whole.

He could feel his lungs straining as if blackness itself was pouring into him, drowning him.

The peal of a carillon, a single forlorn chord pierced the timbre of interring black.

The lonely chime gave Aenguz a point of reference. It cast a distinction between nightmare and consciousness, dream, and memory.

Another chord sounded and it charted a line in the abyss.

A distant part of himself recognized the distinctive ring. But he did not want to recall that memory, did not want to acknowledge what it meant, what it might mean now.

The fragments of consciousness and memory jolted him loose from the immuring terrors.

Other unwanted sensations came to him, but they also inched him closer to the surface.

His mouth was clotted with a gritty paste that tasted like angostura. His tongue choked on stale ash and wet tobacco. He began to convulse. A faint piquant flavor of lavender, from the stubborn sprig of *roona* lodged between back teeth, provided a counterpoint to the acidulous paste.

Aenguz forced the sour mass out of his mouth and dragged his tongue back across his teeth. He spat and hawked the worst of it out.

A desperate hacking punctuated the night like a fusillade, violent as murder. Smoke from fresh wood and steaming sap filled the night air like sacrifice in a hasty ritual.

He dragged his eyes open as if he was waking from the grave.

A careless but raging fire cast orange and yellow shadows.

He was lying on the ground. His hands were bound in front of him by stiff cords.

Where were Selvin and Moodley?

A body lay next to him, turned to the side. An unconscious Warrior jerked and writhed in sudden spasms.

Aenguz tapped the Warrior's back with his bound hands. The tap only added to the terrors in the other's dreams. Aenguz pounded harder. The Warrior lurched from his side. His head flipped and faced Aenguz. White slits flicked in an estranged ecstasy. A gag of black charcoal was smeared across his mouth and he chomped a soundless plea.

It was one of the Finits, he guessed. Aenguz recalled Ridder's accounts. His head looked capable of butting a ram. His face was flat and round. His nose splayed in line with his cheeks. The trunk of his neck hinted at his bulk, but the thin noose cinched around his neck blunted it. The ceremonial Finit shirt had triangles of gray mountains embroidered into it. The feathered cloak was gone.

The sight shocked Aenguz, harkened back to the shapes of his nightmare. For a moment he was unsure if he was awake.

His chest ached as if it was trying to wretch him free from the ghoulish dream. The stiff beats subsided and confirmed for him that he was still awake.

Aenguz reached over and clawed out some of the paste; dug around his tacky tongue. The Warrior recoiled and rolled away. Aenguz's action might have translated into torture within the Finit's trapping nightmare.

Aenguz inched up onto his elbow. The outlines of Warriors were bound and lined up against a wall at the base of a crude parapet. A pair of low walls perched on a prow of rock like gunwales.

Where were Selvin and Moodley?

Black paste was smeared into the mouths of those he could see. A Kriel, Kachota, and a Gambl faced him at points along the line. The rest were turned away. He scoured the line for Ridder or the Deerherds but there were no Deerherd robes, and he couldn't be sure which Warrior might be his friend.

Past the single crenellation, he could make out piles of slate cloaks and leather packs. Where were their weapons? Bundles of cords and grime-smeared sacks were scattered nearby. Bushels of long sticks, like thick arrows, were stacked like harvested barley.

Beyond that, half a dozen or so panicked roe deer stomped and jerked. Tight cords were cinched around their necks.

The hacking of wood came from multiple places and drew his attention. Two creatures straddled a felled trunk at either end.

A cairn tree!

The desecration of these Akkeidii shrines astonished him in a way he could not name or recognize.

Iron axes pumped up and down like pistons into the hollowed cavity. Hunks of living wood flicked up into the night. A further defilement as if chopping down the sacred tree alone was not desecration enough for them.

Their faces were a deep orange like the memory of fire. A line of black cut their faces in two at the corners of their mouths. Divided their heads in two. In the dark, half their heads seemed to float above their shoulders. Their eyes were knife cuts of red and black, feral, and predatory. A mohawk of bent black spines ran atop their orange heads and quivered like crow's wings. Lips pulled back across sharp, sour yellow teeth. The nose was a curved dagger. It seemed to perpetually sneer at the wood and relish the violence. They wore iron vambraces and their cuirasses were scarred and dented.

Aenguz knew that these were Erebim. His knowledge of the old stories told him that much. They attacked the cairn trees and moved about the hallowed land like they owned it, like it belonged to them. But how had they gotten to the Lower Mashu and the Cairngorm? The convergence of the White and Millin was far below. The southern tip of the Lower Mashu was perched above a sheer chasm.

In front of the fallen trunk, three more umber figures tugged at some leather.

Our weapons! Aenguz curled inside, violated, as if he was forced to witness a cruel theft or a murder.

They pulled between one another in a minatory tug of war. Suddenly, they flipped apart. One Erebim flew backward out of control. The leather scabbard flung back into the darkness. The other demon collapsed to the ground. A *montmorillionite* ax thudded to the earth like a stone.

They called others together to lift the ax. They wrapped shreds of burlap around their hands. They pulled and strained the ponderous weapon toward the trunk. It was many times heavier to them than its size belied. Their minatory howls were directed at the obdurate metal. The ax tumbled over into the channel with a muted clang.

Then they grabbed another scabbard and began again.

A short distance from them, near the hasty fire, another creature hacked at a gray stump. Aenguz could make out his weapon pressed against the ground, still buried deep into the tough gray stump. The Erebim was trying to free it.

If he could just get his weapon. Get any weapon.

The third echo of chopping came from further away.

Naked hacked stumps marked the ancient cairns. The profligate violence combined with his helplessness and twisted into a grim core of rage within his heart. From it grew a desire for vengeance so profound that he didn't recognize it coming from within, didn't think it possible.

There was another sound, words of some sort. He looked down his body, over his feet. There floating, drifting with the ineffable currents of night was the Urning. It hovered just before a huge cairn. The stump at its head looked raped.

A roiling pool canted near the cairn. Partway in the ground and partway out it looked like it observed the physics of a bleaker plane. The surface shuddered in a boiling cuneiform. Thick oil rippled and flicked.

If there had been no chopping, Aenguz thought he could hear the Earth groan beneath the corruption.

The spindled arms waved above the viscous hole. Its jerrids or scepters traced above the uncreated night.

At the edge of the pool, Aenguz could see mutilated roe deer.

There too-

He saw-

A pair of Deerherd cloaks.

They bobbed face down in the inky black like a pair of discarded skiffs.

Then-

Other bodies-

Warriors.

Champions.

Face down in the black.

Numbness overwhelmed him. Rage and grief could not penetrate the paralysis. The callous murder combined with his own futility began to alter him, inure him. A vulnerable part of himself that understood compassion was snuffed out. A basic understanding of the value of life was upended and cast out. He was sent adrift on a Sargasso.

Somehow the Urning's words made sense to him. Somehow the residual paste seemed to translate the rhythmic chant. His stilled and numb mind discerned the meaning.

The rhythmic clacks and hisses meted out balefully over the liquid night.

terra di ombra	earth of shadow
terra di nigreos	earth of black
layil ultimus	darkness final
layil oubliette	darkest dungeon
carcere iniurius	wrongful gaol
aeternum yaw-rad	eternal downward
aeternus mo-rawd	eternal descent
secutus adianxit	immured
pavor nocturnus	terror nightmare
olim praeteritum	long ago, past by gone
ego Tyrconell	I, Tyrconell
ego urna	I, Urning
ego famulus	I, servant occult
ego evestigatus	I, discovered
ostium apertio	doorway opening
ruina damnum	ruin loss
ruina vastitas	ruin desolation
ruina dissipantis	ruin dissipate
Ruina Perdere	Ruin Waster
ek apo zaw-rakh	up, out, appear
Shivic, Mezekiah,	Shivic, Mezekiah,
Arkarua, Ophiactii,	Arkarua, Ophiactii,
Tycho	Tycho
Ruin Perederoi	Ruinwasters
Quae una audite	which one can hear me?

proelium ultimus	The Last Battle
iniuctum rego	enjoined prosecute
Regula scilicet creaturae	rule the course of creation
Dominus Morgrom iubeo	Lord Morgrom commands
existo, sum, consum	emerge, be, coexist
ek apo zaw-rakh	up, out, appear
quod existo surgo	be, emerge, arise
ruina damnum	ruin loss
Ruina Perdere	Ruinwaster

Two Erebim shuffled at the edge of the pit. They wore grimy amices that were splattered with blood.

With the subtlest flick from the Urning they left and came up to the line of incapacitated Warriors. They looked like priestly demons charged with a heinous rite. A single sharp rune was branded on their foreheads.

Aenguz collapsed down to the ground and held still as a corpse. His sternum pulsed again as if his heart had a mind of its own and was incapable of processing fear.

He shut his eyes and begged to remain inconsequential, invisible.

The Erebim moved along the Warrior's feet and then they hauled up a body. He listened as feet dragged across the hard bone of earth.

Fear unmanned him. He could not unlock his eyes or grant the slightest respite to his curiosity. Who was being drawn to the pit? But he did not want the confirmation of what he knew was about to happen. Shame and cowardice warred in him. He did not want to be selected. He waited a long time as the words wedged into the night.

aeternum yaw-rad	eternal downward
aeternus mo-rawd	eternal descent
secutus adianxit	immured
pavor nocturnus	terror nightmare

He edged up again on his elbow and looked over his feet at the swallowing pit.

proelium ultimus	The Last Battle
iniuctum rego	enjoined prosecute
Regula scilicet creaturae	rule the course of creation
Morgrom iubeo	Morgrom commands

The firelight cut across the splattered Erebim and their Akkeidii offerings. They held the Warrior on his knees. His head was a straggled mop. Most of the shirt was in shadow but the lines of blue and silver at the neck bespoke the clan.

His clan.

Ridder.

Aenguz's jaw dropped.

He cursed his eyes.

Then one Erebim grabbed a handful of hair and jerked the head back.

Ridder's smeared mouth gaped black. White eyes channeled a grim prophecy. He was held kneeling, offered in supplication. His empty prayer was useless before the Urning and the pit. The black paste sealed his mouth like a curse.

The other Erebim opened Ridder's throat violently, cutting through the hard cords of his neck.

Aenguz blurted out a 'No!' but the remnants of the sour paste kept the word to a strangled cough.

An impossible amount of blood poured out. His opened esophagus sprayed red into the night. For a moment, Ridder regained his eyes. He looked stricken and confused. A shock, unlike anything Aenguz had ever seen made Ridder look foreign or possessed. But his eyes did not remain open long.

The bloody officiants let the body fall headfirst into the pit and the licks of forming night drank the Akkeidii blood.

existo, sum, consum	emerge, be, coexist
ek apo zaw-rakh	up, out, appear
quod existo surgo	be, emerge, arise
ruina damnum	ruin loss
Ruina Perdere	Ruinwaster

Then there was a tone. A plaintive chime arising from an elemental silence. It rose like a wave in the firmament and rang like a carillon. Loud and bright like the first note of creation, the first sound of spring.

The channeled trunk jolted. A cord of light like lightning flashed out. The two hacking Erebim dove off the cairn tree. The others covered their heads.

After a moment, the Erebim around the trunk stepped forward and peered into the hacked channel. They looked mystified and then howling sounds of glee rose.

Ridder was dead. Murdered by Erebim. His weapon, his sword, lost to all time. But the metal was captured, prevented from returning to the earth. The Erebim's profanity strained the limits of Aenguz's astonishment.

This was the second time he heard that chime. The first was when his father died. The violence of both deaths echoed loudly within him.

But mourning and grief were subsumed.

Fresh panic, the urgency of survival, opened a store of adrenaline in him. Aenguz's heart burned as frantic beats breathed life into his fear. He worked at the cords at his wrists. He gnawed at the taut sisal and searched the ground for a nub of rock to cut the tight bonds.

A dolorous groan irrupted from the tip of the Cairngorm. The hacking stopped. Aenguz halted his futile gnawing. The ground thrummed and shuddered against an ill. It sounded like a counterpoint to the released *montmorillionite.*

All of the Erebim stopped and quieted. Their howling speech was swallowed up in the throat of night.

The Urning pulled back from the pit, still as a plague.

The amiced Erebim knuckled their way back from the edge.

The order of the Earth seemed abrogated. Fundamental laws were in upheaval.

The surface of the viscous disk undulated. Leaden waves reached beyond the ragged edges of the pit. The dead Akkeidii looked desiccated and drained. The roe deer were sacks of bones and fur. The moonlight looked warped, unholy.

The cairns scowled down, appalled.

A shape rose from the crèche of night. It was a further negation. A blackness that scorned the imperfect dark of night. The Urning drifted further back. It coaxed the form out from the pool of unformed night. An arm or a tentacle slapped out across the Deerherds. It searched the barren rock of the Cairngorm for purchase.

Another appendage slapped out at an odd angle across the drained roe deer.

A head or the shape of a head pulled out of the bleak tar. The rank oil sluiced off the form and refined the edges of the negation like a malediction.

More of the shape pulled out of the shuddering pool. The Urning led it, drew it, to the opening in the wall. The roe deer were frantic. They darted and jerked not caring about the cords that were cutting into their necks.

He peered over the line of Akkeidii as the shape, now all but invisible, seemed to gather itself. The Urning glode toward the opening and perched over the edge of the Cairngorm.

The Urning turned and led the hollow silhouette through the opening of the parapet. He guided it off the edge of the Cairngorm as if it meant to officiate over a consummation with night.

PART II

PURSUIT

14

～～

THE ONE BRIDGE

The full moon plunged. Soon the cousins of the Mashu in the west would devour the light. The stars withdrew one by one as if lost in their own grief.

The Ruinwaster and the Urning had vanished. Rot piqued the fading night. The smell mixed with the savage smoke from the slaughtered cairn trees. They looked to have stepped off the edge into the chasm below. The crude wall blocked Aenguz from seeing anything further.

The Erebim jolted as if they had been released from a spell. A chaos of howls and barks moved them into motion. Aenguz could see their frantic energy. They were desperate as if an army of Akkeidii Warriors were racing down the hill toward them.

Erebim clustered around the hollowed trunk. Tooled scabbards were scattered around the ground. Some lay half in the fire. A skin of stripped bark was lashed quickly over the hacked channel. Then they slung cords underneath and grabbed chopped limbs and heaved the trunk. The cairn tree dropped after a step or two. Another heave and another drop. They were pulling it to the edge where the Urning and Ruinwaster had disappeared.

Another band of Erebim took up the bundles and baskets. Aenguz could make out some of the Warriors' packs and cloaks amid the piles of supplies. They shouldered their loads and turned toward the opening.

'*Were they all determined to follow their leaders over the edge?*' It was madness pulled out of a nightmare.

One by one the bearer Erebim walked off the edge.

Drovers pulled the lashed roe deer to the edge. The bucks and does balked. They dug their hooves into the glassy earth. Their Erebim drovers pulled and beat them toward the opening as they snorted and bleated.

Aenguz gritted and swore at the Erebim.

"Get your hands off them!"

As he watched the coordinated mass suicide, a cadre of Erebim closed in around the prostrate Champions.

They kicked at the drugged Warriors and pulled at the cords that lashed them together. Ferocious howls and angry barks excoriated the captives. One Erebim stepped down the line and sprayed water in their faces from the Akkeidii waterskins.

Aenguz rolled onto his knees after a pair of brutal kicks. The cord tugged at his neck. He caught a gulp of water during the splash and rinsed out more of the black paste.

"Get back!" he shouted at the violent Erebim. He snatched the water-skin out of an Erebim's hand and went to the Finit Warrior. He bent over and dug the rest of the paste out of his mouth and squeezed in some water.

The Warrior hacked and coughed. His eyes rolled as if he was spinning. An Erebim kicked the Finit viciously.

Aenguz shoved the Erebim back with a curse. The beast whacked Aenguz across his head and scarred arm.

He turned back from the beating and tended the Finit.

"Finit, you must rise. We are captured."

The Warrior blinked hard as if he was dispelling a bad dream. Aenguz pulled him to his feet, but confusion still clung to him.

He looked at the pit. It had ossified into a cooled obsidian. The bodies of the Warriors and the Deerherds lay half-submerged, trapped in the permanent black.

The thump of the cairn tree grew louder.

The bearers were gone. The roe deer bleated somewhere in the night.

One by one the Warriors were kicked or dragged to their feet.

Aenguz reached the next Warrior, a Kriel, while the Finit steadied himself.

He helped the Kriel up and called down the line of Warriors as they woke from their stupor.

Soon the lines yanked at their necks as the Erebim pulled them to the plunge.

The Erebim at the cairn tree barked savagely at the Erebim tending to the captives.

The line grew taut.

Aenguz could make out Mandavu's frame. The Makan Champion was resisting and Erebim were whipping him with long thin staffs.

His brother lunged out at the attackers but the cords at his feet toppled him.

The cacophony was chaotic, maddening.

A pair of Erebim saddled up to each brother and grabbed an arm. The line lurched forward toward the parapet.

The first hint of dawn limned the mountains in the east. All but the surest stars were gone.

Fear and panic would have frozen Aenguz but for the cord at his neck and the rod at his back. The Erebim didn't touch him. They seemed repulsed by his arm.

One by one, the Erebim, with Warriors in tow, stepped out and off the ledge.

But they did not drop.

They rose into the fading night.

A thin gossamer footing cupped the tip of the Cairngorm and vaulted upward.

Over the edge and through the mist, far below, the torrent and churn of the White and Millin carved relentlessly. Swirls and striations blended with the sight below as his eyes adjusted to the height and the depth *and the material of the span*. The span was smooth but within the translucent arm, edges of cumulus roiled.

His first step gave a little as if he stepped onto a taut tarp.

Then he was pulled and prodded up into the night.

The intermittent thuds behind him stopped. The Erebim snorted and barked something akin to curses. The drover at his rear jabbed and whacked.

Aenguz couldn't catch his breath. Every step felt like it was his last. Like he was caught in a looping moment of stepping off the edge again and again. A suicidal moment followed by a suicidal moment.

Up and up, they went.

High over the gorge, the walls on the bridge opened to a wide round balcony. Two other arms raised up to the platform from the east and west like a benediction. The underside of the spans arched and dipped down to a clouded point below the uplifted parapet.

At the center stood a tall, three-legged fane. The thin legs supported a scalloped roof that was as delicate as a leaf.

The fane bloomed and roiled as if it was mined out of summer's first cumulus. The outer lines were smooth and slight but the inside was alive and vibrant.

The Erebim turned left. To the east. Toward the Flayer.

Light haloed the edges of the eastern peaks. The moon rushed to distant Lands.

Their pace grew desperate.

The Erebim were merciless toward the Akkeidii. Constant whipping dogged their every step.

Ahead, the roe deer were frantic to quit the ephemeral bridge. Their drovers let them run in an all-out panic.

Some of the Erebim left the line of Warriors and ran for safety.

The cords that bound the Warriors together made their flight stilted and awkward.

Aenguz shuffled as fast as he could. The barks behind him were no less intense but they faded back.

Suddenly, Aenguz lost his feet and fell headlong onto the taut surface of the bridge.

The cord cinched, cut his neck, and seized his throat shut.

He dragged behind the Finit. His bound hands skimmed across the diaphanous surface. He tried to pull himself up as the garrote stole his air.

His throat knotted; gulps stalled. His eyes were ready to pop.

Rough granite scraped the heels of his hands and toppled Aenguz into a heap onto solid ground.

He struggled at the cord and tried to pry it loose. His face moved from red to purple to blue.

The Finit was fading from view. Aenguz rapped him on the shoulder with his last strength.

Fingers clawed at his neck.

Gulps of air rushed in.

His chest heaved.

The Finit came back into view.

"Thank you," he breathed in between pants. "Finit."

"Ondo. I am Ondo," he said with a restrained, smudged smile.

The last shadows of night receded down into the cleaving surge of the Twin Rivers.

The Erebim bearing the cairn tree lumbered down the span. Their eyes were wide. A full measure of terror had them.

The nose of the trunk crossed to the ledge.

Suddenly, as if an imperceptible chime had sounded, the cairn tree dropped with a heavy thud. Bark and stone scratched on the granite.

The Erebim at the front dropped to the ground with it.

The Erebim at the rear dangled over the chasm. They clung to the branches just steps from the ledge. Their feet bobbed uselessly. They held tight to the tree - for a moment. Their exhausted limbs couldn't hold them long. Some grasped at their neighbors before their combined weight pulled them both down. The gorge swallowed their horrible screams. A small retribution delivered by the cairn tree.

The One Bridge evaporated like a mist in the late morning. It vanished like a trick of the light into the gentle amber of dawn as if it had never existed.

The cleave between the Lands returned, remained.

15

~

HUMP THE LOG

Like a great stone ship, the prow of the Cairngorm cast off. The One Bridge had withdrawn into the ether like a gangplank. In the growing dawn, the boat-like cairns looked useless as if they rested on the deck of a ship bereft of passengers. The wisps of smoke from the dying fire seemed like the remnant of a mortal blow.

The Champions were stranded and abandoned as captives on a foreign land. Even though they could see the southernmost tip of the Mashu, the distance across the chasm was as wide as the distance between continents.

The line of captive Warriors looked broken and defeated. They looked as if the Last Battle had ended in Akkeidii defeat.

The tumbled Warriors scanned around as they righted themselves. They were confirming their losses, searching for their missing companions. Their dislocated gazes unable to process the truth of what they saw.

Oh, Ridder. Selvin and Moodley. He played the confused look of astonishment on Ridder's face as his throat was ripped open. The memory of his black mouth spattering, and spewing blood looped again and again. It was as incused on him as Morgrom's message.

He didn't want Ridder to come on the Challenge. He was as culpable for his murder as if he had drawn the blade itself.

The absence left by him opened a fresh vacancy that mirrored the one left by his father. The vastness of both losses left him hollow and alone as if he was the last Akkeidii on Earth.

There would be no warning for the clans - never mind the message for Corundum or the Counsel Lords.

Aenguz counted the line to see who had survived the ritual.

Light effaced all of the stars.

The lesser night of shadows acknowledged the growing dawn. Color emerged in the gorge.

He looked passed Ondo and searched the captives. Ondo scratched out a whisper, "Shudaak, Shudaak." He searched down the line, calling out for heads to turn.

The black smears across the Champions mouths looked like failed imprecations. It was with an admixture of accusation and dejection when their eyes locked on him for a few desperate moments. Once they realized he wasn't their lost companion they looked through the line to rescan again.

Four Champions were gone.

And Selvin and Moodley.

Six Akkeidii in all.

Slain by the Erebim for the sake of releasing the Ruinwaster. But which one?

The Makan brothers were intact. Kachota tended his older brother. Mandavu had taken a severe beating. His head drooped down as if he was only semi-conscious.

The Baierls had two Champions still. Roberge and Strey. Their faces were narrow and their chins pressed back into their necks. The older one doted over his younger brother. Asked about hurts, checked his state of mind, attempted to allay his fear.

At least these two pairs were not alone.

But the Kriels, Finits, and Gambls, like Aenguz, had all lost one of their clan, one of their own Champions. Perhaps brother-friends. Ondo's searching seemed to imply that they were not just fellow Warriors.

Ondo stopped calling out for his companion.

Once they had taken stock of their losses they looked back out over the distance to the Cairngorm. And at the vacant space left by the One Bridge. It dwarfed them.

The Erebim lurched and inched the dangling cairn tree onto the ledge. They barked and snarled at the captives as they loped passed.

A short distance away they tore through the Akkeidii's belongings. Carefully wrapped bundles were torn apart. The deer meat was devoured, other items were sniffed and tossed aside. Tokens from wives or mothers or sisters or grandmothers were ravaged. At times they growled and fought like a pack of starving dogs.

Clothes were tossed to the side or over the ledge. Nothing the Akkeidii had would fit the long, thick torsos of the Erebim.

Then some of their number portioned out food from the Champions bundles and supplies. They tore at the meaty strips with their sharp teeth as if it was leather.

While they ate, drovers returned with the half dozen roe deer that had bolted down the mountain road. They had to be prodded and cajoled to come close to the larger pack of Erebim.

Aenguz and the Warriors watched as they piled their bundles and bushels on the backs of the deer. At first, the roe deer were unruly. The Erebim were rough. Aenguz's heart wrung as they beat the frightened deer.

An older Erebim, who looked made more from scars than wrinkles, took up a Warriors' cloak and draped it over the buck's back. The drovers followed suit and covered the rest.

This soothed and steadied them. Then they piled on all of their supplies and gear. They were clearly overburdened.

Aenguz wanted to shout but the words stalled in him.

Once the roe deer were laden the drovers started off down the road.

Now the attention of the whole pack of Erebim turned to the captives. And the cairn tree.

They formed up shoulder to shoulder across the road and walked toward the captives.

They cupped the quilled ends of their long sticks into the contoured atl atls. They raised and pumped the air with their heavy arms. They seemed to be drawing up courage in themselves or making a threat. They barked and pulsed in a rising fury.

A cluster of Erebim ran forward and inched the trunk fully onto the ledge and then darted back.

Then the line of Erebim parted to let another set of drovers through. Loops of cords like lassos hung at their waists.

The oily tenders jabbed at the line of sullen captives. With short staffs and coarse howls, they urged the Akkeidii to their feet.

They poked and prodded the Warriors around the cairn tree. Mandavu and Kachota staggered over to one side and the Baierl brothers were positioned opposite them.

The Gambl and the Kriel were lined up behind them. Ondo and Aenguz were position behind the Makans.

The drovers cut and re-tied the cords around their necks and waists. A web of sisal linked them together and to the cairn tree. They wrapped the stripped skin of bark several more times. They seemed to have an unending supply of sisal. Finally, they cut the cords that joined their feet moving quickly down the line. They backed away quickly and carefully from Mandavu and Roberge at the head.

Then they gestured for their captives to lift the *montmorillionite* laden cairn tree. Their howls may have been threats or imprecations. They seemed to be scrabbling for courage. The drovers barked again. The line of Erebim behind them threatened across the distance.

The Warriors were resistant at first and a little confused. The network of loose garrotes mimicked their confusion.

"All of our weapons are in this cairn tree," Aenguz said. "All of them."

Resignation or horror flashed across the defeated Champions' faces.

They found an awkward grasp on a branch or a handful of cord. Then with a heave, they hauled the cairn tree up. They stepped and stuttered forward into an unknown land as captives, as chattel.

The Erebim churned with awe and fear. It had taken nearly three times their number to lift and heft the trunk across the One Bridge. Once the Warriors started, they turned and marched off down the road.

The ancient road traced a weaving course along the cliff face. Harsh brambles and rickety brush found purchase here and there amid the intermittent cobble. Scree and detritus littered the disused road. In places, Aenguz could see landslides that had been recently cleared. Spoor stains marked the edges in places.

How long had they been here? How long had they waited? Aenguz wondered.

The morning wore on. The clouds threatened rain as shades of gray darkened and then lightened. There may have been a rumble that echoed in the distance.

The Warriors could not find a rhythm with the hacked trunk. Aenguz's wrists ached. The healing flesh on his left was numb and raw. Sharp numbs poked at his hip like a spur. A jagged branch scored his thigh.

All of the Warriors seemed to be struggling in one way or another. They shuffled down the road in a pained march.

The scores of Erebim had marched out of sight. Even the over-laden roe deer were gone.

The drovers pulled on the cords at their necks urging the captives to go faster. Mandavu and the Baierl bore the brunt of it.

At times, the trunk jerked and pulled Aenguz off balance sending both captives and the cairn tree crashing to the ground.

At one point, the sharp cracks from the drovers couldn't budge the Warriors so they deigned to let them rest while the drovers ate and drank.

Aenguz panted.

Sweat splatted down on the dusty cobble. It mixed with a feeble trickle of blood. Spittle trailed down into the soup.

The tasseography conjured up a memory.

Years ago, the first days of Warrior training.

They were not allowed to enter the field alone. They had not earned the right to carry any weapons. Their only strength came in numbers.

The Novitiates were divided up and directed over to the stripped and scarred logs.

Aenguz recalled the crude names scratched into the bare Mashuan Stone Pine. Blood, sweat, and piss stained the log.

They had to lift the log and bear it with them everywhere on the training field. Had to run drills or over obstacles together with the log on their shoulders.

'The log,' the older Novitiates said, 'was worth more than them in battle.' So, until they were worth anything they carried the log.

If one of their number collapsed or they all were spent, they lay the log across their stomachs. All the while the older boys would run by shouting, 'The battle is on hold for you until you have had your rest.' Or jabs like that.

Only when they worked as a unit and were deftly able to lift and lower and manage the log, were they given the wooden shield and knotted spear that was little more than a hefty branch.

Aenguz raised his head and looked over the trunk to the bent form of the Kriel.

"Kriel," he panted over the strapped bark.

"I am Lokah. Son of Ruel," Lokah returned a tired and frustrated gaze. His face was smudged with sweat.

"Lokah, Ondo. Hump the log," Aenguz said.

Lokah looked confused for a moment.

"Hump the log," Aenguz said. Almost like a punchline.

Lokah coughed out a short chuckle and smiled back, "Hump the log."

Ondo said back to Aenguz, "Hump the stump."

The three groaned out a hard low laugh.

Lokah and Ondo passed word up the line. Other colorful metaphors chimed up the line.

The Warriors heads swiveled as they met one another's eyes. Old memories swirled through them.

Roberge looked back at Aenguz and Lokah. Humor returned to his face. A smile that contained an easy laughter glowed through the black grime.

"Hump the stump," he said.

Aenguz could not see Mandavu's face, but the giant nodded. He may have uttered something.

"Ready!" Aenguz called out like a Drill Captain.

The Warriors' snapped to their feet. They gripped a branch.

"To the shoulder!"

They squared their feet.

"Heave!"

In one fluid motion, the cairn tree rose up. They nestled it onto their shoulders.

"Ready! Go!"

With a unified step, they marched forward down the road.

Aenguz could hear the startled barks of the drovers. They scrambled to their feet and jogged to catch up with their captives.

They marched through the rest of the afternoon. As a unit, they were able to maneuver over rockslides and through brambles.

Mandavu and Roberge called out obstacles and orders to the others like squad leaders.

The communal effort brought Aenguz and the other Champions back to a memory of youth, a memory of Warriorhood, a memory of home. It gave them enough fortitude to endure the long day. Their first in captivity.

The mass of clouds brought an early dusk to the ravine.

There were glints of firelight on the road ahead in the distance. The roe deer were huddled between the two groups.

The drovers barked for the line to stop far from the other Erebim. A creek lapped alongside the road. They tugged the captives sideways to the culvert.

Mandavu called out the command to lower the trunk. In one gesture, the exhausted Champions lowered and then dropped the log.

The drovers dropped the lines and walked past the roe deer toward the nearest fire.

Aenguz inspected the roe deer in the distance. Their legs were tucked beneath them. They were bedded down for the night. The buck's forked antlers seemed to be keeping watch.

Once the drovers were gone, they hefted the log nearer to the creek so that they could all reach.

Aenguz helped Lokah over the log. The Sidor and the Kriel drank side by side on the ancient road.

They washed out the last of the bitter paste. Spitting, smacking, and gurgling echoed in the craggy trough.

Once they had their fill, they hauled the log out and sat packed together between the cairn tree and the cliff wall.

Aenguz looked at the line of fires along the road. Orange and yellow shadowed shapes teemed around the fires. After a time, they assembled and organized in a fashion. He could see the profiles of sharp noses and spiny manes all facing the cliff wall as if they were making obeisance to stone. Then the Erebim prostrated themselves. And in the cold, bleak night they chanted, '*Morgromote*,' then something unintelligible, '*Morgromote*.'

16

STICKS AND STONES

With their mouths now clear, all thoughts turned to escape - *and rescue*. Ondo found a stone and began working at the cords. The Warriors who couldn't find a stone gnawed or scratched at the tough bands. But the cords were firm.

It was a cruel taunt to have their weapons within reach. *Montmorillionite* would have made short work of the sisal. And the Erebim would have their hands full with eight armed Akkeidii Warriors.

The *'Morgromote'* chant went on for a long time. Aenguz could see a few of the Erebim act as officiants of some sort. The same ones who aided the Urning. They directed the movements of the ritual with a reverent severity. Afterward, their fires slowly died.

The Champions started to put the pieces together from the night before. Until now, murk seemed to sustain the capricious logic compelled by their nightmares. What was happening made sense in this inverted world. Now with the paste washed away, they began to ask questions.

They questioned one another about what each remembered. What had happened? Why was there no warning? How were they captured without a fight?

Mandavu and Kachota turned to Aenguz. Even in the silver light of the imperfect moon, accusations dripped from them.

Aenguz thought about what he might say. What he might reveal. If they had not gone onto the Cairngorm the night before to witness the revelation of the One Bridge, they would all still be there. Ridder and Selvin and Moodley would still be alive. The other Champions would be alive as well.

Aenguz might have avoided the Challenge altogether too.

They would have found the desecration left by the Erebim and the Urning - and the Ruinwaster. He could have dispelled the confusion and shared the message. Ridder would have backed him up. He would have been rid of the responsibility of the message. The evidence would have been plain. They would have run back to Grieg's Gate. The Akkeidii would have been warned.

But he was complicit, albeit indirectly. He was the reason they were all down at the Cairngorm.

"There was an Urning with them. It held us still as stone. We could not make a sound."

The residue of drug-addled nightmares brought the image of the floating monster back to them. Aenguz could see the various shudders and averred glances. They were happy to turn their thoughts from the Urning. They did not want to see it again or perhaps acknowledge that it was real. And they did not question where it had gone. Had likely not even seen it float out over the chasm.

Ondo told them about the bodies. But he could not speculate how they had been affected or how they had fallen.

Aenguz could not bring himself to tell them about the ritual.

The dead Champions and Deerherds seemed to provide the evidence to Aenguz's claims. But the ghoulish arm either made him not worth killing or made him, somehow, akin to them. At least that was what the Makans' darkened gaze seemed to say.

The marvel of the One Bridge was debated next. Was that real? Did that happen? The vagary of the silencing muck left them unsure. Mandavu tried to insist that there must have been some other pass unknown to the Akkeidii. But all recalled being suspended above the gorge on the three arms of the One Bridge. They each confirmed their view of the fane. The details of the shared 'dream' were too similar. The reality of their current circumstance unassailable.

For Aenguz, the residual *roona* and *gingrass* - and perhaps even the *morillion* - had dimmed the worst of the effects.

No one mentioned the ceremony or the Ruinwaster. Aenguz struggled over whether or not to tell them. How could he explain what he had seen? What he knew. In their current circumstance, the message would only serve to wound them all further. There was nothing they could do about it. Except indict him further for his silence and inaction. And for sending them all down to the Cairngorm in the first place.

Instead, their thoughts turned to rescue. Once the Akkeidii found the violation on the Cairngorm, and the dead Champions, they would be at war. They would surmise where the Champions were now.

"Even a blind Finit Ranger could find this path," Ondo remarked.

But first, they would have to cross the gorge by some other means, Aenguz thought.

The Warriors nodded and grunted their assent. Revenge and retribution were a more satisfying muse for them now.

Aenguz acquiesced to their feelings of retribution. The promise of violence and war sustained them and distracted them from their empty stomachs.

"Once they were found and their weapons freed." They promised their revenge to one another against the Erebim.

But first, the Akkeidii had to know that they were gone.

Aenguz had counted the days. It would be at least two days before the victorious Champions would have returned to the Valley of Gathering.

Four and a half days would have passed since they left. By the fifth day, they would likely grow concerned.

They would not send Warriors to search, could not. Dahlward would send Deerherds. The clan lords could agree to that. Likely a Deerherd from each clan.

It would take two days for them to reach the Cairngorm. They probably would not expect to go that far. They would assume that they would intercept the Champions and the victor on the way.

But four or five days would elapse again before they would return to the Valley of Gathering.

And then a host would issue down to witness the desecration for themselves. It would take another two days. Perhaps a day and a half if they believed the Deerherds.

Seven or even eight days might elapse before an Akkeidii chieftain stood on the prow of the Cairngorm.

Who knows where the Champions would be in that time? Then they would have to cross the gorge or somewhere further up the Millin. How long would it take for the Akkeidii to find them?

Aenguz only offered that the clan lords did not know that they were gone yet. He did not want to draw so much attention to the fact that they were there because of him. Or that they were on their own.

They had to slow the pace.

Guiding them on how to lift the cairn tree had been helpful for them. It had brought them together in a small way. But it was clear that they had to slow the pace.

He agreed at points as the Warriors counted the steps in the days that would pass. He let others challenge any unrealistic expectations.

When they arrived at the conclusion that they must now go slow, Aenguz agreed, confirmed, and ratified the decision.

The next day they would go slow.

He did not want to think how far the Erebim might be taking them or what they intended. Or where they might be going. Perhaps the other Warriors felt the same way. They did not voice those questions if they held them. Even on the edge of a strange land, they were further away from home than any of them had ever imagined to be. And nearer to places that they scarcely ever dared dreamed about.

They tried to sleep against the chopped cairn tree. Hands bound, necks lashed, stomachs empty and only hard ground and course wood to shelter them.

Aenguz tried not to think about the Lands around Carrowen Celd.

———— ◆ ————

THE NEXT DAY a pitiful rain began before dawn. Across the webbing, the Warriors confirmed their plan and held still as if they could sleep through a torrent. Not one of them spoke a word to the misery they felt.

Aenguz whispered encouragement to Ondo and Lokah. The Finit and the Kriel put on brave faces, but their lack of sleep and the lack of food were plain in their eyes and on their faces.

They were Warriors, Aenguz thought. *They had endured worse in training.* It was the realization and taunt of their predicament and the unknowns before them that were written on them more than their privation and bondage.

The Erebim stirred. The bulk of their party set off in the rain. Growls and rough barks followed them down the road.

The roe deer were burdened again and prodded into motion. They looked sullen and resigned. Their dark eyes were cast down and their necks were bent. They clattered after the main party on wobbly legs.

When the drovers came to the Akkeidii, the Warriors pretended to only just stir from a peaceful sleep. Roberge stretched his arms and yawned broadly.

The Erebim howled barks at the captives.

The Warriors climbed slowly to their feet.

Roberge responded to them, mocked them.

"Why yes, we would enjoy a morn meal."

More agitated barks.

"Bacon sounds delicious. And fruit breads. Yes, please enough for all of us. What else do you have?"

They raised their knurled staffs and swung at the air.

Roberge turned back to the Champions.

"What else would you like for morn meal?"

A smattering of ridiculous requests came up from the Warriors in the most serious tones.

'I will take this.' Or, 'Such and such sounds good.'

They rattled off an imaginary menu to one another.

The drovers snapped and pulled at the lines and yanked Roberge and Mandavu to the ground.

"Brothers, morn meal will be ready shortly," Roberge said.

They hefted the log but only to the culvert. The drovers barked but the Warriors bent to take water.

When they returned from the culvert, they turned from the cairn tree and relieved themselves.

The Erebim howled all the while but there was little they could do.

"The Rangers will find that for certain," Ondo quipped.

Aenguz watched the roe deer hobble out of sight. He estimated their slow pace.

"Ready for a stroll in the mountains brothers?" Roberge asked.

Aenguz called out the commands to heft the tree up to their shoulders.

"Slow, slow," Aenguz said once the log was up.

The drovers pulled on Mandavu and Roberge's leashes. The Makan swore at the Erebim and pleaded for them to come close.

Roberge entertained a mock conversation with the Erebim as they walked. Through the one-sided dialog he confirmed to himself the Erebim's questionable parentage. The unfortunate ugliness of their fathers. The apparent fault of their noses that left them so odorous.

"You see Strey," he said to his younger brother. "Who knows what rank beast they lay with."

Strey added to his brother's taunt. A foil to the mock conversation.

After a short time Roberge asked, "Oh, you want us to take a break? Brothers, our guides insist we rest."

They let the log down.

The Erebim were incensed. They came up and began beating the pair.

"Uuk, uuk," they coughed out.

Their staffs came down hard on the pair. Their younger brothers stood in to try and take on some of the blows.

Kachota promised a harsh death for the Erebim.

Roberge somehow maintained his demeanor, "Oh, you mean you want us to continue?"

Strey positioned his back to take the rod. Roberge nudged him back.

The Erebim stepped back and barked at one another.

Roberge spat. His voice quivered. "Brothers, apparently they want us to continue."

"Come on," Aenguz said. "Let's go."

They brought the log up again.

The rainy day wore on. Time did not move. Trees replaced the bleak granite. And soon the road entered a forest. Although they were trending gradually downward, they kept the pace slow.

Aenguz looked around Ondo to see if he could see the roe deer. It was hard to tell if his plan was working.

After a time, the Erebim seemed to sense the ploy. Pulling on the leashes wasn't working. Perhaps the pair at the front was too strong they may have thought.

They came to the back of the log and turned their staffs on Aenguz and Lokah.

The first crack was brutal.

Aenguz stumbled.

Lokah cursed at the Erebim.

They cracked again. Pain blazed across his shoulders.

Again, and again.

"I think," Aenguz wheezed, "they mean," a blow cut him off, "for us to go faster."

Another harsh whack brought Aenguz to the ground.

The log dropped. The contents sloshed like oil.

The Warriors shouted back at the drover demanding he stop, promised him death in the bleakest terms.

Ondo bolted to Aenguz side as far as the cords would let him. Hallock stretched his arms across Lokah's back.

Aenguz could see the brothers pulling at the cords over the skin. Scratching, biting, peeling at the bark.

Barks and howls mixed with curses and threats. Suddenly, a thwack!

The log shook.

Thwack!

Aenguz raised his head.

Two long quilled shafts were planted in the nose of the cairn tree.

In the middle distance, half a dozen or so armored Erebim stood. An Erebim was fitting another shaft into his atlatl. He held his arm back and then snapped it down impossibly fast.

The shaft struck the hollowed trunk with a deep 'thunk'

The Warriors recoiled to the ends of their cords.

Aenguz pulled himself up. "Let's go, brothers. Ready," his back screamed from the beating."To the shoulders."

They heaved the trunk up and continued on.

The pack of Erebim kept their distance but stayed within sight. Roberge and Mandavu affirmed their continued presence. They dared not let the log down now.

Aenguz's shoulders and back were a coat of pain.

He wished they could at least flip sides. He wasn't sure how his scarred arm would handle it but the pain was so intense he didn't care what the wood might do. The Warriors tried to shift the weight to give their shoulders a rest. The rain stopped and the hard day wore on.

"They have turned off down a path," Roberge called back under the log.

The drovers led them off the main road and down a narrow-wooded path. Three armored Erebim paused at the turn. They angled and maneuvered the cairn tree like a piece of antique furniture down a flight of narrow steps. Mandavu and Roberge bore the brunt of the weight. But at sharp turns, the tall Warriors had to climb into the forest. Then Aenguz and the others had to turn and walk at the fore.

Eventually, their arms got so sore and so difficult to maneuver that they lowered the cairn tree to their sides. In this way, they climbed down into the gorge.

The armored Erebim followed closely behind.

They barked and shoved Aenguz and Lokah. At times they jabbed with their long arrows.

When the cairn tree flipped, Roberge and Mandavu got the same treatment.

As the shadows of the forest blended with dusk, Aenguz's nose stung with the smell of bright pine and raw timber. Roberge and Mandavu broke through to a clearing and halted. Aenguz could not see what the pair saw.

Mandavu uttered an astonished curse. Roberge said, "Grieg's Balls!"

17

ORLOP OUBLIETTE

"What? What is it?" Aenguz asked.

The Erebim shoved him forward.

Fir sap and tannic bark stung Aenguz's nose as he stepped into the clearing.

The hillside was stripped. Hacked stumps dotted the slope down to the water. A carpet of wood chips covered the trampled bramble.

'I have given the land to the Erebim.'

The drovers steered the captives diagonally down the slope. Mandavu and Roberge navigated the Warriors in and out among the stumps toward the shore.

The White had exited the cataract further up the mountain. The wash grew louder as they lumbered down the descent. The rapids changed. The rush was smoother like several lesser waterfalls in the distance.

The river widened into a lake here. The black surface ran out into oblivion. Dark mountains girded the opposite shore.

Three or four bonfires stretched along the shore. Erebim teemed like ants. Logs floated in the black like corpses. They drifted with the gentle current southward into the void.

Some Erebim were clearing a trunk. When they finished, they waded out into the lake and shoved the tree out toward the rest.

Aenguz could smell roasted deer meat through the aura of raped pine. His shoulders ached as he staggered down the slope. The demands of the burden stretched his wounded shield arm. All of the wounds merged with the lingering pain in his arm. His hurts combined into one encompassing din. The arm may have been better but compared with the other aches and lashes it was just a part of the litany of agonies.

The Erebim on the shore noticed the captives. They pitched hunks of wood and small limbs at the Akkeidii.

Lokah, Hallock, and the Baierls caught the worst of it. Though a few stout branches found their mark beyond those four.

Aenguz was assaulted by the cacophony of howls and arguing barks. It might have been a celebration. A cackled chortle exploded here and there from time to time.

They wended their way down at the ends of leashes. Defeated and disgraced Akkeidii.

And the captured *montmorillionite* they bore.

The captives traversed the final distance to the shore around a bend. Then they came to a line of shorn logs that were lashed together and stretched out into the water.

The bridge reached out to a wooden structure. A pair of square turrets rose on either end. The planks were smooth and fitted together evenly. The bridge reached up to the lower wall that joined them. It looked like a kind of fort.

The base of the structure rested fully within the water. The planks there overlapped like scales. Large black nubs poked out in a row just above the waterline.

The Warriors cursed in astonishment in between labored breaths.

To Aenguz it looked like some kind of river beast had been captured or restrained by the towers. It looked like an unnatural symbiosis.

The drovers led them to the causeway.

Mandavu and Roberge balked. For a second time, they were being forced out into an unknown that upended reason. It enabled a kind of fear that froze them.

They let the cairn tree drop out of a combination of exhaustion and panic-stricken fear. It fell awkwardly out of their hands.

Mandavu and Kachota lashed out. But the drovers were careful to stay out of reach.

Chunks of wood cut and slammed into Aenguz's back. Lokah took a piece in the head. He toppled to the ground. A cackle erupted behind them.

Aenguz climbed over the log and shook the Kriel awake.

Blood matted his hair and coated Aenguz's grisly hand.

The trunk was being hauled up as Aenguz hopped back over. The drovers pulled them on.

After a dozen or so steps, the causeway started to bob. The captives wobbled. The cairn tree sloshed thickly. They leaned away and toward one another.

Aenguz's stomach shifted.

As they walked the final distance, he saw movement on the structure.

Green-gray creatures milled on the deck and stood on the towers. Their oblong heads were smooth. The skin on their faces was taut. Blood red gums crown sharp yellow teeth. Some wore long, distressed gray frocks. Others wore shorter black sleeveless coats.

The creatures on the towers looked down aloof.

The jostling of the captives bowed and swayed the timbered pier. It creaked and groaned under the strain.

Finally, the trunk tipped downward and Aenguz and Lokah stepped over onto the wooden floor. The deck was firm, but it moved with a slight bob. It left him unsteady.

The drovers twisted and pulled the captives around the giant post at the center of the deck. The green-gray creatures cleared the floor. They climbed up into the towers or into the doors at either end. Two rectangular openings held ramps that led down into the dark.

A crossbeam, at the base of the post, cut the air just above their heads. A bone-colored shroud wrapped the beam.

'I have given the waters to the Sallow. Even now, with knowledge I have granted them, they navigate the rivers of the east. In time they will master them all.'

Aenguz shuddered at the sight of the craven Sallow.

The drovers, guided by a pair of Sallow, backed the captives up until Aenguz was pressed against the wall of the tower and the low lip at the edge of the deck. The lake churned shards of moonlight. The stripped trees floated helplessly by.

Mandavu called back to the Warriors, and they let the cairn tree down with a heavy plunk. The deck shifted slightly.

The Erebim crowded around their captives.

Mandavu resisted but it was pointless. Four or five Erebim held him. They cut him loose from the cairn tree, but his hands remained bound.

The Sallow on the ramps led him down.

His eyes were white. He looked like he couldn't swallow enough. His arms were limp in their grasp. He looked like a deer being led to slaughter.

Kachota spat curses and threats at the captors as Mandavu was led away. He pulled to the ends of his cords and pushed his fists at the Erebim.

When the Sallow returned from below, they took Kachota. He peered into the dark after his brother.

Roberge turned to Strey and tried to reassure his younger brother. "Have courage, brother." He looked back to the others with a mixture of courage and helplessness. He may have uttered, "Remember the Mashu."

The demons moved to Strey and Hallock next.

The Gambl was frantic. His eyes darted around in panic. His head turned on a swivel. He reached for the bark on the cairn tree and tried to pull it back. The log tilted. The Erebim matched his panic with their own and jumped on him and beat him into a heap. Their contoured staffs blasted his neck and back.

Strey fought against the horde, but he was quickly restrained.

They dragged Hallock down. His feet trailed behind him.

A bloodied Strey was led down after the unconscious Gambl.

The Erebim clustered around Ondo, Lokah, and Aenguz.

The three looked to one another for answers and for courage against their fear.

Aenguz was useless and helpless. Guilt blanched his soul. He was responsible for their litany of horrors. As the two Champions dropped out of sight, below the water, below the earth, all he could muster was, "Stay strong." He didn't know what he meant.

Aenguz turned his nose at the Sallow's rank breath. They cut the leads and bore him to the ramp.

His eyes did not adjust at once to the pocket of black. The close chamber clouded his nose. Fresh timber like newly milled wood permeated the entire space. Various scents of dank green and foreign herbs filled the air. Heady musk and stale spoor wafted in the space. Aenguz could smell roe deer but there were other animals besides. Animals he could not recognize.

Aenguz was muscled past stacked barrels. Burlap sacks slumped in loose piles. Bushels of darts were stacked about. Dried and drying plants hung from the rafters.

Aenguz squinted into the packed chamber for the Warriors. Where had they gone?

Suddenly he was positioned at another door in the floor. At first, the opening appeared like a negation. A null space of reduced and distilled midnight.

Screams erupted out of the hole.

The terror was primal and desperate.

Aenguz kicked back violently.

They were burying him alive, forcing him into some inconceivable torment.

The Sallow were ready for this.

Ghoulish hands reached out and grabbed his ankles.

Aenguz fell to his butt.

A rank odor made him gag. The pit was foul. A meaty gangrenous stench made him wretch.

He stuttered down rungs into a crèche of blackness. Aenguz closed his nose and hyperventilated in the soupy atmosphere.

His feet found a plank but only for a moment as he was kicked down even further.

Rough edges pounded at his side. Elbows and knees battered him as he was put into place. His boots plashed into shallow water. But his senses told him the fluid was fetid and foul.

The Sallow pulled his right hand to a rod. A hot silty mud squeezed in between his fingers and coated his palm. A hairy brush slathered more of the steaming grease paint around his right hand.

Aenguz tried to snatch his hand away from the burn. But the Sallow held him fast.

The Sallow measured out words.

In a few moments, the squishy mud cooled.

And then hardened.

They released their grip. He felt a knife cut most of the way through the cords that bound his wrists.

The Sallow climbed out of the hole and slid a board into place as if they were sealing a sarcophagus.

The darkness was as complete as the time before the stars or the moon. It was as black as the pit Ridder had died in.

Aenguz was a trapped animal. A primal fear clutched him. He jerked at his immured hand. Tried to climb up and out, to pry it free. He flexed his eyes for any glimmer of light.

Fetid air choked him as if soiled rags were being stuffed down his throat. Water pressed around him and threatened to crush him. A claustrophobic dread swallowed him whole. For a time, he wasn't himself. The need for flight and escape were the only philosophies in this dark hole.

After a time, exhaustion, futility, and a pained wrist slowed his heart. Spent adrenaline left him crippled. The bone-chilling screams were subsiding.

Other voices thrummed in the black. Calming voices.

A hand touched Aenguz's shoulder.

He had a sense of other bodies around him, but the hand startled him out of his skin.

"Hold friend, calm yourself. The *purna* has your hand. The Gildelmun will surely shine."

Aenguz couldn't catch his breath in the soupy air.

"Who are you? What is this place? Where are we?"

He spat questions into the dark.

"I am a prisoner of the *cog*, like you."

"The *cog*?"

"This Sallow-made vessel," the voice answered.

"Who are you?"

"A companion, a friend. Still yourself. The Gildelmun will shine soon."

Aenguz gathered himself to call into the dark for his companions.

Words came from varying distances in the narrow void. Ondo and

Lokah replied. Lokah sounded groggy. The blow to his head still had him. Ondo confirmed that his own hand was trapped and fused to a rod.

Roberge called back for Strey and himself. And the Makans gave back an "Aye." They confirmed that Hallock was there, but he was still unconscious.

Overhead the *cog* rumbled like a growing thunderhead. The tomb swayed.

"Tell me, friend, where are we?" the voice asked.

A rhythm was returning to Aenguz's breathing. He struggled to orient himself in the darkness.

"We are two days from the Lower Mashu on the eastern shore of the White River."

Without a face, Aenguz could not be sure how to interpret the silence.

Another voice in front of him spoke to the first. Aenguz could not understand what they said.

"Are you Akkeidii?" the second voice asked.

"I am. We are."

"Has Grieg's Gate fallen?" the first voice asked. A timbre of dread drained hope from the bleak space.

"No!" The suggestion was akin to blasphemy. But then how did Erebim capture the Akkeidii? Aenguz reasoned for the voice.

"We were outside the gate when we were captured. Grieg's Gate holds."

"Do the Erebim lay siege to the Mashu?"

Who was this?

"No!" Aenguz bit back. Such a suggestion at first balked reason. But now he had to confess that unthinkable things were now conceivable.

"Forgive me, my friend. We have been trapped here for many days with little hope. When you said you were Akkeidii hope and despair collided in me."

"Who are you?"

A loud splash sounded through the wooden walls.

The *cog* shifted and scraped.

Suddenly, a wicked thwack like a sledgehammer on a stubborn spike vibrated through the wood. It thrummed through his immured hand.

"What?" Aenguz demanded of the dark.

Another hard *THWACK!*

"Grab the rod with both hands. It will be easier with you," the voice offered.

Aenguz heard him shift in his seat.

An inchoate glow, a soft amber, emanated from the long square beam that ran along the channel beside him. Warm light rose in a long line at his feet. The spatter of filth and grime could not despoil the golden wood completely. Light rippled and shimmered from within the rich heartwood. The glow held the memory of sparkling water and summer light. The color of yellow flowers infused the glow.

Gradually, silhouettes emerged from the dark. Aenguz inspected the line of bent heads and shoulders nearest the light.

Aenguz didn't recognize the two people in front of him. But he could see Ondo one bench up. Lokah was to his right across the keel plank. The golden light colored the confusion on his face. Blood coated his hair. Hallock was bent over the rod next to the post at the center of the chamber. Kachota was one bench ahead of him. Strey was seated ahead of Ondo next to a bent head. Aenguz could just make out Roberge at the front. He could not see Mandavu, but Kachota's attentions confirmed that the giant Makan was just out of sight around the post. Other wizened bodies were seated and bent in between the Akkeidii.

Then, another *THWACK!* The warm glow brightened by another degree.

Heavy beams lined the low ceiling. They curved down along the sides like the ribs of a great whale. Clinkers dotted the lapstrakes like undigested matter. The rods were anchored in the ribs, and they connected across their laps into the golden keel.

Aenguz turned back to the voice. Gradually, half a silhouette contrasted and warmed against the dark. He was looking directly at Aenguz. The creases at his eyes held the memory of laughter. But now they were repurposed for despair. Compassion and concern shaped his face and tinged his dark skin. He seemed familiar with responsibility. His hair was matted in tight curls. Some of the patches responded to the light. In spite of the dirt, there was a regal air that couldn't be totally masked. His nose was a chisel of focus. A dense beard filled out his hollowed cheeks.

"I am Legerohn, a Moresi. I hail from Inverlieth."

He looked at Aenguz, as if he could not believe he was seeing an Akkeidii. Then his eyes caught the grisly sleeve of Aenguz's arm and bloody hand. Consternation fluttered across the Moresi's face. Aenguz pulled his arm down across his lap.

He noticed a nub of hardened clay on the rod, between him and Legerohn. He didn't process what it meant.

Aenguz balked at the sight of the Moresi. He pulled away again. Confusion and aversion added to the pressing walls of the vice. Morgrom had named them as foes. But tales of the Moresi said that they were traitors of the Venture, of Grieg Sidor. But those apocryphal stories had come later. Had come from Emissaries.

A dim current coursed into his hand and up the wrist.

The inexorable current turned into a drawing of energy from his heart and muscles. He was straining and exerting himself while fixed in place. It drew his mind from the tales of the Moresi betrayal and from the tale of Grieg Sidor the Venturer.

Something about the current felt reluctant as if the wood lamented against its nature. Its power was natural, an extension of its essence. But the drawing from him was strained as if the current was flipped.

"Take the rod with both hands. It will go easier for you," Legerohn counseled.

Suddenly, the *cog* shifted loose.

The drawing increased. A sustained tinnitus grew in his ears. His bones began to thrum with the unwanted current. His muscles and tendons tensed and held him rigid.

His grounding shifted. The *cog* scraped against mud and rock. Then it pulled free, and Aenguz was floating. He was gliding like a leaf on the water, below the water. His stomach crawled up in him as if he was falling.

"Take the rod," Legerohn said firmly.

Aenguz reached out and grasped the rod with his bloody hand. The current passed through him less severely, but it still drained him.

The *cog* curved and glode in a wide arc like an Urning drifting across space.

Aenguz's gut iced over. How could the Akkeidii find them in the water?

18

~~

HARD LABOR

Hammering announced the days - or the nights. The Gildelmun keel provided the only light. When it was gone, the slaves were cast back into darkness. The weight of water seemed more intense in the black.

The '*Morgromote*' chant gave Aenguz a sense of the time, an indication of night. The Erebim were dutiful in their obeisance. The constant discordant rumble above turned into murmuration when the ritual began.

Sallow tenders passed down wooden buckets filled with boiled spent grain and others with stale water. The door to their prison stood open at these times. Aenguz tried to gulp at some fresher air. But the smell of herbs and musk and milled timber from above was no substitute for fresh air. *Remember the Mashu*, he thought.

When the buckets first appeared, Legerohn guided Aenguz to lower one of each down to the bench.

Aenguz was famished. But he was wary.

Legerohn scooped a small handful to his mouth.

After testing the warm gruel Aenguz started shoveling in mouthfuls. But Legerohn stopped him. "This has to last for everyone."

Shame flushed Aenguz's cheeks.

They cupped some water and drank. This time Aenguz held back. It was not enough to quench his thirst.

They passed the buckets up to the two Moresi

"Philamay, Tahnka," they said as they accepted the buckets.

Legerohn reached out and clapped each on their shoulder and forced out a smile.

As the light from the Gildelmun faded, the buckets came back to the pair. They were filled with spoor and urine.

Legerohn's warped gaze confirmed to Aenguz what he thought about the waste that was returned.

The Sallow tenders gathered the buckets, and the captives were left to take what respite they could.

Aenguz was wary of the Moresi. He searched out the heads of the other Akkeidii. He called out to Lokah. The Kriel was slumped against the rib. He raised his right hand to Aenguz and nodded. He looked groggy but he didn't look as near to death.

The captive next to him barely moved.

Aenguz's hand was cramped. He tried picking at the purna.

Aenguz turned his head and bent over the rod to rest. For better or worse, he was used to being denied sleep. His stomach groaned.

Then the hammering would begin again, and the keel would come to life.

This was how the days passed.

Fierce hammering.

Boiled grain and stale water.

Spoor and urine.

Morgromote. Morgromote.

Lokah was too far away to talk with easily.

Legerohn was helpful and reserved. He seemed to sense Aenguz's anger toward him. So, he waited on Aenguz.

But questions harried him. He knew where the other Akkeidii were.

Hallock had woken on the next day. Kachota reached back and assured the Gambl as much as he was able.

Aenguz could see the heads of other Moresi here and there. Their tightly wound hair and dark complexion stood out. But there were other wizened figures in between.

Finally, Aenguz asked. "Who are they?"

"They are fishermen from Straathgard."

More enemies, Aenguz thought. The space in the hold continued to constrict.

"Have the Sallow and Erebim taken Straathgard?"

"No. They strayed too far down the Oso. Leono said."

"Leono?"

"Yes, the fisherman who was here before you."

"How long ago was that?"

"They were here well before us. Leono guessed weeks. But counting days is hard down here."

Aenguz looked back at the shrinking figures. Their heads drooped between their shoulders as if they were a thousand years old.

"Until you came, we sat still for days. We listened to the murdering of trees." Legerohn said the last part more to himself. His soul seemed wounded.

"Were you captured? Or have they-" Aenguz asked tentatively.

"We heard the wailing of the One Forest in Inverlieth. We came to aid the Chosen Freeholder against the massacre."

'*The One Forest stands against me, but it is beset. This generation will not pass before it is felled utterly.*'

Chosen Freeholder? Aenguz thought.

"We were stalled by logs on the Wester and then we were overwhelmed by Erebim and Tsurah. The Tsurah kept some of us and the rest they bore here."

Morgrom's message was coming to fruition.

"How many of you were there?" Aenguz's thoughts went to his own dead.

"Two score Moresi left Inverlieth." The muscles at Legerohn's jaw tightened. "Only a quarter remain here. Half are dead."

Mond, the Moresi in front him, turned and reassured him, tried to console him. White and gray tinged his beard.

The younger Moresi in front of Aenguz whimpered. The darkness seemed to have taken him. A thin beard traced ragged lines on his face.

"We have to get out of here," Aenguz began scratching at his wrist.

Legerohn warned him. "If you break the skin the wound will become infected."

"How do we get out of it?"

"We need some way to counteract the *purna*. If I could but walk into a forest, I could find something to remove it."

If I had my weapon, Aenguz thought.

The grief stilled Legerohn's words. The Moresi turned away from Aenguz and into his own private mourning.

Aenguz bent over the rail and struggled at sleep.

Then after a time, the hammering would start again.

Days went by in this way before a change came to the routine. Aenguz was beginning to lose count. Each day brought them further and further from possible help. No Akkeidii would be able to track them across the water. And the means to free himself was two decks up.

The message would not get delivered. The end of the Earth would come.

The familiar bob of the *cog* altered, eased. The barge turned. Then wood ground on wood. And the hammering halted.

Aenguz could make out scurrying feet and howling calls. Other Erebim from a distance. Rumbles rocked the chamber. Soon, chopping and hacking filled the muffled air. It sounded like they were moored in a forest. And an army of lumberjacks was clearing the trees. Though there were no tree falls. And they were still on the water.

Legerohn turned his head as if the sound of hacking was more than he could bear. Mond looked up into the rafters to search out the source of the chopping. Stokke, the younger Moresi wept.

After a short time, the hammering started. The *cog* pulled away from the wood. The keel brightened. Then the boat jerked to a halt. Aenguz and the others snapped forward. Planks creaked and moaned. The erratic bobbing confirmed for him that they were still on the water. But they were anchored to something.

After a time, the *cog* snapped loose. It swung around again and then the hard tug began again.

Legerohn and Aenguz looked at each other as sweat poured down their faces.

Legerohn reached forward to Mond and Stokke to reassure them. Their heads were sinking to their chests.

In the pauses, Aenguz asked Legerohn, "What are they doing?" Trunks bumped and scraped at the hull. Erebim and Sallow shouted above.

"I fear that they fell trees at such a rate that the Wester is occluded. Their wanton destruction has blocked the river."

When the hammering stopped Aenguz was sure that he was going to die. The golden wood had strained him, had drawn all of his energy. He was losing the will to live.

The *cog* was drawn up against timbers again. The jagged pier knocked at the hull.

The hammering stopped.

The Gildelmun began to dim. Its light seemed to be drawn down into the bottom of the pit.

The door slid back and the Sallow set the buckets down.

Strey yelled at the tenders and demanded their attention. At first, they ignored him. Roberge added his curse-laden voice to his brother's. The

Moresi nearest them also added to the commotion. The tenders came back and made their way to the Baierls.

The Sallow inspected their prisoners. It grabbed one drooped head and pulled it up by what remained of his hair. His nose worked the air. The tender dropped the head and climbed out of the hold.

A few moments later, another pair of Sallow climbed down after him. They leered around the hold in disgust.

They climbed down into the trench and produced a small ax. The new Sallow began hacking down on the dead fisherman's wrist. The sound of crunching bone sounded like a chicken thigh being butchered and rent from its socket.

The Sallow pulled the body out of the trench. They dragged the fisherman unceremoniously down the keel plank. The bloodied and splintered stump whacked Aenguz's head.

They pulled the body up out of the hold. And a few moments later, they heard a flat splash.

Aenguz's heart sank to the bottom of a well.

Light was fading from the keel. The abrupt pall of death cut through the rank, dark space. Waves of grief moved through the captives.

The fisherman choked on feeble sobs as they realized their companion was dead. They looked at one another and broke down further, devastated.

The Akkeidii reached out with their stern but awkward empathy. Aenguz could see Kachota reach to a fisherman ahead of him and clasp his shoulder. Mandavu also consoled him.

The younger Baierl was trying with words Aenguz couldn't hear to console another Straathgardian.

The Moresi reached out with a seasoned grief. Legerohn looked worn and hurt. His eyes were wet. A sound came from some dark corner. It started as a low song and grew plaintively into a threnody. One by one, the Moresi joined in and added to the harmony for the sad dirge.

> *"The river is long that carries me home*
> *Away from my beloved and dear family*
> *The current bears me on*
> *Further and further until*
> *Only her face in memory do I recall."*

The light from the Gildelmun responded. But nothing was drawn from Aenguz. Instead, warmth flowed into him. The light in the chamber grew bright as if the heartwood bore a sliver of the sun.

> *"So long the journey between my two lives*
> *When will my grief find an end?*
> *No rudder or oar to turn me back*
> *Further away and further on*
>
> *The light of my life is gone from me now*
> *Only the gentle swaying soothes me*
> *Along the long river to my forever home*
> *Away from family away from my love*
>
> *Too short is the time of my life*
> *Too sharp is the pain in separating*
> *Too deep is the grief of my loss*
> *Only the gentle swaying gives peace*
>
> *I hold you now in my mind's eye*
> *Your gentle face, without tears or crowded brow*
> *I take your love with me on my long journey*
> *Until the end of time brings us home."*

Home hung on the air in the orlop, and the golden wood seemed to respond. The light from the heartwood lingered a little longer held up by the sad song.

Quiet sobs and gasps along with consoling whispers were swallowed by the dark.

Aenguz took in the dark knob on the rod between him and Legerohn. The realization was grim.

He contemplated the buckets.

Anger seized him.

He took the water bucket and began slamming it down on his fused hand. Water spilled out everywhere. Again, and again he brought it down.

Legerohn was caught by a similar rage. Something snapped in him. He took the bucket of spent grain and slammed it down on the hard casing around his right hand. The rod jarred uncomfortably from the awkward swings. Grain spilled out onto his lap. The buckets began to break apart.

The captives in front called back for a chance to try.

Aenguz and Legerohn passed staves up to the others. They started banging on the rods and chopping dully on the *purna*. The captives shouted and cursed at the Sallow and Erebim.

Aenguz grabbed at his wrist as if he could pull it free from the rod.

"Anything sharp, anything," he said to Legerohn over the ghoulish cacophony.

The lid was slid back into place.

Suddenly there came the 'THWACK!' Then another, and another.

The Gildelmun's light changed.

The current passed through his hand. The heavy hammer continued until the captives, one by one, were driven into the fugue of draining. With no food and no water, and no rest, the *cog* was cut loose and steered out into the water.

Bit by bit the calls stopped. The futile banging dwindled. Each man gripped the rod according to his strength or desperation. They tried to steel themselves against the renewed and reluctant drawing power of the golden wood.

Aenguz lost track of time. He actively welcomed the idea of death.

When the hammering stopped the light dimmed and the *cog* drifted.

It was caught by something not stone or wood. The barge turned sideways into a current. It keened to the side as if it might capsize. Water poured against the outer wall in a rush as if the boat was sinking.

Aenguz collapsed into a drowned unconsciousness before the heart-wood faded.

19

AN IMPERFECT PLAN

In death, there is a gift. A last offering from the dead to the living. In the shock of sudden loss and mounting grief, there is a gift wholly separate from those denuding emotions. A lesson, an experience, a new wisdom, a boon.

Whether it is a function of the natural order, a final gift from the death-bound spirit, or a beneficence granted for those passing to the next world, who can say? But a raw nugget of wisdom and meaning is buried in the loss of each living thing.

But the dead don't choose it. And the living don't always see it. However, always, there is a final unexpected gift.

When Aenguz woke, he thought about the dead fisherman. The hacked stump left a nagging scrape above his temple. He contemplated his brief future and its inevitable end. His failures and losses buried him. They confirmed his self-castigation. He had, with Erebim help, led the Champions into this inescapable dilemma. What kind of leader was he?

Aenguz inched his melted hand along the rod to the hardened nub. He probed the edges and found broken bone. *Leono's hand.*

Death appeared to be the only way out of the pit.

Or was it?

The dead Straathgardian spoke to him, spoke through him. Even though they were foes, in death, he gave Aenguz a final gift. He heard the rending of bone and cartilage over and over again. The memory of the sickening sound knurled his stomach.

There was no way he could pull his hand free. And there was nothing sharp enough in the hold to cut through. He could not bring himself to gnaw through the tendons and bones of his wrist. That logic and capability was the purview of trapped animals. He held no illusions there.

But the twisted body of the fisherman turned on him. In relation to the set nub, it unlocked the means to free himself from the *purna*. He turned the idea over in his mind and contemplated the exigencies, the contingencies. He mulled the consequences and the timing.

The timing would be key.

And there was still the message. It was clear now that the warning was no fantasy. And it was closer than Aenguz believed. The ritual to free the Ruinwaster and the incursions of the Sallow and the Erebim made that plain. If what Legerohn had said about the Tsurah was true, then time was running short. The only hope in countering such malefic evil lie in delivering the message. In engaging the Counsel Lords and imploring them to find the Dagba Stone.

However, Aenguz accepted that he would likely die. There wouldn't be much time after he freed his hand. There would be blood. He would have to pass the message on. Lokah was too far away. And Ondo was out of reach.

He would have to trust Legerohn. He would share the message with the Moresi and trust that he would deliver it to the Counsel Lords at Corundum. If the Champions survived, they could warn the Akkeidii.

What else could he do? He would have to rely on the Moresi.

Whether the Sallow harbored some guilt in the punishment they exacted on the captives or they understood that they needed them to power the *cog*, the Sallow set down a double portion of food and water.

A meager light made its way into the hold.

Aenguz needed his strength.

He passed buckets up to Mond and Stokke and then set grain and water between him and Legerohn.

Aenguz scooped a handful of the boiled grain, raised it slightly to his left and right, and then offered it to Legerohn. Legerohn paused. A mixture of reverence or confusion complicated his face. Then he took the offering and ate. Then the pair scooped handfuls up to their mouths. It almost seemed like a meal.

When they were done, they passed the buckets up.

Aenguz leaned in close to the Moresi.

"Legerohn. I think I have a way to get free," he kept his voice low.

The Moresi pursed his lips. His eyes narrowed.

"But first, I need you to take on a task for me."

Legerohn's head shook slowly as if he didn't comprehend Aenguz.

"You must agree."

"I do not know what you are asking. Or what you are thinking."

Aenguz huffed. Recounting the vision hurt. He steadied himself and continued.

"I had a vision," concern and absurdity flicker across Legerohn's face.

"It was before I came here. When this happened." He turned his melted arm over in the feeble light.

"I was given a message from the Flayer. Lord Morgrom the Divider."

"The First Treacher? Spoke to you? He is dead and banished from the earth."

"He was diminished but he is not dead. He has returned to the Lands of the Earth."

Legerohn pulled back from Aenguz.

Aenguz reached out and snatched Legerohn's fused arm. He demanded that Legerohn heed him.

"Listen, I am not mad. I did not ask for it, but I was given the message and named the Last Emissary of the Divider.

"If my plan works, I may not live. You must take the message to Corundum for me, for the Lands of the Earth."

The Moresi peered deep into Aenguz. He seemed to be weighing multiple approaches.

"What was the message?"

Aenguz began,

"'You will bear a message to the Counsel Lords and the Mono Lord in Corundum. Say to them that the limit of their days upon the Lands of the Earth are before them. Five quinquennia will not pass before my will is sown in every corner of the Earth. The Remnant and the peoples of the Lands squat on lands I have granted to my servants. Your time on the earth is at an end.'"

He rushed through the things that Morgrom had granted the Urnings, the Erebim, the Tsurah, and the Sallow. He meted out the lines as if he read the words from just behind his eyes.

"'Mark me! Before this very year is divided, the Dagba Stone will be lost to this age. You will not be able to use it against me as before. Even if you were able to locate it no mortal hand may wield it. Its power is for my hand alone. When my Ruinwasters have done their work. When you are gone from the Earth, I will locate it and become unfettered from the Earth. And then the universe and Time itself will bow to my dominion.'"

Aenguz let go of Legerohn's hand. He ran through Morgrom's admonishment and promise to Aenguz and the Lands if he failed. With the last words out, Aenguz sagged as if he had let down a ponderous weight.

The whites of Legerohn's eyes piqued against his dark skin.

"How?"

"I do not know how. But the Counsel Lords must be warned. The Akkeidii must be warned. All the peoples of the Lands must be warned. And if it can be found, then they must find the Dagba Stone."

Legerohn's eyes returned. He began to calculate in the dark.

"Will you do this?" Aenguz asked.

"What is your plan?"

"Will you do this? If I fail, will you bear the message?"

The Moresi considered again. He looked out at the captives. He may have been counting the heads of the remaining Moresi, or the ones that were no longer there. Loss and helplessness raged in his weathered eyes.

"I will bear this message. The Remnant must stand together against the First Treacher. Now, what is your plan?"

"The next time we stop, after the food and water are lowered, I am going to free my hand - by force. I am going to climb up and find any axes or weapons above. I will pass down as many as I am able.

"Hack through the rods," dread clogged his throat, "or hands. It may be quicker."

"What then?"

"We fight the Erebim and make an escape."

"It would be suicide."

Aenguz nodded. "Perhaps. But they need us to propel the *cog*. That may give us an advantage." Aenguz paused again before adding. "How would you rather die?"

Legerohn looked to the dark and back as if he could make out hidden horrors. Water rushed against the hull. The *cog* swayed.

"This is madness. But so is sitting here to do nothing to die," Legerohn said.

"How do you plan to free your hand?"

Aenguz placed his left hand on the dead stump between them. "I have learned to live without a hand once. I can do it again."

The Moresi passed the buckets back just then and Aenguz lifted them across his body to the keel plank.

"Just be ready the next time we stop."

The Sallow tenders retrieved the buckets and slid the door into place.

The wicked hammering commenced. The Gildelmun stirred. Light dawned. It glowed incipient at first, but then amber hues shined through the rippled translucent layers of golden wood.

The *cog* dragged alongside its mooring. Something course scraped along the hull.

Then it turned away into a stiff current and the hammering increased.

Aenguz kneaded the details of his plan. He held back as much strength as he dared.

It was a long day traveling into the current. It was a longer stretch than the day before when they tugged at the log jam. He feared the draining would leave nothing in him. But finally, the *cog* nestled up against stone. The incessant pounding stopped. The keel dimmed. The *cog* swayed in the current.

The captives sagged in relief. The Moresi more so than the rest.

There was more commotion on the decks above than the previous stops. Aenguz feared that the Sallow might exact another punishment by withholding food and water. His plan hung in the balance. He wasn't sure he would have the strength or the will in another day. The sounds above faded to a quieter pitch. Then the door was pulled back and the buckets lowered down.

Aenguz brought them down to the bench.

Legerohn looked nervous but ready.

It had to be now.

Neither of them could eat. He passed the buckets up to the other Moresi without taking a bite.

Aenguz turned to his own thoughts and listened for the footfalls above.

There was less rumbling than usual. The decks were quiet. But a distant cackle and howl of Erebim, many Erebim, pierced through the wood. More than were on the *cog*. Perhaps they had found another stop on land with more of their kind to enact their cult-like prayers. That could make his efforts more risky, more futile. He would have to be quick. Surprise from a captive might just be the edge he needed - before he bled out.

The chanting would start soon. He readied himself to act.

But the ritual did not commence as it usually did. What heinous ritual or rite did they hold for? Were they at a site for another summoning? He couldn't entertain that thought for long.

He could not wait any longer.

Aenguz gathered his strength.

He knew he could not simply pull his hand free.

But the gift from the fisherman taught him that he could - rend it free.

Aenguz planted his feet and readied himself to climb into a quick somersault around the fulcrum of his wrist. His breathing shortened. Fear at the center of his mind railed against his intent.

His legs were stiff. His mind told him he was too weak to make the turn.

Legerohn looked at him askance. Bronze light galvanized his suspicion.

"Ready yourself," he breathed to Legerohn.

He had to do this. He had to free himself to free the others. He just had to flip himself. The wrist would rip apart. And then just one hard bite. He only had to break the skin. The rest would tear. Then he could rip his arm free. He would have to cup the stump quickly, but he would be free.

He needed to find weapons or tools for the others. If he was discovered, distract, and deflect as long as possible. Buy them time. His last act would be saving the Akkeidii. And saving all of the others. It would be his final gift. But it was not for him to determine what his final gift might be in death to those left behind. Or what his sacrifice might mean to them.

In the final glow of amber, as Aenguz poised to whip his body around, he caught a glint on Legerohn's fused hand. Something was beneath the *purna*. A small bit had been chiseled away in the riot the day before and it revealed something hidden.

He fought the insidious distraction, but he couldn't ignore the muted shine of brushed nickel. He didn't have time for this. The Sallow could come at any moment. The buckets had already started moving back toward him.

Aenguz reached over and touched the metal at Legerohn's hand. It was a ring, part of a ring. The metal was contoured like cedar bark. An edge was rimmed in smooth silver or white gold.

The numb tips of his fingers tingled. A brisance of lore and fidelity.

Montmorillionite!

The timbre in the metal was slightly different but the power was unmistakable.

How did this Moresi come to have *montmorillionite?* But there was no time for questions.

He didn't fully trust his exhausted mind yet. He knew too well how it could fool him.

He combed through the song to find the Words of Lore and test this ring to see if it was counterfeit.

> *Ev'r keen, ever new, ever bright*
> *Earth's first star to dispel the night*
>
> *Contained but not imprisoned*
> *All metal one, no division*

Shafts of white light shot out. The metal warmed.

The hardened tar softened around Legerohn's knuckles. The *purna* was surrendering its hold to the greater lore. Aenguz pressed his fingers into the clay to touch as much of the familiar metal as possible. Bits of tar started to fall away. Aenguz clawed at the black clay as if he was scribing cuneiform.

He continued prying hunks away from the Moresi's hand. Legerohn's astonishment froze him for an instant. Then he joined in. The white light of *montmorillionite* drew new contours on his face.

Finally, he pulled his hand free. It looked pruned and ghostly as if it was waterlogged. The fingers curled as if they still gripped the rod. He began scratching his hand desperately.

Aenguz grabbed Legerohn's wrist and pulled it over on top of his own fused hand. Legerohn kept scratching as Aenguz pressed the curled fingers down over the knot of black that encased his hand.

He muttered the Words of Lore. The *purna* began to fall away in small chunks.

Aenguz's skin began to crawl. A formication was peeling at his flesh.

In those moments, while the *montmorillion* lore did its work, Aenguz's whole plan shifted.

Instead of finding and throwing crude weapons down, he would take them with him and go above. He would make his way to the top and free the *montmorillionite* from the cairn tree. With blades and lore, the captives could be freed quickly without amputating their own hands, and the Erebim and Sallow could be held at bay.

It was beyond risky, but the temptation of the metal was strong. It called him up.

"Come," he whispered to Legerohn. "There is more *montmorillionite* above." Aenguz buried the mystery of Legerohn's ring for now.

He climbed up onto the keel plank.

Legerohn grasped both of the Moresi in front of him. They both looked back at him and at one another in surprise.

"Mond, Stokke, pass the word on to the others. We are freed. Make ready."

"Yes, Tahnka," Mond replied.

"Be silent."

Mond nodded in reply.

Aenguz reached over the captive and shook Lokah. He looked at Aenguz in disbelief.

"How did you?"

"Tell the others to make ready. And keep quiet. I go to get our weapons."

Joy and relief moved across Lokah's face. He nodded. The first shift to something other than the look of a captive came into Lokah's eyes.

Aenguz crawled to the ladder. He tested the rung against any creaks. He peered up over the edge of their tomb like a dead man anxious to quit his grave.

Sacks and barrels crowded the hold. Bundles of the long arrows were stacked about like bushels of wheat. Coils of the tough sisal were laid on the floor or hung from hooks. Brown tobacco-like leaves hung in the rafters.

But there were no Sallow. No Erebim.

There was no movement in the hold other than the light swaying of loose leaves and dangled rope. Other than the snorts and grunts the space was eerily quiet as if the *cog* had been abandoned.

The twin ramps crisscrossed on either side of the mast. Ambient light shone a pale silver.

The empty space was more unnerving than the prospect of being caught. He searched for any tool, any metal. The only edges were the tips of the long arrows.

Suddenly, a dire horn pealed through the air. It was distant and echoed. The alarm jolted Aenguz. He ducked back down.

"What is it?" Legerohn asked. The Moresi was perched at Aenguz's back.

Heartbeats strained his chest.

A fearsome cheer and blood-curdling howl sounded from far away as if it came from above, from the night itself.

But no footfalls came. No Sallow rushed down the ramp. The *cog* ebbed in stillness.

Aenguz peeked back up. He climbed into the hold.

Legerohn followed.

Aenguz stole over to a bushel, quiet as the grave, and snapped a pair of shafts in half.

He passed one over to Legerohn.

"I do not see any weapons. Do you?" the Moresi asked barely above a whisper.

The hope of *montmorillionite* tugged at Aenguz.

Aenguz gestured to the ramp.

He crawled up. Legerohn stayed close behind.

The pale light was scant but after so long in the pit, it seemed like day. Silver light and limned shadows hinted at diffused moonlight and twinkling starlight.

Aenguz quieted his breath.

He inched his eyes up to the floor of the deck.

If they were seen, the fortunate boon of the *montmorillionite* ring would be for nothing.

There were no Erebim prostrated on the deck. No clothed Sallow standing anywhere. But a chanting, massive and loud commenced in the night. The staccato barks responded to rhythmic chants. A ceremony of evil.

The deck had a few crates and bundles of twine scattered about. But he did not see the cairn tree. His heart dropped into a fathomless well.

Behind him, Legerohn asked distractedly as if he was trying to understand the comings and goings of their captors. "Why do they bear that?"

Back around the mast, behind him, was the cairn tree.

They had not moved the log yet. And bark was still lashed over the channel. Perhaps they needed the Akkeidii, or they were in such a hurry to observe their arcane Rites that they simply left it until after. They had no need to fear that the captives would escape.

As quickly as his heart had dropped, waves of relief and exuberance flooded him.

Aenguz nearly climbed over Legerohn. He slunk across the deck to the dead tree.

Aenguz could feel the *montmorillionite* within. The lore-bound metal seemed to chime through the chieftain's wood.

But it was tempered. The bands of sisal were still wrapped around the log in four or five places. And they only had the stone edges of the arrows.

Aenguz began sawing at the cords. It would take too long.

Legerohn reached out and stayed Aenguz's hand. The Moresi reached to his waist and worked at the belt. He drew out a long thin silver chain with silver loops at either end.

He threaded one loop underneath the cords and fingered the rings. He worked the chain back and forth in quick tight movements. The chain worked its way through the stubborn sisal. In a half a dozen strokes, he was through. He moved to the next cluster.

Aenguz could barely contain himself. He silently urged the Moresi on.

After several moments, Legerohn sawed through the last bonds.

"Mithrite," Legerohn breathed, satisfied.

Aenguz lifted the bark as if he was lifting the lid on a treasure chest. He was almost fearful there would be nothing inside, but he *felt* the metal. Platinum light shone on the underside of the bark. But the trick of the mind kept him slightly unsure.

As he moved up, the thought that the channel might be empty squeezed him. With each inch, his heart sank deeper and deeper.

But then he saw the teeth and the blood of *montmorillionite*.

Daggers and spikes poked out from the channel of liquid metal. Shafts protruded as if they were frozen from being partway withdrawn from the forge.

Legerohn's eyes popped. The Moresi's mouth stood agape as if he was looking on the first secret of creation. "Silvercryst!" he said. His incredulity seemed to stun him.

The mercury-like liquid ebbed in languid waves with the gentle rolling of the *cog*.

There, amid the collection of edges, Aenguz could see it. The outer curve of his weapon. Like a thin sliver of the moon. He knew it instantly.

He lifted it out by the hook. It was like he was drawing it out of the forge for a second time. However, the liquid metal was not raw unrefined ore. A part of him observed an oblique reverence to the silver fluid. This was the released *montmorillionite* severed from the sacrificed Akkeidii Champions. Ridder's weapon was in here. A swirling part of this pool.

Aenguz dropped the broken shaft of the arrow as if it was a twig. He grabbed the body of his weapon and drew it slowly out of the channel. He hefted the familiar weight of his weapon. His eyes traced the length of it, inspected it, adored it.

The last time he held his weapon he thought it would be his last. When he planted it into the dense stump, he thought to never touch it again. He had expected death in the Challenge. All of those who dined with him that night were gone. Ridder, Selvin, and Moodley. He had thought the Erebim had stolen it from him.

Holding his silver weapon now was as curious a revelation as he could conceive.

Aenguz stood. Fear sulked away from his heart. There was no movement in his periphery.

Legerohn rocked back on his haunches. He gazed in wonder and shock as if Aenguz had transformed completely before his eyes into something unfamiliar and new. The Moresi gathered himself enough to breathe a warning to Aenguz to stay low.

For the first time in many days, Aenguz was not a prisoner or a slave. Not a beaten captive. He was an Akkeidii Warrior armed and formidable.

And with *montmorillionite* much could be done. He kneeled back down, but not out of fear or concern, but rather in stealth, like a predator.

20

~~~

GALANGALL WASH

The *mithrite* chain dangled in Legerohn's hands. The *montmorillionite* ring responded to the metal. A subtle shimmer vibrated along the edges of the cedar contour. The Moresi stared at Aenguz in awe or fear. For a moment he appeared lost outside of himself.

"Why did you not use that to free yourself earlier?" Aenguz asked admiring the smooth sharp chain.

"Leono was from Straathgard. I did not know if I could trust him to keep it a secret. The *cog* would slow as we freed ourselves. And we were still too few to hope to escape. We were never alone."

"Come let us free the rest," Aenguz said. The fragments of his plan were flotsam.

"Wait! Let us free the *cog* and put some distance between us and the Sallow and Erebim." Legerohn's words blended with the steady lapping.

"There," he pointed to a heavy rope that was threaded through an eye in the gunwale. "Cut that line. I will cut this one." Legerohn turned to climb over the cairn tree.

Aenguz laid an arm on Legerohn's shoulder and gestured for the Moresi to move out of the way.

Aenguz stepped over the log and set the curved edge of his keen blade against the thick hawser. He leaned into it and turned the blade slightly. The *montmorillionite* cut through the course cable in a single smooth slice as if it was a thin strip of balsa wood. It dropped from the gunwale with a splash.

Aenguz crouched over to the other cable. He gave a short half stroke and cut through the rope. His blade passed through and stuck into the gunwale. The line dropped.

The *cog* turned on the stone jetty and backed into it. Wood ground and creaked. Water muffled some of the splintering. But it was still loud.

Aenguz grimaced at the sound as he made his way back to Legerohn.

For the first time, he looked up at the canopy of night. The jetty was at the base of a titanic pillar.

Bands of edged stone vaulted upward. There were no seams in the rock. This was not stacked stone carved into a shape. Rather, extruded basalt was drawn up from beneath the river. As if reeds of black stone from some subterranean marsh were gathered together out of the deep earth by a titan.

Smaller bands ran up and were cut to form a spiral stair that led up along the pillar. The column shot up to a contoured canopy.

The *cog* turned and revealed more of the wide opening and another pillar to his right. A dark river churned through the opening as if it was escaping from some unknown violation.

"What is this place? Where are we?" Aenguz asked.

"That looks to be Hyrrokkin made," Legerohn answered. "This could be Galangall Wash. We traveled against the current all day. I did not imagine we could be so far east."

"This was the last structure built by the Hyrrokkin for the First Treacher. It teems again. Listen."

Overhead, the line between the two skies gave way.

Clustered stars mused in the narrow night. The moon mimicked the sliver of Aenguz's blade. It perched over the Earth like an executioner's ax.

As the roof receded away, Aenguz saw a series of arches that joined the mountain walls from one end of the gorge to the other. A *cog* was moored to a further pier.

In the open air, the familiar chanting or praying twisted the night. It poured over the top and filled the basin. It sounded like an army of Erebim called for the victory of night.

Aenguz reached back into the trunk and grabbed another weapon out. It was a short ax, like a tomahawk. A studded hammerhead jutted opposite the ax head. Aenguz marveled at it, but he had no idea whose weapon this was.

Legerohn reached out tentatively to take the weapon from Aenguz to help him. The Moresi had squirreled away his chain.

"It will be too heavy for you."

Legerohn nodded, grateful for the reprieve.

They hurried back down the ramp. Aenguz's last glimpse of the outside was of a barren gorge wall.

Aenguz called on the Words of Lore and both weapons burst to life like white torches. The choking darkness was chased back into the corners between the stacked barrels and piled sacks.

The animals were anxious. Their stomps were uncertain. There was a pained bleating. Aenguz could tell one of the roe deer was under duress.

Aenguz turned down the hole.

The faces of the captives were craned toward him.

"Grieg's Balls! You did it!" Roberge said.

The Moresi looked like men witnessing a miracle. The hopes of the message that had moved through them earlier were not false.

The fisherman turned away from the light and closed their eyes.

The Makans and Baierls called for release with hoarse whispers.

Aenguz came down the stair onto the keel plank. The weapons blazed like shards of starlight. He swung the side of his hook down onto Lokah's hand. The *purna* began to smoke and melt instantly.

He threw the ax to Ondo. The *montmorillionite* crossed the space like a shooting star. The Finit grabbed the weapon out of the air and rested it against his hand. He continued the chant of light and power.

Kachota gasped, "Aahh!"

Lokah scratched at the hunks of clay until his hand was released. He spat at the *purna*. He scratched his freed hand maniacally.

"Go, get the rest of our weapons," Aenguz commanded. Lokah kneaded his hand as he climbed out of the trench. A moment later he was gone up the ladder.

Legerohn drew Aenguz to release Mond and Stokke.

Aenguz stepped down into the trench and laid his weapon across both Moresi's hands. The spike and dagger reached both easily.

The *purna* smoked and melted. Legerohn climbed down and clawed at the melting clay.

Ondo was now free, and he set the ax to the hand of the fisherman next to him.

The clamor in the orlop rose as the prospect and promise of escape grew closer. Free arms waved in the white light like the beaks of hungry chicks. Their pleas broke past whispers as they pleaded to be next. Fisherman and Moresi clamored. Baierls and Makans called to Aenguz. A frantic chaos was beginning to displace the quiet. They needed to be quiet.

Soon, Mond and Stokke were free. They scratched their hands and clasped shoulders as Aenguz pulled his weapon back.

"Aenguz! Aenguz!" Lokah shouted down.

The captives were desperate. Mandavu and Kachota shouted out "Sidor! Sidor! Free us!"

Lokah sounded desperate.

He turned and rushed up the ladder and the ramp despite the bitter objections of the captives.

Lokah was perched at the opening as Aenguz ran up.

"What is it?" he snapped.

Lokah pointed behind Aenguz.

The slow arc of the *cog* was curving in on the wall of the gorge. A collision was imminent.

Submerged wood began to scrape against rock. The *cog* bent and groaned. Then it slammed against the wall.

Aenguz fell down the ramp.

Lokah toppled to the deck.

He rolled back onto his feet and ran back up to Lokah.

The Kriel was climbing to his feet. "How do you steer this craft?"

"Get the weapons down there! Free the others!" Aenguz called.

Lokah went back to the tree. He drew out his weapon and pulled out a few into his arms like cordwood and headed down the ramp.

Aenguz went to the gunwale.

The wall of the gorge was on top of him. The sound of crushing and grinding wood was too loud. He pushed the tip of his weapon into the wall and tried to shove the boat back from the stone. *Montmorillionite* sparked against the granite. It looked like he was smithing the anvil of the mountain.

Whatever warped course the cog was on started pulling it away from the wall. But it would only be temporary. It would circle back and slam into the stone again. They would be smashed to pieces.

A blood-curdling scream came from below.

Voices shouted for Aenguz.

He bolted back down the ramp to the trap door. "Be quiet!" he cursed.

Ondo and Stokke clutched the released fisherman. He wailed as if he was possessed. They worked to corral him. Legerohn perched around the two but was unable to help.

Lokah was blocked on the keel plank.

"What are you doing? Let him go! What is he-" Aenguz stopped.

The fisherman's hand was macabre. The skin was gone. A skeletal hand lined with veins and sinew was clutched into a gaping claw like a frozen spell.

It looked familiar to Aenguz. Reminded him of his own hand.

The chaos was deafening.

The sight of the hand sobered him.

He stepped down to the benches and caught the hand by the wrist. Then he set the fisherman's hand down and pressed his foot down against the forearm and bench. He added a fierce heat to his weapon with the Words of Lore. And then with a terse stroke, he severed the hand and cauterized the wound.

The Straathgardian fisherman screamed in one last exhausted breath. Ondo and Stokke released him. The fisherman hugged his stump, scrabbled out of the trench, and curled into a ball at the front of the hold. He collapsed into semi-consciousness or twisted madness.

The clamoring stopped as if a gavel had banged.

Legerohn ordered Stokke over to the fisherman. The young Moresi scrabbled over to him. But the man was lost in his own tumult.

Aenguz looked down at the skeletal hand. It held the phantom rod still.

"What happened?" Legerohn asked and gestured above.

"Can you steer this thing?" Aenguz asked.

Legerohn nodded tentatively.

Aenguz could see that Legerohn was not certain.

He told Lokah to free the rest. Except the Straathgardians, for now.

Legerohn and Mond followed Aenguz out of the hold.

The *cog* was arcing to the wall again.

The Moresi inspected the doors. Mond stared around to orient himself.

They rushed to a door in the turret. They tried to force it open but it would not budge.

"Aenguz Sidor!" Legerohn shouted.

Aenguz waved them away. He lunged forward and swung his weapon underhand with both hands like a battering ram.

The door blasted open. Hinges rent from the frame.

Inside the room was vacant, purposeless. There was no table, no chairs, no furniture. There was no cargo. No barrels or bushels. Nothing hung from the rafters.

The Moresi looked around. Their confusion matched Aenguz's. They searched closer as if their eyes might be fooling them.

Aenguz caught a pattern of meshed moonlight on the floor. A small square window was cut into the floor at the back.

Legerohn traced steps on the floor. The planks were worn in an arc. Lines fanned out in rays on the floor from the rear.

A long arm rattled against the back wall. Sisal lashed it loosely to square timbers.

Legerohn and Mond freed the arm.

It swung out from the wall and caught the two by surprise. They were bowled over.

Aenguz stepped out of reach. The tip whipped past him like the tail of a monster.

The Moresi gathered themselves.

They nestled the pole under their armpits. Their feet danced over the floor.

The *cog's* course altered but in what direction they couldn't say.

"Go up and tell us where to go," Legerohn said.

Aenguz went out and climbed to the turret. He called through the grate.

"Left, left, not so much. Straight, straight."

The *cog* moved away from the gorge wall.

A wiry Moresi joined Aenguz.

"I can guide the *cog* now."

Below, two other Moresi had taken the arm.

The shutters at the rear were flung open. Legerohn and Mond stared back at Galangall.

As he passed, one of the Moresi grabbed Aenguz's arm. His ugly arm. They both thanked him. The taller one held him for a moment. He made certain that Aenguz heard him, saw his abject genuineness, and gratitude at being freed. When he pulled his hand back, Aenguz noticed that they both positioned their hands so that they could scratch the ones that had been trapped in the *purna*.

Aenguz could see the span. Seven massive arches stretched across the gorge. The top edge held a jagged crenellation of stone structures that did not match the construction of the body. The lip looked like a crooked underbite. Jagged and broken. A squat tower stood off-center on the span. It was the tallest thing on the gigantic bridge.

Firelight dotted the rim. Torches poured over the edges where the bridge city met the wall. The flames looked like fiery drool.

And on the water behind him, a *cog* cut through the churning river rapidly toward them.

21

UNFINISHED BUSINESS

Aenguz left Legerohn and Mond and the pursuing *cog* at the window. He had to see what progress had been made with the captives. They would need everyone.

Two more Moresi ran up the ramp. They hugged their hands to their chests and clawed at their flesh. Both thanked "Aenguz Sidor" for freeing them. The tall one introduced himself as Chimere. Their gratefulness singed him. They hurried into the aft chamber.

The *montmorillionite* pushed the formication through his fist to the top of his hand. He scratched intermittently when the sensation reached a fevered pitch.

He started counting heads. That was six Moresi so far.

Roberge and Strey were coming up the ramp. Strey's triple-bladed ax burned white. He held it at the ready. Roberge's weapon glowed. The angled scimitar dropped at his side.

"Well done," Roberge said. "How did you get free?"

"Thank you, my lord," Strey said.

Aenguz took his shoulder like an older brother.

"You can quiet your weapon. You are safe now," Aenguz said.

Strey let the burning light fade to a steady glow. Then he turned in a slow circle as he took in the *cog* and the gorge. His mouth stretched open.

"Legerohn, the Moresi, wears a ring made of *montmorillionite*."

Roberge's face squeezed. "Well, that is strange. I will have to see this ring." He drifted by Aenguz and walked to the cairn tree.

The door Aenguz had smashed was swung outward. Lokah was on his knees behind it against the cairn tree. He was bent over the channel, his back to the Champions. His sleeve was pulled up and his arm was hidden beneath the liquid metal.

Aenguz could hear him muttering an obscure part of the Lay of *Montmorillionite*.

Roberge set the blade down by the other weapons Lokah had retrieved. He took his two-headed ax. The heads were hollow, and the edges curved like a song.

Roberge and Strey, Ondo, Lokah, Aenguz counted to himself. The several days had left growth on all their faces. The cords of their necks stretched through the skin.

Lokah pulled his arm out and turned to meet the two. Although still kneeled, he seemed to rise to meet them.

He looked ashen. The skin on his arm looked like it was covered in a fine powder. At first, he stared through them, beyond them. The housing around his eyes was hardened and fraught. He looked as if he could see into the future or a deep grim past.

"That is all of them," he said, spent as if he had dug too many graves.

On the deck was a sword, a large, long-handled mace, the sword Roberge had dropped, and another tomahawk like the one Aenguz took to Ondo.

Ondo joined them at that moment. He had come down from the prow turret. He held a simple sharp spear that had a hook near the point.

The Champions looked at the Kriel, the flowing *montmorillionite*, and the three weapons before them.

"Where are the Makans and Hallock?" Aenguz asked. He looked back over to the ramp. Two Moresi were helping up the one-handed Straathgardian. They bore him by the Akkeidii into the aft chamber.

When he turned back Roberge said, "You are going to have to settle the Challenge."

"There is no relent in them. Kachota spat at us when we walked out of the hold." Strey's voice rose into a squeak.

"We are being pursued. The Erebim are on our heels. And up there." Aenguz pointed at the line of fire up against the gorge wall. The front of the fiery tongue was nearly even with them. Lokah picked up his long sword and stood to see. It bent into a square head at the tip. He rested it on the deck as if he needed it to stand.

"If you free him, you will have to kill him. Perhaps both of them," Roberge continued.

"We are going to be attacked!" Aenguz pointed around the door. Past the Moresi the pursuing *cog* began to take up more space in the window.

Lokah stepped closer to the ring of Warriors. His demeanor commanded a reverence. Roberge stilled.

Then Lokah spoke. He gripped his weapon as if he was swearing on it.

"My lord, the Kriels are with the Sidors. I follow Aenguz, the son of Sairik. Lord of the Sidor Clan. I reaffirm the bond between Kriels and Sidors."

Roberge took a deep breath. He planted the head of his ax at his feet and gripped the handle. "The Baierls remain friends to the Sidors. Strey and I are beholden to you. We follow Aenguz, son of the Ruler of the Akkeidii."

Ondo set his spear, held it with both hands. "The Finits are allied. I follow the Lord of the Sidor Clan. The Ruler of the Akkeidii."

Aenguz heaved on the verge of tears. But he held his chest still and his mouth clamped. His weapon shook slightly. In that moment, this was the furthest thing from his mind and the most unnecessary. But their fealty moved him, nonetheless. He had expected to die, twice already, maybe three times, if he hadn't seen Legerohn's ring. Their Oath of Fidelity was terse, but it was absolute. They were trying to help him now, counsel him. They would die, if need be, to aid him.

He had to pant to gain control of himself.

"Your Oaths honor and humble me and the Sidors." He gulped. "We have been through much." His eyes fell to the channel. Culpability shredded his voice. "I will strive to be worthy of your faith." He paused. "I am sorry." The words fell out of him. He was apologizing for more things than he could count or name. "Let us say now that we are brothers to one another. Hopefully, your pronouncement will be enough to sway Mandavu and Kachota and Hallock."

Aenguz ordered Lokah, Strey, and Ondo to remain topside to keep an eye on the Erebim. He couldn't look at that threat any longer. And the cairn tree gaped at him like a recrimination. He couldn't face it either.

Then he led Roberge down to the orlop.

Aenguz climbed down the stair. Roberge followed him.

A tomahawk perched into the mast. Its light cast a solemn pall in the chamber. Nubbed and empty rods filled most of the space. They looked like black bones in the belly of the orlop. The light from their weapons flexed shadows against the hull.

The Makans turned. Hallock pivoted back and insisted that he be released.

The Straathgardians did not turn toward the light. Strands of milky hair covered their head in a withered shawl. They looked like Norns of the underworld. They seemed to be pondering into the well of filth at their feet.

Aenguz walked down the keel plank and swung around the mast. The fishermen may have turned their heads at the light.

Aenguz took a knee at the small platform in the nose of the prow. Mandavu and the others followed him the whole way.

Roberge stepped down to the bench behind Hallock.

Mandavu stared up battered and scarred. Black blood clung to him like debris from a storm. It derided the dirt and grime. The silver light revealed faded bruises like rotten plumbs on his face, his arms, at his chest. The scars at his neck were a noose. A failed execution.

But here now he faced a sure death. And he knew it.

"Well?" No futility, no surrender, no weakness. He dared Aenguz. A cultivated anger simmered below the surface.

"We are not free yet," Aenguz said. "The Erebim and Sallow come on our heels."

"Then release me and deliver my weapon." No fear just a hint of command.

"There is an open matter between us."

Kachota growled curses behind his brother. He challenged Aenguz to release them and see about the matter.

Hallock opened his mouth to speak but Roberge rested his weapon on the Gambls shoulder.

There it was. The unresolved Challenge. It was still there for the Makans. The rule of the Akkeidii. Command of the Warriors. Clan Lordship of the clan lords.

Mandavu considered Aenguz as a statue considers the horizon. His eyes betrayed the faintest hint of calculation. He quieted his brother with a turn of his head.

"Release us and deliver our weapons."

"The Kriels, Baierls, and Finits have sworn allegiance to the Sidors and have sworn to follow me. Do you relent?"

This thwarted Mandavu's calculations. The fetid air seethed between them.

"And the Gambls, do not forget about the Gambls," Roberge said. He pressed the white blade against Hallock's neck. "Swear your allegiance to the Sidors and to Aenguz your new lord."

"I swear it, I swear it," Hallock said quickly.

"Would you choose death or exile then?" Aenguz said flatly.

Mandavu flexed his jaw.

"I am already imprisoned. Do you want me to surrender my weapon and swear to never cross the threshold of Grieg's Gate again?" He spat the words through his teeth.

"No." Aenguz held still in the cramped space as if he could kneel there forever.

The air was thicker than the rank that caused it.

Kachota hurled imprecations again. But fear colored his tone now.

"You Sidor cur! Every Makan will covet your death!"

Aenguz ignored him and focused on the giant. "Surrender the Challenge. Surrender it here and now. Surrender it forever."

Confusion fluttered like dazed sparrows across Mandavu's eyes.

Aenguz continued, "We must banish this division between Champions, between clans. Out in the Lands of the Earth we must be one. The Akkeidii must be one people. I will not be your enemy any longer."

Mandavu calmed his brother again and turned back to Aenguz.

He looked as if he struggled with an impossible puzzle. "What are you suggesting?"

"Save your anger for our pursuers. Leave your rage against me. The time for our internal battle is over. We are beset. All the Lands of the Earth are beset."

Aenguz brought his weapon down and pointed the spike at Mandavu's heart. One jab could have killed him.

Kachota wrenched his arm and threw his body over the rod to shield his brother. His wrist cracked.

Aenguz lowered the crook over his immured hand and waited.

Kachota jostled his brother.

Mandavu gave a terse nod.

Aenguz set the hook down like an accolade.

Smoke trailed up between them like a swirling cat's tail. Hunks of *purna* dropped away.

As the last of the vice dripped off, Aenguz went to the ax removed it, and held it out to Mandavu. "Your weapon is above."

As if to seal their tacit pact, he said, "Release the others. We need everyone. We are under pursuit. Mind the Straathgardian's bonds." It was a quiet command but a certain one. He released the weapon and headed out of the orlop. He wasn't sure if or how long the forced truce would last. It just had to last until they got to land - any land.

Knocks sounded as Aenguz and Roberge climbed the ramp.

"Get down!" Ondo called.

Missiles slammed into the *cog* with loud pops. The long arrows poked out here and there like the spines of a raggedy sea urchin.

The walls of the gorge closed in. The path the Erebim followed had descended. They were closing in like a funnel. Pockets of torches dotted the paths in places. When they stopped, arrows fell out of the night like wingless birds.

A Moresi lay dead on the deck. A feathered spear jutted awkwardly out from his side. Fresh blood streaked the deck.

Aenguz needed to see. He rushed up and turned to the prow turret. He crouched down against the low wall.

Lokah and Ondo were in the aft turret with the Moresi Legerohn had commanded. Strey stood at the door below. The two Moresi were still working at the angry tail.

"Can you see what is up ahead?" Lokah shouted over the deck.

Over their heads he saw the pursuing ship. It was gaining on them. Fires hung from torches at the edges and the turrets teemed with vengeful rage.

He peeked over the edge just as a missile slammed into the opposite wall of the turret.

The gorge narrowed further. The *cog* ran down the middle of the cataract.

Up ahead he saw what the Erebim were racing toward.

A pair of low promontories choked the mouth of the Galangall. The flat-topped shoulders of granite looked like twins. Larger fires raged at the edges and a smattering of stacked structures dotted the trailing edge of the plummeting ridge. At the center of both shoulders was a giant spindle. Large creatures, some with two legs some with four, pushed or pulled the arms of the wheel.

Rising out of the water in a kind of forced summoning was a heavy cable. It looked like a serpent being drawn up from the bottom of the Galangall.

Missiles thumped the *cog* on all sides. The pops were rising to a crescendo.

"We need to go faster!" Aenguz hollered back across the deck.

"What is it?" Lokah called back.

"They are barring the way."

They would be caught. The other ship was nearly upon them. They would be caught and overrun.

Wild howls and barks echoed off the walls. The gullet of the Galangall was readying to clamp down on them.

They drew even with the shoulders.

Suddenly, the *cog* pitched upward and seized to a halt. The prow lurched into the air. Aenguz fell forward. Everyone tumbled. The *cog* canted oddly under his feet

Arrows crossed the deck and popped the wood.

'This was it,' Aenguz thought. This would be the end. He gripped his weapon and drew courage out of his *montmorillionite*. He let the light recede into the metal. He would join the others at the rear and meet the marauding Erebim.

He looked across to the others and counted the arrows to time his flight. The cairn tree caught his eye.

Then it came to him.

"Come! Come to the front!" He waved at them. He called to the Warriors to meet him at the log.

They all came to him. Arrows flew all around them. They climbed around the trunk.

Legerohn and Mond and the other Moresi sprinted across the distance and climbed into the prow chamber. The door had since been opened.

They heaved the tree forward up the tilted deck. They staggered forward like the first days of the flight from the One Bridge. Missiles flew over them, between them. Ferocious howls like starved wolves raged and echoed.

They crossed the distance and dropped the trunk and ran to the cover of the room.

The incline lessened.

The boat tipped forward. The cable dragged and slipped under the keel.

They fell back into the room and into each other.

The cord scored the keel and tore at the rudder. A horrible rending sound shook the *cog*.

With a final wretched crack, the boat pulled free.

Aenguz climbed to his feet and looked through to the windows in the aft chamber.

The body of the snake-like cord rose heavily but inexorably out of the water.

It pulled up in a wide smile between the shoulders.

In that moment, the turret of the pursuing boat sailed right underneath the cable.

The monsters on the nubs released the spindles either by command or by surprise. And the smile dropped.

The cable ripped across the turret and dropped down onto the deck. It caught firmly on the mast and stopped the *cog*.

Erebim were crushed. Many poured over the side. The sudden stop brought all of them to the deck.

The captives' *cog* drifted crippled out of range of the arrows into a wide lake. Only the furious howls of the Erebim reached them.

And soon those faded too as the first light of dawn brushed the sky.

22

≈

RELEASE

The rudder flapped in the water like a broken fin. Sharp splinters cut complicated eddies in the water. The *cog* wobbled out of the long lake formed by the convergence of the White, the Galangall Wash, and the Wester. Stripped timber dotted the lake and drifted southward with the crippled barge.

The grateful Moresi who had wrestled with the tiller arm lashed it at an angle to the wall. Legerohn released them to get food and water from the stores that had been brought onto the deck.

Light streamed at an angle through the door. Meshed sunlight cut a wedge against the tiller arm and the wall from the grate above. The arm looked like a kind of sundial capable of only counting the moments to their execution. But for the desecration of the cut timber, the day was beautiful, warm, inviting. There was no sign of the Erebim. But the gray muck of the Galangall tinged the water with the promise of ruin.

Once Aenguz and Legerohn felt certain there was no immediate pursuit they looked to the east and west to gauge and confirm the *cog's* course.

"How do we get to the shore?" Aenguz asked. "I will not feel free until I am free of this," he swept his weapon like a scepter in the chamber like the king of a gaol.

"We could empty the stores from this side," he gestured to port. "That should bring us to the western shore."

They were both nudged out of the way by Mond. He crawled around a small rectangle in the floor near the rudder stock. He shifted to afford more light.

"What is it?" Aenguz asked.

"There is another room down there. I have not yet seen the source of the hammering. And I cannot get that pounding out of my head." The seasoned Moresi stood and faced Legerohn and Aenguz. His furrows multiplied and his lips pursed and stretched.

"Go," Legerohn said. "I will see to the stores."

Aenguz's curiosity led him after Mond down the ramp.

Legerohn halted by the Moresi who had gathered around their dead companion. He was the shorter Moresi who was with Chimere at the rudder. Aenguz never caught his name. Legerohn's shoulders bent with each step. Strey was cutting lengths of canvas from the crossbeam with his ax. He passed them a long piece of tarp and they set it gently over their dead companion.

Ondo was snapping and removing shafts to clear the deck. He helped clear the space around the Moresi. His spear rested near the cairn tree. The other weapons lay scattered beside it.

Lokah and Roberge were pulling items out from the prow chamber where they all had hidden to avoid the deadly volley. They tested the food they found discarding some and setting aside the rest. They stopped as the Moresi gathered.

As Aenguz and Mond descended, Hallock bore a fisherman up the opposite ramp. The Straathgardian's legs were too bent to stand upright. His left hand was still encased in the *purna* and fused to a length of rod.

Aenguz stiffened. He had been freed in a sense. But he was still a prisoner. He might not ever be free.

Mond doubled back and headed for the mouth of the pit. He tested the edges of what looked like a wall. A loop of rope hung for a handle. He pulled it open slowly as if he expected some horror within.

The dark room was a small version of the one above. The smell of grimy Sallow sweat stained the smell of milled timber. A small wedge of light nosed at the opening in the ceiling. It took a moment for their eyes to adjust. A pair of mallets hung on either side of the wall. In the center of the floor, a spike jutted out through a square opening. It looked like a shaft of chiseled obsidian.

Mond dropped to his knees and down to the floor again. He asked Aenguz for light. Aenguz uttered the Words of Lore and brought his weapon to life. Facets gleamed on the black spike.

Mond tested the material. He may have cursed. Then he began working it back and forth.

"Aenguz Sidor. Open this hole up further so that I might relieve the wounded wood." He stepped back to give Aenguz room. "This is how they violate and control the Gildelmun."

Astonishment tempered Mond's fury. He shouted for other Moresi.

Aenguz easily widened the opening by the time they came down. Together the Moresi worked the spike back and forth until finally with a final push, they pulled it out of the heart of the keel. Mond tossed it down with an angry curse. They seemed relieved, vindicated.

Aenguz left them to examine the lower hole.

Another set of legs bore a fisherman up the ramp. A fused club hung at his side from a bent arm.

He couldn't bring himself to look into the orlop. His resistance and revulsion at the pit were too strong. And there was too much death and the promise of death above.

He went to the prow chamber to find the pained roe deer. A similar rope-handled door blended in with the wall. Stacks of buckets rested against sacks and on top of barrels.

An overwhelming stench of spoor and urine knocked him back. He turned his head and closed his nose. It reminded him of the stalls back in the Deerherd shelter when he was a boy only ten times worse. His grandfather made him clean stalls back then when he still hoped to make him a Deerherd. Dahlward would never allow the roe deer to be kept in such filth.

When he was able to turn back he looked into the opening. A short corridor was lined with doors on both sides. Strained snorts and whelps growled behind the doors. Hooves stuttered and shuffled on the floor. The doors and walls rattled and bodies bumped together.

Aenguz noticed smaller doors at the bottoms of the doors and small slit windows rested at eye level.

He went to the first door and held his light up to look within. Round terror-filled eyes pleaded out of the dark. Curved and swirled horns evaporated into the black. He did not recognize the first animals. They were packed into the tiny closet stalls.

They must be parched and hungry, he thought. The Sallow and Erebim abandoned everything to partake in their ritual of evil.

He planted his weapon in the beam above and went back out to the hold.

Aenguz filled buckets with water and slid them past spoor and straw into the cramped stalls. He heard lapping instantly. He did the same at all the doors. Once a bucket was kicked over but he just replaced it with another.

Then he took his weapon and slashed open a sack of grain. He shoved bucket after bucket into the stalls.

As the animals ate he found the remaining roe deer captured from the Lower Mashu.

They came at once to the light. Aenguz cooed to them.

He closed the door behind him to the stalls and then opened the door to their pen. There were two does and one buck. They were all that remained from the half dozen or so captured on the Cairngorm.

Two of the roe deer came up to him and sniffed him closely.

One doe was curled up on the floor in a fouled nest of Warrior's cloaks.

He patted and scratched two deer and spoke to them and calmed them. He took the pails and led them into the short corridor. In turn, they returned to eating and drinking.

Aenguz set his weapon in the rafter and called out a piercing light from the *montmorillionite*.

The doe was in deep distress. Her ears were flat. Aenguz could read pain through her matted fur.

He knelt down and caressed her as he inspected her.

She was in hard labor. A bulbous viscous mass protruded out. A sharp hoof tented the flesh beneath the canal. Aenguz crouched down immediately to deliver the fawn. He spoke steadily to the doe. She squirreled away from his touch but she was so diminished that she could barely move. He could tell that she was fading.

He held a bucket up to his suspended weapon and boiled some water. He scalded his hands to clean them. His grandfather had taught him. Aenguz's left hand barely registered the heat. Then went back and pressed in on the mass and slid his other hand inside. He was firm but gentle. He turned the body and pulled the pointed hoof out.

Then the doe convulsed and the babe came out in a mess of blood and after-birth.

Aenguz pulled the fawn clear. All legs and wet fur. Fluid and blood sluiced out.

The fawn was still. Aenguz touched it gingerly.

It was dead-born. He prodded it more, cleared out the mouth but the tongue poked out lifelessly.

The doe was nearly gone herself. She reached to lick at the babe's fur. Aenguz brought the dead fawn to her.

After a few minutes, she stretched her neck and groaned. Aenguz thought this might be her last throws. But then another babe slid out of the mouth of the canal. With the last of her strength, she pushed out the fawn. Aenguz helped draw the second babe out. Big round, black eyes looked around. Slick slime coated the fur. The silver light confirmed the fawn was alive. Aenguz pulled it beside its dead sibling.

Now she laid her head down, too exhausted to lick.

Water.

Aenguz got some water and cupped handfuls to the mother's mouth until she drank and then until she had enough. Then she was able to lick the dead-born while the other tested its legs.

Aenguz waited until the babe found a teat and then he left to get some grain.

He set some down in a pocket in the cloaks for the doe.

He left the two roe deer in the corridor and closed them in.

Aenguz collapsed on a sack beyond the stalls. His throat contracted. And then the tears came. Dead-born fawns were a fact of life in the wounded world. The Flayer's legacy simply was. Litters were left incomplete. All seeds did not take to the earth. Almost losing the doe, and she still was not free from jeopardy, touched on his own losses. The string of them stretched a line back to his mother. He wept uncontrollably for a time, in a cocoon of sorrow.

He didn't know how he made his way above. He only knew that he was washing blood and after-birth from his hands at a bucket resting against the gunwale.

When he came out of himself, he realized he was standing where the cairn tree had been. Where Lokah had lost himself. He located the trunk angled near the prow where they had dragged it to make their escape.

Mandavu and Kachota were staring into the channel. The liquid metal and the firm *montmorillionite* in their hands seemed to hold them still in the verity of their mortality.

The rest of the Warriors were gathered around the trunk as well like eidolons of woe.

More unreconciled death.

More culpability.

Aenguz walked over to them wooden and somber. He had wiped most of his tears away. The grim core of iron at the center of his heart drew him to the others. The grief and responsibility that kept him away earlier was no longer strong enough to repel him. Anger for the Erebim and loss of the sacrificed Champions drew him forward.

He thrust his weapon, hilt down, into the deck. The sound jolted the Warriors out of their reverie.

Lokah turned and planted his ax-headed sword behind himself.

Ondo set his spear.

Roberge and Strey let their axes fall heads down to bury into the planks.

Hallock set the tip of his sword down and leaned into it and set it firmly into the deck.

Mandavu and Kachota stepped back. Kachota took his twin tomahawks and brought them down together in a single stroke as if he was already planning to slay Erebim. He rolled his stiff wrist.

Mandavu flipped his long mace and drove the spike-end deep into the wood. No one on board could likely have moved it save the giant himself.

Aenguz waited until all the Warriors had set their weapons. His eyes never left the trunk.

Then he spoke.

"The first stones of their cairns have already been laid. Their mothers and fathers, sisters and brothers, uncles and aunts, their mates, their sons and daughters, their grandparents all have mourned them - are mourning them. All the Akkeidii know the loss of those who were more than just Champions. They were Akkeidii Warriors and Deerherds. They were sons and brothers. Some were fathers and mates. They lie now honored forever on the Cairngorm with the heroes and chieftains of old. Their memory will remain forever.

"One last matter remains for our fallen brothers. For their metal to return to the Earth and undo this withholding abomination by our enemies. We right the course and return it to the source of all *montmorillionite*.

"Ridder," Aenguz caught a lump and gulped. "Son of Ragbald."

"Shudaak, son of Stellan," Ondo's voice broke. Tears streamed down his cheeks.

"Slocum, son of Shurn. Champion of the Kriel Clan. Larau mate." Lokah held himself with an uncompromising dignity. As if his last act would be to honor his friend and the Kriels.

"Remille, son of Lestor. Champion of the Gambl Clan. Channi-mate." Hallock's chest heaved beneath his ceremonial shirt.

The Baierls and Makans stirred with guilt. They commiserated with the loss, but they still had their brothers. The loss was slightly removed from them.

"Selvin and Moodley. Sidor and Kriel Deerherds of the Mashu," Aenguz added.

Their shared grief seemed to bring them closer to the others.

Aenguz stepped up to the cairn tree and gripped a branch.

> *Born of the mind bound to the life*
> *Down to Earth with death's final strife*

The Warriors stepped up and grabbed a limb.

They hefted up the hollowed trunk and balanced it on the gunwale. Then, as one, they poured the liquid metal over into the sparkling water.

The mercury-like liquid seemed to jump into the river. It disappeared on its journey back to its source deep beneath the Earth.

They let the cairn-tree tumble over the side and drop into the water. It bobbed and rolled as it joined the other logs that drifted on the current.

They stood at the rail and followed the trunk. Behind them, their weapons hummed a silent threnody only the sacred metal could hear.

Aenguz wiped the bleariness as he turned around to the others. The Moresi and the Straathgardians looked like waifs. Their eyes were a confusion of empathy and mourning. Wonder at the rite they had witnessed left them stricken.

In their own way, they were formal, and they exuded empathy. They understood obliquely what they were witnessing though they were clearly unfamiliar with it. They could not guess what had happened to the Akkeidii on that night on the Cairngorm.

From the aft chamber, a rickety voice called.

"They are coming."

23

~~

A LAST BATTLE

They crowded at the aft window. Akkeidii, Moresi, and a few of the fishermen all stared in grim silence at their pursuers.

A broad *hulk* cut through the water. Dead timbers blasted against the prow and spun away in its wake. The vessel rode low as if it bore stone.

Erebim metastasized on the deck. Occasional darts arced and tested the distance.

Sallow worked amid the throngs of Erebim on the flat decked barge. Their oblong heads bobbed and swirled among the fray. Their armor was the color of coral and turquoise.

The fishermen peeled away from the window and hobbled onto the deck searching for any escape. They looked over the gunwale. They shook their heads at the ramp and the shadowed hold and tore away. Their bent frames and clubbed hands made them look like frightened apes.

Aenguz couldn't worry about them for the moment.

"It comes fast," Chimere said.

"Shut the windows," Aenguz snapped. "Let them guess at our numbers."

"We cannot reach the shore," Legerohn said.

"We will meet them here," Aenguz pushed passed the others and strode out to the deck.

"Clear the deck and raise the ramps."

"Stokke, did you find our bows?" Legerohn asked.

"No, Tahnka."

The Akkeidii and Moresi rushed to clear the space. Barrels and crates were cast overboard. One ramp was drawn up. The dead Moresi was taken into the aft castle. The fisherman hid in the corners in both turrets. In the forecastle chamber, they pulled objects over themselves to hide.

"Seed the nests with the long bolts," Legerohn ordered Mond.

Bushels of the long arrows were lifted into the aft castle and the forecastle.

When the second ramp was drawn up the first arrow knocked the *cog*.

"Stay low. Do not give them any targets," Aenguz said.

"We need to bring them in close so that they cannot use those weapons."

The memory of the shaft-covered deck was fresh for all of them. Aenguz studied the space. He walked a pensive circle around the mast. Warrior tactics and strategy flowed through him. Years of training now come to bear. "Roberge and Strey, ward the forward turret. Ondo, you and Hallock ward the rear." "Mandavu, Kachota, you fight here." Then he turned to Lokah. "Lokah, you and I will fight here." He cut the deck in two halves and set the mast between them.

Mandavu may have chafed at being ordered. Kachota's nod was so terse Aenguz stared until he nodded again. He was wrapping a strap around his ax and hand.

"Now, stay out of sight. Wait 'til the bolts stop and they come alongside. Let them think we quit the *cog* or are cowering below. We will draw them in. Wait for my signal. Then release all of your rage on them."

The Moresi climbed into the turrets. Legerohn, Mond, Stokke, and

Chimere climbed into the aft turret. They kept low and found a place against the rear wall. Ondo and Hallock climbed up after them.

Two wiry Moresi climbed up into the fore. Roberge and Strey followed after them.

A bolt landed on the deck and then two more in quick succession.

Aenguz and Lokah sprinted to the forecastle and Mandavu and Kachota retreated to the rear.

Bolts knocked the *cog* like a drum.

Aenguz cracked the door. Lokah was at his rear. He peered over Aenguz's exposed shoulder.

Behind them, the Straathgardians moaned and wheezed in distress.

In the narrow space, Lokah asked, "What happened to your arm?"

Aenguz tightened. He could feel Lokah studying him.

The space was tight. There was no way to turn or hide the molten wound.

"My grandfather attempted to heal it with *morillion*."

"How did you injure it?"

"I was attempting to honor my father. I tried to fashion a death mask."

"The bone-meld? *Surasanskeld*?"

"Yes," Aenguz said just above a whisper.

"What made you think you knew how?"

Aenguz whispered a chant,

> *"'When honored bones are honor bound*
> *With fallen chieftain wisdom's found,'"*

Lokah finished the stanza.

> *"'Set silver bone to silver hue*
> *And metal's might keep mem'ries true,'"*

"I thought I knew what the *montmorillionite* was trying to say. I thought I understood."

Lokah studied him. He was considering his hairless arm next to Aenguz's. The act of stirring the dead Warrior's unformed metal had affected him in a way that Aenguz could scarcely guess. No Akkeidii had ever done what Lokah had endured. The metal was meant for the Earth. Something about that act left the Kriel altered and preoccupied.

Barking and clamor from the Erebim overruled the wind and the water. The thumps stopped.

Aenguz turned back to the crease. The metal warmed in his hand. The weight lessened. His *montmorillionite* was readying itself. It was the first time the metal reacted this way. It imbued a kind of courage in him. He had been taught this but here it was now. He knew that Lokah and the other Warriors were feeling it too.

The *hulk* drew up quickly.

Hooks and lines grabbed the gunwale.

Then the *hulk* slammed the *cog*.

The force jostled Aenguz into Lokah.

The Erebim and Sallow were out of sight below the gunwale. Soon black hands, obsidian eyes, and half-red heads crested the edge.

His heart was racing. Aenguz swung open the door and shouted, "NOW!"

The Erebim turned and looked at him.

Aenguz walked calmly and quickly to the edge.

Lokah was at his side. His weapon cut the air.

Mandavu blasted the door open. The hinges finally surrendered, and the door limped at the frame. His rage found its first outlet.

The Moresi rose as one. With javelins raised they let a volley down into the horde. Darts came down one after the other like darning needles into the mass of twisting black and shifty coral.

In a few steps, Aenguz was at the first Erebim that crested the gunwale. He swung his ax-edge clean through the iron sword of the first Erebim. He let his momentum carry him in a lightning-quick spin and de-capped the half-orange head. Half the helmeted skull flew off. The Erebim crumpled downward like a dropped marionette.

He thrust the spike forward into the face of another Erebim at his left. Then he plunged the daggered hilt into the neck of a third Erebim at his right. One after the other, the shapes collapsed backward before the severed sword clanged to the deck.

Mandavu swung in a wide arc. The dense metal blasted through the Erebim and crushed them. Light as wood in the Makan's hands. Heavy as the timber that drifted down the Wester to the Erebim. Their armor and shields buckled. Their bones cracked.

Kachota chopped with his tomahawks as if he was tenderizing meat. Hands and arms dropped to the deck with sickening thuds.

Lokah cleaved into shoulders and jabbed through breastplates with ease. His metal singing against the lesser metal.

The Moresi rained death into the Erebim. They also targeted the Sallow. Roberge and Strey provided cover while the Moresi maintained their assault.

The Sallow and Erebim were shocked at the initial barrage. It took them a few moments to collect themselves.

They pushed forward with renewed resolve. They climbed over the gunwales in multiple places. Erebim belched out of the hold in unending numbers. They pulled the bodies down onto the *hulk* and fashioned a grisly stair. Their din was a cackle of demons.

They surged up. Any loose helmet or severed limb flew willy nilly at the Akkeidii. Anything to distract them. Anything to gain an advantage.

The Warriors cleaved and chopped such gore into the air that Aenguz could not breathe without tasting blood. His hair was a mop of black.

The Sallow leaped over and behind the defenders. Mond caught one in the air. Ondo caught another with his long spear. In the tight box, there was not enough space for the Sallow to twist or parry. Hallock felled it instantly.

Aenguz rushed to meet the Sallow. It held a pair of hooked short swords. One low. One high. The Sallow parried Aenguz's first swing with a cartwheel-like move. Aenguz ducked underneath a stroke. The unsteady deck threw him back into the mast. A blade swung at his head, but it caught in the mast. Another buried in at his left. He lunged forward. And spiked the Sallow through brittle armor deep into its chest. The creature clawed at Aenguz with its last shreds and then fell.

Erebim used the advance of the Sallow to gain the deck.

Kachota was driven back behind his brother.

Roberge and Strey fought extravagantly on the turret. Erebim tried to loose their bolts at them but the surging Erebim caught shafts in the back. They had to halt.

Aenguz and Lokah couldn't keep the surge back. Stepping on and over dead Erebim was tricky work with the weaving deck.

The Erebim could not get past Mandavu. They were keen to overcome the giant. Each swing crushed multiple Erebim to blunt death. The gunwale and corner of the turret splintered and broke. The floor of the turret above sagged. Mandavu swung the point back and forth like a two-handed battering ram when he wasn't unleashing wild arcs.

Hordes of Erebim rushed Aenguz. He used the mast to block their strokes. Dull swords whacked futilely as he positioned himself out of the way. He feigned to the left. Kachota slashed low and cut legs off at the knee. Erebim howled and wailed as they fell. Aenguz silenced them with a quick jab.

Lokah bent and whipped with a tamed ferocity. His sword was light in his hands. His practiced style a dance of death.

The tight quarters hampered the Erebim. The Sallow stopped their leaps.

A mound of dead and mutilated bodies left a bridge between the boats. The difference in heights between the two decks lessened.

Roberge straddled both boats. His ax swung like a sickle through metal, armor, bone, and black flesh. Coral and turquoise shattered against his blade.

Black blood and wormy guts sprayed everywhere. The Akkeidii were ghoulish and unpenitent.

The real estate on the deck was receding. Bodies and black blood painted the planks.

The gunwale was at his back.

Suddenly, the deck rose and pitched toward the *hulk*.

The *cog* scraped and groaned.

Aenguz fell forward into a horde of Erebim who had fallen backward.

Mandavu fell like a tree at the final ax blow. His brother was lost in a crowd of black.

In trying to right himself, Lokah stumbled backward and tumbled over the gunwale.

In the last glimpse before the hot stench of Erebim blocked his face, he saw Roberge pitch forward onto the *hulk*.

Aenguz struggled and wrestled against the Erebim. His weapon was pinned.

The Erebim punched and clawed.

Aenguz sought creases in their armor, dug at their black eyes.

A black fist bashed into his head. His gut was kneed or elbowed. There was so much pressure on his legs he was certain that bone was about to break.

He roared in pain.

Aenguz was a heartbeat away from a blow that would end him.

"For Straathgard!" came the rattled battle cry in the fray.

Fishermen poured onto the Erebim on top of Aenguz. They clubbed the Erebim with all the strength they could muster.

In spite of their wrath toward the Akkeidii, they could not ignore the fury of the Straathgardians. As they blocked the blows from the fishermen, Aenguz scrabbled clear. He dragged his weapon out and joined the Straathgardians by stabbing the floundering Erebim. The fishermen harried other Erebim that still struggled to gain their feet.

The *hulk* was pulling against the straining *cog*. Lapstrakes and timbers creaked and warped.

Someone yelled to cut the ships free.

Some of the Moresi had climbed or jumped down from the turrets and were hacking at the hooks.

Hallock was on the deck of the *hulk*. He was fighting his way to Roberge. He turned to chop at the lines.

Kachota hacked through bodies to find the hooks. His *montmorillionite* cut easily through the lesser metal.

The *hulk* pulled away.

Living and dead Erebim plunged into the water as the boats separated.

Strey screamed, "No!"

The *cog* careened back and away from the *hulk*.

Aenguz tripped and lost his balance backward. He slipped on black guts and pitched off the side. His weapon flew out of his hand. Aenguz careened down. His head bashed into the nub, and everything jolted black.

24

FINAL PURSUIT

Brackish water rushed in. Sand swirled and filled his mouth and nose with wet grit. Aenguz turned and flapped to right himself. The world was a malaise of current, sand, and weightlessness.

A hand grabbed him. Aenguz thought it was an Erebim or some nameless creature stirred up from the depths of the Wester.

Lokah pulled him out.

The Kriel dragged Aenguz up to the sandbar.

Aenguz coughed and hacked to clear his lungs.

"Where's my weapon?" he asked as he wiped away the river's dross.

"It is here, there," Lokah pointed.

His weapon had landed hook down below the water line at the edge of the sandbar. The daggered hilt angled like the hand of a sundial. It pointed west directly at the line of trees.

He drew it out as if it was being proffered by the river.

He watched the *hulk* as it drifted the final yards in a tight arc to plow hard into the hump of a further sandbar. The sudden stop threw the surge of black and coral to the deck like a crashing wave.

Aenguz and Lokah saw glints of *montmorillionite*. He counted three. They were surrounded by a maelstrom as if they had riled a nest of asps.

"We have to get to them," Aenguz said urgently. He ran to the point of the sand bar half-submerged in water.

Then suddenly, a chime rose into the air from the Earth's heart. A ring like a harmonized carillon.

His weapon thrummed with a thin vibration like a tuning fork.

Aenguz and Lokah gazed at one another and then back to the barge.

They slogged on; the water seemed to be holding them back.

Then in quick succession, two more marrow thrumming chimes.

They halted in the river. The current ignored them. Sand scraped by them.

The Erebim barked in exaltation. Their cruel hacking continued. Bone and wet flesh were butchered wantonly. A gruesome howl rose.

They walked woodenly back to the *cog*.

Above, Aenguz could see Ondo and Kachota. The two were covered in blood. The distinction between clan and race was effaced by Erebim and Sallow gore. They looked down at Aenguz and Lokah. They all shared the note of death through their weapons.

Mandavu stepped among the Erebim bodies, pile-driving his mace up and down. His rage, unquenched, or newly fired, he went about killing and confirming the dead Erebim again as if he meant to stamp their souls into the Black Earth.

Legerohn weaved among the dead and around Mandavu to the other Moresi. The canted deck was difficult to navigate. Stokke was still alive. He still clung to a spear.

The final throes of Roberge, Strey, and Hallock had bought them a brief reprieve.

Legerohn made his way to the turret as another Moresi climbed down from the carnage of the tight killing box. He reached up to help him down the canted stair.

The three Akkeidii and four Moresi began climbing down off the *cog*. Kachota helped a fisherman off the side. Aenguz grabbed the club at his hand.

As Legerohn reached the sandbar he said, "We have to make for the forest."

Aenguz and Lokah helped them down.

Emboldened by their small victory the Erebim set down a gangplank and rushed down.

The remaining defenders Aenguz, Lokah, Ondo, Mandavu, and Kachota waded into the river toward the shore. Kachota bore the last of the fisherman. None of the other Straathgardians had survived. Legerohn, Mond, Stokke and Chimere raced in. They were hard-pressed to leave their dead behind.

Arrows whizzed over their heads and the course tail feathers split the air.

The water was a cold gritty sludge. Aenguz waded in up to his chest.

Would the bottom drop out? The firm current might drag them right to the advancing Erebim.

But he kept his feet and the water dropped reluctantly away.

They came out one by one onto the virgin shoreline.

The air was rarefied. It seemed sacred. The long strand was a kind of natural narthex at the edge of the forest. Driftwood dotted the shore. A calamity of roots warded the edge.

Aenguz turned to help the others as they made their way up onto the bank.

Erebim were pouring down the gangplank still. Others ran as far as they could along the sandbar and galloped into the water.

Kachota helped the fisherman up to the sand. He waded back to meet Mandavu. Stokke and Mond stomped out of the water.

Legerohn organized the Moresi into a cross. Legerohn faced the forest. Mond faced the river. Stokke faced the Erebim and Chimere pointed north.

They each took a knee in a kind of prayer or obeisance. Aenguz did not understand the Moresi. What were they doing? The churn of Ondo's legs behind him drowned out much of what he could hear anyway.

He waited for the Finit as he strode to the shore.

The blood was only partially washed off him. He looked like a demigod born of the Wester. His long spear a kind of crook.

"Finally, firm ground. I could not get to them." He said to Aenguz. He inclined his head back toward the lost Akkeidii. He spat river water and wiped his round face clean.

"I was thrown from the boat," Aenguz responded.

Then a dire spear caught Ondolfur in the neck. His eyes blinked as if he was casting out a stubborn dream. His free hand brushed at the shaft that ran clear through the tough cords connecting his head to his shoulders. He had no strength. His spear fell to the sand. His tongue convulsed as if he was trying to speak or breathe. Gobs of blood gushed out. He fell forward.

Aenguz grabbed him. The long shaft dug into the shore. Then the unwanted chime rang out.

Ondo's spear wavered momentarily like a serpent. Then it lost its shape entirely and dropped to the sand. It dissolved in between the minuscule grains.

Lokah ran up. Lokah stared at Ondo and the place where his weapon had been. Mandavu ran to them. His helplessness turned to an unhinged rage. Kachota pounded the sand with his hatchet.

Aenguz knew logically that Ondo was gone but he could not believe it. "Ondo. Ondo."

Only the whir of more missiles broke the spell for the Akkeidii.

Lokah took up Aenguz's weapon and drew Aenguz to his feet.

The first Erebim had reached the shore.

Then as if a report had sounded, a flock of birds erupted from the boughs of the trees. They surged and spun up into the sky in a chaotic murmuration. Their squawks and screeches overwhelmed the air. They whirled and flew back over the boughs deeper into the forest.

The sound paused the Erebim.

Legerohn stood up and waved to the Akkeidii and ran to the root wall.

"Make for the One Forest!" he shouted back.

They climbed up as the missiles flew into the earth and root wall. The Erebim raced on.

Aenguz used his weapon to climb into the wood.

Kachota planted his axes into wood and scurried for cover.

The bright day was shut out as if they had crossed a dividing line into another world. The musty atmosphere was thick. Mosses and lichen contemplated the stillness as if the forest was holding its breath.

The Moresi, darted through the thick brush and disappeared almost immediately.

Aenguz and Lokah climbed over thick roots and under wide arms of banyans.

He heard the Makans to his right. But he could not see them. The Moresi were effectively gone. They may have been ten paces ahead of them or one hundred.

The sounds of Erebim hacking grew louder. Their chopping was distinct and discordant. They roared through the forest like a threshing machine. They were making progress on the captives.

Lokah turned to Aenguz, "Let us find some ground to fight lest they catch us from behind."

The world closing in. He had moved from one near-miss to the next. They would be overwhelmed. The numbers coming upon them were too great. His strength and will were almost gone.

They found a small opening where some exposed gray rock had resisted the probing network. Lokah positioned at his flank. "What an unexpected place to die," he said as he looked back into the tremulous brush. The first violated leaves were shaking. The darker shadows of the Erebim canceled the sedate gloaming of the shade.

"Death has been at my heels ever since the hunt. My father interrupted its intent on that day."

"It is a hard thing to be so far from home, from family and kin. Lost in strange Lands with no mountains or peaks, even unfamiliar ones."

"Aye, this forest unsettles me," Aenguz added.

The two Champions readied themselves.

Then suddenly the brush behind them broke and Legerohn and Chimere urged them backward.

The Akkeidii were set for the moment, their resolve girded them. Chimere tugged at Aenguz's arm.

They pulled and led the two Akkeidii through the brush to a wide tangle of a fig tree root network. It spread out like a benign disease on the forest floor. They pushed the two into the ravines between its feet. Legerohn laid over top of Aenguz and Chimere draped over Lokah like a cloak.

Legerohn's arms shifted and became contoured like the bark. It mirrored the contour of the tree's skin around them.

A blast of sudden wind exploded just above him.

A pulse like the beating of heavy wings pulsed the damp air.

The fearsome screech like a stone being drawn across granite.

The cacophony of Erebim howls turned to terror.

The ground shook as if a titan's fist gaveled the forest floor. It made Aenguz feel small, like a mouse hiding beneath the tree.

His curiosity was subsumed by fear of being crushed and squashed. The variegated camouflage covered Aenguz completely.

In the horror of rending flesh and shrieks, the Erebim's final death sounded like enacted ruin.

The servants of Morgrom were experiencing a primal debasement of their oblique humanity.

There may have been courage in some of those rallying howls but in the end, they were snuffed out.

Slow giant-like stomps lumbered a short distance and then the ground buckled as if the largest tree in the forest had been felled. Aenguz did not move an inch while the forest reclaimed the accustomed quiet of undisturbed eons.

PART III
DECISIONS

25

∿

"DEATH WILL BE YOUR RAIMENT."

Aenguz lay pressed into the channel of fig roots as if he had been tossed into a quick and convenient grave. Legerohn still lay on top of him, but the Moresi leader had transformed so completely that it looked like an arm of the tree had covered him and meant to keep him. He looked as if he had surrendered himself, his nature to the greater will of the tree and the One Forest.

The clamor, that had sounded as loud as if a door to chaos had been opened in the forest, was gone. The door to mayhem and bedlam had been mercifully shut and the world granted a reprieve by the puissance of the forest.

The quietude that followed was absolute. No birds ruffled the branches. No song or chirps disrupted the air. Small animals that usually forage and stir the forest floor had fled or held completely frozen. If there were insects or mites, they too had left or burrowed so deep that they made no sound.

The plaintive wheezing of dying Erebim had trailed off. Their course howls and sharp barks were overridden by their final death throes. But the tenor of their harsh voices was still recognizable. The deeper heavier snorts and breaths of the beast that took them slowed and then paused until even that terrorizing sound disappeared.

The silence of the grave claimed Aenguz and drew him further into the tight space. Dead leaves and decaying earth made the air leaden. It was growing harder to breathe. The claustrophobia of premature interment jetted the final reserves of adrenaline into his blood. Aenguz squirreled in the shallow grave. He whispered Legerohn's name over and over again in a rising tempo of panic. His weapon lay beneath him. He could not leverage the physical force of the weapon. His mind was so lost to primal fear that even if he could recount the Lay of *Montmorillionite* the terror had crippled him so completely that it left him unable to find a facet of power within the song to free himself. His metal lay inert and unusable beneath him.

He screamed the Moresi's name now not caring about stealth. He called out to Lokah. And then just wild calls for help.

Legerohn's eyes fluttered open, and sense whirled into them. His bark contoured arm shimmered. The craggy camouflage tightened and the Moresi's dark skin grew taut. He pushed up and away from Aenguz.

Aenguz scrabbled up out of the hole. A tremor vibrated through the root at his right. Chimere stood poised on all fours over Lokah.

"Stay your *silvercryst*," Chimere pleaded. "Do not disrupt the tree." The last shreds of his camouflage had shuddered away.

Lokah pulled himself out of the channel. He gripped his sword and mumbled some Words of Lore at the weapon and halted its incipient shaking. How far might he have taken the metal to vibrate in order to free himself?

He confirmed Aenguz's state with a questioning stare.

Aenguz acknowledged but demurred, embarrassed by his panic in the tight space. As his breathing slowed his curiosity waxed. He was caught in wonder at Legerohn's transformation. And there was the obeisance or prayer or supplication at the forest's edge. *Had they summoned the beast?*

Or begged forbearance of the One Forest? The *montmorillionite* ring was still an open question for Aenguz. As was Legerohn's clear knowledge of Grieg's Gate. Even Grieg Sidor himself. There were mysteries to the Moresi that he needed to answer. But now was not the time. Aenguz needed to take stock of the others.

A warbling call came from the dense green. The only note in a quiet jungle. The sound startled Aenguz. Chimere answered with a similar melodic reply.

Stokke weaved through the thick growth into the open space around the fig. He labored with the Straathgardian fisherman. Aenguz could only make out the straggling strands of hair on the top of his gray head.

"Where is Mond?" Legerohn asked. His initial relief was replaced with immediate concern.

"He followed the Akkeidii brothers back to the shore."

Chimere moved to help Stokke with the fisherman. Then the six of them headed back to the strand.

They skirted the edge of the carnage left by the monster. The heap of the beast was turned from them. A mound of tough skin and verdigris feathers lay on the opposite edge of the bloodied glade. It looked like it tried to carry itself away but the many darts and Erebim cuts ultimately proved fatal. Aenguz didn't get a sense of the actual shape of the animal due to its position and obscurity amid the trees.

Legerohn looked puzzled as he considered the beast. There was a grief there, but some other quandary clenched his eyes and brows as if he had been presented with a riddle.

The forest floor was covered with crushed and torn apart Erebim. Some of their half-red heads were crushed in with pincer-like marks. Black limbs, legs, and arms were cast about. Black blood soaked into the dank leaves. Some bodies were torn fully in half. Sudden terror was frozen on the faces he could see. It was impossible to make a count of how many Erebim had followed them into the jungle but more than a score, maybe the components for two score were shredded about the butchering glade.

They followed the path that the Erebim had cut in their pursuit into the One Forest back to the driftwood dotted strand. A pair of dead Erebim lay face down on the beach. Three more were felled in a line. Kachota was pulling one of his hatchets out from the last one.

Mandavu trailed behind his brother weaving in between the islands of bone-white driftwood. His long mace dripping with fresh Erebim blood. He looked back at the party issuing out of the forest and acknowledged them by pointing at the *hulk*. Two Sallow stood on the sandbar. They were paralyzed by the advance of the Makans.

Mond waited on the company and helped Stokke and Chimere down with the feeble fisherman.

The *cog* and *hulk* lay canted on separate sand bars. They looked in their own way like the dead beast in the forest. These larger and lesser approximations of some kind of prehistoric river monsters looked to have been slain by an unseen titan.

Ondo lay dead on the beach. The long shaft still protruded through his neck.

Aenguz and Lokah jogged after Mandavu and Kachota.

Who could say what went through the minds of the turquoise and coral caparisoned Sallow? *Had they heard the calamity from the mammoth beast in the jungle? Or had they only witnessed the mass of Erebim entering and only two Akkeidii exiting?* And now the rest of the captives. All of them unharmed and with a wounded member besides.

They moved out of their panicked paralysis and began pacing partway up the gangplank, then to the borders of the sandbar. Kachota entered the water like an unrepentant slayer.

The Sallow appeared to argue with one another as Aenguz and Lokah caught up with Mandavu. They quickened their pace to close the distance to Kachota.

The Sallow went to the edge of the sandbar nearest the river. They began to strip off their curious armor. Helmets were dropped unceremoniously. Breastplates were wiggled free. They fumbled with straps at their arms and legs as Kachota climbed onto the near tip of the sandbar.

They screeched when Kachota broke into a run. Then they left on what they couldn't free and waded out into the Wester. They swam out into the center of the river. They found a drifting log and clung to it. And they floated away on the current.

Aenguz, Lokah, and Mandavu joined Kachota as the two Sallow drifted out of sight. He screamed after them. One last bit of fear for the terrified captors.

The plaintive groan of the stranded *hulk* brought the Akkeidii back to their fallen friends and Champions.

With his adrenaline falling and heart receding from fight and flight, Aenguz began to take stock of the consequences of his decisions and omissions. And the costs borne by those around him.

Death will be your raiment.

This was true of him even before the ascription of the message. But now the additional loads of grief and responsibility outweighed him. They were his fault - all of them. The culpability acidulated his soul, soured the fundamental self-worth of his life.

He climbed the gangplank as if he was marching to the gallows or meeting to face accusers. The deck of the hulk was littered with dead Erebim and Sallow. He had had enough anger and revenge in his blood to raise his weapon against them. But back on the *cog*, he had made his first kill. All the Warrior training could not fully prepare him for that bloody extirpating of life. Even if it was Erebim life. The hot rush of anger and adrenaline, and the primal need for survival saw him through the killing.

He was taught that he would have to find his own answer to live with the inevitable outcome of Warriorhood. But now, as he tried to reconcile these new harsh feelings the death of the Champions added shovels of morose grief and sullen depression to his diminishing life.

Two distinct areas emerged after a moment of searching the killing floor. The lighter skin and bright red blood marked the spots. Aenguz stepped over to the nearest one. The shapes of mutilated flesh were not distinguishable as bodies. The Erebim had taken out their rage on the ferocious Akkeidii.

It was Roberge and Strey.

"At least they died together."

Mandavu took in the scene and then moved to the other. Kachota was ahead of him.

The Makans stood over what remained of Hallock. They inspected the movements and lines of blood on the deck. "He made his way as far as he was able to the Baierls."

"The Erebim paid for every step. He was brave to come so far."

The guilt of survival in the wake of their gruesome deaths draped over Aenguz and added another heavier layer to his other guilts and failed responsibilities.

Lokah searched around the deck for any pooled or captured liquid *montmorillionite*. Erebim had captured bits in helmets and some was caught on the deck by crooks of legs or bent torsos. He tipped them over and cleared a path for the metal to run over the openings in the gunwale into the Wester and the earth.

Legerohn and Mond reached the deck as Lokah was finishing. They met Aenguz's eyes, but no words came.

"Will you get some tarp?" Aenguz asked Legerohn.

Lokah left with the Moresi to help with a blade.

Aenguz walked over to Mandavu and looked at Hallock. Kachota explored what remained of the *hulk*.

The giant looked up into the sky as if the Earth was too full of death for him.

When Lokah returned the Akkeidii moved the cloven and hacked companions onto the tarp. Mandavu and Kachota salvaged Hallock. Aenguz and Lokah moved what remained of Roberge and Strey. After they struggled to distinguish between the parts, they decided to keep the brothers together. Something about that decision felt appropriate to them.

In Warrior training, Aenguz and the others in training learned how to carry one another as they pretended to be dead. None would ever be left. Even though the Drill Captains were grave and harsh, the practice was just that a practice. Gallows humor was unavoidable. When someone pretended to be dead and passed wind the exercise would devolve.

But pulling pieces of the dead and scooping falling guts was beyond anything he imagined. Only the experience of butchering roe deer kept Aenguz from retching. Lokah turned and heaved a few times. Mandavu and Kachota had similar hacks as they gathered Hallock.

They bore the Champions down off the hulk and waded with them to shore.

Stokke and Chimere had set a camp on a peninsula of sand girded rock that poked out like a blade into the Wester. It was nearly even with the *hulk* and was the cause for the sandbars and all the captured driftwood up and down the shore.

They had gathered wood for a fire, but no flames were started yet. They had brought Ondo to the camp and removed the long arrow. They had wrapped him carefully in a tarp.

Aenguz and Lokah dragged the tarp with Roberge and Strey up next to Ondo. Mandavu and Lokah set Hallock on the other side of the Finit.

When they were done placing the Akkeidii dead, the Moresi gestured back to the *cog*.

More dead. Aenguz's haphazard plan had led them all to this. His avoidance of the message had also led to this. His capture prevented him from moving to deliver it. But the decision to not share it or the other things that Morgrom had said was his fault. His failing. His lack of courage had indeed surrounded him in death. He wore it like the brackish water of the Wester. Who could say what might have been different if he had the courage early on? If he was brave enough to endure the scorn. If it would have saved these lives. But none of the Moresi or Straathgardians would be alive. They would have all eventually been drained to death in the belly of the boat.

Dead Moresi were being lined up on the sandbar. Legerohn and Mond worked tirelessly. The loss of their companions weighed on them. He began to understand the hard rigor of Legerohn's mien.

Aenguz and the rest climbed up the ramp they set at the gangplank. Wide strips of tarp dangled from the cross beam. Aenguz remembered Strey at the canvas just that morning. Dead Erebim and Sallow were everywhere. The two Moresi had cleared somewhat of a path amid the carnage. They searched out their dead. They were easier to locate and move than the Akkeidii on the *hulk*.

They retrieved the Moresi from the aft chamber. And after three more Straathgardians were found, their clubbed hands and gray heads identified them, they were loaded down onto the sandbar with the rest. Five Moresi and five Straathgardians lay covered in a row on the sandbar.

They ferried the dead across the water and down to the camp. The glow at the top of the tree line was all that was left of day. They were set beside Ondo and the rest.

Death will be your raiment.

Wakes of turkey vultures were tracing circles and descending onto the boats. As Aenguz turned back to the *cog*, there was another wake out over the forest where the beast fell and the slain Erebim lay. Lokah followed after him while the others sat at the fire. Stokke was cleaning one of the birds and readying it to roast.

"What do you return for?" Lokah asked.

"The roe deer are still there. And other animals in pens."

"The grandson of a Deerherd, of the Lord of the Deerherds."

"Aye, I cannot leave them to die."

They climbed up the ramp to the deck and lowered the other ramp to the hold below. They cleared a path to the stalls. Water sloshed in the mouth of the orlop and into the room with the obsidian spike. They set their weapons in the rafters and called out the argent glow. Together they worked to push sacks and crates out of the way. The grounding had thrown everything akimbo.

Aenguz took up some sisal and went to the pens. Lokah followed.

He opened the door carefully.

The doe and the buck looked at him. The doors to the pens shook. Low grunts and stomps rumbled behind them.

Aenguz cooed and spoke to the roe deer. He looped lassos around their necks and led them up the ramp.

With Lokah's help, he lifted them onto the gangplank and skidded them down to the sandbar.

Aenguz left Lokah to lead them to shore. Then he returned for the fawn and the mother.

Back in the pen, he double-checked the dead-born fawn. The doe was still licking it trying to bring it to life. He wrapped the dead-born in the bundled Warriors cloaks the doe had bedded on. "Sleep now dead-born." The living fawn was already covered in filth from the pen. Its legs were too unsteady in the canted space to remain upright for long. The fawn nestled at her teat. He pulled the fawn away and took it up in his arms. It was enough to coax the mother to stand.

He carried the babe and guided the mother onto the deck. He led her down the ramp and through the water to the shore. The roe deer milled on the river's edge. The buck and doe seemed content when the doe and fawn were returned. She drank from the river as the fawn found a teat.

He returned to the barge.

Once there, Aenguz directed Lokah up into the forecastle.

"I do not know what these animals might be. They are hungry and scared. They eat grain so the roe deer will be safe."

Lokah looked grateful to move to a safe place. The sounds in the pens were as disturbing to him as they were to Aenguz. "Be careful."

Aenguz went to the stalls. He cooed to the beasts and explained gently what he meant to do. He unlatched the doors and cinched them open. Then he hid behind the main door to the stalls.

Tentative steps came at first and then a panicked clattering. Their flight rattled the wood and sent shudders through his bones.

Lokah called down after the stampede had stopped.

Aenguz checked carefully to see if there were any beasts left. Two were dead.

He knew their deaths were his fault. The Sallow had not killed them. They did not care for them well, but they meant to keep them alive. While that might not be true, he had no capacity to forgive himself.

Aenguz and Lokah watched them and then followed the white antelope through the water.

Though they were bone-thin, they climbed out of the river and made straight for the forest. There were five or six of the white creatures. Their curved horns looked regal. They searched the root wall for an entrance and then they bolted up into the forest.

It was a small accomplishment.

It was dark when Aenguz and Lokah left the *cog*. The vultures started landing as soon as the pair left.

But they were disturbed up again as the *cog* groaned and turned. The gangplank fell. Lapstrakes warped and creaked. The listing barge slid along the sandbar. It looked as if it was trying with one last effort to make it to deeper water. But the rudder was still lashed. And after several yards, it lodged again with a loud grinding scrape between the twin sandbars. The mast cocked finally to the side. The vultures settled back into their coming feast.

26

~

A CROWDED CAIRN

The driftwood fire lit the bivouac. Lokah and the Makans were shadows to him. They looked denuded as if the strains of the battle, the flight, and the dead had taken everything from them. The Moresi, with one of the Akkeidii's help, had cut large patches of tarp for the freed men to rest on. The Moresi wrapped themselves in them. They looked like phantoms in the orange light. The Straathgardian fisherman was curled up in the bone-white tarp. The shorn end of the fused club poked out. The *purna* covered hand looked like a massive scab. He was turned away from the dead that lined the stone field on the peninsula. He huddled as if he was afraid they might take him. His sleep was quiet but troubled. The moonless night and sagging stars offered no consolation.

Aenguz took the last tarp across from the fisherman. He was too tired to eat. Saving the animals had given him small respite from the crashing waves of death. But claiming the dead, and the silence in the work left him alone too much with his own thoughts, his self-assumed litany of crimes. When he laid down, he found he couldn't face the fisherman or the dead beyond. Even with his eyes forced shut, their silent recriminations kept him from sleep. He turned to face the Wester. The pointed squawks and scuffling of the carrion birds on both barges were continuous. The rending of wet flesh was sickening. The placid shore of the Wester brought the sounds straight to him.

He rolled over to face the enigmatic edge of the One Forest. He had witnessed what the forest was capable of. Had seen or more accurately heard something so primal and fierce that even the Erebim were dehumanized by it. More than that though, if he accepted the role of the Last Emissary and the path intended for him, then the route westward lay through that wood. He had no reserves to contemplate that choice. Had no strength to imagine what traveling alone through the One Forest might do to him. How long could he hope to survive after what he saw there? Whatever pieces of his life that remained as an Akkeidii Warrior and ersatz leader of his people would be left here on the shore. He would become the Last Emissary of the Flayer. It was too much. He was outsized by forces and needs that no single person could hope to bear. He rolled to the north and turned his back to the fire. The driftwood along the darkened shore looked like heaps of old bones. They created a kind of buffer from the deaths he was culpable for in the distance, in the north on the Cairngorm. Had Selene learned of Selvin's death? She must have. But the last thoughts he pushed away were not the time behind him but the time ahead. Was there enough time to deliver the message? Could the Counsel Lords be warned and the search for the Dagba Stone begun? Or would the accelerated fate of the Earth be the final casualty in his long line of failures?

———— ◆ ————

THE NEXT DAY THE fisherman died.

When Aenguz woke, the shell of the Straathgardian was being set next to the others. Aenguz counted the coarse shrouds. Fourteen. The same number that had departed from the Upper Mashu. It felt like more than a coincidence. It felt like a prophecy fulfilled.

Death shall be your raiment.

But there were fifteen bodies. Roberge and Strey were kept together. Was that a sign that more were set to die? Perhaps it was another premonitory edict from Morgrom. If Aenguz accepted the charge and turned his mind toward the west, maybe he could save what remained of the Akkeidii and Moresi. With the message delivered, then warnings could go out through all the Lands of the Earth. Defenses could be marshaled. At least until the Dagba Stone could be located. All of the Akkeidii and Moresi and the other peoples of the Lands might be saved. The Flayer's victory might not be so easy or assured.

But accepting that would mean accepting the mantle of being the Last Emissary. It would mean going alone.

He went over to the line of shrouded bodies. Their heads lined the rock field. The Moresi were placed with care. Stokke and Chimere set the fisherman next to their number. They had suffered together for a longer time in the dark hold. Ondo marked the middle of the three tarps and four bodies of the Akkeidii. The awkward sack of the remains of Roberge and Strey looked monstrous. There was not an easy way to make it look human. Hallock's remains rested beside Ondo. His body was a lump as well. Mandavu and Kachota were adamant that no piece of the Gambl be left on the barge. In the end, Hallock had distinguished himself by trying to reach and aid the Baierls. The smaller wraps of the fisherman flanked them. Their courage had saved Aenguz at the last.

Once Stokke and Chimere moved away, Aenguz spoke to the dead. He apologized and begged for their forgiveness. The unreconciled grief in him pulled him to the rock field. He found a stone, hefted it, and set it next to the Straathgardians. His cuts and bone bruises from the day before jabbed at his sore frame. But the exertion felt condign. He lifted another stone and set it beside the other. He started tracing a cordon in stone around the bodies. Lokah joined him in setting the foundation of the sepulchre.

Mandavu and Kachota went to the rock field. They inspected the stone and then in turn added them to the cairn. Stokke and Chimere returned and added their strength. Their griefs were plain on them. Legerohn walked over as if he bore a stone for every Moresi he had lost. Mond followed dutifully behind him. He looked like he struggled with his own inadequacy to relieve his leader's grief.

The Moresi set rocks carefully on the bodies from foot to head. Then the Akkeidii piled heavy stone after heavy stone. The Moresi set stones in between the larger ones and filled out the barrow as it grew out of the sand.

The Akkeidii pulled off their ceremonial shirts. The day grew hot, and they were too torn and worn to be of any use. They draped scraps of tarp over the rocks they hauled up to protect their chests. The exertions gave them purpose and a release for their grief.

Other than a few directions here and there, the company worked in silence. The sound of grinding and scraping stone was the only language between them. Tears and sweat were wiped away often. Each man tended to his own private grief. A sense that each could have done more, should have done more to prevent the loss of those they honored.

The Akkeidii climbed on the mound deftly and passed stones up to one another. None said it but there was a sense that they were also laying stones for the Champions that had been lost on the Cairngorm. Aenguz felt the Mashu as if a familiar smell of his homeland had opened his memory. He counted stones for his father and Ridder and the Champions that the Urning took. The heartache of all the laborers was expansive.

The sun was high when the Akkeidii pulled away. Their exhaustion drained their grief along with their strength. It distracted them and made their losses bearable again. The cairn reached the edge of the bivouac. The mound looked like an elongated giant tortoise shell. A beast on par with the river creatures being picked at by the vultures.

They had not yet set a bowl for the cairn tree. That piece would be last.

They scooped up water from the barrel the Moresi had secured from the *cog*. In the pause, as they accepted the expiation of their labors, Aenguz thought about how they might set a tree so close to the One Forest. Who would go in to find a seed? What kind of seed or sapling could they find? And would such a setting of a tree be an affront to the forest?

As thoughts darted through his head, the Moresi started gathering up pieces and hunks of driftwood from the shore. They could not know that the Akkeidii were not done. Had not completed the rite. They wedged pieces of the bone wood into stones. They ringed the base of the cairn. The interwoven network of white tendrils circled the barrow like a crown.

Aenguz looked to Lokah, Mandavu, and Kachota. They acquiesced and even approved of the Moresi's unintended answer for the cairn tree. They shared terse nods and the corners of their mouths curled downward in approbation.

Aenguz left the cairn, stripped off his boots and his leggings. He checked the pocket and confirmed that Selene's ribbon was still there. But the impressions of the flowers at the end were all but gone. Then he went down to the river and washed the dust, sweat, and grime away. The exertion had helped. And honoring the dead had held some relief. But his dilemma still remained.

One by one the others followed suit and washed in the river. They found space between the shore and sandbar to wade and recuperate. Then one by one they came back to the camp. Aenguz started a fire with the scrap driftwood. Pieces that were deemed unworthy for the barrow. Then he wrapped himself in the tarp and sat by the fire as the sun raced to the west.

Mond speared a pair of vultures. They were easy targets. He chose birds that had only just descended to the barge. Too much Erebim flesh might make them inedible he reasoned. He gave them to Stokke. And the young Moresi cleaned them and set them over the fire.

In time, they all returned to the fire after a baptism in the Wester.

27

THE MESSAGE REVEALED

I t was late afternoon when the word 'home' was spoken for the first time. It was mentioned casually while they ate as if to test the tenor of the exhausted and grieving company. The topic was broached in relation to a question about pursuit from the other Erebim and Sallow from Galangall. How long did they have there? How long before the pursuers were missed?

Aenguz knew it was coming. Dreaded the line of reasoning. The incused grief hid the thoughts that accumulated in his mind. They all deserved to return home. Their losses were profound. They all had families and peoples that would be worried and wondering if they were still alive. Aenguz wanted to return to the Mashu. The foreign shore he found himself deposited on seemed on the other side of the world. The mountains of the Mashu would provide a succor his soul craved. But he was sure more dead would follow if he did not take up the unwanted mantle of the Last Emissary. No rationale of warning the Akkeidii first or assembling a suitable delegation could sway him. He believed that there would be more dead if he did not turn toward Corundum. If he reached the Mashu, he would reach it alone with the dead of the company trailing behind him. And there was the matter of the time. Midyear would come and go if he made such a detour.

Who knows how long the clan lords would deliberate a course of action? Who knows if they would even believe him? Going home was simply an impossibility on more levels than he could name. Denial and irrationality could not overcome the obviousness of those facts.

Kachota offered that there were barrels of axes and saws in the hold of the barge. He guessed that they planned to work on razing the forest once they had captured them. But it was accepted by all that other Erebim would eventually come.

Legerohn and Mond speculated about the difficulty of traveling northward. Entering the One Forest even at the edges was perilous as they had seen. They knew the Erebim were assaulting the One Forest in the north. "And who could say how far east their line stretched across the border."

Following the Wester north to the lake seemed to make sense to the party. They could work together. Mandavu and Kachota spoke as if their bravery and anger alone would be enough to cut through the Erebim regardless of their number. North of the Wester they could part ways and return home. But there was uncertainty in their voices that undid the bravado.

Suddenly, Aenguz spoke.

"I cannot go home."

All eyes turned to him.

The Moresi looked confused. Their eyes narrowed. Chimere's head cocked as if Aenguz spoke in another language.

Lokah looked to the Makans. A sheepishness fell over their faulty bravado.

Legerohn tried to interpret the signs in the Akkeidii's faces.

Then Lokah said. "The Erebim have brought war on themselves. The Akkeidii may already be marching east. There will be no Challenge while there is war."

Mandavu jerked to reply but then he caught himself. The tenuous bond that Aenguz had exacted in the orlop was not an oath. The giant had sworn no allegiance to Aenguz. Aenguz had plotted to kill him. He had passed over a chance to kill him while Mandavu's hand was still attached via the *purna* to the rod. His release and rescue could easily be turned and viewed as weakness rather than benevolence. Mandavu's brow held a clenched anger. Kachota seemed poised to swear. But he held back in honor of his brother.

Finally, Mandavu said, "Even in this wilderness our laws still hold. Lokah is right. The Challenge may be stayed in times of war."

Kachota tightened and shifted as if he did not know how to reconcile his brother's patience. In the periphery, Aenguz saw the mistrust Kachota still held toward him.

"Then we head to the Mashu and join our brothers in war." Lokah said. They turned back to Aenguz.

"I still cannot go home." He hugged the tarp around him as if he meant to hide his shame. "I have to go to Corundum. I have a message for the Counsel Lords there."

Confusion rippled across all their faces. It was as if Aenguz was slipping into madness.

Legerohn said, "Ah, the message. I had forgotten."

Now the Akkeidii and the Moresi turned to Legerohn.

"What are you talking about, Tahnka?" Mond asked.

"What message?" Lokah added.

Here it was. The truth he had hidden and sought to eschew.

Aenguz took deep breaths. He tried to draw courage or resolve from the fire. "I have been bidden to deliver a message to the Counsel Lords at Corundum."

Chimere and Stokke listened in rapt silence.

The Akkeidii looked confused and concerned as if they were trying to translate unknown runes.

"Tell them the message, Aenguz Sidor. Tell them what you implored me with." Legerohn wanted to enlighten the Moresi.

But Aenguz looked at the Akkeidii when he spoke.

"The night my arm was...healed, I had a vision. I was taken before the Flayer. He is not gone from the Earth. He will soon be freed from the contortion that Grieg Sidor has placed on him. At least one Ruinwaster is abroad in the Lands. Maybe more."

Their faces were drawn. Lokah looked at Aenguz as if he was a stranger. Mandavu and Kachota exuded open revulsion. Their eyes were wide with shock and disbelief. He glanced at the Moresi. Chimere's mouth was agape. Stokke's lips parted as if his last breath had escaped.

Aenguz described the horrors of Carrowen Celd and his terrible plummet there. Then he let his eyes drop to the fire and he recited the message as if the flames were living parchment.

In the end, he added Morgrom's warning to him.

"'If you fail to deliver my message, death will be your raiment. And I will only require one Ruinwaster to bring about the ruin of the Earth. One Ruinwaster alone would be enough to rend the Vaults of Corundum.'"

"I am the Last Emissary now. I must bear this message to Corundum."

The fire sank into white ash. Dusk gave way to darkness and tinted everything black.

Legerohn's gaze revealed that he could not decipher the Akkeidii's confusion. "How do you not know this message?" he asked the Akkeidii. His furrowed eyes started to contemplate that Aenguz might indeed be mad. He had wanted Aenguz to share the message for the Moresi's benefit only.

Chimere added wood to the fire. His reactions were blunted in the dark.

Mandavu asked, "When was this? When did you have this *vision?*"

Here it was. Another sin. His crimes were stretching back to the source. A line of culpability reaching back to the Mashu and the root of his selfish choices.

"The night before the Assembly."

"Before the Assembly?" Mandavu erupted. "Why did you not tell us then?" he demanded. "Look at this. Dead Akkeidii are strewn across the Lands." The giant waved an arm at the cairn and out into the night. "And these Moresi and the lost Straathgardians."

Kachota cursed at Aenguz as if all his concerns were proven true.

Lokah's face wilted.

Shame and guilt weighed on Aenguz as heavily as the stones on the cairn. It took all of his strength to pull his head up. "And would you have believed me?"

Kachota shouted back. His justifications of distrust litigated his conclusions about Aenguz. "Is that why you drew us to the Cairngorm?" his question dripped with accusation. 'Are you one of them?' his question begged.

"I was thinking about my father." Aenguz's words were heavy as if each one was a load stone. "I was thinking about laying him to rest with the honored dead. I was thinking about my clan. I was thinking about how to delay the Challenge."

"You were not thinking about anything, save yourself!" Mandavu declared. "Roberge and Strey and Hallock. Ondo and the other Champions are all dead! Because of you."

"I know," Aenguz whispered.

"Why did you not tell us?" Kachota pleaded.

"In the Assembly, once the Challenge was called, would you have heeded me? Would you have believed the message?"

The Makans growled. Caught in the truth of Aenguz's assertion they could only grind their fury in grumbles.

Lokah pondered the cairn. He traced the fingers of driftwood that caressed the stones with his eyes. "I have sworn an oath to you. By my metal, I will keep it. On behalf of the Kriels, I have sworn an oath to the Sidors. I will honor it." Lokah took his sword from behind him and offered the handle to Aenguz. The Erebim and Sallow blood were gone. Washed away by the inscrutable properties of *montmorillionite*.

The hilt of Lokah's weapon reminded him of Ridder's. Aenguz reached out with his left hand. He wanted to reveal the ugliest part of himself. He wanted to give Lokah a chance to see what kind of person he was aligning himself with. Aenguz reached for the handle tentatively, gave Lokah a chance to withdraw. A chance to comprehend the flawed leader he had sworn an oath to. Lokah held the blade of his weapon. The razor edges would not scratch him. Aenguz gripped the handle. Nodded and released it. It was an affirmation. There was nothing to add or say. Sidors and Kriels.

Lokah rested his sword across his lap. The stout head pointed at the brothers. Then he continued.

"None in the Assembly would have believed you. I would not have believed you. But what we have seen and heard confirms what you saw and heard in the depths of the Earth. Who could have foreseen that the Erebim would have come across the One Bridge onto the Cairngorm? None have ventured into the east in years. Even we crossed the essence of the One Bridge which was altered by theurgy unrecognized by us."

Lokah's eyes moved over Aenguz's arm. "You have communed with the metal in a way I cannot fathom." His hairless right arm shined in the firelight. His submersion in the liquid metal to verify proof of life mirrored Aenguz's in a fashion. "In spite of your wound, or because of it, the metal has not rejected you. How can I reject you? How could he bear *montmorillionite* and be false with the message.

"Whether by coincidence or design, all that has befallen us has been due to the Flayer and the Erebim. Two cairns are raised now for the Champions. They are the first Warriors to die in this war. They are heroes. I believe Aenguz to be true, though I do not know how he endures such a burden. Our dead tells me it is true. If by some reasoning that were not enough, my scars would tell me it is true.

"If Aenguz must venture to Corundum, then I, Lokah, a Kriel from the line of Hernus Kriel, will accompany our Lord Aenguz son of Sairik, our fallen Ruler of the Akkeidii, to Corundum."

Then he turned away from the brothers and spoke to the Moresi.

"The Lands' need falls to the Akkeidii once again. And the Akkeidii will bear it."

Legerohn rose to meet Lokah's words as if he stood.

"I too have sworn to deliver this message. Though it was to be in the wake of your death. You were prepared to give your life to free us, in spite of the futility. I do not forget that. I swore a promise to you. And the word of a Prince of the Moresi is true." He worked at his belt and pulled out the *mithrite* chain. He reached over and handed it to Aenguz. He closed his fist and held the cedar-contoured *montmorillionite* ring up. The metal in the ring responded to the chain and the smooth bands gave off an inchoate glow. "With this gift, the faith and honor between the Moresi and the Akkeidii is re-sealed. Between a leader of the Moresi and the Akkeidii Aenguz Sidor. We will travel to Corundum with you and by our lives see that this message is delivered to those who can give battle to the First Treacher." Then he dropped the chain into Aenguz's hand.

Mond, Stokke, and Chimere said at once. "Your words, our will."

Aenguz gripped the *mithrite* chain and nodded a thanks to the Moresi. "The courage of the Moresi is beyond reproach." They had been through much together already. The fact that he intended to still honor his promise moved Aenguz. As much as he did not want to hazard the journey alone, he could not ask them to accept the risk. He could not ensure their safety.

Mandavu and Kachota fumed.

After a moment, Mandavu spoke. "Were Roberge and Strey still here, they would join you. So would Ondo and Hallock. Their oaths would compel them." Mandavu's jab felt like Akkeidii steel between his ribs. The Makan's slight was warranted. But he could not out do the culpability that

Aenguz already bore. It was a burden that was already more than he could sustain. Ridder, Selvin, Moodley, and the other Champions all bore the cost of his reticence and cowardice.

"My heart says that we should return to the Mashu. But I do not covet what it would say about me or the Makans should we abandon you to this wilderness or this task. I vouchsafe that Lokah speaks the truth. We will not break faith with the metal. War is upon us. The first casualties have fallen. If aid is to be found in the west, then Makans will see that it is found."

Aenguz had jumped so quickly from the fear of going alone to having all the survivors decide to join him that he didn't know what to say. In the Assembly, before the Challenge was called, he started to feel the burden and responsibility of leadership. The responsibility of life and death. So he didn't want to make the same mistake. He wouldn't. Despite the innominate perils, he did not want them to accept without understanding the risks.

"Your oaths surpass me. I do not warrant your faith. Too many are dead on my account. Whether I would have been believed or not, my withholding of the message has had consequences that cannot be undone. I will not hold you to your oaths. You do not know what you may be accepting. I cannot ensure your safety. And time is short. Erebim will soon be at our backs, and I cannot risk going north. Before you freely choose to come, whether by oath or no, you must understand that Corundum lies to the west. My path leads that way." Aenguz reached his grisly arm and pointed toward the glowering wall of trees.

28

SACRILEGE

The Moresi devolved. Mond begged leave of Legerohn to speak freely. Stokke and Chimere turned on Legerohn too and also begged to be heard. Consternation transformed them. They retreated out of earshot. The dark consumed them. The edges of the firelight caught their soiled shifts. They looked like a cabal of disturbed spirits.

At the same moment, Mandavu and Kachota objected in no uncertain terms. Had they not seen what happened in the forest? How could they prevail against such a monster? The forest could be used for cover to head north. Stealth was the only tactic available to them. Lokah was calm and resolute as he challenged the brothers. The virtues that governed him transcended his fears. He drew more from the lore than Aenguz could guess. His dip in the liquid metal had changed him in ways Aenguz could scarcely decipher. His own communion with *montmorillionite* had left a mark so complete, had affected so much of his mind that it made up the hidden underlayment of his conception of life and the construction of the world. But he could not see it, did not fully understand it, or feel it. Lokah seemed to have been presented with a vision or a revelation in the form of a mystery his lorewise mind could knead and plumb. He was nonplussed by the prospect of entering the realm of the creature that slew two score Erebim.

Aenguz used the fire to wash the message from the front of his mind. He listened to the Warriors as they descended into argument.

The brothers were steeled against fears they knew and fears they could only imagine. What else lay in the forest? What other dangers might the wood hold? Their unbalanced numbers only emboldened them to advocate for a clear battle against Erebim that would be north of them. A clear fight. Perhaps Akkeidii Rangers were already making their way down the Wester. There may be help to the north.

The Moresi stayed huddled together in the dark. The sibilance of their exigent whispers added a whirlwind to the night. Aenguz could make out Mond. He nodded and shook his head as if he couldn't decide between assent and objection. Legerohn listened to Chimere intently. His chin rose in the moments when he spoke or questioned Chimere. Stokke looked like he was about to be undone. As if executioners were haggling over his life.

This was the fruit of the Divider's work. The party was split. This was the world Morgrom sought to create. And with division sought to bring down. The Flayer had been acute and exact in his warning. If they could not come to terms, Aenguz would be forced to enter the forest alone. He had already accepted that inevitability. Returning to it and the familiar fear was stripped of some of its power. And he would not trick them or coerce them to go with him. He would not bear that kind of deception again. If they separated from him then he would go alone. And they might be safer without him than they were with him.

Lokah appealed methodically to the oaths that already bound them. Their oaths as Warriors, their oaths to *montmorillionite*. Their oaths as Akkeidii. He walked them through the avenues that were open to them. The directions they might take. The cairn silently added its own verity to the Kriel's apology. Roberge and Strey and the others would have joined Aenguz. But of course, they could not come. Their logic simply said that there were fewer of them against a certainly larger number of Erebim than they had already encountered. And perhaps even Urnings as well.

His appeal to the role of the Akkeidii in defending the Lands touched on an ancestral honor that tugged at the brothers. How had Grieg Sidor responded when, after the Venture, the Flayer threatened all life? How had the Akkeidii who warred on the Cairngorm?

But that exigency was both too far in the past and too near to be fully internalized by the Makans. And it asked more of them than just their skill as Warriors. They could not guess what challenges they might face. None of them could. The Flayer held powers that were beyond the strength of flesh and blood. He was a god that battled against the will and inertia of creation. And against mythic figures that were enlarged by lore and time. The brothers saw themselves as creatures so infinitesimal as to be meaningless. They would need all the Akkeidii. How could they alone make any difference in such a war?

"I, for one, will not abandon our lord to this onerous task. We are not alone in this adventure. The metal still guides us. We are not powerless." Lokah shifted his blade on his lap as if to give his *montmorillionite* a voice.

Mandavu and Kachota mulled Lokah's words. They were like cornered animals. Their only way out was through the forest. Finally, Mandavu spoke. "We may fare better than the Erebim in the woods. I cannot say. It is clear there is no better way westward."

Aenguz accepted their assent, but his shame and guilt only left enough for a nod.

"It is settled then," Lokah finished.

The Moresi returned from their conclave.

Aenguz wondered and worried that they may have come to a different determination now that they had to cross the forest. Their whispers had been strained. Their arguments barely subdued. They sat at the fire. Mond to Legeron's right and Chimere and Stokke to is left.

Then Legerohn began. "Aenguz Sidor. It is with no small intrepidity that we join you on this journey. Though our home lies in the west, the One Forest is sacred to the Moresi. All life in all the Lands of the Earth issue from the One Forest. Every animal that has flown, walked, ran, or crawled to every corner of the Lands has issued at one time from this forest. To cross the crèche of creation trespasses beyond the boundaries of our faith."

Chimere's earnestness galvanized Legerohn's words. Stokke nodded devoutly. The young Moresi stood on a precipice.

"The shortest way to Corundum, the only way, is through. We meant to aid the One Forest when we departed from Inverlieth. We meant to counter the attack on the forest by force or through joining with the Chosen Freeholder of the One Forest. It was the Forest Warden who we attempted to reach with our call yesterday. And too to ask leave of the forest to trespass. We do not know if our call summoned the beast against us or for us. We do not know if the One Wood hears us. It is slow to respond, and our lives measure faster than the rings of life." He paused to clear his throat. His words scraped like sandpaper. "Our aid now takes another form. But we must observe all caution." Authority radiated from him. This was the bargain he navigated with his men to hazard the task. "Everything we will need we must bring with us. There is to be no hunting in the forest. Every step must be watched and warded. No living thing may be harmed. Your weapons must be wrapped. No edge may be shown to the trees."

"How can we defend ourselves?" Kachota blurted out. "You saw what that monster did to the Erebim. What are we to do if we encounter another? Will you protect us with those sticks?"

"If we encounter something, I will not hesitate to fight," Mandavu stated flatly.

"Nor will I," Kachota added.

Lokah looked like the Moresi had asked him to pitch his weapon into the deepest part of the Wester.

"Without leave of the Chosen Freeholder, or if we kill anything, we may not pass safely," Chimere added.

Aenguz experienced a similar shock as the other Warriors. His weapon provided a surety that defined him. He had already been stripped of it once. The lore and power in the metal beyond its use as a weapon made it a necessary tool. Especially embarking on a journey like the one they had agreed to go on. But there were other larger forces at work. Between Morgrom and the creative powers of the Earth, a few *montmorillionite* blades would count for little. Something told him that subtler powers, esoteric ones were needed for this venture.

An argument stoked again. Before it blazed, before division rose again, Aenguz said simply, "It will be done. We will cover our weapons."

Kachota objected with garbled curses. Mandavu smoldered but relented. Kachota acquiesced to his brother's direction.

"Very well then. We will cross the One Forest once our preparations are complete." Legerohn spoke as if his words were the only thing holding the company together.

Lokah added his affirmation to Legerohn's. "We will cross through the One Forest."

Aenguz's confessions drained him. The whole company was exhausted from building the barrow. And they had not fully recovered from the battle. Mond set the watch. They did not want to be surprised in case reinforcements came down the Wester. Or up it. Two Sallow had escaped. There was fear directed toward the forest but anything that issued from it would wake them all. Once the watch was set Aenguz fell fast asleep wrapped in the tarp that felt like old skin.

Preparations were made at first light. Vultures were speared and smoked. Waterskins recovered from the barges were filled from the barrels. Other provender from the boats was packed away. Simple tunics and ponchos were trimmed from the abundant canvas. Akkeidii blades made the work go easier. The Moresi shed their coverlets. The blood, stains, and tears made them as useless as the Akkeidii's shirts which they had discarded the day before. They did set rocks upon those same shirts and set them by the barrow. If Akkeidii Rangers did make it this far south, they would know that Champions had been here. They would surmise that they were the ones who set the cairn. But that hope was thin.

The Moresi heeded their own warnings and wrapped up the Erebim javelins. Bundles of Erebim sisal were looped and wrapped. Strong rope could always be useful. Aenguz set his pristine weapon in a double layer of the tarp. He wrapped it tightly from tip to tip and tied off a strap with the cord to sling over his shoulder.

Chimere sat cross-legged at the forest's edge. He may have rocked or spoke to the trees. Perhaps it was a chant. The wall of wood swallowed his words.

Legerohn came up as Aenguz looked on Chimere.

"He asks leave of the forest for us to pass and leave of the Forest Warden."

Aenguz felt mildly foolish when he asked, "Does he receive a reply?"

"The forest is slow to respond. If there was a reply, it would take days to hear."

Aenguz nodded unsure of the value of such a request. But any help was welcome.

"It is why the Erebim can attempt such an assault. If the First Treacher is to be believed, he has given it to them." Legerohn's skepticism hovered between mockery and uncertainty. "I am sure the Chosen Freeholder is held to the north to try and bar or stop their advance. Roots are rent from the earth. Gildelmun are felled. Sap boils. It is not clear the Forest Warden can hear us through such slaughter. We can only hope to go quietly and unnoticed. The One Forest is long and narrow. What yet remains of it.

Once it covered the whole Earth. It was the first life that graced the dawn of creation. Now I fear it may one day be gone. And the rest of life with it. Our quest to stop the Erebim has failed. Hopefully, your charge to deliver the message may yet save it. And our purpose not lost to utter failure."

Legerohn left to check on Chimere.

The world closed in again. The space contracted. But it was not bounded by the walls of the Mashu. It was formed by walls in the wilderness of the Lands of the Earth. Erebim to the north. Sallow possibly from the south. The East was a wall of despite. And the forest was as unwelcoming as a pending winter storm. Time too was running out. The heat confirmed that summer had begun, and that spring had faded. Aenguz judged the half-moon the night before. The long days of midyear were several weeks away. And the distance to Corundum was weeks away as well, as best he could guess. The Moresi had traveled by boat down the Wester. It was faster than travel by foot in the north. And Inverlieth, their home, was nearer to Corundum than the plot of ground they found themselves on now. If they weren't delayed, he may reach Corundum in time to deliver the message before the Flayer's grim deadline. But would it leave the Counsel Lords enough time to mount a search? Aenguz only felt the urgency in his charge. In getting the message there in time for them to act as quickly as possible.

The company looked like ascetics about to depart on a secret and dire pilgrimage. They looked like they were devoted to an order dedicated to bone and death. The driftwood-ringed barrow looked like their crude monastery.

The fires were put out and covered with sand.

After a moment, they approached Chimere at the forest's edge.

Chimere was gaunt. He was still coming back to himself. Mond asked if it was safe to pass.

"I have done all that I am able. The forest suffers. Fire and ax rage to the north."

29

THE ONE FOREST

Aenguz held for a moment offering them all a last chance to relent, a chance to object and turn toward home. He met all their eyes. His amber flecked eyes measured them and gave them every ounce of his gratitude. He was grateful to not be venturing alone.

"All right then. To Corundum." With that, he stepped into the One Forest.

The air was thick and damp as if they had waded into a lesser Wester. The atmosphere in the forest brooded over them. Wet moss and earthy bark choked the air. It seemed as if they had crossed into another world. The vague scent of decaying leaves undercut the still air. Aenguz struggled to breathe at first. His lungs stretched and reached for air as if he was being slowly drowned. The cover of broad-leafed underbrush hampered their progress for a time. The leaves slapped and objected to the intrusion.

Then the wall of stifling green gave way to a network of craggy roots. The bases of massive fig and banyan trees spread out across the forest floor. Their knotty trunks supported the opaque canopy like thick pillars holding up an ornate cathedral ceiling.

The company was forced to crawl more than walk at times. Combined with the stifling air their progress was slow.

Aenguz was lost within the first few steps. The Moresi moved ahead deftly and led the way. Chimere and Stokke were ordered ahead by Mond while he stayed with Legerohn. The two Moresi maintained the connection with the Akkeidii. Aenguz was as uncomfortable in the One Forest as he was being the Last Emissary. With his role and charge now revealed it seemed like he had left his old life under a heavy rock on the beach. The relief in opening up about the dolorous charge evaporated as soon as he entered the wood. It was not without a cost. With the Wester behind him, the last connection to his home and his life were gone.

They wended their way until dusk settled on the boughs. Stokke found a clearing as the light dimmed. And they settled in for the night. Different strains drained the Akkeidii and Moresi. Trespass for the Moresi. Unknown fears and muted weapons for the Akkeidii.

The Moresi mimicked the Akkeidii motion of raising their food, but it was awkward. And they didn't pass on their first bits. They nibbled on the smoked turkey. Lokah and the brothers shared their meal as familiarly as if they had sat at the same table since birth. But they did not talk much. An incipient fear of the dark forest soured them. The Moresi's fear was more esoteric but still tangible in a way. It was not that they were afraid of the dark but rather afraid of what they might see at all.

There was no rustling from animals or bird calls. The forest seemed to be scrutinizing them. A watch was set. But they all slept lightly when darkness finally came.

The next day was quiet and uneventful. It looked to Aenguz like the concern about the absence of animals clouded Legerohn more than the rest. Had the One Forest heard Chimere? Was some other power at work? Was the way being cleared for their slaughter, a surrogate retribution to satisfy the rage of the forest? There was no time for him to lay with the roots and interpret the forest's intent.

That night, Mandavu squawked to expose the heal of his weapon to shine some light. But the Moresi responded with such adamant gravity that he gave up his request and laid awake for hours grumbling now and again about being forced to lay down so soon and in darkness that could be easily dispelled.

On the third day, after a few hours of hiking, they came to a sharp ledge. Stokke and Chimere appeared out of the forest panting in a frantic urgency. The party moved together through the woods to the lip. A wall of sound greeted him as he parted the leaves.

The cacophony sounded like a contained storm. Or too, like a thousand waterfalls. A green canyon opened before them. The edge dropped down abruptly as if the Earth had been carved out. Aenguz expected a massive river or some kind of cataract.

Instead, myriads and myriads of birds hopscotched across the boughs below and filled the air above and within. They twisted and flew like whipped billows of smoke toward the south. Twisting rainbows of feather and claw rippled through the air. A pandemonium of colored birds flew in murmurations hopping from one cluster of high-branched trees to another.

Skeins of geese pierced the air forming ragged arrows as they struggled against their inborn drive to head northward in the summer. Aenguz could only guess what they might be flying away from or how they might be being directed or commanded.

Sieges of gray and white herons flew like gliders above the fray. Their great wings lifted them easily to eagle's heights. They pumped their broad wings and raced southward.

Cauldrons of hawks and falcons dove and cut through the air. Their instincts to hunt the finches and wrens halted or stayed by some unknown decree. Even the convocation of eagles that traced heady figure eights, nearly eye level with Aenguz, seemed to spy prey only to turn on the wind and glide southward.

To the north, a white ribbon waterfall cut into the emerald and disappeared at the gorge floor. There, the green roiled like a miasma as if the forest was being charmed into verdancy.

Aenguz's heart stalled.

At the gorge floor, the green surged and heaved like a flood. He glimpsed brown backs and gray heads. Herds and prides of tan fur and coarse scales moved here and there amid the green and the shadows. All moving along the course of the river that peeked out in places. All the animals were moving southward. They made their own kind of river.

An impassable one.

The strong musk of a thousand different animals flowed and swirled in the open space. It mixed with the dank air and permeated it. Wings stirred it. The smell of countless untended menageries compressed into this desperate space.

Awe among the company was palpable. There were too many sights to comment on any single one. Foremost in their thoughts was the cause of this exodus that necessitated such a retreat southward. What was happening to the One Forest in the north? What else might be rushing southward? And how could they hope to cross it?

Legerohn ordered Chimere and Stokke to scout the ridgeline in either direction for a way down.

When they returned, the two Moresi compared reports and chose Stokke's path. He led the company to a plummeting ravine.

Aenguz put his hand on Stokke before the young Moresi could descend. This was his burden, his course. He climbed over the lip without any idea of what they might encounter below. Or how they might cross.

Lokah followed behind Aenguz. He had flanked him automatically like a First since entering the One Forest. Then the Moresi came. The brothers brought up the rear. They gripped their weapons futilely through their tarps.

The calls and squawks of countless fowl washed out the sound of his breath.

Aenguz carved a path switching back and forth down along the ravine until he reached the bottom.

Just above the valley floor, a writhing torrent seethed. Small animals scurried through the crushed ferns and trampled bracken. Smudges of red and gray and brindled brown darted under stalks and over patches of exposed stone. Wild dogs of a sort. Snakes and mice rippled the ground running and slithering side by side.

Larger shapes moved through the trees in the distance.

"Not one fang or claw rends here," Aenguz said back to Lokah.

"I have never seen the like."

The implication for them was the same. What was driving them? And, would whatever power or peace that kept these animals from devouring one another extend to them? Would they view the company as kin to them or as cousins to those that had caused their flight?

"We need to be larger."

"What?"

"We need to be larger. 'Cloquet.' Aenguz shouted. "We need to stay together. Stay close." It was shorthand for 'Close quarters advance.' Another drill designed to keep the squad together and allow them to advance through a crowd or a mob and not get separated. Once the young boys mastered the log together. They were then tested with crossing a clotted distance without it. They were ordered to pass through older Novitiates who were surging against one another in their advancing and retreat practice. A riot could separate the members of a squad and make them vulnerable.

Lokah replied, "Cloquet"

He signaled back to the Makans. They responded with a hand signal. The Moresi were read into the Akkeidii's training.

"Grab the collar of the man in front of you. Stay close and tight."

Lokah clutched Aenguz's collar.

Mond took Lokah's. Legerohn grabbed at Mond's neck. Chimere, then Stokke, and then the Makans followed suit at the rear.

With a wave from the rear Aenguz led the company down into the maelstrom.

He was careful with each step. He couldn't be certain that killing even the smallest creature might draw attention to them.

He wanted his weapon out, wanted the thrum of lore in his veins to quell the fear. But he needed to make himself as invisible as possible. *Montmorillion* lore might act like a siren to these fleeing creatures.

The branches above him were alive with all manner of apes. At first, he thought the shuddering was from birds. But they swung and grappled at the branches in a suspended highway. Black, gray, red, and fusions of colors swung above. The branches and trunks vibrated as if they were being struck over and over again. Leaves and moss rained down.

Boars and various jungle cats darted around them. They were wary of the many-legged animal that crossed in front of them. Aenguz was nearly knocked off his feet a few times. But none stopped to tear at the company. From time to time, muskrats or raccoons would dart between them.

Aenguz tried to focus on a power that he wasn't certain he possessed. That those with him would be safe. That their long chain had the intended effect.

It was a stilted advance. Canvas cut at his throat. It was making it harder to breathe. He halted to give his throat a rest and tell Lokah to ease his grip.

The ground was unsure. There seemed to be another dip. Suddenly,

Mond slipped. He pulled Lokah back. Aenguz lost his footing and fell forward off into a small clearing. The company was lost behind him.

Red and gray squirrels scurried around him. A snake slithered over his arm. The ground thumped like boulders were being dropped. A large creature jostled in the trees ahead.

There was no immediate cover as the branches splintered and parted.

Legs like pillars pounded the flattened brush. Knots of muscle bulged around the chest of the towering beast. Sharp rhino-like horns clustered all around the shoulders and bent forward rife with the promise of goring.

Tendrils dangled around the mouth of its battering ram head. Aenguz could make out the long tight rows of teeth within the wedge-shaped jaw.

The tentacles probed the air with a mind of their own. When the beast snorted to take in the scent, Aenguz's hair fluttered back.

Every muscle in the armor-fleshed beast flexed.

Aenguz's heart burned with adrenaline. But naked terror rooted him. The coloration reminded him of the beast that fell near the shredded Erebim.

It stuttered forward impossibly quick and came right up to him. Its breath was fetid. The tendrils relished froth and foulness at its lips.

Aenguz contemplated his weapon. He might be able to make himself a problematic target, buy time for the others to attack or flee. But by the time he freed it, he would be dead. None of the powers of the metal would avail him.

Other animals gave the monster a wide berth. The trees at the edges of the clearing quaked.

There was nowhere to run.

This was it. His failed journey's end.

At least he had shared Morgrom's message with the others. They could finish the charge.

The beast stepped so close that the writhing fingers nearly touched him.

He closed his nose against the smell and panted in his last few moments.

The beast shifted its weight and plodded over him and disappeared out of the clearing toward the south.

His heart didn't let go for several moments after the beast passed. He couldn't process what it might mean that he went untouched. He feared that being the Last Emissary had made him a pariah to all living things.

The company rushed down and watched as the beast passed out of sight. Their awe stilled their lips. If they swore, it was not loud enough to reach him.

They lined up again and continued on. In time, they reached the shallow river. They located a ford and crossed while fish and frogs wriggled by their feet. They stopped long enough to fill their waterskins. The Moresi reasoned that it would be safe to do so. They were reverent and gentle with the water.

Aenguz led the company to the further side of the canyon through more streams of panicked animals. Lokah kept an even tighter grip. Aenguz could feel the Kriel breathing at his neck. When they reached the western wall of the gorge, he released his hold. They climbed up the western face of the canyon and out of the calamity in darkness. The rising moon swelled and lit the way for the fleeing flocks. They camped out of earshot in the glowering forest.

They had all grown quiet by what they had witnessed. From then on, for the next few days, rests and meals were held in silence. Even Mandavu gave up his complaining. The plight of the animals had impacted on them. The threat to so much life all at once by forces they could only imagine touched on terrors they hardly knew how to reconcile or relieve. *Would they one day be forced from their homes? Would their peoples be driven on an exodus to some other far away and unknown lands?* Morgrom had wanted his so-called enemies to feel the full scope of his vengeance. Did that intent extend to all animal-kind as well?

The forest exhaled them as if it was ridding itself of trespassers or a virus. Thick underbrush hearkened the western border of the One Forest. So, with slight warning, they exited the cloaked and troubled wood.

30

TSURAH

Aenguz followed Mond and Legerohn through the underbrush out of the One Forest. The two joined Chimere and Stokke. Legerohn placed a hand on Stokke's shoulder and sought to reassure all of them against the grimaced relief that contorted their faces. Mond nodded with approval at the younger Moresi.

They waited until Lokah and the brothers exited the wall of green before they pulled away to expiate their trespass. Chimere took a knee and faced the forest. The other three turned their backs and kneeled out to the four corners of the world. This was the same ritual they enacted in their flight from the pursuing Erebim on the shores of the Wester. Uninterrupted now, they continued their oblique ritual. Aenguz could only guess if they were making an obeisance, offering gratitude, asking for forgiveness, or making atonement. They stood after a time and Chimere bent his arms in mimicry or honor of various types of trees. He wondered if they would get the answer they sought from the beleaguered forest.

Mandavu and Kachota tore at the tarp-covered weapons immediately. They walked away from the Moresi and their cryptic practice. They included them in their unveiled disgust at the One Forest.

The Erebim twine had knotted around their *montmorillionite* over the days of hard travel. Where the tarp touched an edge, it split away easily. But at the shafts the cords held tough. They struggled alone in a rising pitch of frustration against the knots until they realized they would have to work together to carefully cut the cords they couldn't rend free.

Lokah watched them for a time as if he was trying to unravel their angst. He propped the hilt of his weapon at his feet and pulled the tarp away from his blade in one long smooth stroke. He stayed only a few steps from Aenguz as he flipped the blade and held the tip over the hard ground. Then Lokah leaned into his weapon and drove the tip into the stony earth as if it was clay. He looked up at the sun and then down at the nub of shadow at the ground. He cupped his ear to the hilt and listened as if he was trying to discern the heartbeat of the Earth. He whispered couplets to the metal.

The brothers broke into an impromptu *salaage*. They stepped through a few of the five forms but then they whipped into an ad hoc conglomeration of strokes, thrusts, and parries. Their *salaage* looked more like release than practice.

Aenguz was glad that he had not lost anyone to the One Forest. They had made it through but at what cost? He had exacted something sacred from the Moresi in crossing the forest. He did not want to accept the mantle of Last Emissary but if it meant their protection, he would accept its power. But the cost to those around him was akin to an infection. They were being drawn and torn in ways they could not suspect. The Akkeidii had been effectively muted. Their key source of power and protection had to be covered and removed from them. They could not provide the most conventional protection their weapons could provide. Aenguz led them like unarmed Novitiates through the canyon. Backward or forward he was undoing the meaning of his life and theirs. He sat down to rest and to halt the flow of unraveling in either direction.

His left arm looked garish against the canvas. He inspected it as he pulled the blade against the tarp and freed his weapon. The stiffness and tautness were all but gone. A new color had blanched the translucence. Still, he seemed to be able to look through the thin skin. All of the trials and imprisoned time had allowed the *morillion* to do as much as it would. His arm and hand were usable and intact. It just looked gruesome and ghoulish. A fitting mark for an Emissary of the Flayer. The Last Emissary.

Coarse garrigue marked the western edge of the forest. A border of thick sumac and juniper mirrored the One Forest with a lesser wall of foliage. The sun stood straight above, and its heat pressed down like a platen as if it meant to make a permanent mark in the earth of their transgression. Strange trunks like the one Aenguz sat on dotted the area. They looked like the remnants of a broken temple. Complicated striations marked the stone-like wood. An interruption of a merging between wood and stone. An attempt at protection in conversion that had failed. At least the sky was open. Aenguz wished for any mountains to orient his heart. But there were none.

Lokah raised his head from his hilt and said, "Like an echo and a premonition of water." The riddle was plain on his face.

"Is there any water nearby?"

Lokah's eyes darted between Aenguz and the stumps as he sought to decipher. "I see drought." The yellow dirt confirmed the parched stretch. "I do not understand what it means."

The dry garrigue and pressing heat countered any thoughts of water. So, when the whiff of smoke came it contradicted Lokah's riddled words even more.

Aenguz looked back at the Moresi. Mond's nose tested the air. He turned like an old windvane. Legerohn and Chimere turned their noses to the One Forest in a desperate hope that the smoke wasn't coming from there. Even at a distance, the effluent dank was still intact.

Lokah called to the brothers. They halted their whirling. The smoke had not reached them. Then their heads cocked.

The Moresi and Akkeidii came together.

"There's a fire to the south and west. It is not coming from the One Forest," Legerohn said confidently.

"Mond, Chimere, find the source and come back in haste," Legerohn commanded. "We will wend north until you return." Mond and Chimere disappeared into the sumac. Legerohn and Stokke took up their packs after the pair each pulled out an Erebim shaft.

They moved northward along the shrub line. They stepped over and around the hardened trunks. A haze started to thicken the air like a dry fog. Aenguz's eyes began to burn. Going north was not safe. They had to move west. Who knew how far the Erebim may have come?

After a time, Aenguz heard a warbling call. Legerohn halted. Mond and Chimere broke through the scrub far to their south. They looked like dark phantoms escaping a dream as they ran toward the company.

The pair stifled hoarse coughs. Tears streaked down their cheeks. "It is Tsurah," Chimere said. Panic twisted his tone.

"How far?"

"Five hundred paces or so. They walk behind a line of fire," Mond hacked hoarsely. "There is a dry river valley just west of here." He was lost again to fits of coughing.

Aenguz passed them his waterskin.

"How many?" Legerohn asked Mond.

Mond gulped the water and coughed back. "I do not know my lord. The smoke was too thick. There is a line of them walking northward. And there are others moving through the trees. Behind us."

Legerohn and Stokke handed them their white packs. Urgency gripped the party. They led the Akkeidii into the low sumac. The ground sloped downward a short way from the clearing. The Moresi found a covert nestled

on the ridge. They crowded together and peered through the winding
canopy of branches and searched southward.

A spotty wall of smoke drifted in a line across the dry riverbed. Behind
it the ground was charred. Solitary trees burned along the edges near the
slope. Bushes smoldered.

Shapes darted and scurried ahead of the smoke. A handful of white
antelope, Saiga, like the ones that Aenguz had freed from the hold of the
cog, ran northward. Other antelope and smaller brown animals rushed
to escape the fire.

"Tsurah," Mond said darkly. He pointed through the smoke.

Figures walked behind the fire line.

Their pallid flesh made them look sickly but thick muscles and corded
necks revealed hale and strong bodies. Their heads were like armored nubs
atop their broad torsos. They looked like they might tip over on their thin
legs. White-furred loincloths hung at their hips. Or they were at one time
white. They were now charred with black and smudged with blood. They
bore torches like shepherds of hell.

Aenguz rubbed his bleary eyes. A second set of smaller arms were set
in their torsos like child's limbs. The smaller set issued out through the
complicated joints at their armpits. The second hands worked coils of a
lasso at their stomachs.

"They corral the fleeing animals northward, back toward their lands."
Legerohn reasoned. "And they do not hazard the One Forest yet."

To the Tsurah I have given dominion over animal-kind.

An animal broke back through the line of fire. A frightened brown
thing, its fur trailed smoke.

The Tsurah nearest sprang on the terrified beast, tipped it, and tied
the creature's legs together deftly. Legs and sand and smoke flew up until
the poor animal was subdued. He left it there and rejoined the solemn line
of dour hunters.

The smoke was raw on his throat. Soon they were all covering hoarse coughs. The sumac to their left was loud in the distance with Tsurah flushing the brush.

"Where can we go?" Mandavu asked. "You said the north was not safe."

The implication was clear. Asking them to go back into the One Forest would be too much for all of them. He guessed the One Forest would harbor them but if they were seen would they then threaten the forest? But that wasn't his chief fear. If he moved away from his course would the supposed edict still protect them? The Lands south of the Wester were not safe. North might be the only option.

Aenguz moved out of the covert without answering Mandavu. The others followed as quickly as they were able ahead of the smoke and the Tsurah. Chimere and Stokke moved deftly ahead of Aenguz. They needed little motivation to get out of the reach of the smoke. Mond and Legerohn moved ahead of Aenguz but stayed close enough to not lose the Akkeidii.

The Moresi were gathered into another patch. They stared northward.

Aenguz and Lokah moved closer and looked out over an open gorge at a massive structure. Mandavu and Kachota came in and warded their backs. They seemed anxious for blood.

Stacked rows of arches bisected the parched riverbed. At the base, stout curves of black hexagonal bands stretched out of the earth and into humps across the distance in a bridge. They looked like pylons drawn out of the rock. They reminded Aenguz of the pillars at Galangall Wash. Except the bridge supported three bridges atop it. A half a dozen Tsurah stood on the black bridge below. They seemed to be checking the progress of the others.

On top of the pylon bridge were three more tiers of arches. Each row was smaller than the one below. They were made of blond polygonal fitted limestone. The top-most arches were the smallest. The top of the structure cut flat as if it was setting its own horizon line. It ran to the ridge peak on the further side of the wide ravine and disappeared into the scrub.

"What is it?" Aenguz asked.

"It looks like a kind of bridge," Lokah whispered.

"Do you think it is the water bridge, Tahnka?" Stokke asked.

"It may be. It might be."

"I did not guess that the old structures still remained," Mond said.

"What?" Aenguz asked.

"In the Before Times water bridges bore water to the City of the Sho-tah. The Hyrrokkin and Sho-tah built it together."

"If the old wisdom serves, this water bridge will lead us to the City of the Sho-tah," Mond added.

"And then to the Rursh Keleg, the old road to Corundum."

"How do we get by the Tsurah?"

"There may be a way."

They pulled back from the copse and made their way to the crest where the top-most arches met the land.

The smoke was getting stronger again. At times, strange calls from the Tsurah seemed impossibly close.

They came upon a parched bowl of dusty rock and patchy scrub. A thick fallen wall of mud-colored brick was built against the stone. It looked to be a kind of cistern. A broken cistern. Bone dry dust mixed with remnants of charring. Ruins' work.

They climbed down into it and followed the dusty course to a short tunnel carved into and through the ridge. Stokke and Mond scouted the opening. Then they waved the others through. Aenguz and Legerohn walked side by side. Lokah and Mond flanked their lords. Mandavu and Kachota trailed at the rear and kept their heads on a swivel and listened for Tsurah.

The tunnel was short. Sand covered the floor. Large blocks girded the entrance on the further side. It opened to the edge of the gorge and connected to a channel that ran along the flat top of the water bridge.

Flagstones covered the top. The dark rectangle opened like the door of a tomb. It was only wide enough for them to enter single file.

Aenguz gestured for the Moresi to go on ahead.

Stokke froze. He pressed his back up against the tunnel and stared out into the sky and refused to look at the channel. His head shook in a perpetual 'No'.

The Moresi could not budge him. The young Moresi started to wail from any press or insistence from Mond or Chimere.

"You go," Legerohn said. "We will bring him."

But Aenguz couldn't leave them. Wouldn't leave them.

He called Mandavu and Kachota to him.

"Go ahead."

Mandavu was confused or perhaps thwarted. The brothers were ready for a fight and Aenguz's command countered their intent. There was a lilt in Mandavu's eyes at being commanded at all.

Aenguz peered into Mandavu's eyes like a squad leader, daring him to disobey.

Mandavu nodded and the brothers stole across the distance and disappeared into the black.

"Lokah, go back and cover our tracks. I do not want the Tsurah trailing us in."

"Yes, my lord." Lokah went to the opposite opening and with his sword began sweeping over the ground and above the dust.

Then Aenguz turned to Legerohn.

"We have to go."

"The space is too narrow for Stokke."

Mond and Chimere had taken some tarp and gagged the young Moresi. The strain against the channel and not wanting to wail tore him in two. But any pull from the others brought an unwholesome sound to his throat.

"Go," Aenguz said to Mond and Chimere.

Legerohn hesitated for an instant and then nodded his assent.

Lokah was halfway through the tunnel. Dust was churning and settling. The floor looked rippled by wind and rain behind him.

"The Tsurah are close."

Aenguz said to Legerohn. "Describe Inverlieth."

Legerohn looked puzzled.

"Describe Inverlieth to him."

Legerohn whispered in close to Stokke.

Aenguz tore a strip of tarp and tested the length. He tied the band around Stokke's eyes and knotted it tight. Stokke either relented or was too lost to prevent him.

"Keep telling him."

Lokah was at their back. He waited on the three. "We have to go."

Aenguz motioned to Legerohn and the two took Stokke up in their arms and rushed across to the channel.

Legerohn went in first and pulled Stokke in behind him.

Aenguz waited at the mouth for Lokah. The Kriel Loremaster covered their tracks with sweeping waves of subtle power from his long sword. The sand and dust smoothed and fell, and their tracks were effaced.

They pressed into the dark. Parched dust and new smoke choked the narrow chamber. Aenguz urged them on until the light at the mouth behind them was as small as a star. Legerohn continued to whisper into Stokke's ears.

"Still," Aenguz whispered loudly. And the company halted.

Lokah held his blade up. He may have been mouthing Words of Lore.

Over Lokah's shoulder, the pinprick of light fluttered. Then a dark shadow blotted the light. His heartbeat was the only sound that registered.

The light shimmered and twinkled, and then returned. The Tsurah had passed.

31

CITY OF THE SHO-TAH

Aenguz wanted to get to the front of the line, to head off any danger that might yet befall the company. But the space was too narrow. When he gave the 'all clear' to Mandavu, the giant Makan called light to his weapon and led the company forward to the City of the Sho-tah. And then hopefully to the old road that led from the old city to Corundum.

Mond and Legerohn warded Stokke. The young Moresi looked like a blind prophet caught in a revelation of unvarnished prophecy. In an unexpected gesture of solicitude, Kachota handed one of his axes back to Chimere and Mond. They carried it between them like a lantern.

But the confined space wore on all the Moresi as if the walls were slowly constricting in on them. In the glimpses that Aenguz caught of Legerohn and Mond, their faces looked strained as if they were holding their breath underwater. The motes of dust visible in the white *montmorillionite* light made it look as if the channel was full of water.

The Akkeidii were more at ease in the mine-like shaft even though they had to crouch. The walls were too smooth and perfect and the passage too small. And there were no veins of raw *montmorillionite* ore to light the channel. But it made it easy for Aenguz to imagine that he was in the

Mashu even if it was only an impression. Every step took him further from his home and his grandparents and Selene.

They shuffled on with no sense of time or distance. Mond and Chimere appreciated the gift of light, but they had to stop and rest their arms from time to time.

For the Moresi's sake and Stokke specifically, Aenguz wanted to slide or break through the flagstones, but they were too vulnerable in the space. If they were seen they would be caught or killed. The water bridge was a boon. And so, they would have to suffer it like they had suffered the One Forest.

At a point, the line came to a halt. Mandavu quieted his light. Both axes went dark. Aenguz and Lokah stilled their light. As his eyes adjusted from the bright light, silver light poured into the tunnel ahead. A handful of flagstones had fallen in the channel and lay in pieces.

Mandavu poked his head carefully out and turned around in all directions. Then he moved across the stones and Kachota took a look and drew in some air. Then they cleared the way for the Moresi and let them poke their heads out to look at the night sky. The open air was enough for Stokke. When Legerohn moved to undo his blindfold Stokke shook his head violently. It was taking all he had to stay in control of his fear.

There was no smoke in the air any longer when Aenguz and Lokah peered out. Legerohn lingered beside them. The waxing moon hovered in the east and strange stars lay scattered across the night sky to the south. Cicadas scarred the summer night with their scratching song. Aenguz peered over the edge. Savanna spread forth in a vast unbroken sweep. The smattering of round, thick-trunked trees with a crown of branches at the very tops were leafless and charred. Ash and burned grass covered the ground in a blanket of ruin as if the Tsurah meant to bring night into the Earth.

The flagstones stretched away in either direction. Behind him, the line disappeared behind a silvered ridge. Ahead the thin line bent in a careful arc toward the north. The night horizon swallowed its terminus. It was difficult to gauge how far they had come or how far they had to go.

"The woe these Lands bear," Legerohn said. His helplessness left him plaintive and worn. "They have taken what they wanted and retreated to their homes in the north," His disgust with the Tsurah was plain.

They spent the night by the opening. The fresh air renewed all of them. When dawn came, they continued down the long, elevated channel.

At times, the channel opened to deep gutters that ran alongside low mountains. At these times, the Moresi were relieved and took in the air from the low-growing vegetation and curious but hardy trees. Here it was safe to uncover Stokke's eyes. The strain left him drawn as if he had forgone food. Though Mond and Legerohn helped him eat the smoked fowl they brought with them. Unsure of their progress, they meted out their remaining food and measured their water usage more carefully. Fortunately, the channel was shielded from the sun and cool and so rationing was endurable.

Aenguz also took the opportunity to take the lead from Mandavu and Kachota under the auspice of sharing the responsibility and giving the brothers a rest. But in truth it was to act as the first barrier should they encounter an animal or an enemy. He was determined to not let anyone else die on this journey. Watching Stokke suffer was difficult enough. When the gutters left the ground, they blindfolded him again before entering into the covered channel.

The atmosphere in the tunnel and the dry landscape peeled away the thoughts of home. He was in a foreign land an unfamiliar land. And unknowns stretched ahead of him like the inscrutable dark ahead. Aenguz marched on with the light at his side determined to not waste any time and relieve himself of Morgrom's message. With that burden gone they could return to the Mashu and relate all that had happened and prepare the Akkeidii for what was to come.

Aenguz was grateful when he spied sunlight ahead. He poked his head up and looked out at their path ahead.

The water bridge extended like an arrow shot straight across the plain to a wounded plateau. Wisps of cirrus looked like smoke wafting up from the ruined city.

The plateau lifted in the south and listed toward the forest in the north as if it was sinking into a green ocean. The mountains in the south billowed southward in plumes of burnt umber, like smoke. The City of the Sho-tah looked perpetually wounded, perpetually sinking.

Tumbled walls and collapsed buildings covered the flat top like gangrene and scabs. Wisps of dust twirled like unformed spirits.

The water bridge appeared to splay out with arches on either side of the plateau just beneath the surface of the crumbled city. Foundation supports, sewers or the mouths of catacombs struggled to hold up what remained. The rugged face of the cliff ran down onto the dry plain.

The rest of the company took turns looking out from the hole.

Then they rested and lingered in the shade by the light and wondered about the ruins that stood between them and the head of the Rursh Keleg.

"The Rursh Keleg is to the north?" Aenguz asked Legerohn.

Legerohn searched the stone as if his memories were written there.

"It runs along the southern shore of the Wester and leads to Corundum. It starts in the city somewhere. In the north."

"It looks like a maze," Lokah said. "How will we find it?"

Legerohn shook his head. There was nothing left to offer.

"Should we wait until nightfall?" Aenguz asked down the line.

"I believe we will need light to navigate those streets," Lokah offered.

"We have light," Mandavu chimed in.

"We might stand out if we opened our light to the ruins," Lokah countered.

"What about beyond the city? What if we go straight across and track up the further side? Pick up the Rursh Keleg to the north?" Aenguz posited.

"No. Whatever we do, we cannot pass on the other side." Legerohn's response was sharp and absolute.

Aenguz questioned Legerohn with a look. A familiar respect had grown between the two. Aenguz was surprised and grateful for the closeness and the trust. The incused suspicion of the Moresi had dissipated. While the ring on his finger had brokered a truce, it was the actions time and time again that proved them to be friends.

"The Ganzir lies beyond the city." Legerohn halted as if he had pronounced the surest route to their deaths. "Nothing can survive the Ganzir. It was the last assault that Tycho Ruinwaster left on the Earth after he ruined the City of the Sho-tah. It was his last act on his way to Corundum before the First Treacher's defeat in the Last Battle." He paused and gathered himself. As if to not be governed by superstition he added, "At this time of year, even in Inverlieth, the hot winds from the Ganzir reach our home. It is said that 'the sun never sets on the Ganzir'. We must at all costs avoid it."

"So, we cut across to the city and straight north to the Rursh Keleg." Aenguz said with more certainty than he felt. He was anxious to lighten their load. Reaching a sure old road would certainly ease their way by giving them a clear path.

They packed their food, ducked down, and continued the final distance to the City of the Sho-tah.

Aenguz spied the end of the water bridge's long journey from the One Forest. He silenced his weapon and made his way out onto the cracked wall at one side of a wide square basin. It was cut out of solid rock. But it was riven mortally near where the water bridge would have emptied into it. All it held now was fine powder that swirled and skitted at the bottom. They crossed the riven cistern to the plateau proper.

He stepped out on the ledge and waited for the others to exit. The threshold to the wasted city was frangible. Dust held the stones together.

A broken wind ran through the streets stirring up motes of yellow dirt and dust. Though the city was barren and dead, the remnants of life or what might have been life in the city were dotted here and there. Stubborn shutters teetered on fragile hinges. Doorless doorways looked merely open and not simply hollow. Hollowed buildings with crumbled and roofless walls made for slow going. It looked like the top of the city had been torn off. The walls and windows of the whole place looked to have been shaken.

At points, they would come to a convergence of streets that opened into a square. The recollections of community clung here. A dry basin around a square fountain rested in the middle. Debris that might have been the more mundane detritus of life was strewn in the corners. Shattered jars, desiccated bolted wood, bands of fiber that might have been rope clotted in the edges of wall and ground. The wind could no longer budge the pieces.

Everywhere, no part of the city was left untouched by the Ruinwaster's devastation.

There were dead ends everywhere. At times they doubled back when a road or alley became impassible. The nature of the roads seemed designed to corral them. Other times, they found themselves following a road that bent south and east. But they had to doubled back and choose a different road. Each time they came into a dead square they made certain to locate the mountains and choose a road that led north. Thin lines of cirrus seethed at the edges of the sky over the Ganzir.

At one point, they stopped to orient themselves again and spy around some corners.

Aenguz chose a road and took a few steps down it. Suddenly, something, a light shadow darted to his right. The wind and echoes covered its sound. Not everyone saw it. But his startled response set the company on high alert.

Then the sound of clatter grew like brook stones flooding over the streets.

Suddenly, a score of horned Siaga burst into the square where the company had paused. Their hooves skated on the stone. But their desperate flight took them down an alley.

The panic of the animals infected the company.

At once, the Akkeidii felt the ring in their ears. *Montmorillionite* was warning them. Their heads turned slightly but simultaneously.

Another small herd of animals poured into the square and the company was forced into a run south back into the city.

The frothy panic of the frightened animals added to the clear warning of the *montmorillionite*.

In the chaos, Aenguz watched as the company split in half. Mandavu and the Moresi split off down a different street. Kachota and Lokah ran with Aenguz.

In another unfamiliar square, the animals broke off into various directions down different streets. Aenguz and Lokah and Kachota were being corralled against their will.

In the calamity, Aenguz turned and got separated from the other two. He tried to fight against the herd, but he was carried down a different street. Lokah called out, but he was hurried off a different way. He had to continue or get trampled by the stampeding creatures.

He entered into a narrow lane where the side streets were barred by collapsed walls or hastily stacked rock barriers.

The frightened herd rushed into the alleyway. They skidded to a halt and looked around terrified and confused.

Aenguz doubled back out from the stalled herd. Tried to find Lokah. A pallid shadow blinked overhead.

He ran on, his heart racing, his pack jostled wildly on his back.

He turned here and there with no idea where he was headed.

Suddenly, he turned down a narrow alley. A single Saiga stood there.

A dead end.

Montmorillionite was screaming in his ears.

Aenguz climbed up the steep pile of rocks at the further end of the alley.

He reached the hook of his weapon to grab rock to pull himself up.

Suddenly, the tumble of rocks shifted, and against logic and gravity the wall of stones fell forward and toppled over him. Panic and terror at being crushed and buried alive shut out all other thoughts as boulders collapsed around him.

32

MARCH OF THE HYRROKKIN

A primal shriek erupted, sounded foreign. Preternatural terror effaced all thoughts. Crushed. Buried alive. Adrenaline ruptured his heart and threatened to rend his sternum. Rough brown rocks pressed his legs, caught his arms. His head fell into a vice. His nose would break. His final breath carried the terrible scream and the rocks choked it out.

His heart was loud as a thunderhead. His chest cratered.

Veins were on the verge of bursting.

Tattered hyperventilating breaths remained. His lungs fought against the crushing press for the tiniest gulps of air. The last bits of his life were strangled, enclosed. But Aenguz did not black out.

Through some turn of chance, the stones held poised. They kept him an inch away from being crushed.

He squeaked a meager groan against the stone. His panic was still too imminent to be ignored or closed out completely. A tinnitus from his weapon rung deep within him. *A warning of some sort from his* montmorillionite? *Was this how death came to a Warrior? What would this mean for the others? Would they be left unprotected? Would the vagaries of the Lands take them now? Had they escaped the Tsurah?*

Then a sound, almost like a breath. A subtle rift like shifting sand. Then plinks sounded like a cascade of small stones over pins.

"Shhhhhhh." It grew, then it receded. First the breath, then the plinks, then finally the sand.

It sounded like a 'shush' and not a random sliding of detritus.

But the primal fear of being trapped near a poisonous snake, powerless to move away, set his heart thumping again. Fear and strain stretched him to the breaking point.

He twisted to find and free his weapon.

Another "Shhhhhhhh" came with a cascade of stone and plinks.

His weapon quieted and the fiber of his bones stilled.

At a seam between the rocks, Aenguz spied the frightened Saiga in the alley. Caught in fears akin to his own, the beast stared at the wall, appeared frozen. Its only response, to stand still.

Just then, a Tsurah appeared at the entrance of the alley.

Aenguz jolted within his skin. But he did not slide an inch against the rocks.

The pallid, burly arms lifted a mass of netting at the entrance and drew it across the opening. The smaller lithe hands worked it onto a hook on the opposite end. Then the childlike hands produced a rope and measured out a lasso while the larger arms opened to calm the beast.

The Tsurah closed the distance soothing the air. And the boy-arms sized up the lasso and lifted it.

The Saiga snorted and stuttered. It turned to the approaching Tsurah. Its eyes were wild with terror. The whites made it look crazed. The antelope shook its horns and staggered backward awkwardly toward the rock wall.

Aenguz wanted to rise and protect the animal but he was helpless under the rocks.

Then suddenly, the pile of mocha stone shifted around Aenguz and-

Lifted.

He was pulled up into the air as if the ground sought to usurp the sky as if the city itself was revolting against the intrusion. He arched into the air; threads of cirrus stretched like a loom for an instant. Then he crossed over the frozen Saiga and came down onto the terrified Tsurah. All four arms shot up in shock. The lasso dropped. Then a crunch and a squish that Aenguz heard and felt through the stone. The pile of rocks effaced the Tsurah. The coppery smell of Tsurah blood and meaty biles seeped in.

Aenguz faced the Saiga. The beast gathered itself and bolted off out of the opposite end of the alley with a start.

"What? What?" was all Aenguz could muster.

Another 'shush' came. But then words formed in the falling of the pebbles.

"The Tsurah are shrewd. They will find us if you do not hold still and stay silent as stone."

The rocks kept him firm, but he had a little more space. His nose was no longer in danger of being crushed. *What was talking to him?* The voice surrounded him more completely than the stone, but there was no other reply and soon the adrenaline faded and left him drained. He was trapped again under common rocks, and he was left with the impression that he had imagined the tumble through the air. Perhaps a blow to the head? A hallucination?

Nervous hooves and ordered footfalls sounded in the road behind him.

He listened for the others. For any sound that might hint at their state.

But there was nothing. But there were also no chimes from *montmorillionite*. At least none that he could hear. Nothing came through his weapon at his back.

But that did not quell his fears for his companions. Had they evaded the Tsurah? How could they find him if they had? And if the Tsurah had captured them, what might they do to them?

In the waning light of the afternoon, the sounds of hooves and Tsurah continued through the city and faded. Shadows filled the alley and the creases between the rocks.

Then without warning the pile of rocks rolled and turned. At first, he thought his hallucination vanished and the true rockslide commenced. But Aenguz spun around, end over end, intact until he was upright. He was held suspended in the air in a giant fist of brown stone.

A pair of eyes, motes of wine dark blue were set into a rigid brow. The contour of a face, chiseled and pensive confronted Aenguz, studied him.

"Who are you? Are you in league with the Tsurah?" the plinks and shifting sand asked.

"No, no, we are not in league with them," Aenguz pleaded. "I am Akkeidii. Aenguz of the Sidor Clan."

"Where do you hail from?"

"My home is in the Mashu."

"Why do you travel in the Ruinwasted city?"

How much should he reveal? This creature could end him in a blink. If it thought that he was in league with Morgrom his journey might come to an end right here. This pile of rocks could become an unmarked cairn in this ruined city. He would be lost. His bones would join the dust of this forsaken ruin.

"We travel to the Rursh Keleg to reach Corundum."

His *montmorillionite* may have made a barely imperceptible sound like leaves grazing water.

The stones paused and held still as if it might not utter another word before the fall of the Earth.

"Why do you go to Corundum, Mashuan?"

What if he had to explain how he knew that Morgrom was still alive? Would this creature believe him?

"Erebim and Sallow are abroad in the Lands. And other evils. We go to warn the Counsel Lords to gain aid against them."

Stillness again from the stone. The day faded into dusk. The parched sounds of the ruined city curled through the growing dark. How could he get free? If the others were alive, they would need his help.

"Why do you not take the northern road?" the rocks continued.

"We were taken by the Erebim. A month ago we were taken from the Mashu."

More silence. The hand held him for moments measured only by stone. The light continued to fade. The city grew ominous. A tension returned that undercut the faint winds. Stone rippled and brushed at his back. The first stars poked through the veil of dusk.

"Your words are true. The Ichor of the Earth proves you true. But there is more in both of you. I can tell."

"Ichor of the Earth?" What else did this stone see?

"The liquid metal."

Montmorillionite.

The fist relaxed. Aenguz opened his lungs and took the first full breath since the stone toppled on him. Death moved away from him.

"What are you?"

"I am Hyrrokkin. I am Ochroch. A Stonethrall."

"The Hyrrokkin are thought to be gone from the Lands of the Earth."

"Such is a consequence from the curse of the Reaver. We are diminished. We are not what we once were. We seek now only to preserve the city against the Tsurah who defile it. For the sake of our lost stone-brethren. The Sho-tah."

Then, rock ground and scraped behind him. Another pile of rocks. Another Hyrrokkin came up to Ochroch. The second Hyrrokkin covered the dead Tsurah and then Ochroch rolled into motion.

Aenguz turned with the Hyrrokkin. Half in a somersault and half a canted stride. Like a wounded warrior using a round shield as a crutch. He roll-walked in the grasp of the Hyrrokkin out of the alley.

The full moon silvered the ruins and cast long deep shadows. The fractured light across broken walls and step-turns in Ochroch's fist made Aenguz dizzy. He wasn't sure which direction the Hyrrokkin was headed. He wanted to reach the others but how to get free? The only time Ochroch moved toward hurting him was when he spoke. *Did he know where the others were? If they were still alive? Would he help him if they were?* But there was no breaking free. And anything above a breath garnered a firm squeeze. There were a myriad of other questions about the Hyrrokkin Aenguz wanted to ask as Ochroch crossed the benighted city. *Where had they gone? And why? What of the curse? Could they be implored to help the Counsel Lords in opposing Morgrom?* If his companion's need was not so dire, and he did not bear the necessities of the dour message he could imagine remaining with the Hyrrokkin for weeks or even months. He knew nothing of the Stonemage's lore, but his Akkeidii heart responded to this race of living rock creatures.

Ochroch's course through the city was erratic, it seemed, to Aenguz at first. The path he chose, brought him to a tumble of rocks. He stopped there. Merged with the pile. Then shifting sand and plinks were exchanged and the pile rose and roll-walked away into the night. Ochroch remained for a time and then he would continue his march.

He relieved a dozen or more Hyrrokkin on his way northward. All of the Hyrrokkin he encountered headed the same way downward to the forested edge of the city.

Ochroch roll-climbed up steps to a wide terrace. The pillars of agora were toppled and scattered. The rise afforded a sweeping view of most of the northern region of the city. It must have served as a kind of open space for the Sho-tah to gather. A score or more bonfires dotted the north. Walls blocked some so that only the stone glowed. Others nestled in among the trees further away to the north. The trunks and bows were canopies of orange and yellow. Shadows danced around the flames with too many arms.

Ochroch's wine dark eyes glinted with splinters of silvered white. Motes of umber flicked here and there beneath his worried brow.

Without warning, he spoke.

"Will you help us fight against the Tsurah, Mashuan?"

Aenguz sensed worry in the Hyrrokkin's question. What could these creatures have to fear against the Tsurah? He witnessed firsthand how easily they were crushed.

"They desecrate the city and the memory of the Sho-tah. Will you aid us in our battle tonight?"

Ochroch sensed Aenguz's pause. "We are not invulnerable, Mashuan. And our numbers lack."

There was a deep ache in Ochroch's confession. Part of him wanted to help the Hyrrokkin. But he couldn't abandon his friends. If he died there would be no hope for them. He thought of a way to serve both ends. "There are more of us. If you help me find my friends, then we can all help you fight."

Ochroch's eyes held firm and flickered like dark facets of malachite.

"The other Mashuans and Inverliethians have been taken to the pens of the Tsurah."

Aenguz sensed there was more to what he said than the other being simply held as captives.

"There they breed and warp the line of animals into horrors for the Reaver for a new Earth. If we prevail against them, we will destroy their pens and pools at the edges of the Wester. But that is a battle for another day. I am sorry. They are gone. Will you help the Hyrrokkin?"

Aenguz squirmed violently against Ochroch's fist. He torqued his joints and bent and strained against the hand. He squirreled his hand around his hip to reach his weapon. He growled a roar that threatened to grow loud.

Compassion and sorrow moved Ochroch to unwrap his hand. He set Aenguz down on the terrace.

Aenguz staggered and nearly fell. He looked up at the squatting tower of rock. Was there still time? Could he even find them? "I need my weapon. I must find my friends and free them if I am able. I cannot leave them to the Tsurah. I cannot abandon them."

Ochroch's resignation tempered the moonlight that washed over him. His hand fluttered and the daggered end of Aenguz's weapon poked out. Aenguz took the hilt and drew it carefully away from Ochroch's bouldered fist.

Aenguz stood and searched around the terrace for a way down.

"Mashuan, Venturer, beware the *trullen*."

Aenguz stopped his scan and looked back at Ochroch. "What are *trullen*? Some Tsurah creature?"

"No." Ochroch winced. The chiseled crags on his face seemed to lose their substance. "They are our offspring. They are our diminishment made manifest. The Reaver's penance to us for refusing his aims."

Aenguz's grimaced. He reached out from his rooted position to console the Hyrrokkin. He could not form a reply to Ochroch.

Ochroch continued, "They roam the ruins at night now. They abhor the sun. It returns them to the substance of Hyrrokkin, but their new flesh cannot bear it. They do not recognize friend or foe. They do not recognize their parents." Ochroch ground out something akin to a tear or a hard sigh. "Anger and brutishness is their only wisdom." He looked out over the city again as if he saw back across time. "It has taken generations for this to come to pass. A punishment from the Reaver who measures time differently than us and who draws our grief through an age. Our children are an ugly mirror of what the Hyrrokkin will become in the Lands of the Earth. All that we have built will be forgotten. *Trullen* will be our legacy." He gathered himself in a fashion. Shoulders pulled back. Haunches squared. He gestured to his left with his heavy stone arm, and said, "Stay to the western edge of the city. Your passing will be slower, but you will be safer there. Stay clear of the Tsurah, and the *trullen*, and head north. You will find the head of the Rursh Keleg there beyond the World Stair." With that Ochroch rolled to his right down the stairs and into a pool of shadow.

Aenguz wished he could have helped the Hyrrokkin. The force that altered the course of their lines was beyond him. Morgrom exerted powers that extended beyond reason.

"War is not the worst thing you should fear. Nadirs of despair will unwind the fabric of your souls. All will be divided against all."

Aenguz went to the edge and looked out again at the fires. Without Ochroch's height, the nearest ones were now out of sight. He searched to his left heeding Ochroch's words and found a stair back down into the crumbled maze.

The western edge of the city bore the brunt of the Ruinwaster's wrath. There were few exposed flat spaces. But climbing over and among rocks was part and parcel of his life in the Mashu.

The edge of the city ended abruptly as if it had been shorn off. The dark beyond tricked his eyes. An abyss opened up. Beyond it, a narrow line of flat-topped canyons extended out to the Ganzir. They held up the moonlight on platters like broken sheets of ice. An echo of severe heat hung in the night air that hinted at the harshness of the Ganzir like a furnace door had been recently closed. The epicenter of the Ruinwaster's might lay beyond. But there was night. The sun did set there but perhaps not the heat.

He found a rhythm of walking and climbing that included a pause to listen for any movement in the night. Even though Ochroch had assured him, Aenguz was still suspect of certain piles of stone. When he needed to use his hook, he tried to divine if the pile was Hyrrokkin. Regardless, he whispered an apology to stone for the sharp edge of *montmorillionite*.

Eventually, he came to a fallen building. Only a thin strip of floor remained between the edge of the wall and the collapsed roof. The maw opened up beside him with an unsated ache for more of the city. He could not see the bottom. The light from the full moon didn't reach the chasm. If he slipped here...

In front of him, the plateau was torn away. A rockfall spilled and looked like a natural amphitheater. There were more sounds in the city to his right. But the stones twisted the stray wisps and grunts. He couldn't tell if they were Tsurah, Hyrrokkin, or *trullen*. But there was something moving in the dark just beyond where the bowl kissed the city. The aura of firelight traced the fallen tops of buildings like a preternatural dusk.

Aenguz chose to climb down and cross the distance at the edge of the void rather than follow the rim into the city. He made his way across carefully unsure of the soundness of the rockfall. Moonlight splashed into the crumpled bowl. His hands ached. His fingers were scraped raw. Blood trickled from the backs of both hands. He wished Ochroch was here. The Hyrrokkin could have navigated this slope with ease.

Aenguz made his way up the further side. He avoided looking into the dark at his left like a person terrified of heights. Finally, he came to a series of arches that supported the foundation of the city.

He was able to move more easily here. There were massive supporting blocks here and there intermittently. The detritus of buildings were either absent or lost to the black below.

Aenguz came to a broken arch of stone that dangled a megalithic block. A buttress of stone that resisted ruin. Mortar barely clung to the seams. The arch seemed to contemplate a release and a plunge into the abyss. Green and yellow firelight tickled at the underside of the curve. The shorn foundations of the city stood beneath the exposed buildings above as if their garments had been ripped away.

Aenguz lowered down and slid in between blocks and then inched up to the opening. On a ledge beyond and above the arch, scores of Tsurah writhed. A calamity of arms, large and small, thickly muscled and comically childish, churned the dark and the firelight into a malaise of shadows.

Behind them, other fires raged but he could only make out the glows against the dark and the ecstatic tracing of shadows.

Before him was a small pocket at the edge of the plateau. The floor of some subbasement or foundational footing in the raw rock. A simple solitary stair ran down to it from the line of Tsurah above. They were focused on something at the lip that was just out of sight for Aenguz.

Then the Tsurah parted and made way... *for robed Erebim*. The forehead branded officiants led a pair of Saiga down the narrow stair. A sickly green glow like a diseased swamp tinged the silhouettes of their shadows. If there were Erebim here... They walked past his window and the Tsurah resumed their churlish dance.

Aenguz pulled back and climbed into a different pocket of rock closer to the edge of the void. More of the black confronted him seemed to draw him toward it. He nestled in peeked out from the lee side in the shadow. As his eyes adjusted, out over the void, was a translucent fane. Cloud material bloomed and rolled on a rising temple of concentric disks. A circular stair that ran down in all directions into the impenetrable dark and merged with the near edge of the plateau a short distance away. On top were the thin spindled legs of the diaphanous fane. The scalloped roof looked like it could be carried away by a strong wind. Moonlight gave life to the seething clouds and provided solidity to its translucence. A different kind of structure than the One Bridge but crafted by the same hands. What was this structure's purpose? What did it bridge? Where did it lead?

Between the ethereal white and the abyss below was a black pit perched on the ledge. A full third of it extended out over the chasm. It canted slightly. It ignored or repudiated the edicts of gravity. It held its observance of another physical law. A lower one.

The Urning glode in a smooth circle around the pit. It waved its jerrid and scepter like a harsh maestro. A complexity of lines traced the border. A subtle, arcane geometry. A language written in threads of molten fire.

The lines scored Aenguz's mind, seized him. The pattern and the detail mesmerized him. The lines carved like the script of Morgrom's message. The Urning drifted out over the black in a focused trance and carved out an unhale polygon in the night between the worlds. The lines seethed yellow and red. The asps in the pit lashed with licks of ecstasy. A rhythm of ill only they could hear. The Urning returned on its glide to the ledge and connected more lines along the borders.

At the edges, beneath its tattered and dangling feet, lay stark carnage. Carcasses clotted the edge, piled like offal. Saiga blood stained the stone. Other figures, human in shape were contorted and lifeless. Aenguz searched the stricken faces of animal and man. His supplication was too raw to be a prayer. *No, no, no* repeated in the tight chamber of his mind. His eyes caught a pile of netting at the base of the blocks just below him. It looked to be covering bodies. In between the holes, he saw dark skin and bone-white fabric.

33

~~

THE EDGES OF THE WORLDS

Aenguz's heart jumped as the piles took form. The facets of faces, the color and texture of arms, thin legs, and thick ones, revealed themselves. Bodies he had become familiar with in unconscious ways during the days of traveling in close quarters became clear to him. Their writhing also hearkened to their internal straits. He recalled the bound and captured Champions from that night on the Cairngorm. The stupor that held them and their shrill terrors as well as his own. The fact that his companions were still alive brought unexpected water to his eyes. He squeezed the bleariness out.

Against the wall, between the drugged captives and the stair were a pair of amphora. The handle of Mandavu's mace poked out of the top of one. And the hilt of Lokah's weapon crowned the other. Kachota's axes must be hidden below. The Erebim meant to keep the released *montmorillionite* once their captives were slain.

With their weapons, they had a chance at freedom and flight. Though the only way out led up the stairs past a wall of Erebim and Tsurah. And there was the pit and the ritual. What would the Urning do once he saw them? Was there a way to stop the release of a Ruinwaster? A way to thwart or delay Morgrom's designs? The powers pulsing on the crucible of the ledge below him offered small hope.

Aenguz crawled headfirst in between the heavy foundation stones. The dust and yellow soot of the city covered his poncho. The grist and powder of the Hyrrokkin coated his arms and his face. Aenguz squirreled in between the crevices right down to the unconscious company. He covered his weapon with what free canvas he had. Any ring or shine now from his metal might reveal him. Even as he climbed down toward futility, he was determined to free them regardless of the cost. With the fate of the Earth and the undelivered message hanging in the balance, he was resolved to not let them die alone in their reverie due to his inaction or inability. If they fell here, it would be with weapons in hand doing all they could to get free of the city and warn the Counsel Lords to oppose the Flayer.

He was eye level with the brow-branded Erebim. Half-orange heads bobbed like the firelight. It readied its dagger. The other acolytes corralled the Saiga. They waited for the command from the Urning. Their black feet trailed blood. Their red-stained hands mottled their robes at the waist. Salty copper and smoke filled the air, seemed concentrated there. The panicked Saiga struggled amid its slain kindred, but it was held firm by the Erebim officiants.

He crawled in between the canted block and the heavy Tsurah netting. Aenguz pulled up the daggered edge of his *montmorillionite* careful to keep the silver sheen in shadow. Any glint now might be fatal. He slid it easily through the thick cords of the netting.

He pulled it back and revealed Legerohn's face. The Moresi leader's eyes were clamped shut and a smear of black paste covered his mouth. Aenguz remembered the strong grip of sleep and dark dreams that held him on the Cairngorm. He shuddered for the terrors that Legerohn must be lost in. A nightmare of ravaged forests. An end to all life replayed over and over again. Aenguz could only guess. He dug out the damp mush and drew up his waterskin slowly and squeezed water into Legerohn's mouth. The Moresi's eyes blinked groggily. Initially, he didn't regard Aenguz at all. Perception was not in them. Then by degrees, his eyes focused, and recognition came to the Prince of the Moresi. Then the panic of 'Where am I?' came to them. Aenguz poured more water into Legerohn's mouth to quiet him. He slid the daggered end of his *montmorillionite* through the cords at Legerohn's wrists. With the ax end, he freed his feet. The blade sliced as easily as if he was cutting through a petal or a stalk of wheat.

When Aenguz met Legerohn's eyes again he pulled in close and whispered, "We are surrounded by Erebim and Tsurah. An Urning is here." Aenguz paused long enough for Legerohn to digest and separate dream from reality. "It is summoning a Ruinwaster. We will be taken next. Are you strong enough to fight?"

Legerohn nodded. Something like chagrin flicked across his face. Perhaps it was because he found himself once again being indebted to Aenguz for his life. Other questions crowded behind his eyes, but his attention quickly went to the others. He looked above and below his feet.

"They are all here," Aenguz answered. "Stay still. I will free them. Ready yourself."

Legerohn nodded.

Aenguz continued quietly up the line slicing through the netting and the bonds at feet and hands. He freed Stokke, Mond, and Chimere. He cleared their mouths and kept them covered when they coughed and spat out the dark paste. Legerohn steadied Stokke and then through him to the others as they came back from their imposed nightmares.

The Saiga was dead. The Urning called in its own inscrutable way for more blood. Human blood. The robed Erebim barked across to the armored Erebim.

Then Aenguz reached Lokah. After consciousness came to him a sense of relief at the sight of Aenguz passed over his face. Then a grim look of a Warrior's calculation settled in. He said with a contained fury, "Where is my weapon?"

Aenguz inclined his head to the clay jars as he added, "We are surrounded. There is an Urning here. And Erebim here and above us. There are Tsurah above all around. Lokah nodded and scraped out more of the paste as Aenguz started to move on. Lokah's eyes worked to dispel his confusion, but he was a Warrior and his training left him dutiful. "The Rursh Keleg is near. Up the stairs and to the left behind you."

The Tsurah on the ledge turned away from the ritual. A spray of sparks erupted into the night behind them. All of the Erebim turned to the muffled distraction beyond. The armored Erebim held their ground. The Urning continued his dire circuit. The oily flames of the pit rippled and licked.

Aenguz dipped back to Lokah. "The Hyrrokkin may be making their assault," Aenguz said. "When I pull back the net, be ready." He did not have time to dispel Lokah's confusion or explain.

Aenguz moved on and freed Kachota. The cynical creases at his eyes were replaced with disbelief and relief. Gratitude stumbled across his face along with the shreds of unnamed nightmare. Lokah reached up and helped to steady the younger Makan.

Then Aenguz came to Mandavu and sliced the cords at his feet and hands. He clawed the crude paste out of the giant's mouth and patted his cheek. He took the depleted waterskin and tilted it as high as he dared.

As Mandavu came out of his dark reverie he asked, "How is it that you are alive? Where are we? Why are not-"

"There is no time, Mandavu. Are you able to fight?" Aenguz explained their situation. The dross of nightmares kept Mandavu groggy.

The robed Erebim barked for their armored companions to come and bring a body. The two that came had arms thick as thighs. In a handful of strides, they would be at the captives.

"More water," Mandavu eeked out. Aenguz left the skin with him. Then the Makan asked, "Where is my weapon?"

"Look to me. Make ready." A hard look flashed for an instant between the two Akkeidii. Gratitude and confusion altered Mandavu's complexion more than the black paste. The unreconciled conflict he held toward Aenguz and the surrendered opportunities to take the Makan's life created fissures in the image he maintained of the Sidor. Instead of killing him, this leader who he had wanted to kill was preserving his life, again. Yes, there was exigency but there was something more to Aenguz that he hadn't fully considered or understood.

Aenguz gripped Mandavu's shoulder. He tried to convey his understanding to the giant. The precepts of the Akkeidii they had both been inculcated with left doubts in both of them.

"There are Erebim behind you and Tsurah up above. We will be beset immediately. We must go up the stair. Hyrrokkin attack the Tsurah. The head of the Rursh Keleg is near here to the north. If we can clear the ledge we can make for the head of the road. The Tsurah may well be too occupied with the Hyrrokkin to block our flight."

Mandavu shifted and looked up at the scene and took in their foes. His eyes caught the amphora and came back to Aenguz.

The beefy Erebim were nearly on them.

In a fluid movement, Aenguz stepped to his feet and whipped the black netting off the captives in a single heavy wave. He extended his weapon out like he was unfurling a wing. The armored Erebim were stalled in a moment of shock. The robed Erebim squawked a shriek. Seeing an armed Akkeidii balked reason for them. Old fears left permanent in their blood or the stark stories they held to this day touched on them. Or it was simply the fact that not only were they startled, but they had left their weapons. They had no need for them with subdued offerings.

Aenguz looked at the two Erebim with a Warrior's hardened gaze. But strode to the amphora and swung his weapon with a snap. His movement away from them while still looking at them also held the Erebim a half moment longer.

Aenguz smashed both amphora with a single backhanded stroke.

Shards of starlight burst from the broken clay.

Mandavu was at his back. He picked up his mace before the sounds of breaking ended. Lokah and Kachota followed behind him. Lokah's sword remained poised against the wall as if it was waiting for its master. Kachota rooted around quickly in the pieces for his tomahawks. Then he spun their heads around and cocked his arms.

The two Erebim gained their senses and rushed Aenguz.

He stepped and extended. His version of the third form and swung. He slashed the necks of both Erebim in a single swipe. His quickness was too much for them. Black blood gushed out. Their fingers clutched their throats to try and keep life in.

Legerohn and the other Moresi met the robed Erebim. Their ceremonial daggers were no match for the Moresi even though they were unarmed. They overpowered them. Mond brought his knee down onto the head of one and Chimere twisted the neck of the other until it snapped. Then they added their might to the Akkeidii and warded their flank. They were familiar with fighting next to Akkeidii Warriors.

The Urning continued its circuit and its cryptic chant. It turned a complicated motion with its jerrid. And the blood from the fallen Erebim crawled across the ground and offal to the ravenous pit.

The other Erebim on the ledge rushed the Akkeidii. They did not forget their weapons. The Erebim at the top of the stair poured down. A group of Tsurah, with their backs to the ledge, were pushed suddenly over. They fell hard but with their added arms they quickly turned to their feet and joined the fray.

Mandavu drifted to the base of the stair and slammed the first Erebim into the wall. Their momentum had brought them down right into the giant. He wielded the *montmorillionite* lightly as if it was a thin length of lead wood. But to the Erebim, it was a steel beam. Bones and armor crunched and cracked.

Kachota kept the Tsurah from his brother's back. The bulky Tsurah flailed their arms wildly and made themselves hard targets. But Kachota was quick.

Lokah's *montmorillionite* rang against the Erebim's lesser metal. When his blade lodged a partial way in a shield, the strong Erebim would try and rend or pry the weapon free or take a jab at the Akkeidii. Lokah pirouetted on the balls of his feet seemingly against momentum and gravity. At times he would feign and turn and other times he brought his full weight into the body of the fierce Erebim.

Aenguz gave cover to the Moresi while they pulled short swords and dull hammers from the fallen Erebim. Aenguz caught blades in the crook of his weapon and with a flick whipped them free. With his spike, he jabbed legs, faces, shields as if it was a darning needle. The sleek dagger at his hilt added a killing stroke to his withdrawals. There was no reset, only death blows with each move.

Erebim and Tsurah jumped down from the upper part of the stair. The Erebim were driven by the Urning. The Tsurah seemed to be escaping the growing calamity above. Aenguz glimpsed a brutish figure that was smaller than a Hyrrokkin but larger than any Akkeidii. Sandy pale arms, rough with crags, swung menacingly in the air and at the Tsurah. Dull eyes searched with an undirected anger. It turned its hump of a back and was gone as quick as it had appeared.

Space on the ledge was evaporating. The Moresi were making their way back onto the blocks Aenguz had crawled through minutes ago. Legerohn and Mond beat back the press. The uneven ground, littered with death, tripped up the Erebim.

Mandavu fought back in the broken pieces of amphora. A Tsurah had reached and grappled him with all four arms. His mace was pressed against his legs. Another added its arms to the first. They tried to slam their heads into Mandavu's head, but they only battered his chest and shoulder blades.

They were running out of space. The stair was unreachable. The asps in the pit were rising. Blood poured in from the dead. The Urning was exultant. His lappet writhed. The chant culminated.

Aenguz swung at the Erebim, but they kept their distance and waited for the courage of numbers. They stood on the bodies of the fallen and towered over the company.

They would soon be overwhelmed. The impossible, distorted journey was coming to an abrupt end. Morgrom had warned him that the Lands to the south of the Wester were lost. And now another Ruinwaster would find an opening from the Black Earth.

The fane atop the round pyramid seethed with cloud as if it flowed with a different wind. Moonlight silvered and solidified it until it was almost opaque. Only the flat top of the canyon behind it shown through.

Aenguz scanned through the Lay of *Montmorillionite* for an answer, a power that might help. But his blood and adrenaline would not allow the kind of focus he would need even if there was an answer in the metal.

The Erebim inched closer.

The pit was resplendent in unholy black.

There was an opening to the pit still. The Erebim did not crowd near to it. Fear or reverence kept them from the Urning's circuit.

Needs and exigencies compressed him. Inadequacies and failures stripped his self-worth away. Ignoble thoughts collided with overwrought responsibilities for the others.

When he spoke, it sounded like a command, but it was the only thought that distilled through.

"The Urning must be stopped."

Lokah was piqued. Death surrounded them. He was panting hard and splattered with blood. He responded to Aenguz, or his oath to Aenguz, or even the harsh commands of Drill Captains incused in him over years of training.

He bolted past Aenguz, racing and extended the ax-tip of his sword toward the floating incarnation of evil.

The Urning turned partway and held his bent scepter upright before him.

Lokah froze in a lunge.

The first inchoate tendrils of the Urning's might reached him. Volition started to cede. Strength began to forget purpose.

Before Aenguz lost himself, he tossed his blade to his left hand and then brought his *montmorillionite* down hard onto Lokah's sword.

A blast of argence erupted and dwarfed the light of the moon. The incandescent silver evaporated all shadow instantly. The green firelight was inconsequential. All eyes stared into the sun at once. The Erebim and Tsurah were blown over. Lokah and the others were tossed back like dry leaves.

The Urning was thrown back. The scepters disintegrated, became ash. The blast carried the Urning back over the pit. It lost its command of the air, its hold on the earth. The elemental pull of the Black Earth tore it down like a ravenous claw. Thin arms whipped in a spasm. Its body stretched as if it was being extruded through a straw. Then the Urning dropped into the whirling pool and out of existence in a blink. The pit peaked with a wave and then fell flat and hardened like a callous.

White fire erupted and exploded in a cataclysm. Earth and sky were replaced with a consuming arc of argent flame. Aenguz was suspended, cocooned in a sleeve of calm. His left arm sprouted electric shafts of light as if it was coated in millions of white gems. The rest of his body was effaced, unable to survive the eruption of light and power. But the arm acted as a kind of resistor. And the sentient metal that abhorred division or any fracturing of its oneness did not register malice or hate in Aenguz's stroke. The singular element possessed senses not easily gleaned. Part of the response was self-preservation. The metal's desire to cling to the form and the life with the Warrior for the brief moment in time above ground. Aenguz's communion and apotheosis with *montmorillionite* had exposed him to a connection that gave him some understanding, some measure of empathy.

He bore no hate toward Lokah. Was not planning a killing stroke. Lokah was paralyzed. He was not considering Aenguz as a threat at all. Only the Urning and Aenguz's call to stop it. Aenguz's mind was fraught with fealty and rescue. Connection and compassion for the company. Hope and an abject desperation of powerlessness against the Urning and Morgrom. His choices led him again to places where only forbidden options and impossible actions remained. But the Ichor of the Earth intuited him and the mettle of his heart and wounded soul. It stayed the fullness of its objection and channeled the brunt of it through the mitigating arm. Aenguz sensed the elemental sentience and awareness around him. And one more thing too, his purpose had not yet been fulfilled. *Montmorillionite* was not done with him.

The hurricane of bright power faded. The stars returned to their perches. His arm dulled and the encrusting gems disappeared. The mottled, milky gray barely covered the veins and arteries. Tendons stretched like thin dim shadows beneath the skin. His arm melded and mimicked the callous covering of the pit and the gruesome contours of Erebim dead and spilled blood. It connected him in a way to murder and desecration.

His *montmorillionite* was as clean as rarefied platinum. It might have been an illusion of light were he not holding onto it. As he oriented himself using the silent round shrine before him, he noted again how the blade pointed due west, toward Corundum.

The quiescence evaporated like the last light of day. The imperfect silence of the ledge replaced it. The shouts of battle above rolled over like a wave. Grunts and roars like rending stone fought against the fierce sibilance of Tsurah hunters.

Aenguz surveyed the mute pit. Had he stopped the Ruinwaster from coming free? There was no sign that he could discern. No black miasma on the translucent temple or among the unconscious Erebim. If it had somehow come free, he could not tell where it had gone.

Lokah lay on his back across slain Erebim. His weapon lay between them across shivered armor and severed limbs. Erebim blood was burned in splotches across the magic silver. Kachota was splayed over Mandavu. Even unconscious he protected his brother. He still clutched his axes. Mandavu was a twisted heap. Dismembered Tsurah had bled out beside him. But life was still in him. In all of them.

The Moresi were tucked into crevices in between the blocks. Chimere stirred but his eyes were closed. Legerohn and the others were intact. The metal had not snuffed out their lives.

Aenguz went to Lokah and uttered some healing couplets from the Lay. The Kriel opened his eyes and blinked as if Aenguz was still bathed in light. "By Grieg!" Questions formed in his throat, but amazement held them there as his mind worked to process what he had seen.

Aenguz did not know what Lokah might have seen in the blast. He had mirrored, in a different way, some of the experiences Aenguz had with *montmorillionite's* power. But Lokah's experiences were wholly unique and altering in their own way. Aenguz hoped there would be time one day to fully plumb their experiences and ask questions of one another and of the metal. He handed Lokah his weapon and said, "Let us get to the Rursh Keleg." He reached out a hand and pulled Lokah to his feet.

The chaos on the ledge above was growing louder. A limp Tsurah cartwheeled over the ledge. Stone crushed flesh. Exploding cinders and sprays of sparks were ubiquitous.

Lokah went to Mandavu and Kachota. Aenguz turned to the Moresi.

A cascade of burning logs forced him to step back. He nearly fell over the Erebim dead.

Then suddenly a massive boulder of rock, covered in Tsurah rolled over the edge past Lokah and over Aenguz. He only had time to close his eyes before the Hyrrokkon swallowed him.

Then they together pitched over the edge and down into the bottomless black.

A cascade of embers and burning logs toppled all around him. Explosions tore at the slope as the glowing debris hit the rock face. Sparks reached in between the slats and stung Aenguz.

The fane and the moon blinked in and out of sight trading places with an unfathomable black. The sounds of the fray above were lost in the fall.

The Tsurah that clung to the Hyrrokkin were crushed and flung free. A wet splintering sound and then dull slaps that disappeared into the ocean of night.

There were long dreadful moments of weightlessness, of dropping. Then crashes of stone on stone. They were spaces between the twin hells of the pit and the bottomless void.

Aenguz tumbled tightly in the Hyrrokkin's fist. Finally, one final blow blew him out like a candle.

34

THE GANZIR

The pain at his side jolted him awake. A year or an eon might have elapsed. His breaths brought a pain that wrenched and pierced. He could only draw the shallowest puffs.

The fist held him as gently and delicately as a babe. The fingers were pulled back like the petals of some prehistoric flower. Before stone and petal were separated.

"Wha-" his head throbbed, a pain to match the agony at his ribs.

The bloom of rocks wheezed. Desiccated plinks drizzled.

"What? What?" Aenguz groaned. He tried to roll to his side. The pain in his ribs prevented him.

Aenguz curled and worked to gather himself. Any movement was agony.

"I am grieved to not have preserved you whole. The height was too great. I-" the plinks trailed off.

Pieces came back. The summoning. The ledge. The Urning. The *trullen*.

The weak gravel came back. "Did you see the *trullen* Mashuan? They remembered themselves. They fought against the Tsurah of their own accord."

"Ochroch?"

He thought he recognized the particulars of the Hyrrokkin's voice. "Are you-? Can you rise? How damaged are you?" Aenguz winced. The words wrung out of him like a damp rag. "I have to get back," he had to pause. He was beading sweat. The pain was squeezing moisture out of him.

"I am afraid I-"

The two laid there. Embers smoldered and faded around them. Crushed Tsurah lay broken and dead on the rocks.

"Alas, we are not invulnerable. I am not." The plinks trailed off and the sand poured like the final grains from an hourglass.

"How do I help you?" Aenguz asked.

The sand trailed for a while. Then with a kind of breath.

"I think I will commune with the stones here. I can see that they have known deep water. Look here. I think I will listen to their song for a time."

Aenguz could not guess what Ochroch might mean.

'A time' might be an eon for the Hyrrokkin. Aenguz pulled at the rock and begged Ochroch to rise. Everyone he touched came to an end. He couldn't bear to let the Hyrrokkin fade or die. And his friends were up above in the midst of a war in the ruined city. He had to get up there.

"I cannot move right now. You must go," Ochroch breathed. "Follow the *wadi*."

"This canyon leads to the Ganzir. It is death for me. I cannot survive it."

"Ah fleshling, Mashuan. Would that you could hear the stone. It was so peaceful. And surrounded by placid life. Can you see it?"

"What?" he rasped. More riddles from the Hyrrokkin. "Ochroch, you must rise; I must get back up to my friends and the Rursh Keleg."

The shifting sand was hoarse.

"Follow the wadi. You will come to Tycho's Dune. You can follow it," the voice faded.

"I do not understand. I cannot go into the Ganzir. I am not made like the Hyrrokkin."

"The Tsurah will come. They are tenacious." Ochroch creaked out sandy breaths.

"May the Oasis of the Ganzir find you. Mayhap there is still a *wakeel* in the Ganzir."

"Ochroch, I do not know what you mean. I cannot go that way. Tell me another way. Do not go!"

The sand breaths slid down into the pool of darkness that lay around them.

Aenguz edged his way off the petals of stone. He tried to cradle his side but there was little relief.

He stared back up the abseil, but the ledge was out of sight. How far had they fallen? He wondered and worried about his companions. Had they escaped? Had they found a way out of the battle? What of the pit? Did the Urning finish its work before it was sucked into the abyss?

The questions were pointless. He was trapped at the bottom of the world. The part of him that was born in the mountains looked for ways to climb back up. It was so far above that he might as well have been contemplating how to climb up to the moon.

Detritus splashed down around him. Hints of the battle and confusion above. Sounds that might have been Tsurah echoed down into the deep ravine. He turned from the silent Hyrrokkin and climbed slowly down the wadi. The only way forward was to the Ganzir.

Aenguz slid on his backside down abseils in the dark. At times, he pitched forward onto all fours, and jolts of pain roared through his battered side. He fought back gasps and groans, but the echoes multiplied in the crevasse.

The dawn was slow to come. The moon appeared here and there as he wended down the narrow ravine. The sky lightened but the shadows were persistent. And they did not stop the heat.

Before midday, a warning thrummed in his weapon. He couldn't be sure if it was warning him about what was before him or what was behind. But he couldn't go back.

The ravine widened. Pockets of spiny brown grasses and thin-leaved trees clung to the dry sand and silt.

Then a stone whizzed by his head and skitted into the trees.

A party of Tsurah slung rocks at him. The heavy arms held a sling. The tiny arms set a stone in the pouch. And then with a snap, both arms stretched taut sending the stone out in a shot.

Aenguz turned and ran into the trees grimacing at the pain at his side.

A stone caught him in the back and knocked him over. Stones cut through the trees, glanced off bark.

Soon the floor of the wadi was covered in a fine white sand. It slowed him. His feet dragged. His cracked ribs screamed with every breath.

Soon the feet of the trees were covered. He slogged on as stones whizzed by and nearly felled him.

The sand carried him up as it swallowed the trees.

He rose up until he was even with the boughs around him. He broke out of the shade and came to a wall of sand.

It consumed the trees whole on either side. The arms of the canyon were overwhelmed by the parched white wave.

Stones blasted the sand around him.

Aenguz ran up the wall of the dune. The trees dropped away and the sunbaked him as if he were climbing the steps to the temple of the sun.

The Tsurah pumped their thin legs through the fine sand. But their progress was slow.

Aenguz strained against heat and pain and exhaustion.

He glimpsed back. The Tsurah were caught in a slow-motion chase up the wall of white sand. But all four arms helped them in their climb. A pair of Tsurah ran atop the plateau at the edge of the canyon and jumped onto the sand. They raced toward him.

The crest started to level; he strained the final distance to the top.

And there before him was the baked and desolate expanse of the Ganzir. The ground was a parched wound. The heat was an escaping air from a furnace.

The Dune of Tycho stretched to his left and right as far as he could see. It swallowed the arms of the flat-topped canyons. The devastating wind was blowing up off the Ganzir and across the dune, inching it eastward on a path of inexorable ruination.

The Tsurah on the crest were closing in on him. He could hear those behind him.

He was caught between two deaths. He might be able to fend off one or two of the Tsurah. But with their slings, he might not get close enough.

He ducked as one of them let a stone fly with a crack of leather.

Then with only half a thought, he turned down the westward slope and took off into a full run down the dune and entered the Ganzir. The pain at his side tore at him.

He varied his path as he ran. His feet sank into the sand and tried to swallow him like the canyons and the trees.

The heat coming off the Ganzir was an open furnace.

He ran until the dune leveled onto the hard-packed desert floor.

He sprinted as stones came now in a desperate flurry. Turning and zagging rent his side. One glanced off his head. He stumbled forward onto the hot floor of the Ganzir.

He looked back but the Tsurah came no further. He climbed to his feet as they let their final stones fly. They stood as if they had come to a wall. Something in their stance looked like surrender or defeat. Their child's arms drooped dejectedly.

Aenguz hobbled forward until the wary Tsurah were too small to make out on top of Tycho's Dune.

Aenguz turned north to make his way out from under the ruinous heat. But with no markers in the distance, he wandered into the waste.

Smaller dunes of baked dust and sand rose up like schools of humpbacks out of the cracked plain. He didn't have the strength to climb them. His eyes melted the landscape. The ground shimmered and diffused. In the distance, he made out a small bleached white building. Little more than a shed. It disappeared amid the shimmer and the blaze.

Acute thirst and hollowing hunger struck notes in him that measured the time to his death. He understood that he was going to die here. His sunbaked bones would join the dust of the dunes.

His lips cracked and his blood was thick like sap. His blistered skin tried to ooze fluids he could ill afford to lose. His throat scratched and scraped. The Ganzir was slowly choking him.

He scanned the horizon for a direction to turn but the world had become the desert. Aenguz held the daggered end just above the hard pack and pressed it in. He stilled his mind and called his focus. He cupped his ear around the spike and with parched words uttered some Words of Lore.

"In the midst of the desert's plight
Healing water, creation's might.

Far above earth, and far below
Rain wells rise down life giving flow"

A few more couplets sputtered out like fine powder. The sky was barren. Reservoirs were too distant or deep to matter. No springs or wells or arroyos hearkened to the call of metal and lore. Only the memory of water in the past. Perhaps the Mashu or the Wester but it could easily be from before his birth. And in the future, again perhaps a distant future, still water. Impossibly still. But in this moment, *montmorillionite* held no answer for Aenguz's thirst.

His weapon did provide heat when the sun did finally set. The desert grew impossibly cold. Aenguz pulled sand over his legs to stay warm and coaxed heat from the metal for comfort. But sleep was elusive. It was not so different from after his accident at the forge. The disconnectedness of thought. The lucid logic that warped the world. At least the Moresi saying was only a myth. The sun did set here.

The next day, in his sun-blasted delirium, he began to understand that his charge had come to an end. Legerohn had been explicit about avoiding the desert. Aenguz saw the fear in the Prince's eyes. Morgrom had called out the Ganzir too. *"Hear me, when Tycho Ruinwaster is found...the Ganzir...will seem like a garden."*

Deviating from the course, albeit indirectly meant his death. There was only a thin line to follow to avoid failure and death. Any help that the Counsel Lords could provide would have to come from the others. If they got free of the city and stayed on the old road they should be saved, if they encountered no other obstacle.

He saw the white windowless building again. His mind labored wondering what hovel might exist out here. He half-believed that it was a delusion. But it appeared real. Wedges of shadow punctuated the corners. It couldn't be the same building although it looked to be the same. A domed roof and four short arms like a cross beneath. All he thought was the prospect of shade. Except it led further into the desert. If it was real, it might at least provide some respite. But deeper down he understood it was a place to die. A place that might mark the spot where he fell. A kind of cairn so that he would not be utterly forgotten in all the Lands of the Earth.

If it vanished again as it had before, the Ganzir would take him.

With the last drabs of his strength, he staggered to the squat white structure. He must be hallucinating. The building seemed to drift on the shimmer just above the earth. He might have abandoned this last effort if he was more whole. The vision teased and taunted him.

Then, of a sudden, he seemed to cross the distance to it in a few strides. Aenguz was delirious.

He reached out with his cracked and burned hands to touch the bleached white stucco. Four short arms, like a cross, supported a simple dome. Not only were there no windows but no doors. It was some kind of Ebenezer or memorial. It was a foolish hope. Nothing would or could live out here.

He found the one corner where a wedge of shade started to grow. But not fast enough. The desert air burned his lungs, scoured his throat. He set his weapon against the wall and sat down, ready for the Ganzir to take him.

"I am sorry your time was so short," he uttered to his *montmorillionite.* "I had hoped for so much more for both of us." He thought for a minute that the metal was already wavering, already surrendering its shape. "May your journey to the source be swift."

He wanted to touch it one last time.

The weapon pulled away and fell into the corner.

Fell beyond it.

His delirium teased his eyes. He blinked out the dust and last of the moisture.

The corner of the stucco blended seamlessly with the wall deeper in.

He turned his head and saw the slightest discrepancy between the contours of both walls.

Aenguz fell to his side. His ribs screamed. He climbed over his weapon. He inched forward to test the depth. He touched the wall. A deeper wall.

To his left was shade, glorious shade.

He dragged himself to relief and pulled his weapon after him. His legs were stubborn.

The narrow opening was longer than the wing of the building. Surely his addled mind was mistaken.

The air was cooler than the Ganzir. Still warm but far better than the pitiless heat of the unfettered desert.

Perhaps this was a mid-road to the White Earth. It didn't make sense. The corridor turned at a right angle that should have taken him outside the borders of the monument. There was no logic in the design. But that's how the transition was right? It couldn't make sense to the still living.

The parched wind was replaced with a steady gurgle. Another turn, which should have put him yards outside the structure but instead it led him to cobble. Aenguz pulled his head up with a final effort and saw *green*.

He must be close now to the White Earth. He collapsed on the cobbled courtyard. He lost touch with his weapon. A final farewell.

35

FREEHOLDER

Sensations were discordant. Weathered knuckles brushed his lips, stroked the hair on his face. A timorous female voice uttered questions, exclamations. Her face was sun-browned and lined with creases like tree rings. Her hair was the color of old iron. It was pulled back into a comfortable ponytail. Green eyes looked like brilliant moss in a quiet patch of forest.

He was lifted up. Shouldered like a sack of potatoes. His feet dragged across stone, dragged up stairs. *Stairs?*

When she let him go, he flopped onto a soft bed.

Then there was mineral-rich water at his lips. Then the sweet juice from a berry. 'A treasure berry,' she had said. Or he thought that's what she said.

Sleep fell like a hammer. It felt as absolute as death. What would waking into the White Earth be like?

GOSSAMER RODE THE BREEZE. Teak shutters countered the white walls. The sharp tips of palms tickled the blue outside. A long shaft of sunlight cut against the door by the window.

How long had he slept? Where was he? What time is it?

The orange light faded to pink while torpid thoughts and questions slogged through him.

There was a bandage on his head. His chest was wrapped too. Exhausted, Aenguz was ready to dip back into sleep. Ready for night and more rest.

The ambient light shifted. The glow changed.

A new shaft of light cut a shape on the wall. Dawn was growing. The day was brightening.

He could not trust his mind. Dreams or some other state had him.

He relaxed into exhaustion and away from the disorientation. Sleep was the only truth. The only necessity.

Aenguz leaned into the teak rail outside his room. A lush garden crowded at the center of the square courtyard. A grotto at the heart of it gushed water. Natural basins overflowed and poured into others. The laden trees and bushes drank it up. All manner of fruits and berries piqued the green. Many he didn't recognize. Others he knew the taste of instinctively, had tasted recently.

A woman emerged from the garden with a sturdy wagon brimming with fruit and squash. She drew the wagon through an archway out of sight.

She was familiar and foreign all at once.

"How are you today?" she asked at Aenguz's side.

He nearly jumped out of his skin. "How? What?" His heart skipped out of his chest. His grip on the rail kept him from tumbling.

"Wait? Where am I? Who are you?"

Then the disjointed vagaries of a dream started to drop, and the sure-footedness of reality made the dream world odd. Sense and the fantastic collided. His grip on the rail was not enough. Sleep rather than waking overruled.

———◆———

A SONG CAME TO him.

> *"Chosen, responsible, unfettered, free,*
> *Preserve the treasures of the lost Earth*
> *Against foes and woe and lost belief,*
> *Halt the damage, halt the dearth*
>
> *Freely hold the chosen charge*
> *Till time and healing gain*
> *Alone, wakeel, warden writ large*
> *Tender, warder, protector same."*

———◆———

THERE WAS NO NIGHT. No stars. No moon. Night never fell here.

The sun barely set. It cast long shafts of light across the compound and then rose again in another quarter. New shafts. New shadows. Seasons of a sort ebbed and flowed like waters in a tidal pool. But it seemed normal. As normal as the natural order he had known, had learned.

Planting and harvesting overlapped with nurturing and tending. Seeds were gathered and stored.

Meals were as abundant as on any festival day every day. And the diet was as simple as an ascetic's.

Mere Gurudev moved with impossible celerity. This too seemed only vaguely strange now. It had become familiar.

Aenguz was used to seeing her seemingly in two places at once. She was always present at a call. Digging, planting, pruning, tying off vines was laborious work. But whenever there was a question, Mere Gurudev was there.

Pollinating and knowing when to harvest took understanding. When a question arose, he wasn't even sure he had uttered it. Then she was there. Her apron was a mash of runes in mud and hand-print splotches.

"Are these ripe? What do I do here?"

"Ah, yes. Seed to Life. These need more time but this one here," she stepped to the next tree where the yellow flowers called out to be pollinated. She rooted around in her apron for a thin pointed dowel.

She gestured Aenguz in closer. Her skin looked like worn leather.

She bent the pistol around the dowel and stripped the pollen back. "See there," her voice creaked like it might shatter. "Here. Now you try."

Aenguz took the dowel and focused on the next flower. As he bent the pistol around the dowel, he studied his mottled purple fingers. The veins worked under the translucent skin.

"Good. You have it. Now do that with all the flowers you find. The beans on these trees are not ready yet. Perhaps in a day or two."

A nameless consternation sprouted in his mind.

"Wait. What am I doing here? Where am I? I- I-" he trailed off and stepped back from the tree.

Mere turned and stared dead into Aenguz's eyes. Her green orbs belying spring life and hale leaves.

"You have a grave and great purpose. Your venture is not done. My purpose will draw to an end when yours succeeds. Seed to Life."

Aenguz pulled back as the illogic of his whereabouts deconstructed the dream-like impressions. A branch brushed his side at the place where a bandage had been. Where were the bandages? Why had he needed a bandage? How had he been hurt?

The fall. Ochroch.

Sudden as a snap, instead of waking, he was out.

THE OASIS OF THE Ganzir was a maze. The compound was a collection of different courtyards, chambers, rooms, gardens, and orchards. Stairs led up to tiers of crenellated walls.

Following Mere Gurudev around the Oasis was difficult. After turning a corner and climbing a stair she would be ten, thirty, fifty paces ahead. Half the time the effort was just finding where she was next.

"Come Venturer!" she called with a rickety wave pulling him forward.

Free-standing bell towers, their clappers gone, were here and there. She pointed out past the bell frame. Five bells hung inside. Aenguz knew they had no clappers. Had not rung, would not ring. He did not know how he knew that. He just knew. He had seen them during his many chores and errands in the Oasis.

"What is this Oasis? Below it is little more than a formed white stucco rock. Here it is vast," he swept his arm back to the Oasis. "And the sun. Where is the night?"

"The Oasis resides in a place between. Neither on the Earth nor out of it. It is but a sliver of what this land once was. One of the last acts of the Azari before the Ruinwasters came. Before the call to preserve.

"It was a green land. The trees were happy. So were the birds. There were more lakes than could be counted." Mere Gurudev waved her hand over the barren expanse beyond the walls of the monastic fortress. The Ganzir scorched the ground as far as he could see.

She listed off different landmarks. The names of which she rattled off with ease. Valleys with strange names and rivers with melodic titles. Soft prairies filled with flowers where she roamed as a girl. She counted off those too one after the other and after the other until melancholy took her voice.

Even amid the parched vista of the Ganzir the horizon pulsed and changed. The Oasis turned and faced north and west, east, and south. It moved and drifted in a gyre above the waste like a leaf on a lazy wind.

"We could not defend against Tycho Ruinwaster. Lord Morgrom commanded our ruin and set his servant against our Lands. His hunger for control over the course of creation was- is boundless. Even with all his eyes, there is much he cannot see." She sounded bereft.

"Our last gift, the One Sight, a remnant benefice of the One Race. All the Azari shared all they saw. At one time he participated in that gift. He saw everything we saw." She sighed as ancient memory flooded her. "But he was craven. Sought only his own gain. His own need for power and mastery. He craved our secrets such as they were. We withdrew from him. In time, in his abjection, he sent Tycho forth. The Last Battle had already begun."

Like the Hyrrokkin or the Sho-tah, Aenguz thought.

———— ◆ ————

"Now I preserve what I may and harvest the seeds. Here they are all hale. Here they all hold life."

What would the Earth look like without the blight of dead seeds? Aenguz wondered. Without the dead and blank spaces here and there amid the Earth. The picture wobbled him. But his mind was still set on the Ruinwasters.

"Are all the Ruinwasters like Tycho?"

"No, they hold different manifestations, different purposes, and powers. What you have witnessed in the summoning bodes ill for the Earth and the course of creation if it is true. Ultimately, Obilivion destroys so that he might shape the face of the earth and everything in it according to his desires, his will. And he would have all things serve him."

"How do I know which Ruinwasters have been released? And how many?"

"If Tycho was freed the Earth would already be in ruin. The Oases would be razed.

"They dwell in a maze within the precinct of the Black Earth. Who can say what theurgy the Urnings use to draw them forth? Mayhap they cannot choose which one they call but rather cast their missive into the abyss. Or something holds him or restrains him. Prevents his escape. Who can say?

"Shivic leads Oblivion's armies. He cannot move about the Lands of the Earth himself as he is, at least not yet. The Venturer saw to that. Shivic gives his minions a general and a tactician. Shivic will require a form to inhabit.

"They are all just spirits of malice and woe. Mezekiah's power is more subtle. His work breaks the walls between worlds. The separations between the White and the Black would be eradicated were he freed to work his ill. He may also facilitate the release of others in kind. A free and open portal to the Earth."

"What of the other two?" Aenguz could only guess which Ruinwasters might be free. He could only hope that the last Urning had failed. That his stroke against Lokah's blade had worked. But there could be others out there. How long had he been at the Oasis?

"Ah, two are brothers, twins of a sort. Arkarua and Ophiactii. These are murderers, traitors, and possessors. They inhabit other creatures as well but seek to hide. They sow dissent and mistrust. These two were the First Emissaries. When they are separated, they are at their weakest but still deadly. Always they seek to be together. They seek to mock Oneness with a simulacrum of joining. But like their master, they have trouble seeing clearly. Especially one another. When they meet and join, they are almost as powerful as Tycho."

"How do I know which ones are freed?"

"Only the Earth knows. Their coming presages the Earth's doom."

———— ◆ ————

HE STROLLED THROUGH A groomed vineyard. The vines were plump with dark berries.

The thought of the One Bridge and the fane at the second summoning came to him.

"Why do they perform those rituals by the One Bridge and the stair by the City of the Sho-tah?"

"Ah, the *verrandulum*. The constructions of the One Race. Before Morgrom revealed his evil, the *verrandulum* were portals to travel across the Earth. Perhaps even further. Vast distances could be crossed in an instant. Often, they were built with other structures like the One Bridge and the World Stair so that all could reach them. During the Last Battle, they were obliterated, mostly. Some were too strong to be completely destroyed. Only the full moon sees them now. The Dagba Stone enabled their ruin."

Clouds gathered on Mere's brow. The bright sky dimmed. "The *verradulum* cannot fall into the service of Oblivion. All that I have striven to preserve here would be lost. Seed to Life. And even more than that. The portals under command of the Ruinwasters could lead to the threshold of the White Earth. Morgrom could undo the universe. Destruction and desecration would supplant creation and life forever."

———— • ————

THE COURTYARD WAS LINED with workbenches. They were in various states as if a dozen planting projects were left midstream. Pots and amphora were stacked and piled everywhere. Gardening implements were strewn about.

The ground was covered with dirt and leaves, the detritus of pruning. Mounds of soil spilled over here and there.

At the center was a long teak table, big enough for twenty people. A score of benches were lined around it. A banquet of fruits and vegetables and various herbed flat breads and leavened breads filled the table. Crocks of rich brown stew were here and there. There was enough food laid out for fifty people.

Overhead the sun blazed but its heat was akin to a pleasant summer day. The Ganzir could not reach this place. The Oasis was elevated, removed.

Mere tore pieces of bread from a small loaf and ate from a small cluster of treasure berries.

Aenguz ate as if it was the first food he had eaten since coming to the Oasis. He washed down mouthfuls with the mineral-rich spring water.

At once, this felt like the first meal and his last. Such was the dream-like feeling of the place. His bandages were gone. His ribs held only a dull ache. The scars on his head had closed over. Memories of old wounds, old hurts were distant.

"I have to go," Aenguz said finally. But he did not want to disappoint Mere.

"Why do you think we are celebrating?"

As always, the assumed logic of the Oasis turned things on their ear. Aenguz was reconciled to his task to deliver the message. And he had resolved, as if he had always known, to find the Stone. His despondency was for his friends. He had led them right into the teeth of danger. He would finish his task for them as much as for the Lands of the Earth. Already he had spent too much time here. Each lost day brought Morgrom's designs closer to fruition. How many Ruinwasters were free?

——— ◆ ———

"I WAS CHOSEN FOR this task."

"Were you?"

He recognized her tone. There was something she was seeing that he wasn't.

"Do you understand the riddle of choice?"

He was beginning to slip. On the edges of his mind logic from the waking world began to impinge on his thoughts.

He shook his head careful to not drop completely out of consciousness.

"There are two parties in such a matter, not just one. You alone cannot be chosen for something."

His lips pursed. His eyebrows crunched.

"You must choose the thing that chose you."

But he had done that. Had accepted the Morgrom's charge on the banks of the Wester.

"I have accepted my charge as the Last Emissary. I will even search for the Dagba Stone if I am able."

"You were a choice of convenience. But you were chosen before that. Have you accepted that?"

The vision caused by *morillion* of all *montmorillionite*. The metal was not done with him yet. What did the sentient metal choose him for? What would it mean for him to accept? What might it mean for his life?

Mere raised her eyes. A wry smile creased her cheeks. She spooned more vegetable stew and considered the unfinished work around her. Then she continued. "There is of course a sacrifice for accepting what you are chosen for." She looked up into the bright blue. "I miss the stars, the night sky, the moon. Rest. The eyes of my people. These old bones..."

Aenguz was lost to unconsciousness.

———— ◆ ————

MERE SLUNG ANOTHER PACK on Aenguz. It reminded him of the packs that Jorgen slung on him before the Challenge. A pair of waterskins, and another. There was enough food and water to carry him all the way back to the Mashu. But he couldn't refuse her any more than he could refuse his grandmother.

He was in a smaller courtyard. An archway lay behind and a crease in the stucco was the only other feature.

"Thank you. This is more than enough."

"Remember to save the seeds. There are more in there." She patted one of the satchels. "Bear them to Corundum. These will aid against Oblivion's blight. Seed to Life."

Aenguz nodded. His strength had returned. When he arrived, his old poncho was enough to bring him down.

Now he had light clothes made of a soft white fabric. His boots had been mended and cleaned to almost new.

Finally, his mind turned to his weapon.

She seemed to know his thoughts. "Here." She laid her hand on a scabbard. "This was left from another of your people." The leather was black with half a dozen bands of silver. At the top, a different leather was stitched on. Aenguz flipped it up to see the crook and spike of his perfect weapon. *Who was she talking about? Whose was this?* But he kept his questions at bay. This was a farewell, and he didn't want to suddenly be lost to dreams and sleep.

"Thank you for helping me."

She brushed away his thanks and continued readying him as if he was running late. She took up a loosely knitted shawl of white gossamer like a bolt of Spanish moss. She flung it up over his head in a sweep and adjusted it like a doting mother.

"This will help protect you from the heat." She also handed him some light white gloves from a pocket in her apron. "These will help protect your hands.

"Now, the Oasis has moved to the north and the west. Go out here and head due north. Keep the Spine of the Earth to your left but do not walk toward it. The dividing line between the Upper and Lower Lands is still too far. Make for the mountains to the north that border the Rursh Keleg. They are closer. Then find the road and your journey to Corundum will be nearly complete." She tugged on his arm and led him to the opening.

"Seed to Life, Sidor Venturer. Save what must be saved."

She waved off his final thanks as if she was brushing away gnats.

Then he stepped into the crease between the walls. The narrow corridor bent around like a convoluted wardrobe. The ill-logic of the turns twisted Aenguz around and crossed back on themselves. He disregarded his need to unravel, to call out the contortion. His desire to impose logic on the Oasis only led to unconsciousness.

The air in the dark space transformed. The heat of the Ganzir asserted itself and permeated the cool shade. Blistering light and heat scorched the white stucco walls of the windowless structure.

PART IV
RESISTANCE

36

~~~

STRANGERS

The shimmering furnace punished the earth. Aenguz shielded his eyes as he sought his bearings. The flat-topped canyons were nowhere to be seen to his right. To his left, the Spine dominated the horizon. The peaks looked sharp enough to sever the sky from the earth. They set a barrier that seemed to mark the edge of the world. Their size made them appear close. But he was not deceived by that. Life in the Mashu had taught him as much. Mere had said to go north. Ahead of him, a line of low squat mountains ran out of the east to the base of the Spine to his left. They seemed small by comparison and passable. He turned back but the stucco marker was gone. Cast to some further corner of the ruin wastes. It left a parting disorientation in him. If his meager understanding of the Lands of the Earth was sound, the Oasis had transported him days across the Ganzir. How long had he been in the Oasis?

Beyond the low mountains ahead, northward, lay the Rursh Keleg. The old road to Corundum and the end of his long journey. Once he delivered the message, he could then return home to the Mashu.

Heat radiated up through his boots. Mere's gossamer soaked up the sun's rays and made the desert's piercing heat bearable. Hints of the Oasis's verdant air clung to his light clothing and the shawl. The packs shaded his legs.

Logic and reason reasserted themselves slowly as the mountains ahead grew. The desert gave no hint as to the season. His ribs had been broken. But now they were healed. And the bruises and hurts from the Tsurah stones were old scars now. How long had he been with Mere? How much time had elapsed? What would he find when he got clear of the Ganzir? Summer? Fall? Or winter? Had midyear come and gone? Perhaps she had hurried him on his way because midyear had already passed. Would it even matter for the Counsel Lords to find the Dagba Stone before Morgrom's threats came to pass?

Rhythmic markings emerged in the hard pack. They seemed to mark an old path through the mountains. It led the final distance into a wide fold between the mountains. An arroyo opened in the desert alongside it.

The sun drifted to the west. Its course was familiar, appropriate. Dusk and night would come. The certainty of that was more comforting than the Mashu hearkening peaks of the Spine. He was in the world again, but for how long would the world as he knew it remain?

His thoughts went to his companions as the worst of the Ganzir's heat faded. The shawl clung to him tightly and kept him cool as shadow filled the pass. He had walked them right into the teeth of the Tsurah and their battle with the Hyrrokkin. He tried to imagine them fighting their way free from the City of the Sho-tah. But the fray above the ledge was brutal. And there were the *trullen*. They would not know them like the Hyrrokkin did.

The charge to deliver the message and prevent the Lands' destruction drove him. Mere's words implored him and gave new meaning to the charge. They made him more than simply the Last Emissary. She had called him Sidor Venturer. She had drawn a line between *montmorillionite* and himself that he had overlooked. His purpose had taken a different shape because of her. But it was for the honor and memory of his friends that impelled him the final distance to Corundum. Their sacrifices would not be in vain. He would honor them by completing the task.

Once he delivered the message, before returning home, he would journey to Inverlieth and tell the Moresi there about Legerohn's company. About Mond, Chimere, Stokke and the rest. The brave and grateful Moresi who fought so hard for their freedom side by side with the Akkeidii. And who kept faith with their promise to save the One Forest by helping him deliver the message. He would produce the *mithrite* chain and affirm the bond between the two peoples. Legerohn's ring was lost, however. Aenguz would describe it and affirm it as well.

He would then go to Straathgard and relay what had befallen Leono and the other fishermen. How they had suffered and survived the cruelty of the Sallow. How they had fought and saved his life. He would relay their final days to their families and their people.

Then he could return home to the Mashu. Who knew what he might find there? *Were the Akkeidii at war like Lokah had surmised? Were Akkeidii scouts abroad in the Lands of the Earth still looking for them? Was his grandfather able to maintain control while Aenguz was away? How was his grandmother? Were the Akkeidii waiting? Had they chosen a new leader? Was Selene still unbetrothed?* Still waiting? He had promised her he would return. And once this task was complete, he would return to her. At least Grieg's Gate would keep the Flayer's hordes from the Hearth Valleys in the Upper Mashu if they even dared to come on the Mashu again.

Aenguz stopped and checked his pockets. Thoughts of Selene and the Moresi made him check for the ribbon and the chain. He dug for a moment in the unfamiliar pocket but then, there it was. The ribbon and the chain were knotted together in a ball. A promise and an oath intertwined. He put them back and resolved to untangle them later.

The Spine cut off the sun as he walked the last distance down out of the mountains to the Wester river valley and the Rursh Keleg. It was so different from the southern branch he had left weeks ago.

The old highway and the sickly Wester were apt companions for one another. The road was in disrepair. It ran like an ancient, sand-colored snake. It hugged the line of mountains like a dry river. Stubborn scrub and nascent trees ruptured the weakened cobble. A border wall that might have warded against a forgotten shore was broken more than intact. Rubble from the mountains piled and scattered everywhere. The slight wind halted for a moment and seemed surprised at Aenguz's presence.

The Wester did not glint or smile. Silt yellowed the water. The two lines in the valley seemed to mimic one another, intertwinig in a way between their two natures. Between the river and the road, there was a wilderland of scrabble and rock. It was barren and looked like a swath of blight between the two. Their withered paths were contrary and parallel. The river issued from the base of the sharp Spine eastward. And the Rursh Keleg led to it. The contortion and strain between them were written on the Earth like a living scar.

The fading light still brightened the dome of the sky when Aenguz reached the road. He found an alcove. A kind of way stop or camp. Square stones ringed a fire pit. He unshouldered all of his packs and skins from Mere wondering again why she had given him so much. Corundum was less than a day away. He set his scabbard down against the stone and admired the craftsmanship. It was a princely gift.

He searched the road for some wood and started a fire in the scarred pit with Words of Lore. He returned his weapon to the scabbard and admired the silver bands. They were engraved with fine patterns. He walked across the road to a still standing length of the wall and looked out at the Wester, the further shore, and the Spine.

Suddenly, "Ho traveler! From where do you hail?"

The voice startled him. He nearly lost his footing when he spun.

He cursed at his carelessness. His weapon rested by the fire. The solitude of the Rursh Keleg and the desolation of the Wester gave him the impression that he was alone in the Earth.

"Show yourself." He stepped to the middle of the road cutting the distance between himself and his *montmorillionite*.

The voice came from the east. Aenguz couldn't see anyone.

"Hold! Are you from Corundum?" the voice asked.

Whatever he was, he wasn't an Erebim or a Tsurah.

"I am not from Corundum. But I travel there with heavy purpose."

Silence. The voice waited.

Aenguz continued. "My home is in the Mashu. I am Akkeidii," Aenguz called back as if he was answering to his own past.

After a pause, the voice may have whispered to someone else.

"What Hearth Valley do you hail from?"

"I am a Sidor and that is my Hearth Valley." The mountains warped the voice, echoed it off toward the Wester in a broken wave.

"Who is the Sidor Clan Lord?"

"What is this? Show yourself!" The question stung him, more than he expected. Aenguz's past clawed at him, reminded him of his dead father. But this person, if they knew of the Akkeidii, they would know of Sairik. *Was this an Akkeidii Ranger? Had they come this far?*

The voice waited.

"Sairik is the Lord of the Sidor Clan," his throat failed him, and he gulped before continuing. "Lord of the Akkeidii. Ruler of the Two Lands. Polemarch of the Warriors."

More silence and whispering. "Stranger. Who are you?"

There was a pang of grief mixed with a rush of anger. His weapon drew him back. He wanted to get *montmorillionite* in his hands. He stepped back toward his camp.

"Hold your place, Stranger! You prove yourself false."

Who were these people? Aenguz chastised himself again for letting his
guard down. This conversation would be much different if he had his blade.
And if these were rangers, this would all be over in a moment.

"I am Aenguz, son of Sairik, who was the Lord of the Akkeidii.
Challenged Champion of the Sidors."

"Give up your lies, stranger. Our lord is dead. Choose your next words
carefully. We know that evil is abroad in the Lands of the Earth."

Our?

"Who are you? I have answered you. Now show yourself."

There seemed to be confusion behind the voice. The sun had changed
the dusk by subtle degrees. The stones of the disused road held still as if
they feared what might come next.

The voice called out, "Remove your gloves."

He pulled off his gloves. He held his hands up. Then with a realization
that bordered on hope, he pushed up his left sleeve.

"Grieg's Balls!" From around the rock, Kachota appeared. "Can it be
you?" The Makan held his twin tomahawks. They looked like they might
drop at any moment. The dust of the Rursh Keleg covered him. His face
was powdered with it. He was so decimated, he looked like a denizen of
the ruin wastes.

Lokah stepped out from behind him. The Kriel was gaunt. The canvas
tunic barely hung to him. Old wounds and dried blood marked him like
a disease. His sword seemed ponderous in his hand. The realization of
Aenguz being alive couldn't reach through the veil of hard travel.

"How can it be you?" he breathed. Disbelief radiated from him.

Aenguz crossed the distance to them in a state of shock. Their privation
horrified him. But their presence welled his heart so much that he thought
he might burst. He had assumed them all dead.

Legerohn and Mond came out next. Their eyes were dry wells. They
held an admixture of consternation and disbelief. They might have been

looking at a miracle. Legerohn was drawn. The Moresi leader appeared to be at the end of his strength.

Chimere leaned on Stokke. The younger Moresi helped him forward. Both were ashen. They all looked like they hadn't eaten in days, weeks even. The vestiges of their innocence had been stripped away from them. They were Moresi warriors now, tempered by their hard labors.

Mandavu stepped out last. He leaned on his mace like a walking stick. The giant was diminished. Only a strip of canvas hung around his neck. His ribs pressed against his skin. His familiar anger was tamped with disbelief. Wear and disconsolation colored his whole affect. He stared hard at Aenguz as if he had given up on trusting his eyes. His companions looked two steps away from death. Hope seemed lost to them.

They came together but were too unsure to embrace. Aenguz ached to hold them, confirm that they were not a dream. He thought he might break them. Also, their eyes confirmed to him that he was too strange to them, too altered.

"What is in your hair? How are you here?" Lokah asked. He continued to affirm his hope.

Aenguz brushed at the gift from Mere Gurudev. "Protection against the sun. I came through the Ganzir."

"You were in the Ganzir? How could you survive?" Legerohn asked. His incredulity was echoed by them all. Heads nodded limply at Legerohn's question.

"I came upon the Oasis of Ganzir."

"The Oasis is a myth." Legerohn began to wonder at Aenguz.

"Well, it rides above the Ganzir."

Questions and multiplying consternations stalled their tongues.

"Come. There will be time enough for the tale. I have food and water. Enough for all of you." He motioned them back to the camp. "And Corundum is near."

Aenguz led them back to the alcove like an anxious child. He raised and passed out sacks of food and waterskins to the beleaguered company. He gestured for them to eat, pleased at all the provender he had for them. *Had Mere known?* His gesture was an abundant approximation of the Akkeidii pre-meal tradition.

Their thirst and hunger overrode their uncertainty. After a drink and a few bites, they dove in like the famished company they were.

There was enough water for them to wash the Rursh Keleg from their faces. Their hollow cheeks and corded necks rent his heart.

"Mind your seeds. Make sure to save them, all of them. We must bear them to Corundum."

Lokah spit seeds into his hand and pocketed them while giving Aenguz a sidelong glance.

Mandavu studied Aenguz as he ate. "I saw you; we saw you crushed by the living rock. How did you survive?"

"I was not crushed. I was caught. Well, I was caught before and then caught a second time by the Hyrrokkin."

Confusion and concern rippled through the Moresi and the Akkeidii. Had the heat of the Ganzir done something to him?

"I cannot believe my eyes," Mond said. "It is you and it is not you."

"How did you live? You were crushed. How did you survive the fall and the desert beyond?" Legerohn interjected. "You look rested and refreshed. You look clean. Your clothes..."

"The Hyrrokkin saved me. Twice."

Kachota whispered something to Mandavu about the stability of Aenguz's sanity.

Aenguz ignored him and pretended not to hear. The Makan's suspicion was so welcome again.

But Aenguz's answers only served to confuse them. He took in their concern and thought how best to explain his unexpected detours.

As they continued to eat, he told them how he had come upon Ochroch in the ruined city. How he had saved the Saiga from the Tsurah. He told them about his interrogation and their curse. He described the Hyrrokkin march through the city. They knew about the ritual, but he could not say if it was successful. He described the fall into the gorge and how Ochroch had died or rather communed with the stone. He told them about how the Tsurah chased him. And about the Ruinwaster dune that marked the border of the Ganzir. Then he told them about how the desert almost took him. How he was sure he was going to die. But then he recounted how the building turned into the Oasis.

He watched their faces return to confusion and concern as he recounted the disjointed memories of the Oasis. The size of the compound. Its flittering course across the Ganzir. The absence of night. And Mere Gurudev. He couldn't make sense of his time there. How could he make it make sense for them? They looked back and forth to one another as if Aenguz had become a stranger again. But his clothes and the food and the water seemed to validate his story. And his excited, amber flecked eyes and enthusiastic curiosity suited him, seemed appropriate. The distance between their different states created the biggest disconnect in their fragile belief. It was Aenguz but he was altered somehow.

Aenguz had his own questions about how they escaped the battle in the city. But the soporific effect of the Oasis fare was taking effect. They looked about ready to drop. The fire warmed the alcove and made a welcoming space that invited rest.

"How many days have passed since you fled the city?"

"It has been at least a score of days," Mond answered. His fatigue tightened his old bones.

Aenguz insisted they sleep while he took the watch. He would find out what happened to them on the morrow. They nestled in around the fire as if they had done so a hundred times. Stokke and Mond saw to Chimere.

Legerohn kept a watchful eye. Lokah and the brothers positioned themselves strategically. Not clustered together and placing themselves between
the Moresi and the road.

Aenguz could not sleep, was not tired. The unbroken days in the Oasis
left his internal clock upended. If his calculations were correct there was
still time to deliver the message. But precious little to find the lost artifact
of the Last Battle.

37

~~~

ECHOES OF THE LAST BATTLE

Aenguz stayed awake all night. Once the company had fallen asleep, he fed the fire and then left them to consider the night. He was determined not to get caught unawares again. He called a slight glow to his weapon and traced regular loops on the road warding the camp. Keeping watch made him feel like a young Warrior again. But so much had changed since those days.

The moon was gone. Only the curious stars held the sky. Without the moon, he couldn't determine how close he was to midyear. The summer stars were out, and the cool night felt like summer. But he wasn't sure his sense of temperature had adjusted fully after traversing the northern edge of the Ganzir.

The Spine was ominous here. It looked like the end of the world. 'Turn back,' they intimated with their imposing peaks. 'Come no further.' Shreds of cloud passed between the peaks at dusk but disappeared. But one obdurate tuft remained on the forested face of the slope just above the Wester. On one of his circuits, he thought he spied a blue spark like a minuscule blink of blue lightning. But it was brief, and it did not return.

What would Corundum hold? The epicenter of the Last Battle.

How would the Counsel Lords react to him? To an Emissary from Lord Morgrom? Would they believe him? Would they be like the clan lords? Would there be internal divisions and strife that might delay the search for the Dagba Stone? If there was none of that dissension, would they even know where to look? Would they send messengers out to the Lands to warn the peoples of the Lands? Lokah, Legerohn, and the others would need rest. They would be in no condition to turn around and do that right away.

They could at least go home once they were ready. Aenguz would help the Counsel Lords search for the Dagba Stone. He had the strength and the will. And if he aided in finding the stone, he might shed the mantle of Last Emissary.

The first light of day emblazoned the Spine and made it more tangible. Snow speckled the gray with a kind of camouflage. The stubborn plume remained, caught by the pines. And the blue spark returned. It worked like an arc in the torpid tuft of cloud.

Aenguz proffered provender to the company as they stirred. A night of rest did them some good, but he could see they were on the final edges of their strength. *What had happened to them after he fell? How did they get free? How long had they traveled exactly to get here?*

The time apart had changed him, had changed them. The journey through the Lands had done much to alter their perceptions, their understanding about the Lands of the Earth and the natural order of the world.

After they had eaten and freshened themselves, they headed off on the final distance to Corundum. They tacitly divided up the satchels leaving Aenguz only his weapon and a small pack that held the seeds Mere had given him.

Lokah flanked him. He carried his silver sword over his shoulder like a fishing pole. The packs seemed to weigh him down. The Makan brothers and the Moresi walked behind. They were familiar with one another. Their rhythm and pace already set from long days of travel together.

Aenguz's legs were strong and fresh. He was anxious to go faster but kept his tempo in line with the company.

They hobbled down the road together the last distance to Corundum. The yellow Wester seemed to be fleeing from it. Aenguz was mired in his own thoughts of what he might find there when Lokah halted.

A line of soldiers barred the road. They stretched up the slope to his left, across the Rursh Keleg, and down into the squalid scrub of the wilderland. Their rectangular bronze shields curved around them. The upper part of the shields held the pattern of the Spine behind them. They looked to be an extension of the mountain wall. Their spears were pointed up and tipped in black. The sigil upon their breastplates was a jagged triangle that ran down from their necks and presumably to their waists. Their helmets obscured their eyes, left only black slits. Their burgundy cloaks trailed in the wind like forlorn pennons.

Two soldiers stood ahead of the line on the road before the company. One held the shield and spear for the other. A gold insignia like a frond marked the cloak at his neck. The older man at the fore held his helmet under his arm. A sword was strapped to his waist. His hair was the color of gray salt. Armor rested comfortably on him as if he never took it off. The bracers on his arms were cinched tight. His legs were thick as stumps.

Lokah's weapon moved off his shoulder. He brought the tip down to the ground in a smooth arc that belied his exhaustion.

Aenguz could feel the *montmorillionite* mace in the Makan's hand come up. Mandavu's walking stick was no more. And Kachota's axes cut the wind.

The Moresi were unarmed but they looked ready to fight. They stepped aside to give the brothers room. They were familiar with fighting with the Akkeidii. Chimere stood on one leg to free Stokke. Legerohn stepped up to Aenguz. Mond flanked him.

Aenguz's Warrior training was a part of him. 'Draw your weapon.

Form up. Side your peer.' But he was not here to fight. And he was not willing to risk those behind him. A nascent part of himself demanded he draw his weapon. Instead, he left his hands loose at his side.

For a moment, there was silence and stillness across the distance.

The old soldier stepped forward. His hand rested comfortably on the pommel of his sword.

"Why do you come?" the old soldier sounded like a bear. "The Well is closed. There will be no more sacrifice."

Aenguz couldn't guess what the old soldier meant. He called back, "I bear a message to the Counsel Lords of Corundum."

"What message? For whom do you deliver?" he growled.

Aenguz gestured the others to stay, and he stepped forward calmly. He turned his palms to the old soldier. The distance between them closed and he was careful not to be threatening.

"I am, I was the Lord of the Akkeidii. I am an Emissary sent by the Divider. The Last Emissary."

The line of soldiers rustled as if a gale appeared.

The soldier behind the older man turned his head to the side with a snap and the line behind him steadied and stilled.

"Then you bear ruin. Lay your message with me and return to from wherever you came."

"I cannot. I am bidden to deliver it to the Counsel Lords."

"My duty is clear. I am Stair Mark Uran of the Stair Guard. We ward the paths to Corundum. The Stair of Fohrnthulen. And the Vaults of Corundum. We serve the Counsel Lords and the Lands of the Earth."

"Is it your duty to prevent friends of the Lands from bearing warnings to the Counsel Lords from the Divider?"

"Friends of the Divider or friends of the Lands? You cannot be both?"

He was right, of course. His suspicion singed the roar at the edges of his tone.

The contradiction had been an internal one for so long, that hearing it now as an accusation confounded him. "This charge was placed unwillingly upon me. Our purpose is in service to the Law of Creation and the Lands of the Earth."

Stair Mark Uran deliberated with the confidence of a man who had a platoon at his back.

"Treachery is the chief tool of the Divider."

"We are Akkeidii and Moresi. Friends of the Lands and enemies of the Divider. I do not wish to challenge your honor or service, but we have come too far to be rebuffed now at the foot of Corundum."

"If you will not lay down your message, then lay down your arms. In that way, you may come to the Stair." He seemed to realize something. Perhaps a proof or a test for the stranger.

"Come and take them," Mandavu said coolly over Aenguz's shoulder.

Kachota's axes held on the edge like a triphammer. Lokah held as still as the dead road around him. Legerohn took deep breaths, readied himself to grab the first fallen spear.

The soldier behind Stair Mark Uran called a command and the line of spears came down and pointed at the company. Their shields rose from the ground.

The company was in no condition to fight. Even if they were, they would not be able to fight their way up to Corundum. And even if they did, how would the Counsel Lords hear any message from him? It would all be for nothing. But he also could not betray the Akkeidii and ask them to surrender their weapons. He held enough of his former self to know that this was a mountain too far.

With a look and a gesture, he stayed the Akkeidii and the Moresi.

Aenguz walked forward calmly. He kept his arms loose.

He pulled the black and silver scabbard easily off his shoulder and set it down lightly between them and stepped back. Mandavu may have gasped.

Uran considered Aenguz and the scabbard. His eyes were filled with suspicion or calculation. His hand worked the pommel.

He commanded the soldier behind him to take up Aenguz's scabbard.

He called up a pair of soldiers behind him to come up and take the shields and spears.

Then he walked by Uran to take the weapon.

He grabbed the strap. It grew taut as if the scabbard was caught on something. He took both hands and pulled. The scabbard slid only slightly. Then he put his back into it and inched the metal banded scabbard forward.

"Handle the weapon, Pogacar," Uran said without taking his eyes off Aenguz.

Pogacar reached under the flap and tried to draw out the weapon. He squatted and strained to lift it. A groan seeped out from the helmet.

"Release it," Uran growled.

The weapon dropped with a muted thud.

"What theurgy is this?" he demanded as he pulled back from Aenguz's weapon. Uran waved him back with the other two.

"Is this the metal of the Mashu Lands?"

"Yes."

"Only Akkeidii may wield it." His fist worked the pommel like a combination.

"Yes. I am Akkeidii as I have said. Do you believe Akkeidii and Moresi to be friends of the Lands? Friends to the Counsel Lords and denizens of Corundum?"

"Only a fool would say otherwise. But dark things happen in the Lands these days."

"They do indeed. That is why I must speak with the Counsel Lords."

Uran nodded. "The Akkeidii and the Moresi are friends of the Lands. But I fear what your coming means for us." He took his helmet back from the other and waved it in the air.

The Stair Guard raised their spears and lowered their shields. The blue arcing in the stubborn mist halted.

Aenguz reached down and slung his weapon lightly over his shoulder.

The line of Stair Guard jogged down from the hilltop and up from the wilderland. They climbed onto the bony trail and filled in behind the company and ahead of them. Stair Mark Uran gave some orders, and a squad of Stair Guard ran on ahead.

Then they marched on along the last desolate expanse of the Rursh Keleg. Though the soldiers were armored and greatly outnumbered the company they stood just a hair's breadth on this side of courage.

The low mountains did not reach the final distance. The road straightened and blended with a scarred plain just before the cliff. They might have been at the base of a quarry. The cliff wall blotted out the Spine. It filled the west as if it was the foundation of the horizon. The day was warm but low contoured clouds moved in and etched the sky. They left the ground bleak and gray. The Rursh Keleg ended at the foot of a stair cut into the cliff face.

The squad of Stair Guard that Uran had sent ahead jogged back and forth up the irregular switchbacks that wended up the impenetrable height. Back and forth they went. Quick turns here a long stretch there. The rhythm of the Stair followed along rifts that the cliff offered.

At the rim, a line of spears, like a sharp forest looked down on them. They appeared like eidolons in service to the great height. The defense of the Counsel Lords, the Vaults, and the Stairs themselves.

Lokah leaned in close to Aenguz, out of earshot from Uran. "If this is welcome, I wonder what warm embrace might look like."

"Mind their fear. A hasty hand on either side might make short work of us, especially on that stair."

"Aye," Lokah answered.

The soldiers at the fore moved at a trot up the steps. The base of the stair was wide. It opened toward the Wester. Bashed plinths marked the stone rails. They left a pang of violence in the air. Aenguz could only guess what might have been there. A statue. An obelisk. Some other sculpture. Erebim entered his thoughts.

Aenguz studied the stair a moment as Captain Uran climbed. The Stair Guard behind him were nervous and anxious. They had to work to keep from crowding the company.

Here was the end of his long, unexpected journey. He met the eyes of everyone in his company. Their eyes were too drawn for trepidation. If they felt any, they didn't show it.

Then he paused like he had before they had entered the One Forest. "Rhet?" he asked.

The Akkeidii replied, "Rhet."

Legerohn nodded and made sure Mond and Stokke had Chimere.

Then Aenguz turned and climbed the Stair of Forhnthulen.

The stair switched back immediately on itself and ran up a long stretch before zigging back again.

Aenguz watched the company as they hobbled up the steps. He was able to keep pace with Uran. But it was a strain for the others. The guards in the rear were not used to climbing so slow.

Lokah said, "Go on. If they kill you, we will kill them when we get up there."

He looked back to the brothers. They shot a look at the soldiers behind them. They were bunched up behind the Moresi. Mandavu glowered at the Stair Guard.

The company stopped briefly to rest and take water. The fruit and bread had helped them get this far but they were far from replenished, breaks were necessary. Then Aenguz climbed on ahead. If they killed him now the others would at least have warning.

When Aenguz reached the top of the cliff, the line of spears was gone. A pair of bare pedestals marked the top of the stair. Stair Guard lined a winding path across a flat that led to another set of stairs cut into the mountainside. It ascended into the wall of mountain pines. The soldiers stood at attention. Stair Mark Uran waited with his second a short way from the top.

Aenguz looked back across the Lands as he waited for the others. From here the Lands looked abandoned. The winding course of the Wester danced with the Rursh Keleg. The unrelenting sun of the Ganzir beat on the backs of the low mountains in the distance. Unbroken forest stretched to the north. Beyond was Inverlieth somewhere.

Aenguz had never seen so much of the Lands at any one time. Had never thought to cross such a distance. He wondered about the cost. He pondered Grieg Sidor. The Venturer must have stood here at one time and looked out over the Lands of the Earth. Faced with the inevitability of the Last Battle.

When Lokah joined him, he thought about Grieg Sidor's friend, Hernus Kriel. The two Akkeidii heroes of old.

Lokah looked every bit of the hard miles he had crossed to get here. He might have been a beggar or Hearthless in his torn poncho. Scratched and scarred, smeared by dust and dirt. Only his face was clean. Untended cuts and stubborn bruises marked him like inscriptions. He was gaunt but alert. He observed the place of a First and stood at Aenguz's side. Where Ridder would have been. Still, he held his weapon insouciantly as if he could cut down a hundred men.

He looked at the line of soldiers and the winding path. "Wonderful, more stairs."

They waited for the rest of the company. Aenguz made sure they had the time they needed to drink and catch their breath. It broke his heart to see them so decimated. They would have a chance to rest. Once the message was delivered, they could recuperate. They could return to their homes once they were hale and whole again.

When they were ready, Aenguz led on and followed behind Uran and his second. The middle stair led through the forest. In places, it was clearly defined. In others, it was little more than a rocky path. The space would tighten and then it would open to a winding paved stair.

Halfway up, or what Aenguz guessed to be halfway, a company of Stair Guard stood at attention by a simple shelter. A middle watch. Flashes of white peeked out from within their eye slits as he walked by.

The stair wended to the right, toward the Counsel Lord's Keep.

At the final distance, the stair widened. It looked like a broad stair that led down from a manor's veranda to a garden as wide as the Earth. Twenty men could walk abreast.

They took the final steps slowly. At the top, a boulevard ran into a mist presumably to Corundum. It was lined on each side with smooth-barked trees. They vanished in the fog. Between each tree was a wide stump from a grand old tree.

Aenguz waited for the company to gather.

Uran waited on the edge of the mist. His second was a phantom further on.

Leaves rustled. Birds darted both curiously and suspiciously. There was no song. The atmosphere hung by a thread.

Once they were ready, they walked into the mist.

Uran remained just in sight. The second disappeared.

When they reached the spot where Uran had stood, the translucent yellow stone of Corundum rose up and truncated the forest. It was clouded in the obdurate haze. Striations of crystal ran at an angle in a mighty vault up and out of sight in a wall of sour crystal. At the base, a wide rectangular opening marked the entrance. Too wide for any door with no sign of a gate.

Aenguz could make out shapes in the shadowed opening and the muted glints of the Stair Guards' bronze armor. They were off in the distance beyond where the boulevard stopped short.

Aenguz came to the end of the path. His eyes trailed down to the space between the boulevard and the shadowy opening.

Below along the sheer face of Corundum a mighty mountain river ran frozen as if the mechanics of gravity and time had been banished, stilled. This was not white ice but stilled water. The absence of the sound was suddenly overpowering.

The limpid murk devoured the uppermost course. And downward, the frozen falls spilled into a gray void. Hunks of stone hung suspended half in the glass. The remnants of a shattered bridge held the echo of cataclysm. What power could do this? Could hold water so?

A line of planed timbers cut a path through the bouldered blocks down from the boulevard and up to the other side. An ignoble entrance to the mouth of Corundum.

Aenguz stepped onto the jagged timbers amid the stilled waters. His thoughts went immediately to Grieg's Gate. For all the power of the Akkeidii Stonemage governed headwater, the Water Gate would be rendered useless if water itself could be stayed. Erebim, Sallow, any foe, could pour into the Upper Mashu and lay siege within the Valley of Gathering. Morgrom's powers dwarfed him. A single Akkeidii Warrior, a *montmorillionite* blade, a dolorous message. What rebuff could he offer against a power that could do this to a river? Or occlude the keep in a sempiternal mist?

38

JOURNEY'S END

Aenguz climbed up out of the mist and into the wide entrance of Corundum. Two footings from the shattered bridge marked the edge in the wide chamber. The rectangular space looked canted as if a giant block of crystal had been withdrawn out of the space. The chamber walls followed the angle of the striation. Against the low ceiling, it gave the space a distinct tilt.

Three pairs of unlit braziers ran to the center of the chamber. They looked like Hyrrokkin hands back-to-back. One clawing the floor and the other holding the ready wood.

At the end of the line, there were seven robed figures ringed by elite Stair Guard. A black sash crossed their chests in a sign of mourning. Three were women. Four were men. They spanned a range of ages. They all bore similar staffs. Edged wood that tapered from hilt to floor. And above the hilt, the wood twisted in a kind of chiseled braid. Wood that looked like it was cut from stone.

Stair Mark Uran stood before them. Another man, dressed in a simple short tunic, stood apart from the line of Counsel Lords. Impassive eyes were flat and unblinking. But they scrutinized everything. His hair was jet and cut short and square. He stood with his legs wide and his arms clasped behind him. If he wasn't so self-assured, he might have been confused for a prisoner.

Aenguz waited at the edge for the others to come up as he surveyed the chamber. Lokah said as he stepped up, "What death marks this place?" He helped up Chimere to ease Mond's joints. Kachota came and they shouldered their gimpy companion.

Aenguz reached for Mandavu's scarred, bloodied forearm and guided the giant up.

"Watch your head," he said trying to lighten the Makan's mood.

Mandavu took in the entrance and Aenguz's comment with a wry smile.

"What do you think? Ten to one? Fifteen to one perhaps."

"Still, they look more afraid of us."

"Aye," he answered as he straightened. Some in the hall gasped as the giant stood.

Once they had all crossed, Aenguz walked to the robed figures. Lokah fell in beside him and Legerohn walked at his left. Mond followed behind. Stokke took Chimere from Kachota. Mandavu and Kachota stretched to the side.

They were a haggard group. Not like a delegation that would warrant such a meeting as filled the entrance to Corundum. They looked to have walked through a gauntlet to reach the Counsel Lords. They dropped the sacks and skins to the floor as if they could carry them no further.

Aenguz looked like he was not a part of them. His white leggings and soft white shirt from the Oasis looked new. Strands of gossamer still filled his hair and made him look older than he was. His oversized scabbard at his back and simple satchel at his side made him look benign, like a Deerherd before the line of Counsel Lords.

He stepped forward a few paces from Lokah and Legerohn. The ceiling opened up abruptly and Aenguz could see a balcony that ran atop the back wall. It was lined with men and women. The few children were held close by their mothers. They jostled and whispered. Their voices trailed up into the heights. A single stair ran from the left edge of the balcony down the wall to the center at the back of the chamber.

Captain Uran waited in front of the Counsel Lords.

At the center of the line was the oldest of the group. His black sash seemed heavy on him like a chain. He was flanked by a woman with a mane of brilliant red hair. It flowed down onto her chest in waves of broad curls. Her light blue eyes were mesmerizing and penetrating. They conspired to give her a formidable air.

On his left, was a man who wore a sharp beard and stood tall and erect as if he held formation with the Stair Guard. His face was firm, but his eyes calm and confident. He examined the company as if he sought to understand meaning in every movement.

The ancient man between them looked like a grandfather. His staff helped him maintain a stolid pose. Something about his posture said that he was observing the pomp for the benefit of the rest. That if it were just him, his feeble hands would reach out for an embrace. Grief languished here and it had all but taken the old man. Aenguz could see that much in his bent frame.

He stopped before the Stair Mark. The old soldier tensed to keep Aenguz at a safe distance.

"Mono Lord Venrahl, Lord Lana, Lord Bremball, Counsel Lords," he nodded to the pairs on either side of the three. "Stroud," he nodded to the man in the simple tunic. "This is Aenguz of the Akkeidii-"

Lokah strode up and cut off Uran. "Counsel Lords of Corundum, Warders of the Stair of Forhnthulen, Denizens of the Crystal Keep, before you stands Lord Aenguz, Ruler of the Akkeidii, Lord of the Sidor Clan, Ruler of the Upper and the Lower Mashu, Polemarch of the Warriors of the Akkeidii. He has traveled to you across the Lands of the Earth with a dire message, unbidden, unasked for. We have heard it. We have sworn to bear the burden with him for the sake of the Earth. Many have fallen in the wake of this errand. Hear now what an Akkeidii has been charged to bear."

His bellow silenced the people above. The Stair Guard snapped to a tighter stance. The Counsel Lords looked at Lokah. A deference fell over them.

"We are honored by your coming," Mono Lord Venrahl started. His voice was unsteady, but he was precise with his words. "Moresi and Akkeidii traveling together on the old road. These are unusual times. Few travel to Corundum anymore. Access to the Well of Sorrows is forbidden." The words shook his waddle, flapped his cheeks.

What was the Well of Sorrows? How did that matter?

Aenguz had crossed hell and blood to stand here now. He had come to deliver Morgrom's message and be rid of it. And with it, the mantle of Last Emissary. Then he could get help for his friends and return home.

"Stair Mark Uran says you bear a message from the Divider for us. He says that you are not, and we trust the Stair Mark, but I must ask, are you in league with Lord Morgrom the Divider?"

The lines of the message from Carrowen Celd rose in lines of fire in Aenguz's mind. But before he began, he asked, "First, my companions have hurts and injuries. And they need food and rest."

"Of course, aid will be given. Stewards have been summoned. Rooms will be prepared. You may rest and recover from your long journey as long as recuperation needs."

Good, Aenguz thought. They could rest. Aenguz met the eyes of each of the Counsel Lords. He glanced up at the people staring down at him. The eyes of the Stair Guard were impervious, but he brushed over their helmets with a sweeping look. Warriors, he was familiar with.

"One other thing. We have been on the road for many days. Has midyear passed?"

"You have come before midyear," the Mono Lord answered. "In three days midyear will come."

There was time, to deliver the message at least. Searching for the Dagba Stone would be another matter but at least he arrived before midyear.

The entrance of Corundum quieted. "I was selected through chance into the presence of Lord Morgrom the Divider and Flayer. The First Treacher to the Lands of the Earth. He is not gone from the Earth. He remains. I was drawn to the deepest parts of Carrowen Celd. I have seen him."

Shock widened and clenched their eyes. Some of the Counsel Lords checked their grips on their staffs.

"I do not know how this was done apart from my body for I did not leave the Mashu. That lore is beyond my ken. I do know that I was there, deep beneath a barren plain and curved ridge that looked like a scythe upon that plain. There, I was bidden to deliver a message to you."

The words stalled for a moment. The entire host held its breath.

"I am the Last Emissary that Lord Morgrom will send to the Lands of the Earth. It is an unwanted charge, but it is so.

"This is the message I was bidden to deliver to you.

"'You will bear a message to the Counsel Lords and the Mono Lord in Corundum. Say to them that the limit of their days upon the Lands of the Earth are before them. Five quinquennia will not pass before my will is sown in every corner of the Earth. The Remnant and the peoples of the Lands squat on lands I have granted to my servants. Your time on the Earth is at an end.

"'To the Urnings I have granted the air. They are masters of it. I have sent them forth to find the portals and free all five Ruinwasters. With the aid of my wisdom, they have divined the means of their escape. Before twenty-five moons grow full all five will be freed. Four will wreak havoc on all the hope and beauty in the Earth you hold so dear. Hear me, when

Tycho Ruinwaster is found and his shackle removed, the Blasted Flats, the Shattered Lands, and even the Ganzir will seem like a garden.'"

Aenguz recited how the land, the water, and animal-kind were given to the Erebim, Sallow, and Tsurah.

"'Mark me! Before this very year is divided, the Dagba Stone will be lost to this age. You will not be able to use it against me as before. Even if you were able to locate it no mortal hand may wield it. Its power is for my hand alone. When my Ruinwasters have done their work. When you are gone from the Earth, I will locate it and become unfettered from the Earth. And then the universe and Time itself will bow to my dominion.'"

Aenguz pondered the admonition leveled against him specifically. Then he added.

"'If you fail to deliver my message, death will be your raiment. And I will only require one Ruinwaster to bring about the ruin of the Earth. One Ruinwaster alone would be enough to rend the Vaults of Corundum.'"

He had done it. He delivered the message. The deaths, the long miles, the harsh trials. But he had saved the last of the company. But it was an incomplete relief. The weight he had expected to be lifted held on him still.

Horror and upheaval roiled the chamber. Someone in the gallery fainted. There was a high shriek. The Stair Guard trembled as if they had just been called to war. Uran looked lost. He had no enemy to direct his strength or his forces against.

The Counsel Lords turned to one another. Panic shook them. They looked to each other for strength or courage. They seemed inadequate compared to the Divider.

The four Counsel Lords at the flanks said to the denizens of Corundum, "Remember your Oaths," to try and calm the commotion.

Aenguz's hope drained out of him. His blood chilled. A sudden shiver quaked him. Their shouts and moans were like stones cast at him.

"Master yourselves! Are we so undone by the words of the Divider?" Counsel Lord Bremball said to the host.

"What of the stone, High Lord?" Lord Lana said to Venrahl.

He was driven back by their ache as if to the edge of the stilled waters.

"I will help," Aenguz said at first to quiet the discord. "I will help find the Dagba Stone!" he shouted.

The chamber snapped quiet.

He sensed at once that he had said something wrong. His thoughts of the waters of Grieg's Gate and his long absence from home and his desire to stop Morgrom collided in him. Quickly he added, "There is still time to search. But we must begin immediately. Where might we begin to look?" His mind went to the magnitude of the Spine. Such a thing might be impossible to recover in time in so vast a span of mountains. "What does it look like? Are there any powers that you hold that may guide us?"

Lord Lana dropped her gaze. Her cheeks sank.

Lord Bremball clenched his jaw. His sharp beard flexed.

The Mono Lord wiped the warble from his voice and enunciated as if he was pronouncing a law. "The Dagba Stone is lost. The Bane of Corundum will claim no more lives. That is the end of the matter."

"The Well of Sorrows-

"Will be-

"Sealed-

"Tomorrow! Forever!"

He banged the heel of his staff on the yellow crystal and a whirl of blue flame arced into the chamber like blue starlight and bright whale song.

Chaos and light splashed across Aenguz's face. He clamped his eyes shut.

The gallery shrieked and gasped in unison. Shields and spears clattered.

After time measured in strained breaths, the reverberations finally withdrew like a receding wave. Aenguz opened his eyes. The crystalline walls held remnants of the blue light.

The diminutive Mono Lord leaned into his quieted staff. Counsel Lord Lana raced to his side, held him up, and led him away behind the line of Stair Guard.

Lord Bremball stepped up to Aenguz and said, "Battling against the Glaize has drained him. Lord Aenguz, the Dagba Stone has been lost beneath Corundum since the final day of the Last Battle. The Well of Sorrows is the only passage that leads to the underbelly of Corundum. It has taken Mono Lord Venrahl's granddaughter and many others besides. It is to be sealed tomorrow at midday once and for all."

Aenguz's heart plummeted.

He had failed.

The Earth was doomed.

39

PRISONERS OF CORUNDUM

Doom and ruin.

The end of all things.

With the Mono Lord's departure, the people of Corundum started to disperse. Lord Bremball took the lead after Lord Lana drew Venrahl away. He spoke to the other Counsel Lords briefly and then they too disbanded.

Stair Guard stood at ease. Bremball and Uran spoke. They agreed to return the watch on the Stair to its normal complement. The threat from the company was over.

Uran gave orders to his Step Marks. Most of the Stair Guard disbanded. Only half a score or so remained.

The denizens above drifted away like flotsam. Purposeless and morose. Stewards drifted down the solitary stair into the clouded chamber. They waited on the fringes for Lord Bremball's command.

Bremball approached Aenguz and the company. "Message Bearer. Forgive the Mono Lord. His grief and long days of striving against the Glaize to keep open the eyes of the Divine Oculum have left him drained."

Stewards came at a wave. Half a dozen or so young women and men came up and gathered the sacks and skins from the Oasis. Two took

Chimere onto their shoulders. Stokke still stayed close to ensure that Chimere was all right with their support. A young woman kneeled by his foot and examined the ankle.

Aenguz held a hand up when one reached for his satchel of seeds. Mere's gift would stay on him.

With a wave of his arm, Bremball guided the company to the stair. "If you will follow me, we will take you to quarters and tend your friends' hurts." The stewards walked with them, and the Stair Guard followed behind. Uran left presumably for other Stair Guard matters.

Questions bombarded Aenguz. He could sense that Bremball was waiting on more privacy to explain away the questions on Aenguz's face. At the top of the stairs just beyond the balcony, the wall opened to a wide refectory. Rows of crystalline tables filled the hall. Groups of people sat here and there. Some consoled women who wept openly. Few children ambled about, warded closely by adults. They seemed forlorn and confused. Their presence was a reminder of the barrenness the blight had wrought.

Couples gathered with families in places and tried to take in the consolation of fathers and mothers. Their helplessness and futility wilted them. It was pockets of grief and tears here and there. Others bore themselves away too familiar with grief and despair to shed more tears. Childless couples left the refectory with only one another to hold them up.

Food was set on the counter at the edge of the kitchen, but none ate. Stewards organized platters but otherwise, the food was wasted on a hollow banquet.

"What has happened here?" Aenguz asked.

Bremball led Aenguz and the others up a stair past the kitchen and then answered. "Mia. The Mono Lord's granddaughter died. Lost to the Well."

Aenguz bit down. Frustration, impatience, and anger contorted his face. *What by Grieg is the Well of Sorrows?*

"The blight strikes hardest on women."

Aenguz knew the anxiety and desperation when children didn't come. The abjection of barren women who begged to become mother-aunts for the fortunate women who bore children. They subjugated themselves. Very nearly became slaves. It was the only answer many of them could find that would keep them from their own loss and desolation. "Aye," Aenguz answered dejectedly. He recalled the mother-aunts who bawled when he said goodbye to Selene in the Valley of Gathering.

Bremball laid hands on shoulders of some as they passed through corridors, consoling as he could.

"Mia was no different from most. Though, she thought as a grand-daughter of the Mono Lord she might be spared the blight to her womb. Do you have grandparents, Message Bearer? Do you know the joy and pride they feel in their grandchildren?"

Aenguz knew. The worry that his own grandparents must be experiencing in his absence was a chronic ache in his heart. When a line continued, the blessing and joy for the clan was profound. He thought, likely like Mia, that as the son of a clan lord, and the grandson of the Lord of the Deerherds and the Clan Mother of the Akkeidii that the blight would pass over him and Selene. But all couples thought that, hoped for that. Especially those left in the refectory below.

"Mia brought that joy to her parents and the Mono Lord. But when she and her mate could not conceive, she turned to the Well and the belief in the Stone."

The stairways narrowed and the ceilings closed down as they rose deeper into the keep. Fewer people passed the company. The corridors grew dusty and unused. Ambient light from crystals spaced far apart in the halls barely guided the way.

"At the culmination of the Last Battle, the Stone was rent from the Divider's hand. It fell to the Spine." Bremball met Aenguz's eyes. He lowered his tone as if he was delivering a secret. "It came to be believed that it was not lost in the mountains but rather lost down a narrow shaft in Corundum." He continued on in a steady tone. "The curse of the blight was not understood then. Much was lost. But when fewer children came, and animals and terraced fields grew fallow, focus turned back to the Dagba Stone, the Keystone of Creation. Some believed that it would hold the answer. That it could relieve the blight and the barrenness in the Lands of the Earth. Though none could say how such an artifact might be used." Bremball looked at Aenguz to affirm that he understood the tale. Aenguz knew. All Akkeidii knew. It was Grieg Sidor who had rent the stone from the Flayer's hands. The panels in the facade in the Valley of Gathering told the story via deft Stonemage craftsmanship.

The turns and stairs wended in a maze up and up. They passed doors upon doors. There were not enough souls to fill the abundance of the Crystal Citadel. No one dwelled so far up.

"In a time we do not like to recall, many people hazarded the shaft to try and find the Stone. None returned. But hope and despair leave pernicious marks on the soul. Combined, they confound reason. Over time, the shaft earned the name 'Well of Sorrows.'" Again, Bremball lowered his tone. "The old Counsel Lords, in order to stop the loss of life, conceived a way to dampen the hope that claimed so many. At one point, a system of lots was introduced to limit access to the Well. There were fewer children and fewer people in the Lands. The location of the Stone in the Well of Sorrows was disputed, its power questioned, even its existence diminished. But hope could not be wholly eradicated. Generations of Counsel Lords sought to lessen its import. Barring all hope was simply not possible. Can you imagine how grim such a drawing must have been?" Then suddenly Bremball asked, "Do you have children, Message Bearer?"

Aenguz shook his head. "No." He began to doubt that he and Selene would be different.

Bremball led the haggard company up a long, narrow stair. They came to a long hall high up in the uppermost reaches of the keep. A line of rooms with open doors lined a dark dead-ended hallway. Light flickered out. Stewards stood in front of the doors like ushers. Others shuttled in and out. Aenguz could smell fires and hints of roasted meat and fresh bread.

"Hope and despair collided in Mia and became toxic. She was the granddaughter of the Mono Lord after all. How could she be afflicted so? The Mono Lord's heart was decimated by his granddaughter's empty need and his own powerlessness. He was caught between two exigencies. The meaning and purpose of his life's work and his granddaughter's depression. She succumbed to the cult of the Well and was lost. Mono Lord Venrahl found the only answer left to him. The culmination of his life's work. He commanded that the Well of Sorrows be sealed once and for all. After tomorrow, no more lives will be taken by the Bane of Corundum."

Aenguz and Bremball stepped aside to let the company pass. A cadre of healers ushered them into the nearest suite. It was set up as a triage center. They took Chimere to a divan. The others were guided to chairs around the dining table. They began washing and dressing their wounds. They discarded their shredded ponchos and stewards were sent for fresh clothes. They hobbled past Aenguz and Bremball.

Aenguz saw all of the company tended to. Then he pulled back and spoke in a harsh tone to Bremball.

"You cannot seal this Well. Surely you understand that we need the Dagba Stone to repel Lord Morgrom. The message holds the answer to his defeat. If a Ruinwaster descends on Corundum, his minions will only have to sift through the rubble to find it."

"He will not be swayed," Bremball shook his head. Resolve squared off his short beard. "We will have to find another way to combat the Divider. There is much in your story that we must discern if we are to make a defense for the Lands. We do not travel as we once did, choosing to protect what we can here in Corundum. You hold knowledge that may aid us in the coming battle. There are answers to be gleaned in your journey. It will take time for us to plumb all that you have seen and heard."

"What time? Midyear is upon us. We must strive to find the stone now!"

"There will be no swaying all the Counsel Lords before the Well of Sorrows is sealed. But they will come back to themselves, and we will listen. There is still hope in the Lands. Akkeidii and Moresi travel together. Who knows what might be learned once we hear your tale?"

"Where is this shaft? I am Akkeidii. The roots of mountains are familiar to me. Let me attempt it." Down from the head of the stair, at the bottom, the Stair Guard lined up at attention. He met Lord Bremball's eyes.

"We are used to people trying to seek the Well of Sorrows. We ward you against yourselves. Stay here tonight. Rest."

"Are we prisoners?"

"Tomorrow, once the Well is sealed, you will be free to move about Corundum. The Bane of Corundum drives some to madness. We will find another way to combat the Divider and save the Lands of the Earth."

Bremball turned to leave. He paused on the edge of the stair. "If you found the stone, how could you be sure that you would know how to use it? How do you know that you would not be compelled to deliver it to the Divider? You were compelled to cross the Lands against your will just to deliver a message. How can you be sure that you might not come to the conclusion that the best course to preserve your life, or that of the Akkeidii would not be to deliver it to his hand?"

"How could you think I would want the Earth to become a hell forever? That I would relent to such a desecration of the Lands? How would I gain from such an act? I am Akkeidii from the line of Grieg Sidor."

"I could not imagine that Mia would fling herself unto death. Or any of the others before her. But they did. How could you keep the Stone safer than the mountains beneath Corundum? What would you do if you held such a power?"

Aenguz didn't have a ready answer for the Counsel Lord. He was a Warrior. His only lore centered around *montmorillionite* and Deerherd lore. How could he use such power if he found it? Something made and held by gods.

"The Well will be sealed at midday tomorrow. After that, there can be no temptation. With your help, we will plan how we might resist the Divider. There is much from you we would want to hear if you would tell us. There are always options and allies."

"It will not matter after tomorrow."

"There is still hope, Message Bearer. Rest while we put the dire legacy of the Well behind us."

Just then a young steward came up. "There is food for you, my lord," she said. Her long brown braid rested on her like a finely kept horse's tail.

"Rest, eat. I will see you tomorrow." Bremball went down the stairs and past the Stair Guard. Helmets nodded tightly as he passed.

40

～～

A DESPERATE PLAN

The young woman led Aenguz to the further suite while the others were being tended. His rage and disbelief left him numb. Also, something in Bremball's tone left him surly. The Counsel Lord talked to him with a lilt as if he was a child. As if he did not have enough wisdom or experience to understand the exigencies that drove the Counsel Lords to their decisions and actions. Or that Aenguz was too callow to understand that there might be another way to oppose the Divider. And too there was the cadre of Stair Guard at the bottom of the stair. There was no negotiation where there was force. Only greater might against lesser. And against a greater foe, only a more cunning force could prevail. He was deceived by being led to such an aerie in Corundum. If he wasn't in such shock over learning the location of the Dagba Stone and the residue of the Mono Lords' considerable power, he might have seen what Bremball was doing. Still, he was too easily fooled.

He half listened as the young woman showed him the empty suite. A long crystalline dining table lunged out of the floor. High-backed chairs, angled on the same bias, made of the same yellow stone, ringed around it. Every corner, every doorway, each alcove was set on the bias. A world of parallelograms.

The table held a platter of roasted meat and another with white and gold cheeses. Bread and dried fruit filled another platter. Heavy angular pitchers and slanted goblets of the same dimmed crystal crowded the table. The sacks and packs from the Oasis were stacked on it. He unshouldered his weapon and his satchel of seeds and laid it down beside the others. At least here he had succeeded. The seeds from the Oasis were here but if the Counsel Lords didn't travel out into the Lands how could they serve to mete the blight?

She highlighted the broad room next to the dining table that held other couches and chairs. Fresh cushions and coverlets were thrown carefully over the blocky furniture. The slight slant only barely mitigated by the colorful coverings.

Opposite the sitting area was a refreshing room and fatter pitchers and basins just inside. A hearth glowed to the right of that door. And next to that a small kitchen with a place for a cook fire. It was cold and dark. A large family could easily live in the suite but it, until recently, had long stood empty. She was mechanical and deliberate. Nervousness tinged her voice. When she met Aenguz's eyes she just as quickly looked away and focused on her introduction to the room.

The message was delivered but the heaviness was not gone. It weighed on him like a black funerary bolt. Bremball had not stood in Carrowen Celd. He had not seen and heard the eyes and all their voices. He did not see how Morgrom reacted when he spoke about the Stone. He did not feel the umbrage the Flayer displayed in order to hide his fear of the arcane talisman. The Dagba Stone had to be found. Aenguz had crossed the Lands of the Earth to deliver the message and he knew what the Flayer was capable of.

Aenguz pulled off the gloves Mere had given him. The young woman's eyes winced in their sockets when she glimpsed his left hand. Aenguz turned from her. He went to the wall opposite the door.

Heavy drapes that stretched floor to ceiling were drawn closed against the wall. He found the seam on the thick drapes and parted them. An opening led to a balcony carved out of the rock the width of the room. Beyond the edge, the Glaize voided the night. It looked as if he was perched on the edge of an abyss. The air was dank with only the merest hint of pine. No cascading water soothed the night. Just a damp, stale stillness.

"Is there anything you require?" the steward asked.

The means to oppose the Flayer, he thought as he closed the curtains against the consuming dark. He examined the platters of food. It reminded him vaguely of the Oasis and his meals with Mere. How many had there been? He took up a piece of herbed flatbread. He held it up to his left and his right. "For the Upper and the Lower. For the Millin and White." Then he walked over and handed it to the young woman.

She balked at first and looked puzzled. Aenguz reached the bread out to her. She took it tentatively. He nodded until she nibbled. "Akkeidii tradition." Then he retrieved his own piece and took a bite. The bread was still warm.

"Did you know Mia?"

Her round eyes drooped. "Everyone here knew Mia."

"Did you understand her struggles?"

Her hands dropped to her midsection. Aenguz thought that he had perhaps touched on something too intimate. She was young but not so young as to not understand the course of life as it was meant to be. The life command in her belly was present and immutable.

"Yes." She hovered for a moment wrestling with things Aenguz could only guess at. "As the granddaughter of the Mono Lord she thought she would be able..."

"How did she approach the Well of Sorrows? Was it not barred?"

"The Well sits out in the open atop the Keep. Now the top of Corundum is barred. The Mono Lord has commanded Stair Guard to block the way. Before, his word alone was enough. Should have been enough."

Aenguz glimpsed the sorrow that Mia must have held, that all the women of Corundum must hold for the curse of the blight and barrenness with the answer so near and so lost. He was too late to save Mia. He counted through the delays and his guilts. Another death due to him.

He wondered if his mother had gone through the same worry and uncertainty. How cruel her life had been to take her as a consequence of his birth. She had overcome the blight only to be felled by her only child. 'Sometimes the mother dies.' If he could find the Stone he could turn the course. Turn impending death to life.

Her eyes were timid. Moisture tinged them. "If you require anything. Just tell the Stair Guard. A runner stands by and will be dispatched should you have any need." With that, she left.

Lokah entered as she passed. He wore a beige coverlet that looked like a nightshirt. Bandages bulged here and there. He set his sword against the wall. Aenguz tore more bread and handed it over to him. Lokah picked up some dried fruit to hand to Aenguz, but he waved it away. Then Lokah sat down and ate in earnest. He smelled the pitcher and poured some malt wine. He proffered it to Aenguz. Again, Aenguz shook his head.

Mandavu walked in next. He wore an ill-fitting beige robe of undyed hemp. The sleeves were too short, and the robe didn't cover his chest. He surveyed the table as Lokah extended a piece of cheese. The Makan took it, raised it to his right and left, and then joined Lokah.

"What did Lord Bremball tell you?" Lokah said in between bites.

"I learned that we are captives here."

Lokah and Mandavu stopped mid-chew.

"We are to be kept here until the Well of Sorrows is sealed. Many had descended into the Well, but none have returned."

"They need the Stone to battle the Flayer," Lokah said.

Mandavu's eyes seemed to calculate the distance and difficulty to take the Stair Guard.

Aenguz understood the giant's look. "No, listen." Aenguz waved them over to the drapes, parted them, and stepped through. "We will not reach it that way. They would cut us down."

"Then how?" Mandavu asked. "Where is it?"

"The Well is on top of the keep. I am going to climb up, find it... and... descend in."

"What do you mean?" Lokah raised his voice.

Aenguz pressed his hands down to quiet the Kriel.

"If I am in the Well, they cannot close it. It will give us time to search for it."

Mandavu's eyes began a new calculation. "How do they plan to seal it?"

"I do not know. If the Dagba Stone is beneath Corundum, then this is the only way to find it. And the last chance to do it. But I need your help."

Lokah blinked slowly. He drew in a breath and exuded calm. "You do not know where the Well of Sorrows is."

"It is on top of the keep. The steward told me."

Lokah continued over Aenguz. "You do not know if the Stone is even down there. It is a myth."

"No Akkeidii has looked for it. No *montmorillionite*."

Lokah weighed Aenguz's words. But he was unconvinced.

"What does the Dagba Stone look like?" Mandavu asked.

"I, I do not know."

"Then how will you know when you have found it?"

Aenguz searched the faces of the two Warriors hoping for an answer. He had no idea.

"Then my descent will stop them from closing the Well until we can be sure it is not down there. If there is a chance, then we have to keep it open."

Lokah and Mandavu looked at one another. The Makan said to Lokah, "You said the fate of the Lands' need fell to the Akkeidii and the Akkeidii shall bear it."

"Are we to let another Lord of the Akkeidii die? What will the Song of the Kriels and the Song of the Makans say about us?"

Mandavu thought for a moment. His conflicts seemed to find some resolution. His uncertainties seemed to ameliorate. "If it is to be the end of the world, then there will be no songs."

Lokah considered Mandavu. His jaw worked side to side as he pondered. He looked at Aenguz. "What do you command of us?"

"At dawn, demand to speak with Counsel Lord Bremball or the Mono Lord. Do whatever it takes to reach them. But do not kill anyone. You must prevent them from sealing the Well at midday. If they are right, it is the only way out. If they know I am down there, they will have to wait to seal it.

"Lokah, I am trusting you with the satchel from the Oasis of the Ganzir. It is full of viable seeds. It is for the future of the Lands regardless of what happens. Should I fail, they will counter the blight.

"Keep your weapons close. If I do fail. You will know." His eyes became leaden. They knew the sound and vibration of released *montmorillionite.* "If I fail, then return to the Mashu with all haste and prepare the Akkeidii."

The pair nodded reticently. They knew that this could be the last order from him.

Aenguz continued, "I need your help with a distraction. When the others come in here, we will break bread. You must talk into the late hours. I will need time to scale the keep and find the Well of Sorrows. The Stair Guard must think that we are all here. I am sure our voices carry in these corridors." Aenguz looked over the side wall of the balcony and judged the crystal.

Lokah and Mandavu nodded again as if their heads were made of stone.

"I do not have my metal here to offer you. Here is my hand." He reached up with his right hand and they took it. Mandavu's covered Lokah's and Aenguz's. They agreed with their grasp. Also, they knew he was putting his life in their hands.

"Now, for the show."

Aenguz stepped away from them and parted the curtain.

"They have set a feast for us. Let us fill our bellies on the first real meal we have had in weeks. Mandavu. Call the others!" Aenguz bellowed.

Mandavu walked slowly to the door.

"Come Lokah, pour some malt wine. Put these stewards to task. They have not had an Akkeidii's thirst in Corundum for an age."

Aenguz took his scabbard and draped it over his shoulder.

He whispered, "If they do come in, just call to the refresh room as if I am in there. Tell the others what I mean to attempt, quietly."

Lokah nodded dully.

Kachota came in with clothes that made him look like a docent. Legerohn and Mond were also studies in beige.

"Let us drink and eat for we are alive at the end of the world."

They looked confused but Mandavu followed in after them and closed the balanced crystal door partway.

"Come tell me of your escape from the City of the Sho-tah."

Legerohn and Mond looked confused as if they found themselves in a room filled with strangers.

Aenguz took up the waterskin from the Oasis and a sack. He began to stuff it with some bread and cheese as he invited the others to sit.

Kachota said to Mandavu, "His head has been cooked by the Ganzir. He invites us to sit but makes as if to-"

Mandavu clapped his hand over his brother's mouth.

"His brain is scrambled, that is for certain. Let us drink to it, brother." Mandavu pulled his hand away and stared into Kachota's eyes.

Aenguz backed up to the curtain.

"Come, I have told my tale and we have delivered the message. I am done with words for now. Tell me how you escaped the battle and what the Rursh Keleg held for you. Let us see if we cannot make a drain on the casks in Corundum."

With that, Aenguz stepped between the curtains and vanished into the Glaize.

41

~~

THE WELL OF SORROWS

A thick, damp fume wrapped the keep. The dulled black was stagnant and old like an undisturbed swamp. No stars or moonlight pierced the encompassing void. The hard crystalline keep was like a footing for the world. A cornerstone for all matter. Aenguz stood on the threshold between solidity and formlessness on the silent battle line between the Glaize and Corundum. The certainty of life and the inscrutability of the unknown.

The vestigial voices beyond the curtains kept Aenguz steady against the effects of the dwarfing powers. The muffled edges of his companion's ruse played the part of a celebration. But he couldn't shake the feeling that he listened back through the veil onto his own eulogy.

The reverie was brief. Time was short and he had no idea how large Corundum might be. Or how far he was from the top of the keep. And as for finding the Well of Sorrows... But, if he could get in in time, the Counsel Lords would be forced to halt their sealing of the Well.

He turned his mind from the murky abyss and focused on the contour of the wall at the edge of the balcony. He had climbed at night before, but never alone. Warrior training necessitated it. And not without rope lashed around him. Rangers learned to climb without it. They had to.

He pressed his hands against the rough crystal and took in the contours of the allotropic stone. The surface was damp. He brought his boot up to the ledge and wiped dust from the Rursh Keleg onto his hands. Front and back. His heart was familiar with the hard skin of mountains, but this crystal was different.

He unsheathed his weapon and hooked it over his shoulder. He might need ready access. The scabbard would be too clumsy. And a part of himself admitted that it might be the only thing left of him. He left Mere's gift on the floor of the balcony.

He stood on the angular edge and reached for the seams on the face of Corundum. Striations in the crystal vaulted on a slightly upward angle. He checked his grip, stretched his foot out, and with a practiced air, pulled himself out onto the outer wall. *"Take what the mountain gives you,"* he recalled his Drill Captain's instruction.

Rather than climbing up, he inched along the seams. His cheek splayed against the wall.

There was no time in the null space. Corundum might have stretched into eternity. But he had seen the tuft of cloud against the Spine from the Rursh Keleg. It was tangible. It had borders and edges. It was nestled in the Spine. The dividing mountains were not overcome by either the Glaize or the keep.

No matter how imposing a mountain was, a strong and patient hand might navigate it. But not without risk or peril. Respect was important.

The coarse washboard grew smoother. He brushed his fingers over the backs of his hands. The parchment skin of his left held the dust better. No sweat muddled it.

He reached ahead with the numb fingers-

-and slipped

His heart fell.

Nothing but dropping and imminent death.

But in a blink, he hit against smooth rock and stumbled down to his knees more out of shock than a loss of footing.

He held there, on all fours, on the contoured floor of the abyss. His heart was lost below somewhere.

Aenguz probed the hard wet stone and climbed to his feet careful of the slick surface.

But this wasn't stone. The mountain river, stilled by Morgrom's perverse hand, poured down and around Corundum. He was caught on a frozen swell. Behind him, the tepid ice poured down out of sight. It likely ran down right past their rooms. A muffled chuckle fell against the stilled water.

He continued up between the silent and surging river and the outer wall of Corundum. He reached his right hand up and felt for the top of the keep. They had walked up flights and flights of stairs. He held onto a hope that he had to be close.

Eventually, his fingers found the contoured lip of the wall. He pulled himself up and found a squat forest of crystal nubs and agate stumps. There was no way to discern where he was other than the belief that the Spine towered to his left. He climbed over and into the jagged landscape.

The sharp agate jabbed and cut his hands. His knees were battered, and his ankles twisted in the tight crevices. The clothes from the desert were not intended for climbing over such a vista.

At times, he tried to penetrate the Glaize and find any hint of the Well.

In following what the crystal forest gave him, he was no longer certain where the Spine was. He wanted to draw on his weapon, sing to it to guide him, and call forth light from the *montmorillionite* but he had to maintain stealth. He was not sure how much time had elapsed.

Then a sound caught his attention.

He drew in a long breath and held perfectly still. *"No one will be expecting you from the heights. Be still. Listen. The mountains carry words,"* the words of the Drill Captain pounded.

There it was.

Voices.

Doubly careful now, he climbed toward the sounds. His chest scraped across the sharp nubs of crystal. It shredded his white sweat-soaked shirt.

Across the glass forest, there was firelight. A little brazier was set among a bouquet of crystal arms.

A dozen or so Stair Guard, wrapped in their burgundy cloaks, chatted by the fire. The course landscape carved their words. Half of the watch split off and walked in a line through the short forest of angled glass. He had come up to the changing of the guard.

The Well of Sorrows had to be close. He couldn't see it. But, perched above the forest was a large obelisk of tourmaline. The fire tickled the underside of the stone. Dark shards of light like a sour rainbow glinted off the under face. The Glaize sought to take the topside.

A contraption of ropes and timbers balanced the obelisk at an angle. It looked like some prize that had been captured from the void.

Aenguz used the cover of their parting chatter to get in closer. This might be the last watch before morning. If there was no Glaize, he might even be able to see the first vestiges of dawn.

He had to hurry. The Glaize wouldn't stop the sun entirely.

Aenguz used the obelisk to shield his way and block the firelight.

Beside a timber, he stopped and peered at the maw. The opening was ringed with crystal teeth.

The Well of Sorrows.

His mind dropped suddenly to Carrowen Celd.

A dread gripped him.

His breath quickened and sharp panic added to the edges against his hands and knees.

Resistance rooted him. Froze him like the waters surrounding Corundum.

'Even if you were able to locate it no mortal hand may wield it. Its power is for my hand alone.'

This was madness. No one ever returned from here. No one. He stared into a pit as sure as the grave. He would go back. Find some other way. But not without killing. The Stair Guard and Counsel Lords would repel them. The Akkeidii would be criminals. The Song of the Sidors tainted forever.

At his back was a thrum. A steadying current. His weapon calmed him, reached out to quell the denuding fear. It was enough to help him gather his wits.

His breathing slowed.

He spotted a coil of rope. Part of the lashing that held the giant shard in place.

He took it and climbed over the last distance, quiet as stone.

He tied a firm knot around a stout purple stub of crystal. Then he pushed the mass into the hole, swung his legs quietly over the edge, and descended into oblivion.

42

~

LOREMASTER

Late into the night, Lokah went to the heavy curtains to spy the first hint of light. The company made a show of sharing tales with the specter of Aenguz. Stewards brought more pitchers of malt wine at intervals. Kachota met them at the door and retrieved them. Once they left, he emptied them one by one into the basin by the cook fire. And then he placed the empty pitchers on the table. The Akkeidii and Moresi only drank water.

The first moments after Aenguz left, Lokah whispered Aenguz's intent to Legerohn and Mond under the cover of Mandavu and Kachota's voices. Chimere and Stokke had not come in from the other suite yet. Legerohn was incredulous. His mouth attempted words and disbelief collided with his understanding of the Akkeidii who had undertook to rend his hand free of the *purna*. Lokah explained the plan to summon the Counsel Lords in the morning. That should give Aenguz enough time to find and enter the Well. Legerohn froze at the table. Then he joined in with the brothers and their pointless rants. Mond pulled Chimere and Stokke aside and explained the plan to them as well. Lokah watched the faces of the young Moresi as they digested Mond's words. Lokah saw them whisper 'Your words, our will.' Then they too joined in on the ersatz celebration.

Each time Lokah peeked through he secretly hoped he would find Aenguz there. That he would have been thwarted from the futile risk and forced to return. But as the night wore on he began to understand Aenguz's resolve.

When he saw what he thought was first light in the soupy Glaize, he walked out onto the balcony to confirm the translucent sunrise. There on the floor was Aenguz's empty scabbard. The supposed gift from the Chosen Freeholder. His heart drew tight. Aenguz would have wanted his weapon free. It appeared final, like a coda to Aenguz's unbidden journey.

Lokah brought the silver bound scabbard in and set it before the empty chair at the head of the table. The company grew quiet. Exhaustion fortified their dread. Their eyes drooped and demanded sleep.

Lokah continued out the door and down the stairs. Three Stair Guard waited at the base of the narrow stairway. Two brutes with thick legs and powerful arms that made their shields and spears look light. A Step Mark was with them. A yellow flourish like a seal marked the collar of his burgundy cloak.

Lokah asked to speak with the Mono Lord and Counsel Lord Bremball. The Step Mark nodded and waited for Lokah to return up the stair before turning down the corridor.

"Now we wait," he said when he returned to the suite.

The company refreshed themselves and worked to chase the sleep from their eyes and their limbs. Legerohn pulled the curtains back to let what milky light in there was.

Lokah recalled lines from the Lay of *Montmorillionite* to steady his impatience. Reciting couplets in his mind steadied him. But he was still having trouble focusing. The light grew and the time poured past. The Mono Lord was old and likely burdened with other responsibilities. Counsel Lord Bremball could have come by now.

He went to probe the Stair Guard on the progress of the Counsel Lords.

In the corridor at the bottom of the narrow stair, Lokah saw at least two dozen Stair Guard. Their helmeted heads turned to him. Lokah felt helpless as if his use and purpose had been stripped from him. He hadn't expected this response from the Counsel Lords.

"Are the Counsel Lords coming?" Lokah knew the answer.

"Not until the Well of Sorrows is sealed," The Step Mark answered. The two brutes were rooted as if they had been planted in the crystal.

"We must speak with them about the Well of Sorrows."

"They will speak with you after the Well is sealed."

"We have to speak with them! We have to stop them!" Aenguz is in the Well! But Lokah knew any explanation would fall on reticence. They had their orders.

The Step Mark shook his head. The squad bristled.

Lokah lumbered back up to the suite. Every eye was on him and seemed to discern his incapability. "The Counsel Lords are not coming until the Well of Sorrows is sealed." Lokah explained that the corridor was filled with guards.

Mandavu bolted out of his chair. Kachota followed him and went to the top of the stair. The brothers came back huffing and seething at the guards. Mandavu took up his mace and then set it down. Picked it up again and set it back down. Kachota looked at his axes as if they were made of common metal or too heavy to lift.

Legerohn knew of Aenguz's admonishment. There would be no killing. He went down and appealed to the Stair Guard. Frustration knotted his face when he returned.

"What can we do?" Mandavu spouted. He spoke more to the vestiges of Aenguz's words than Lokah or anyone in the dining room. He went to the balcony and surveyed the walls of Corundum. Kachota examined the crystal beside his brother.

"There is no time for that."

Lokah searched his exhausted mind for an answer. For an escape from the sensation of uselessness. Aenguz had charged them to save him from the Well. And to do so without shedding blood. Lokah had assumed the role of a First but if he was honest with himself, he had failed at that role. Twice in the City of the Sho-tah Aenguz had been lost to them. In the One Forest, he had let him go. He had sworn an oath back on the *cog*. He could not do nothing and remain helpless. And he could not kill any of the Stair Guard. Even if he abandoned that charge, there were too many of them. Lokah chanted parts of the Lay to himself. He ran through the more cryptic and arcane verses. The rhythmic couplets had a meditative effect. They steadied his mind and relaxed his self-flagellation and rebuffed his fears of helplessness. Sections, he knew, could be pulled apart and stitched together in different ways. Certain components were set and fixed. Always called the same particular powers from the metal like different intensities of light and heat. There was no value in corrupting those lines. But other stanzas could be pieced together into their own unique phrases. Their own unique wisdoms. Like a subtle combination, the secreted powers of the metal could be revealed to the lorewise. It was by this self-same process, Lokah believed, that Aenguz likely had come to perform the *Surasanskeld*. It was the first time he thought there was something more to this son of a clan lord than he had considered. An admiration had sprouted. And a respect for the son of Sairik beyond the position and role.

Lokah rose up. "Wait here." He took some scraps of cheese from the platter. Grabbed his sword and rebuffed the brothers who started after him. "And close the door."

He went down to meet the squad. He stopped two steps above them. The space was packed with Stair Guard. Armed as he was, they fixed their stance and readied their spears.

Lokah held his sword, tip down, before him. It looked like a pendulum. He wanted to look as unthreatening as possible.

"Are the Counsel Lords coming?"

"Not until the Well of Sorrows is sealed."

"Will you let us pass? We must stop it."

"You have the only answer we will give."

"Very well."

Lokah called the lines to himself. He made sure he had what he needed and nothing unnecessary. Nothing that might dilute the power. His lips parted and slowly the couplets came out.

> *"Can you hear the song of the stars?*
> *Do you know the measure and the bars?*
>
> *Who can hear the sound of mountains?*
> *Or the waters roar, Earth's fountains?*
>
> *In silence, all listening found.*
> *In cacophony, Earth abounds.*
>
> *The voice of silver is alone.*
> *The Mashu's blood and Mashu's bone.*
>
> *Thrumming beneath the Mashu's roots,*
> *All other sound needs become mute."*

Lokah held his sword just up from the step and flicked the blade with his fingernail. At first, he heard nothing. The cheese was packed in tight. But the harmonic vibration coursed through his arm and spine. Then the solitary chime like the ring of a tuning fork reached inside his ears.

And it rose.

The Stair Guard looked to one another and staggered. The two brutes may have been threatening him. Lokah couldn't hear them. They did not reach out to strike him or his sword. They may have been under a similar command to not kill or hurt the company.

The pitch of the metal rose and pierced the fabric of the air. Lokah covered one ear with his free hand.

The Stair Guard stepped back. And then in twos and threes, they toppled. Spears clattered and shields dropped. The two brutes dropped to their knees and fell forward. The Step Mark feinted.

Lokah climbed back up to the room and swung open the heavy crystal door. Dug the cheese out of his ears and said, "Let's go."

The brothers and the Moresi pulled their hands tentatively away from their heads. Mandavu and Kachota lifted up from their curled positions. They looked at Lokah with a reverence and awe as if they were praying. They stood and took up their weapons.

Legerohn had a kind of knowing smile as if he had come to be unsurprised by Akkeidii theurgy. They left Chimere at the long table. He wished the company luck and also luck for those from the keep that these Akkeidii may encounter.

"No killing," Lokah said as he led them down the narrow stair.

Legerohn, Mond, and Stokke took up spears as they stepped over and around the unconscious Stair Guard.

Lokah didn't know which way to go other than down. He had followed behind Aenguz and Bremball without thinking. He stole down a corridor until he came to a stair and then he raced down it. The halls were empty. Dust gathered in corners.

He turned down another corner and came upon a boy playing on an empty stair. He stretched on the steps in a slow-motion lunge. He pretended at fighting invisible invaders. His eyes went wide when he saw Lokah and the rest. His imaginary world seized him.

Lokah grabbed the boy by his shirt. "Take us to the Well of Sorrows now!" He held him firm as he pushed the boy down the stairs.

The boy's feet grazed the floor as Lokah ran. He pointed the way left and down until they got back down to the refectory. The denizens of Corundum jumped back and gasped at the party of Akkeidii and Moresi. A woman screamed and shouted for the Stair Guard as they ran through the hall.

The boy led them across the refectory in front of the kitchens. Shouts and gasps came from within. Pans fell. Pots clanged. People jumped out of the way. The muted light from the Glaize hid the time. But the activity in the kitchen told Lokah that morn meal was over.

The boy pointed them up a further set of stairs beyond the kitchens. Lokah carried the boy ahead of him. His short legs would not go fast enough. The turns and switchbacks were a maze in the crystal citadel. If he lost hold of the boy, it would take time to even return to the refectory. People splayed against the walls in shock as the company ran past.

Up and up they went until finally, the boy led them to a yellowed crystal door. Lokah passed the boy back and thrust the door open. Fogged light poured in. "Where now?" Lokah demanded of the frightened boy.

The boy cowered and pointed down the path as if he was afflicted. His arm shook in a frightened palsy.

The company rushed along a path girded by a squat crystal forest. Purple and white stumps bolted at angles in the open space on either side. The Glaize was a void of gray. Lokah rushed up the winding path.

Soon the shapes of Stair Guard appeared in the mist. And the blue-robed Counsel Lords materialized.

"Stop!" Lokah shouted. "Hold!"

The specters turned to them.

Mandavu and Kachota were ready for a fight. Their weapons bounced lightly in their hands. Legerohn and Mond gripped their spears and poised ready to lunge. Stokke was somewhere behind them guarding their rear.

The Stair Guard turned to fight.

"Do not seal the Well!" Lokah jogged closer.

Lord Bremball waved the Stair Guard back.

The Counsel Lords parted.

Lokah could see thick beams perched up amid the crystal trunks.

Ropes dangled and draped lifelessly. The steepled lever came into focus with each step.

Mono Lord Venrahl leaned on his staff before the fat nub of tourmaline. A woman wept at his feet. "It is done," he wheezed. Tears filled the creases on his face.

Lokah's steps were heavy. Each step a moment of inculcation, of inability and uselessness.

The company stepped up woodenly to the nub and stared dumbly at it. "You fools!" Lokah raged. "Aenguz is down there!"

The realization came in waves to the Counsel Lords. They searched one another's faces. Lokah's emotion and certainty cut through any question they might have had.

Venrahl looked up with a grim realization and slumped again. All of his strength was gone.

Lokah searched out the bright spot in the Glaize perched at an angle in the east. It was not yet midday. It was barely mid-morning.

Bremball stepped toward him helplessly. "The Mono Lord determined to seal the Well early so that none might be hurt."

Lana's blue eyes trembled. New tears formed. She stood by the old Mono Lord as if she was ready to catch him.

Kachota ringed the fat tourmaline plug. He called to Lokah and the others. A line of rope was wrapped around a stout crystal. Lokah recognized the Akkeidii climbing knot. The other end was trapped taut in the sealed mouth of the Well.

Mandavu roared. His pent up rage took force and form. He swung his mace at the tourmaline plug. Shards splintered off. He wound up and swung again and again. Metal and crystal rang. Shattered chips flew everywhere. The company pulled back.

Kachota was lost, unable to console his brother.

Lokah asked Bremball in between the strokes, "There must be another way beneath."

"I am sorry. There is no other way down. We have looked."

"Well, we have not."

43

~~

A REFUSAL OF REQUIEM

The Counsel Lords departed the Well. The fulfillment of their life's work had only given the Well of Sorrows one final victim. Lana escorted the Mono Lord away. Bremball took the grieving woman beside him. He extended what consolation he could to the shocked company. The Stair Guard abandoned the tangled scaffolding and steered clear of Mandavu. They considered the giant and the nub of tourmaline as they passed. Two immovable forces. One aspect of their purpose in warding the Well was over. They disappeared in the mist after the Counsel Lords.

Mandavu's blows shattered the dampening calm of the Glaize. Lokah and Kachota came together and negotiated a pause to the giant's rage.

The devastated Akkeidii came back to the sullen Moresi. Legerohn looked bereft. His head floated from side to side as if he was searching for an answer in the minute space around him. Mond clenched his jaw and pursed his lips as if he was suppressing a groan or a wail. Stokke's brows steepled as if he was about to cry. Perhaps the prospect of the tight space touched on his own deep fears.

Lokah drew the company together. He calmed himself with the rhythm of the Lay. But he was caught with a sense that he was not wise enough to uncover something, anything in the Lay that might help. He was not a Stonemage. Did not have or know how to use a *durann*. But he would not be thwarted. His mind worked. "We are not done. Aenguz is still alive. And we will find a way to reach him. He has food and water and *montmorillionite*. He can last for days down there. But we cannot wait. We must scour Corundum for any egress to the underbelly of the keep."

"Bremball said there was no other entrance," Mandavu said, challenging Lokah. His chest rose in anger in his ill-fitted robe.

"We are Akkeidii and Moresi. We have not looked. Stone is not perfect. And even the tiniest opening might be exploited."

"Is there any other opening that you know of beyond this one?" Mandavu's ire rose.

"No, but by Grieg's eyes, we will survey the length and breadth of Corundum. Inside and out for any crack or cave or seam."

"How big is this Corundum? Do you know?"

"No, but-"

"Do you know how long it would take?"

"No, but-"

"Then this is the only opening that we here now know of."

"Yes."

"Then do what you will, my search starts and ends here."

Lokah looked to Kachota for any insight to reach Mandavu. Kachota's eyes bounced as if they had lost their mooring. He looked sheepish like a child afraid of cross parents.

"If we work together to survey the keep-"

"He could have killed me. Twice. He should have killed me. Instead, he freed me. Twice. And on the one occasion that he asked anything of me, of us," He directed his ire at Lokah. The company did not exist to him. "We failed him. We could not prevent these fools from sealing him in. A simple task. Nothing next to the trials he led us through." Mandavu searched the suffocating Glaize. Gray light dampened the crystal forest. "You spoke of the Song of the Kriels. What do you think the Song of the Kriels and the Song of the Makans will say about us? What would our fathers say about us? Our mothers? Our clans? That Aenguz led us across the length of the Lands of the Earth. From the southern arm of the Wester all the way to the Spine." Mandavu reached out to point east to west, but the Glaize or clouds beyond hid the sun and took his sense of direction. It fed his unchecked rage. He whipped his hand in a whirl unsure of anything. "How many horrors did he save us from? How many days did he look to our safety? We stand on the very structure he set out for those many days ago." Mandavu gulped down a lump. "Not even one day. One day has not passed and we lost him. We swore on the balcony, as if no other oath held us, to prevent the Well from being sealed. One minor task. But *we* could not be troubled to arrive in time." The indictment was directed at Lokah but Mandavu spoke as much to himself. "I know what the songs will say when our role in the loss of our lord is known. That the Makan and Kriel Champions could not save the Ruler of the Akkeidii. That they did not raise their blades once in his protection or defense. That a Sidor, from the line of Grieg Sidor no less, charged with a burden by the Flayer, who had saved our lives ten times over," he swept his arm over the morose company. "Was lost to the very place he traveled to for help." His brow relaxed for an instant. "It is well that he did not name you as his First. That failure, especially for a Kriel would not be born well among the Kriels. I know what it would mean for a Makan." His anger and accusation could not wholly mask his own shame.

Lokah felt the shame and failure too. Aenguz had charged them not to kill. And he had to allow time for Aenguz to reach the Well of Sorrows. He could not know the Counsel Lords would seal the Well early. But the outcomes would speak for themselves. They had presided over the death of another Akkeidii lord after he had done so much to preserve them. "Still, I must search while life and faith holds."

"Then search Loremaster. You will find me here. And By Grieg, our lord will know that we are here, and that we are trying to reach him." With that, Mandavu returned to the megalithic plug.

Lokah understood Mandavu's rationale. But he saw his own failure as one of reasoning and not force. Yes, the Well was sealed but Aenguz was not dead. And the keep was not surveyed yet. In his own estimation there was still a chance, still a reason for hope. The Counsel Lords could be wrong. They did not know the mountains the way the Akkeidii did. But he would need all of the rest of them. Mandavu could not be reached.

"Kachota, begin up here. Find where the crystal meets the Spine. Determine the size of this place if you can. See if you cannot find some seams in the rock face. Mark anything that holds promise. We will chisel our way in if possible." Lokah started to say, 'Keep an eye on Mandavu,' but Kachota nodded tersely and dismissed the counsel.

"Legerohn, will you and Mond and Stokke search the lower face of the keep? Look for anything that might be exploited. Water ran here once. If there is any kind of an opening, we will make our way in. We have *silvercryst*."

Legerohn agreed. He commanded Stokke to bring Chimere to the refectory. If anything was found, they could tell Chimere. That way he could act as a central point for them all.

Lokah agreed with Legerohn's reasoning. And he appreciated the Prince's hope of a speedy answer to their search. "We will gather there at dusk or when the Glaize dims and see what has been learned. Then we can focus our efforts. I will search the interior of the citadel and see if there are cellars or other basements that might touch on rock or a wall that borders this shaft."

Legerohn said, "It will be done."

Mond answered, "Your words, our will."

Lokah turned to Kachota. The younger brother nodded and turned up the trail and headed into the murk of the Glaize. He slowed as he passed his older brother and then continued on without a word. Lokah left with the Moresi. The pings of chiseling tourmaline followed them down the trail to the maze of Corundum.

44

~~

OBLIVION

A primordial darkness swallowed him. A blackness that existed before the first blessing of light passed over the void.

The line was an umbilical cord connecting Aenguz to reality and the certainty of creation.

The flicks of firelight could not reach past the lip. The Glaize above sealed him in as if shovel fulls of murk covered him.

Aenguz lowered himself quietly down into the shaft. It was angled like everything else in the Keep.

Part of him hoped that he would hear Mandavu and Lokah arguing, fighting, preventing the Counsel Lords from enacting their world-ending designs. But even the vague conversations of the Stair Guard were devoured by the black.

He was gripped by the sense that there might be no floor to the well. That some other wound in Corundum, caused by the calamity of the Last Battle had left a puncture into the true void. An empty space where bodies might drift for an eternity.

When he came to the end of the rope, he was sure that his fear had been proven true.

Aenguz reasoned it was safe to cast some light.

He braced his feet against the wall. The shaft had narrowed considerably.

Aenguz was careful with his weapon.

The tips grazed the walls of the shaft.

> *"Ev'r keen, ever new, ever bright*
> *Earth's first star to dispel the night*
>
> *Born of the mind bound to the life*
> *Down to Earth with death's final strife*
>
> *Light in the dark and in the hand*
> *Pow'r concentrated from the Lands."*

His *montmorillionite* came to life. White light filled the shaft.

A sudden claustrophobic fright raced his breaths. A narrow channel of vertigo drew his heart through a siphon.

He could not see the opening.

Below was an even more concentrated black. It drank the light with ease.

He inspected the walls for a way to climb down or press. The shaft was tighter. He might be able to brace against it. If only the rope was a little longer.

Then suddenly, a horrible screeching sound. A tectonic shift blasted the tunnel. The walls shook. The air punched him down like a hammer's blow.

The rope slipped from his hands.

His weapon dropped.

The light snuffed out.

And Aenguz fell.

Aenguz grasped out desperately at the walls. Anything to stem the fall. His garments scraped and ripped. His skin grated against the crystal.

In time measured only in panicked heartbeats, the walls left him. He was lost. Dropped into the abyss. A forever fall. Adrift. Alone. All darkness compressed around him.

Then Aenguz crashed onto a pile of brittle scree and detritus. It caught him and started an avalanche in the black. A sharp and shifting river gulped him downward. This must be some secret portal to the Black Earth. A wound in Corundum that ferried him past death into that bleak shadow world.

In the slide, he could hear the scree pouring off a further edge. Gnawing rocks plinked down elsewhere some deeper black below him. A subterranean chamber within filled with the blackest night. The crèche of uncreated night.

He spread his arms out and his legs to stem the slide. Cuts and jabs poked him on the deathly river like malicious claws in the darkness. It brought him to a stop. His heart was loud enough to drown out the clattering just ahead.

Then the brume of death came and choked him. The stilled air of the under gloom was fetid and foul. Blood and bile. The unmistakable scent of corpses. Spoiled salt. Rank and rot.

He coughed uncontrollably and covered his mouth and nose to find a breath. He pulled shreds of his sleeve up over his mouth. The fibers filtered the air just as they had ameliorated the Ganzir's heat. The panic of suffocation was stayed partially.

Strange dry stones shifted and rattled around him.

The plinks slowed and dropped off into the deep.

When his heart relented from paroxysm, Aenguz reached out in the darkness for something surer than the river of scree.

His foot found something. He edged toward it and braced against it. He dug his feet in below the surface. Then he took account of the barbs and shards that were still lodged in his skin. Damp sticky blood and deep cuts carved up his legs and arms.

The wall he braced against was smooth but not like crystal. It was hard but not like stone. He needed light. Where was his weapon?

His waterskin had, thankfully, shielded his head and much of his back. But it was wet, and light.

A shard had pierced through the bladder. Water was pouring out of the skin. He touched the sharp edges and rounded nubs and knew reluctantly that this was bone. The entire landslide must be comprised of bones. All the failed attempts at the Well of Sorrows gathered here. He tried to climb out of the pool of bones. Tried to steel his mind against it.

> *This was not the Black Earth. He was not in hell.*
> *At least not the one where damned souls dwell.*
> *This was the Bane of Corundum.*
>
> *He needed his weapon. Needed light.*
> *He called out in the stifling grave of despair.*
>
> *"Light of the Earth burnished and true*
> *Warrior forger silver hue*
>
> *Forged in the mind, crafted in soul*
> *Singular kind for one alone*
>
> *Ev'r keen, ever new, ever bright*
> *Earth's first star to dispel the night."*

At first, there was nothing.

Just the eternity between heartbeats.

Despair reached him, assured him of his own death.

Alone. Soon to join the rest here.

Then his wide eyes caught a gleam.

Despair cast doubt in him. Insisted what he saw was false, that his eyes were being tricked.

Aenguz chanted the words again. Breathed them through the cloth.

The light grew. Like white gems in a king's vault.

Montmorillionite shone through a ghoulish pile of gaping skulls and riven bones. The dead guardians of this rank tomb tried to take it or draw life from it.

Aenguz waded to the light. His hand anchored against the smooth wall.

He set the slide in motion again. The bones worked to take his weapon down.

He could not go too fast. But he also could not lose his weapon.

Desperation drove him forward to the strangled light.

The dry bones clutched at him, drew him down as if he was surrounded by drowning skeletons.

He lunged the final distance.

But death's ghouls would not be thwarted.

They carried the weapon over the edge into a deeper nothingness.

Hope fell with his weapon.

He reached the shattered edge of stone and watched the light drop. Bones poured after it.

The dead at his back pushed on him but he was anchored at the opening.

But the silver light did not vanish. It swung in the air as if it had caught on a branch.

The grasping ghouls plummeted down cracking and clattering through a sieve.

The silver cast strange shadows like a lantern on a storm-tossed ship.

The space was filled with interconnected arms as if globes had filled the chamber and then liquid bone was filled in between and then hardened. And then the globes were melted away.

Even as bright as the light was, it did not reach the floor or walls of this other-worldly chamber.

He reached around and tested an arm. He pulled himself out into the strange cavern.

The thinnest arms were brittle. Every step and grapple was uncertain. Branches broke. Others held.

Bones rattled at his back and down into the nether black.

The shifting light turned the fulcrum of his balance, but it held in the air suspended by the hook. Finally, thankfully, he reached his weapon.

He braced in a crook of joints around it but didn't reach for it. It still swung and cast slow, ugly shadows.

He rooted in his pocket and pulled out the knotted *mithrite* chain and Selene's ribbon. He untangled the two lines and wrapped the ribbon around his wrist. Soft pale blue covered the sickly flesh. The mottled skin that she ignored, didn't care one jot about.

Then Aenguz looped the chain through the ring and knotted it around his wrist. The gift from Legerohn that had effected their escape by releasing the captured weapons. Once again the Moresi was saving Akkeidii metal. He grabbed his weapon by the spike and pulled it across his lap. The waving shadows stopped and stilled in the strange dark world. He looped the other end of *mithrite* around the hilt, tested the chain, and tightened it to see that it would hang securely from his wrist. Both metals held.

He checked his waterskin. It was all but empty. He drank the last of it and tied the bladder around the arm to mark the spot by the opening.

His food was gone. Lost in the fall or buried in the bones. He inspected his cuts and hurts. Red dotted the white fabric. The gossamer acted like a kind of gauze against the bone wounds. He was in no immediate danger. But the loss of the water was...

He considered the sound above that precipitated his fall. It had to be the perched obelisk. The Well of Sorrows had been sealed. But it wasn't near midday. So much time couldn't have passed yet. Had Lokah and Mandavu failed? Were they prevented? Dead? He didn't think the Counsel Lords were so callous. Or had the Mono Lord hurried the sealing? Either way, his only way in or out was gone. If he found the Dagba Stone, how could he get out? Now, the only way to let the others know that the Stone was or wasn't here would be by his own death.

45

ALTHOUGH I CANNOT SEE

Lokah fortified himself with the knowledge that Aenguz was still alive. His weapon had not vibrated with the death chime. He had food and water and *montmorillionite*. If his search for the stone failed, he would be looking for cracks and fissures as well. If either of them found a promising spot, they would hear a pinging or a clarion from the metal. Listening would be as important as searching. He would remind the others when he got back. He stamped down the sense that it was a feeble hope.

The heart of the keep was solid. Rooms and corridors fanned out in a haphazard way from the center. Like their flight to the Well of Sorrows, he had to go down and through the refectory and up. There was no direct way across. His equilibrium was strained against the angles and the striations of the keep. The canted walls left Lokah feeling like the citadel was listing to the side. The emptiness of the place overwhelmed him as much as the incongruent twists and turns. When he encountered denizens or stewards, they pointed down a hall or a stair but could not offer much else about what he might find.

When the Glaize dimmed, Lokah returned to the refectory. He worked to keep a mental map of the pathways of Corundum. He pondered a way to mark key corridors and eliminate others. He heard no sounds. Found no promising seams.

A cadre of eight Stair Guard passed him and descended the stair to the entrance of Corundum. He gave them space. He wasn't sure if any of these were ones he had toppled or if word of what had happened had reached all of them. Better to keep back. He looked out over the inner balcony and followed them until they were out of sight. A young boy, a novice, stood at sharp attention as they passed. He wore an animal horn around his neck. Lokah presumed that this was the night watch heading down to relieve the Stair Guard at the top of the cliff and at the middle watch, halfway up the Stair of Forhnthulen.

Lokah turned back into the refectory. Clusters of families spread out in the cavernous dining hall. They cooed and fluttered around the few children in their number. They hung on every bright note and laugh. The little ones were the centers of their miniature separate universes. The parents and aunts and uncles put on brave faces and drank up the joy the children provided. The distances between families appeared vast.

Cleaning occupied the attendants in the kitchen. Men and women moved about organizing, scrubbing, stacking pots and crocks. Remnant odors mixed with soapy water. Two hulking men with heavy aprons teetered about as if the joints in their hips and knees were arthritic. They rocked and pivoted around the others and helped where heavy lifting was required.

Lokah fumed at his own anger. Life was already returning back to normal in the keep. Far too soon. Aenguz was still lost. But the dual sorrows of barrenness and lost hope still infused the place with a grim pall like the yellowed walls of Corundum.

He found Chimere and the Moresi at a table away from the denizens of the keep. In the massive dining hall, it was easy to sit apart. Kachota was giving orders to a steward. The young man nodded and nodded as Kachota spoke. The Moresi ate. Chimere had seen to the food and drink.

He was navigating and talking with other stewards. Platters and pitchers were spread out on the table. Mandavu was not there. Lokah scanned the opposite end of the hall on the further side of the refectory, but he did not see the stubborn Makan.

Kachota reached for some food to give as Lokah approached, but Chimere was closer. Lokah accepted the seedy roll and raised it up to the Two Lands and Twin Rivers and silently asked the Mashu for any kind of guidance.

They all continued eating and gave Lokah a chance to drink and eat. They were still hungry from their long days of traveling to Corundum. And Lokah saw how none of them had slept since the day before. Eyelids hung at half-mast. Heads looked impossibly heavy. Stokke yawned in between bites. Chimere rested his head in his hand. His leg lay up on the bench.

Kachota chomped on cheese and mutton quickly and washed it down with a deep gulp of malt wine. He was still chewing when he spoke. "The Glaize is a curse. I am blinded up there. I do not know the breadth of the place yet. I did find where the headwaters split around the keep. The glass water is as ill as the air up there." He tore a hunk of bread off before he continued. "If the waters ran, there might be some rift or channel. I cannot say. I need more time."

Legerohn chimed in as Kachota took a drink. "We followed the waters along a narrow stair down from the entrance. The river drops away and down the mountainside, but the stair leads to a toothed pool beneath an overhang. Frozen water fills it. We were able to walk on it and see where it issued out. But it is clogged with a glass wave. It may hold promise, but we could find nothing. Perhaps your eyes may see more."

Lokah nodded. "I will come with you there tomorrow." He contemplated the waters. If the crystal wasn't enough to seal the keep, the stilled waters throughout the keep acted like a diamond mortar that held everything tight in its grip. If they had flowed, there might be an answer but the power that stayed the Glaize and the waters around Corundum were beyond him, were certainly beyond any of the powers in the Lay.

He recounted his search and his general understanding of his conception of the structure around the center of the keep. He confessed that he too would need more time just to finish the south side. There were no places of promise thus far. There was less hope in his voice than he intended to show. They were all determined, but they were tired. Lokah knew it was hard for anyone to think after the day's events. "Get some rest. We have not slept since we found Aenguz." They had all experienced the shock and surprise at finding him out from the Ganzir. And too quick he was gone again. "We have only just begun. Rest and tomorrow we will search with the knowledge we have gained today."

A pair of stewards came up with some bundles and supplies. All eyes turned to Kachota as he inspected what they had brought. He granted them a terse thanks and then turned back to the others.

"My brother will not rest in a bed while Aenguz sleeps on stone. He will bed down in the hall where we came unto the topside of the keep. I bring food and water to him and some better fitting clothes. And I will join him." He took another deep draught. "He continues on the obelisk. It is hard stone. They meant for it to be sealed forever." He looked at some more food and passed over it. "Although I cannot see, I have no fear of being lost. I hear his mace pounding in the bleak." With that, he stood up and gathered up all he could carry. "I will come to Chimere if I find anything. Otherwise, I will find you here tomorrow at day's end." He turned and walked off through the tables and past the few families that remained.

The next morning, Lokah followed Legerohn and Mond down the stair to the entrance of Corundum. There was so much to cover, and time was racing by. Midyear was only two days away. The Dagba Stone and message felt tertiary. His focus was on locating an exit for Aenguz. He was still alive, but they had not found any sign yet. Lokah wished Aenguz knew that he wasn't alone and left for dead.

His inadequacies haunted him. He had panicked the night before when they returned to the rooms. The stewards had cleared the table while they were away and the satchel of seeds, Aenguz's last charge of him, was missing. The innocent act left him in a muted apoplexy. The Moresi were frightened at first by his panic. They helped and found all of the remaining sacks, including the one with the seeds. They were placed on a shelf by the small kitchen. Lokah slung it over his shoulder and slept with it.

The night watch was returning from the Stair of Fohrnthulen as he and Legerohn and Mond crossed the entrance. The two braziers were dying, and the incipient light of dawn was illuminating the Glaize. The eight Stair Guard glanced at the searchers with a tiredness that mirrored their own.

Legerohn and Mond led Lokah to the corner of the entrance. Stokke helped Chimere to his post in the refectory. A narrow path was carved into the face of Corundum. It followed a rough angle down along the still river. The Moresi leaned against the crystal as if they were afraid they might fall into the water as if it still surged. Or as if the Glaize might reach out and take them. After forty steps or so, the river dropped down out of sight. The trail reached around the keep until it came to a round pool elevated in the void. Stone teeth ringed it. Frozen glass poured between them and held still. The water within roiled in a frozen churn. A massive overhang of rock and crystal seventy or eighty feet high covered the pool. Legerohn climbed onto the frozen lake. Mond warded his Tahnka.

They didn't speak until they were clear of the stair. "I asked the stewards. This pond is called Mimirmere. Above us is the bottom of the Divine Oculum. This space," he cast his arms about in the void, "is called Rainbow's Crèche." The Prince looked at Lokah with a chagrin that bordered on ridiculousness. The Glaize took meaning from everything.

He led Lokah into the maw of Rainbow's Crèche. A wall of water filled the hole and choked it. Lokah began examining the edge where water touched stone. The frozen water sealed every crease like sudden amber. Lokah stepped back to the center of Mimirmere to take in the entirety of the blocked cavern.

Stokke reached the water as he did. He informed them that food was being readied for them. Chimere was seeing to it.

Legerohn and Mond waited on Lokah for some sign or indication how to proceed. They had found nothing but surely an Akkeidii could see things they could not in the fissures around the hole.

Lokah tested the water with his sword. Stone would be easier to chisel. But the water filled in everywhere. He walked to the other side of the pool. He caught the edge of a second path. He thought of the breastplates of the Stair Guard and the relief of two stairs. *Two stairs.*

Legerohn and Mond nodded in approval. They trailed behind Lokah. It was a vague hope, but his hope was desperate for any hold on possibility.

The path led around like the other one. But it ended abruptly. The side of Corundum was shorn off. He could make out a mass of boulders just on the edge of the Glaize below and up the mountainside. Hunks of water splashed frozen here and there amid the landslide. He saw the corner of an opening like the entrance on the south side. But it was the wall of Corundum that stretched straight down and disappeared into the rockfall below. There was less hope here.

They walked back to Mimirmere. Lokah examined the south side and peered over the edge. He guessed that anywhere the water touched the opening would be sealed. But he would find a way to look, nonetheless.

They went back up to the refectory to eat and recalibrate their search. He told them to listen as well as look. Aenguz may be making a sound near an opening. The ringing from Lokah's weapon the day before reminded them and bolstered them.

Lokah needed help on the inside and the outside. He needed help from the Counsel Lords and the Stair Guard. But they ignored the search happening around them. Other than the absence of the Counsel Lords, life in the keep was inching back toward a new normal. He could feel it in the rhythms and routines of life in the giant refectory. Their return to normalcy conflicted with his growing urgency. He asked a steward about the Counsel Lords. The steward informed them that the Counsel Lords were in conclave deciding how best to oppose the Divider. They had not been seen in the keep since the Well was sealed.

The company split up again and continued their search. Lokah directed the Moresi to search inside. He would search up the slope outside the keep. It was the only place left that could be reached by foot. Perhaps the water pulled away from the keep somewhere. He would check on Mandavu and Kachota later. There was too much to cover and too little time.

46

~~

HONOR BOUND

Lokah passed the night watch on the tree-lined boulevard as the Glaize soaked up the last of the light. His search had yielded nothing. Uselessness gnawed at him as he walked behind them.

Two braziers burned in the entrance. The Stair Guard saluted Counsel Lord Bremball as they passed. The boy with the curled horn stood beside him until the watch passed by.

"The Glaize reasserts itself after being battled for so long. The Mono Lord strove against it for days once we saw your approach from the Divine Oculum." Bremball said as Lokah walked up. *Days? What powers allowed them to see so far?* Bremball continued. "Corundum was fashioned firmly." The statement seemed to imply an answer to Lokah's feelings of helplessness.

Lokah brushed needles and burrs off his beige robe.

"Generations have explored Corundum. Mates and spouses especially. It is difficult for us to watch. But we have become inured to it in a way. We know Corundum."

Lokah reasoned that Bremball was not here to dissuade him. Nor was he here to rub salt. There was some other purpose.

"Have you determined a way to fight the Flayer? Is that what you have come to share?"

"There is much yet to still discuss. The Mono Lord is still recovering from his battle against the Glaize." Bremball looked into the static mist and then back to Lokah. "There is a way you can help find the purpose in your lord's sacrifice. Your knowledge of the Lands in the east would serve a great benefit to us and the Lands of the Earth."

Lokah considered Bremball's veiled implication that Aenguz was lost. And the Counsel Lord's need for intelligence. But what force could they muster against all the Erebim, Sallow, and Tsurah they had seen. There was no army here.

"I am concerned only with freeing Aenguz. Once he is freed, we will tell you the tale of our journey from the Wester and before."

Bremball's pursed lips worked through his words. "Time is our foe in this matter. We hope to take some measure by midyear to oppose the Divider. In that way, we hope to answer the call of the message."

Lokah glanced back at the darkened Glaize and the shimmerless waters. "No power has aided you against the Divider's power here. This is only one expression of his might. Have you not striven against it?"

"We have. But there has been no permanent surcease to the Glaize. And no release for the waters."

"Then what can you hope to bring against the Flayer?"

Bremball looked intently at Lokah. "Is it so different from your own hope?"

Lokah wondered about the futility. Bremball intimated that his efforts were for the world while Lokah's was for only one man. And Lokah had not striven against the Glaize. It made him question the limits of his lore wisdom. His helplessness to save Aenguz or the incapability to help the Counsel Lords. "Let me see how the others have fared today." His determination buoyed his flagging hope. "If they have found a place to expand or carve through, we will share what we have seen and encountered in the Lands of the Earth."

Bremball accepted the answer and nodded compassionately as Lokah left.

The Moresi were at a table away from the groups of families. In comparison to the clusters of life, the Moresi were sullen. Kachota was nowhere to be seen.

Legerohn recounted the fruitlessness of the day's search. Stokke listened all day at the pool but heard nothing.

Lokah was beginning to realize that Bremball was right. Generations had searched for any other way to save countless others who had hazarded the Well of Sorrows. His hope and determination and lore simply weren't going to be enough.

They would continue to search and listen, but their hope dwindled. None mentioned the fact that midyear day would fall on the morrow.

How could life continue in Corundum so oblivious?

Chimere cocked his head. Something came to him. Lokah noticed the young Moresi. His mouth hung open for a moment before he spoke. "What about the Vaults of Corundum? Have you found them?"

Disjointed pieces fell into place for Lokah. The path around the heart of Corundum. The refectory as a throughway. The stewards restrained helpfulness. The Counsel Lords reticence. The two brutes in the kitchen. Lokah assembled them like parts of Corundum's cryptic map. The steward that hovered near them stepped back gingerly from the company. He knew. And he wouldn't be fooled by the Counsel Lords again.

"I need the brothers." He got up and headed toward the top of the keep. The Moresi looked at one another and tried to decipher what they had missed.

Lokah pushed open the yellow door on top of Corundum. The fading light held the wavy contour of the Spine. A mighty ping rang out. The feeble echoes failed in the Glaize.

Lokah followed the sound to the Well. The tourmaline plug no longer towered in the hole. He could make out Mandavu on the further side as he approached. Broken hunks of tourmaline hid the edges of the Well. It looked like he was smashing rock as a penance or punishment. Flecks of the colored stone covered him head to toe. He wore a shirt that fit him better than the undersized robe, but it looked like a kind of stone-mail armor coated as it was.

"Mandavu," Lokah called.

The giant stopped. He set the point of his *montmorillionite* mace down and leaned against it. Minor debris clung to his mace, but no edge was dulled no facet scratched. The spike at the top was as sharp as the day it was forged. Mandavu sagged. His chest heaved. He wiped powder and sweat away from his face. "What is it? Have you found a way down?"

"No."

Kachota came out of the dark mist beyond and echoed his brother's question.

Mandavu pulled up his mace to resume.

"Wait. Perhaps."

Mandavu stopped. Kachota drew in close.

"I will need your strength," he said to them both. "We have not seen the Vaults of Corundum and they may hold an answer."

Mandavu set his mace back and listened. Impatience teetered in him.

Lokah explained what he reasoned. "It may not hold a way but, we must be sure."

Mandavu agreed but he would not be pulled away from the plug he had set his will against. He waited for more.

"We may be unable to observe Aenguz's wish. They may not take us there willingly."

Mandavu shrugged as if a collar had been released from his neck. He wiped his face again, pulled up his mace, and walked away from the piles of scattered tourmaline.

"All ways must be explored." He hefted his mace as he walked to Lokah. "This offers a more direct force sometimes, Loremaster."

The three Akkeidii descended into the keep.

When they returned to the refectory the space was empty. A score or more of Stair Guard ringed the Moresi. Bremball, Counsel Lord Lana and Stair Mark Uran stood just outside the cordon. A line of Stair Guard stood at the edge of the kitchen. The two aproned brutes held massive cudgels behind the counter.

The Stair Guard left a space for the Akkeidii to pass and join the Moresi.

"Another greeting," Mandavu said.

"A warning," Stair Mark Uran answered.

"We must search every possible way." Lokah inclined his head toward the kitchen. "The Vaults may hold an answer."

"There is none. The heart of the keep is solid."

"Please, do not ask this of us," Bremball said. "Our purpose here is clear."

"Would you risk our knowledge for that purpose? One we care nothing for. We hold no interest for whatever treasures you keep there. We possess the greatest treasure in all the Lands of the Earth." Lokah held his sword before him, tip down as if the obviousness of *montmorillionite's* value was plain.

Mandavu and Kachota exuded an "Aye." They held their weapons as if they were the greatest prize in Corundum.

"Our Oaths to protect the Vaults is sacrosanct. We do not wish to battle you, but we will. We must."

Lokah surveyed the Stair Guard and the Counsel Lords. He looked to Legerohn and the Moresi. They were ready. Mond was taut. He gave

Lokah a tight nod. Stokke held Chimere but they both looked ready to tackle the nearest Stair Guard.

He turned his head to Mandavu. "For the Song of the Kriels."

"And the Makans," Mandavu and Kachota answered.

Legerohn stepped forward and raised his voice. "Counsel Lords, Stair Mark Uran. We are not your enemies. We are all victims of the First Treacher's conceit. His words serve only to divide. We must stand together."

"As long as you stay clear of the Vaults we have no enmity with you," Uran replied.

"We have no interest in what you hold there," Lokah said calmly. "We must exhaust all means to reach our lord."

"Your lord is lost and gone," Uran replied with a hard finality.

"He is still alive," Lokah said.

Mandavu and Kachota assented.

Legerohn continued. "I do not presume to know all of the mysteries of the Akkeidii's metal, but I have come to know with certainty that its power is true. Aenguz Sidor is not dead. But if we do not find a way beneath Corundum he will be." The Prince gathered himself.

"I have traveled with many Akkeidii on this long and dire journey. I am here to tell you that they will not be dissuaded. Have you not seen how Mandavu chisels away at the blocking crystal? Or the scouring that Kachota has done in the mountains above? Have you not seen the lengths that Lokah has gone to in order to gain some entry point to the depths below? It has only been two days. Do you think they will stop? I have watched them endure far worse for far longer than this. And they had endured even more before I met them. Before they freed us from the grips of the Sallow.

"They are honor bound to find their lord or bury him. If now is their time to die in service of that end, then they will die. But it will be known beyond any doubt that they died trying to save their lord. No other memory of their efforts will serve." He paused briefly. "And it will be remembered that it is you who prevented them. The Moresi will remember."

As Legerohn spoke, Mond straightened. Stokke drew up courage even with Chimere resting on his shoulder.

There was silence. Spears shifted. The Counsel Lords gripped their staffs. There was no movement.

Lokah glanced briefly on Legerohn with satisfaction. He balanced the tip of his weapon on the ground before Legerohn and bade the Moresi to take it. Legerohn clutched it with both hands and kept it poised. The honor and respect exchanged by that act between the two was palpable.

"Before we begin," Lokah began. He pulled the satchel strap over his head. "This was the last thing Aenguz asked of me. If he does indeed die, let this be the last thing that you remember of him here in Corundum. Not the message. Let it be remembered that Akkeidii and Moresi bore the message here."

He walked over to a table between them and lifted the flap and said, "These are seeds from the Oasis of Ganzir. From the Chosen Freeholder there."

Then he reached in his pocket and emptied the few seeds onto the table. The rest of the company did the same recalling Aenguz's admonishment to preserve them on the Rursh Keleg. Mond gathered the seeds from the Moresi's pockets. Legerohn dared not move for fear of losing his grip. Stokke and Chimere were hung together.

Counsel Lord Lana looked to Bremball and whispered, "Could it be?" She relaxed her staff into the crook of her shoulder. She walked past the Stair Guard and went to the table. She looked at the seeds and into the sack.

"These are all seeds?" she said incredulously. "All seeds from the Oasis of Ganzir?"

"This was the last wish of Aenguz Sidor. Now our lord is in peril. Will you lead us to the Vault to confirm there is indeed no other way beneath Corundum?"

Lana looked back at Bremball. His eyes softened and he deferred to her. Lana turned to Uran and said, "Let them pass."

The Stair Guard parted. There was no small sense of relief that fluttered through the ranks.

Lana gathered up the loose seeds and the satchel that Lokah set down. Then she said, "Follow me." The line of soldiers led the way directly to the kitchen.

Within, the two aproned brutes set their cudgels down on a wide butcher's block. They stood at crooked attention as Counsel Lord Lana and Uran entered. Their rickety joints left them stiff.

Before Lokah crossed the opening into the realm of the kitchen, he turned back to Bremball. He wondered if this was yet another trap. The line halted behind him. Lana turned and looked back at Uran.

The Stair Mark ordered the soldiers to fall out. They withdrew out of the kitchen and drifted out into the empty hall.

"I only held you back to protect you not to imprison you. You have been to every corner of Corundum. I have seen your efforts and it is clear you love your lord or owe him some life debt that cannot be easily paid.

"I do not know if you will find an egress that so far has not been found. But I do not, I will not halt your honor from being fulfilled. I am sorry for your loss. Aenguz bore a hard charge. In a way, he was already shorn from the world of men. Perhaps his pursuit into the depths was the outward manifestation of that separation. Perhaps he cannot return. Was not meant to return. How can a man bear the doom of the earth and remain whole?

"But if there is a way, I know that you will find it even if it is only through the same hole he went down."

Lana led on past the different island tables and standing cook fires, stacks of wood, shelves, further into a dusty pantry.

The Counsel Lord pushed at the back of the pantry and the shelf swung in.

Darkness and must greeted Lokah. It seemed as if he was entering into some kind of secreted root cellar.

Lana coaxed blue light from the chiseled wood at the head of her staff. She walked self-confidently down the hall.

Soon ambient light ahead framed her. Lokah followed down to a brightly lit landing. Stone arches framed a compact rectangular courtyard. Ambient light poured down from above. The opening was out of sight. Darkness filled the low arches.

A pair of Stair Guard stood in the center.

They were at ease at the sight of the Counsel Lord but as Lokah appeared from behind they squared their stance.

Lana assured them.

She led them to the left and under the heavy arch.

The corridor turned immediately to the right and ran down into the black.

The Akkeidii followed suit with light from their weapons.

The corridor ran downward at a gentle grade deeper and deeper into the secret heart of Corundum.

The atmosphere held the must of ancient rock.

She came to a stop.

By some means that Lokah could not see, the Counsel Lord opened the massive doors. The crease opened and was lost in the dark above. In the last stretch, the ceiling pulled up and away from the company.

The tight space opened so completely and suddenly it was like moving from the confines of a nutshell to the dome of the world.

Delicate clusters of crystal decorated the ceiling. They hung down into pillarless vaults. Crystals clumped like braziers high up on the walls. Every shade and spectrum of purple and lavender were captured in the hard glass. Greens and blues accented here and there in cubic mosaics. The space was a sanctuary that held the silent rhythm of prayer.

Tall, narrow limestone shelves fanned out in rows. Their ends were distant and lost in the colored dark. Their flanks disappeared on either side interrupted in places by bulks of crystal and rock. Railed ladders were mounted on the shelves.

Lana went to a simple workspace that was set off from the door. A wide tabletop was set on limestone blocks. Papers, quills, and a few tomes were organized on the table. A solitary chair was pushed back. She set the satchel down on the table. Gravitas and enthusiasm tore at her. Once she affirmed to herself that the seeds were safe, she turned to the company and said, "the Vaults of Corundum."

"Grieg's Balls," Kachota uttered.

"By Grieg." Lokah was overwhelmed by the vast cavern of crystal and light. He drifted as if drawn to the shelves. Upon closer inspection, there were little cubbyholes on the tall shelves.

Seeds.

Myriads upon myriads upon myriads of seeds.

He relaxed his light. The crystals gave off enough light near the front. Further down the light was effaced in lavender and emerald in the terminus between the shelves.

"How do we search such a place?" Mandavu asked Lokah.

"We find the ends and the edges. See if there are cracks or fissures. Feel for air. Look for frozen water. Listen for any sounds."

It will take us days to cover this space, Lokah said to himself.

The company staggered out into the Vaults while Counsel Lord Lana counted Mere's gift.

47

THE BATTLE OF CORUNDUM

Only a few Stair Guard remained when Lokah and the others came up from the Vaults. Counsel Lord Lana remained behind. She inspected the seeds by the light of a glowing crystal and scratched notes in a tome.

Stair Mark Uran and Counsel Lord Bremball stood in the empty refectory. The two brutes were gone, and the kitchen was empty.

They began their survey of the seed vault but knew they would need more time to check the dark corners of the crystal cavern. They were still depleted and although they were at midyear's eve they didn't expect to reach Aenguz even if they heard anything.

Lokah clutched his sword for any inchoate feeling his weapon might provide. Any connection or inkling of Aenguz's straights. But the metal was its usual self. When the light left his blade, as they left the hidden corridor, his *montmorillionite* looked inert as if it had never held any power at all. The Lay also offered him no answers.

"We will continue our search tomorrow," he said to Uran and Bremball.

Uran tensed. His jaw hardened but he did not object.

"Counsel Lord Lana is the seedmaster of the Vaults of Corundum.

She has allowed it. It will be so. Come tomorrow. The two guards will not bar your way."

Lokah nodded. He was prepared to fight and die against these two moments earlier but now he just felt heavy as if the Spine pressed down on him through the Glaize and the yellow crystal.

The company waited on Lokah's command. They looked drawn and defeated. Denial and hope could only be sustained in them so long. They would not give up, but their sullen eyes confessed that they had, in some way, accepted that this was the end for Aenguz.

They sauntered toward the stair when a sputtering sound crumpled up to the refectory. Staccato spurts followed on the first imperfect wail.

The Stair Mark said to Bremball, "That sounds like-"

"-the horn of Forhthulen." Bremball finished Uran's words.

They all ran to the head of the stair. Long bolts clattered into the wall and rattled to the floor. Uran ran down the stair with Bremball close behind. Lokah peered down as he ran. The wall of crystal that hung down from the ceiling blocked the entrance.

The Stair Mark ran to the boy. A shaft poked out from his chest at an awkward angle. The two Stair Guard nearest the braziers were dead. Long quilled shafts rose out of them like erect saplings.

The boy was spitting blood. The strap of the horn was caught underneath the shaft. He lay prostrate trying to breathe his last breaths to warn Corundum.

Uran cradled the boy's head. Grief and rage shook the old Stair Mark. He whispered some praise to the boy. The young novice's eyes were glassy and lost. Then he took the horn of Forhnthulen from around his neck and let out a clarion so loud that Lokah covered his ear as he passed.

Bremball ran to the edge of the entrance where the two guards had fallen. He peered into the dark Glaize and invoked blue light against the bleak. Two Erebim galloped down the boulevard. As the blue light strengthened,

Lokah could see the first edges of a wave of an Erebim horde. He could make out Tsurah too. Stones cut the air around them.

Bremball looked to Lokah. "Ready the defense. I will set a Warding."

Then he stepped down onto the frozen river and perched himself up on the corner of a half-submerged block of limestone.

He brought up his braided staff and called a different power from the chiseled staff. A wide dome of blue like a thin but powerful veil expanded from him over the further edge of the shore and the mouth of Corundum.

Just as the mist took shape and hordes of Erebim vomited out of the Glaize.

Shafts and stones were rebuffed. When the first Erebim reached the Warding, they slammed into it and were thrust back. They tested it with their dull axes and hammers. They howled and barked wildly frustrated by the wall of blue.

Stair Guard clamored down the stairs in paltry groups. The main body had not yet been raised. They formed into incomplete rows. Their dead companions stole the strength from their legs. They were drawn back from the edge while the others formed up.

Uran growled orders loud as the horn. He passed it off to the first Stair Guard and ordered him to keep blowing. Uran then wailed for the Stair Guard to hurry. When Step Marks arrived, he called out orders to them to form up their squads. Some still fumbled with their cloaks, others worked at the straps and buckles on their armor.

Counsel Lord Lana shuttled down the stair and ran through the growing throng of Stair Guard. She navigated past, taking note of the dead at the base of the stair. She called her staff to life and added her power to Bremball's. She set the staff before her as if nothing in heaven or earth would move her. Her red mane was a flurry of dark fire.

Lokah and the company were herded to the edge of the entrance as the lines of Stair Guard formed. Mond or Legerohn gave orders to Stokke. The young Moresi had taken Chimere back up to the balcony and had returned with bows and bunches of arrows for Legerohn and Mond. He told them that archers were lining the walkway above. Chimere was with them. The denizens of the keep were helping to ready the defense.

The other Counsel Lords came down and squeezed through the lines. The Stair Guard was starting to take stock of their courage. Lokah could see their fear. The Counsel Lords joined Lana and added their power to Bremball's.

The Mono Lord waddled through the lines. He looked stricken. His eyes found Lokah and the company. He seemed to be assuring himself that they were not betrayed by the Akkeidii and the Moresi. He asked Uran when he passed, "How much more time do you need?"

Stair Guard were still filing down the stairs. The back rows were filling up.

"Just a bit more. As much as you can give me." Uran ordered the braziers to be lined up across the front of the opening and set ablaze.

The chaos in the entrance was a kind of mirror to the chaos at the edge of the Warding.

Erebim and Tsurah closed in. They probed the edges of the protective dome. They climbed onto the frozen river at either side.

Furious hacking filled the air.

The Erebim parted and others brought up the bodies of the fallen Stair Guard from the watches. They hauled up their stripped bodies and pressed them against the blue veil. The effect on the Stair Guard was a mixture of horror and anger that denuded them in a way their training had not prepared them for. Lokah could see it.

One of the tall trees fell onto the blue dome.

The strain on Bremball was plain. The cords of his neck creased and stretched. His back leg quivered through the robe. The uneven block twisted his stance, torqued his knees and ankles.

Then the line of Erebim parted and through the murk, a figure floated. Their wild barks turned to temerity.

Gliding through air as if the Glaize was a revelation of mastery over atmosphere. The Urning glode through the horde and sneered at the Warding. Its contorted arms and jerrids flexed. The roiling fingers of its lappet responded in unison.

Another tree fell on the Warding. It formed a kind of chevron over the dome. It pointed like a wedge to pry open Corundum. The Urning started to unravel the spell that Bremball had cast and the power the Counsel Lords had enforced.

48

～～

APOTHEOSIS

Maintaining the *montmorillionite's* light was draining. Keeping the white light glowing as he climbed down through the cicatriced chamber required all of his focus. The bladder that Aenguz left had disappeared above. If there were walls the arms prevented the light from reaching them. Climbing down into the rank and rot of old death was counterintuitive too. He had to fight instincts to move away with each move lower.

The smell of rotted flesh grew intense. He tore off a sleeve and covered his mouth and tied it around his head. Holding couplets in his mind that might of mitigated the worst of the stench strained him too far. Aenguz hadn't slept since leaving the Oasis of Ganzir and now fatigue was abrogating him. And too, the thought that he would have to search through bones and despair to see if any had found the Dagba Stone but were either destroyed by it or too weakened to climb up and out denuded him. There were impaled skeletons here and there. The brittle space was treacherous.

When he found the floor, he was so drained that there was no relief for the opening that led below to the familiar feel of stone. Aenguz pushed past the rotted, meaty stench to an alcove of stone where he could breathe and rest. He would start again when he regained his strength.

When Aenguz woke, his first thought was water. The lack of it was going to be a problem. He was already thirsty from his climb down to stone. With the water he had, he could have searched for days. Now, without any, his time was shortened considerably. But water found ways into and through stone. He would climb down further.

He called a trifling light to his weapon and gathered himself. To steady himself, he sat up and rolled the blade back and forth on his palms in a kind of simple *salaage*. When he was ready, he called the brightest light he could summon from his blade. Shades of granite and basalt emerged and floated from the black, seemed impervious and unfamiliar with light. Below him was more black, but now it was framed by stone. If there was water it would be further down. The air was dry and still. Motes like bits of powder held in the air and contributed to the unearthly silence. The slight shifts and noises Aenguz made were the only sounds in the vast cavern. They were as unfamiliar as light in this place.

He drew back his power to a simple steady light and started the process to climb further down. Climbing downward was challenging but the rough granite was surer than the fragile arms above. He found creases to grab and notches to hold onto. He let himself down slowly and carefully. When he needed it, he used his weapon to cut away at the rock. The sound echoed briefly in the black and was forgotten.

The floor of the cavern held an odd sheen. When he brought his light up his heart sank. The bottom of the cavern was cast in stilled waters. A river had flowed beneath Corundum - at one time. Like the waters that flowed past the citadel, these were stilled too by a power far and above anything Aenguz could grasp. He walked on the river of glass looking for any pooled water, any signs of moisture gathered on the faces of the stone. It was dry as a tomb.

He walked downward as futility grew. The silence, the dust, the parched air told him that the cavern was sealed tight. No air moved. The space was large, but he would die of thirst before he suffocated. And another problem became obvious to him. If the Dagba Stone was down here, if it had reached the bottom somehow, if he even knew what it looked like, it might be resting beneath a river of liquid diamond. Even his *montmorillionite* barely chipped the surface when he tested it.

He searched along the stayed watercourse until he was too tired to hold the light. Time had no meaning in the cave. He slept when he was too exhausted to hold his eyes open.

Aenguz grew lightheaded. His mind drifted and his normally sure balance was failing. He stopped to rest more. His fatigue was its own comfort. But even at rest, his heart thumped as if he ran. His mouth was as dry as the rock. His normally sure muscles cramped. The thirst was denuding but hunger seemed only to nag. He couldn't be sure how much he had covered or how much there was to cover. At times he used light to peer into the glass but nothing unique shown in the impassive river.

The thirst without the heat of the Ganzir left him disoriented. Aenguz began to understand that he had failed.

He climbed up to a rounded ball of rock. In spite of the fascinating but frozen seethe and surge, the roiled water was too various and disquieting to rest on. His weapon dangled at his wrist. The failing light barely reached him. He couldn't hold it any longer. His hands were his eyes. He pulled himself up and draped over the rock as if he was thrown over the back of a horse.

He drew up the chain and pulled his weapon beside him.

His mottled arm was a rippled echo of the colored stone around him.

He would have lost his metal a dozen times if it weren't for the *mithrite* chain. His wrist bled but Selene's ribbon stemmed the worst of the cuts. The blue was blotted with dried black blood.

He had so hoped to return to her. Imagined that it would happen.

Imagined that the blight would pass over them. That they would have a life. That he would rock against her like when they first embraced. But now...

He let the delirium take him. The rock would hold him still.

Light flickered and feathered across his skin.

A blink in a normally steady light.

He shifted the blade.

There it was again.

He noticed a soft light. He thought it was a reflection from his own dying weapon, but it issued from a tiny crease behind him.

He turned toward the mouth of the fissure.

A warm light filled the crease. It was not reflected light. It was not silver. Not crystal gleaming in the bitter dark.

He sat up and twisted around and bent in to look inside.

A tuft of fine green grass, like the first sprout of grass seed, like baby's hair, filled the pocket. Tiny delicate flowers like the ones that grew high in the Mashu dotted the green. Lavender Spring Crocus and gentle blue Germander Speedwell nestled in the grass. Yellow mountain avens and cinquefoil reached for the source of the life-giving light.

At the heart of this verdant crèche was an object.

It looked like a kind of cochlear bone. Three rounded arms reached up from the base to a concave oval top. A roundish nub sat on the top of it. It was open in between. It seemed sculpted. A kind of melted bone or impeccably preserved fossil. Thin streaks of gray, like wisps of smoke, brushed lines through the stone. A fugue of faint red colored a third of it.

The Dagba Stone.

Aenguz wasn't sure he could trust his eyes.

It sat on its side just out of reach in the little alcove. What fluke brought it down here from the Well he couldn't guess. But the light and life around it only confirmed it as the Dagba Stone.

Aenguz reached in with his right hand but the Stone was too far down. And the position was not optimal. The only way he could reach in and see was via his left side. He transferred the mithrite end of the chain to his left wrist along with Selene's ribbon.

He eased his weapon down into the crevice. The waning silver light was drowned out by the Stone's warm yellow glow.

He passed the hook over the Stone and brought it under one of the three arms in the hollow space.

All of a sudden he wondered if he should touch such a thing.

'-no mortal hand may wield it.'

What alternative did he have?

Aenguz hooked the Dagba Stone.

An eruption of power exploded through the conduit of his body. Light arced like untamed lightening through him, effaced him. A pillar of force sent a shock wave that shook the earth and threatened the walls between the worlds. The cavern buckled and rent. Massive hunks of rock broke loose. Those sounds alone would have been cataclysmic. But next to the raw power of the Dagba Stone they were pebbles skipping across water.

A hurricane of force expanded, uncontrollable, unquenchable. A holocaust of light and power. All light gathered here in this moment and expended in an exaltation of creation.

Aenguz moved out of life and past death. The merest part of himself, the tiniest mote that he might call himself held to existence, or what had been existence.

There was no breath, no life, no survival, just effacing argence and erupting power.

All life, life in potential. Creation bottled and all at once released. The very beginning of time and the final dust of eschaton expressed, fulfilled, culminated, and released.

There was no processing of this, just moments of witnessing. No comprehension with thought or reason.

Aenguz was lost in a moment of apotheosis, an eon of expanding revelation.

Another force. One more present and more anxious for release surrounded him, enveloped him, and devoured him whole.

Freed waters exploded into motion like the white fire. Potential rushed and released. Restrained flowing, ceased pouring, elemental falls stayed now exalted and cascaded all at once. A jubilance bigger than the rise of all the mountains in all the Lands of the Earth climaxed. Release, rightness, natural order resumed.

The waters took him and everything else in the cavern away in an epochal flood.

49

WATERS

Stair Mark Uran talked with the dozen or so Stair Guard he had called to his side at the edge. He was telling them how to protect and retrieve Bremball. The Counsel Lord was fading. Flesh and bone could only endure so much power. The battle would soon be upon them. They would have to catch Bremball and fight the Erebim. "Draw him back, quickly. Do not stop to help your brothers. The Counsel Lord is your first priority."

The horde seemed to sense that the Counsel Lord was fading. They had a clearer view of his face than Lokah had. The burned and scorched bodies of the dead Stair Guard smoldered at the shore.

The Stair Guard left room for the Akkeidii and the Moresi at the right side of the entrance.

Mandavu and Kachota looked grim. They uttered the names of the Akkeidii that the Erebim and Sallow had killed.

"For Ondo. For Roberge. For Hallock," and so on, through the line of their dead. Over and over, they counted up the numbers of Erebim they intended to slay in retribution.

Legerohn, Mond, and Stokke tested the strength of the Stair Guard's bows. They kept a bushel of arrows between them, and they flanked the Akkeidii.

"Ready yourselves," Lokah said. "Bremball is about to fall."

Then suddenly a concussion buckled the floor. The keep cracked as if old stones were settling under fresh weight. Light blazed through the walls. The home of the sun was within Corundum. The line of invaders looked grotesque and silly in the bright light. They shut and covered their eyes and faces. The asps on the Urning shot out straight and then dropped.

Bremball's Warding snapped out like a dead spark.

Then the waters released.

The sound of rapids started, continued, as if the whole host had been deaf until that moment.

The horrible barks and howls of the Erebim in the face of the dying light were effaced. The front most of their number fell forward in twos and threes. Those clamoring at the edges of the river dropped into the surge.

Bremball was carried down on the block.

He looked like a captain on the prow of a doomed vessel.

His eyes passed over Lokah and found Counsel Lord Lana. She had somehow kept her feet.

She followed Bremball's gaze. A word formed on his mouth for her. Then the block sank, and the river took him, submerged him.

The last thing Lokah saw of Bremball was his blue robe pitching over the falls.

Mond, and Stokke let a volley fly into the horde. In a smooth rhythm, they let shaft after shaft fly.

It was enough to shake the Stair Guard out of their shock. The archers added their bows to the Moresi's.

The Erebim regrouped and began snapping their arms down on their atl atls. Bolts flew into the ranks of the Stair Guard, bounced off shields.

The trunks dropped when the Warding fell. They reached across the span over the rising froth. They crossed between the footings at the entrance.

The Stair Guard tried to move them, but the massive trees were too heavy. And levered javelins took those soldiers who tried to move them first.

There seemed to be an unending supply of Erebim.

The Urning floated to the side and used one of the logs to glide over and reach the keep. The Counsel Lords were barely on their knees. Lana stared down the falls as if her life had already fallen. The Stair Guard pitched spears and arrows at the Urning. He caught them still in the air and let them drop.

Lokah and Legerohn moved in to meet the dark form. He felt the first tendrils of the paralyzing force. The Stair Guard nearest him became like statues. Mandavu and Kachota were too far away. He could not strike their weapons as Aenguz had done to him. He would be paralyzed like the rest. Erebim climbed on the logs after the Urning. Corundum was about to be taken.

Lokah felt a low rumble like a deep earthquake. Almost like the opening of Grieg's Gate.

His arms were hardening with a rictus. The Urning was closing in. A roar greater than the rapids reached him. What was that sound? What ill had the Erebim concocted?

He looked up the slope. His head was not yet gripped.

A wall of water cascaded in an avalanche down the mountainside.

His eyes splayed open. He called out the only words from the Lay to the others and shouted, "Anchor's might-" and he grabbed Legerohn and took him to the ground. His sword changed and instantly weighed a ton. It dropped to the crystal floor. He drew in a loud breath accenting it for the others to hear.

There was no time to explain. He only hoped the Makans understood the two words from the Lay.

A new white effaced the forest's edge, sprayed the corner of the entrance.

Mandavu gripped Mond and then let his mace carry the two to the ground.

Kachota tossed one of his tomahawks to Stokke who was too far to reach. He snatched it out of the air. The ax pulled him to the ground like a stone. Kachota let the irrefusable weight of his ax pin him to the ground.

The Urning had no theurgy against such raw natural power. Something pent up in the waters seemed to make it rush more quickly. The stalled kinetic energy was expending in an irrefusable crush. The water took the Urning without any interruption and carried it over the falls.

Then the flood drowned Lokah and gorged on the entrance in a violent surge.

Lokah felt Legerohn squeeze him with all his might.

They were flung up.

Their legs fluttered like pennons in a gale beneath the waters.

Lokah took the opportunity to wrap his legs around Legerohn. The Prince was slipping.

Somehow his other hand found his hilt and he hung on with every ounce of his strength.

The force of the water threatened to rip him loose. His lungs strained to the point of breaking. Lokah fought against the desire to gasp. Would surely drown if he gave in.

Then the direction of the water turned, and he and Legerohn dropped back to the crystal floor.

His lungs burst just as the water pulled away from his face. Legerohn was coughing at his chest.

He rolled his drenched head to look at the mouth of Corundum. Mandavu clutched Mond. The two were coughing out water. Kachota and Stokke clung to each ax as if it was some kind of float drawing them in toward the keep.

The entrance was nearly empty. A few mounds of burgundy clung together. Water slipped around them as if they were islands in a shallow river. A smattering of shields and spears were scattered across the floor.

Four of the braziers were gone. Lost to the flood. A pair were knotted together and tumbled against the wall near the narrow stair at the mouth. A drenched mound of blue was wedged in a toppled brazier. Red hair matted and mopped the floor. Stroud was tangled in beside her. He may have protected Lord Lana. Lokah could see no other blue in the entrance.

Archers and Stair Guard rushed down the stair. As the surge receded and was replaced by the roar of the mountain river, Lokah heard someone yell for 'Rope'.

50

≈≈

POIESIS

Water filled Aenguz's nose and mouth. His lungs were on the verge of surrendering. On the verge of an enormous gulp of newly enlivened water. As if from the Earth's first moments of creation. The cascade of tumbling and rolling in a torrent had no meaning.

He craved air. His lungs demanded it. The collapse and rush of newly released waters were drowning him. The release was as cataclysmic as a detonation that could rend the Earth once and for all.

He was drowning in the mouth of Grieg's Gate. The current had him and was pulling him under to an unknown depth. Flecks of ice scratched against his skin, caught in his hair. There was a vague worry of getting caught, of getting found out but he was too outside of himself to remember why or to care about that in the midst of submersion. The world was water, and he was not meant for it.

He was submerged in the Wester and unconscious. Sand and grit brushed over him. The thick current had him.

When he slammed into rock, his arms wrapped automatically around the stone. His cartwheel tossed him hard against it. This stone was not the smooth stone-metal of Grieg's Gate. Nor was it the hard back of a sandbar. He clung to it like the finger of a Hyrrokkin. His clothes were all but gone. Shreds of fabric like frayed string trailed and whipped. Their shielding purpose was for the sun, not water.

The froth and spray of rapids were all around him. His air-starved lungs exploded. He was able to breathe in between violent choking gasps.

There was light.

By increments, the distance between his soul and his body closed.

Aenguz inched up higher to take a better hold of the rock and take in more air. Rivers of water poured around him.

His eyes fluttered open, bleary from the agitated froth. Light and rainbows shot across his vision. The cynosure of the sun was perched on the edge of the horizon like a proclamation. The dawn of midyear. It blazed out as if this was the first dawn. Firmament waters had cleared the air. The lines between night and day were reaffirmed, Earth and sky reestablished; confirmed as natural and right.

The Glaize was gone.

He clung to the rock as if it was the only solid thing in existence. As if it was the last scrap of the earth at the end of the apocalypse. He was at the edge of a pool ringed by teeth like the one he clung to. A roof of rock reached overhead.

The apotheosis of colored light and firmament waters had taken him up and out of himself. Had taken him to where the distinctions between life and death were nullified by the laws and edicts that governed the shaping of the world. The nascent but immutable laws that crafted the universe and shaped the Law of Creation itself.

Aenguz found himself at the head of a waterfall perched over the Lands of the Earth. The tail of the falls spilled out of sight. Below him, the white torrent was deafening. The crash of water was the only sound in this new world.

Ahead, beyond the complication of rainbows, a single massive rainbow bridged the Wester. Thousands of other rainbows filled the air in a flock of light. It seemed that if he looked hard enough, he might be able to peer into the ether of the White Earth.

Below, down the perilous plummet, he could see rich brown loam being churned up in the Wester. The river whose true banks had been dry and essentially barren for an age were now flooding along the shores. A glut of water was moving eastward. The Rursh Keleg was submerged. The old road was no more for the time being. Water poured into the folds and wedges in between the hills. The forest on the left bank was inundated. The whole wider world was stretched out before him and threatened by a flood. A sudden but vibrant flood.

Aenguz sensed that this surge would rectify things along the river. The animals penned on the edge of the Wester by the Tsurah would be freed. The fell creatures that dwelled in the silty channel at the heart of the Wester would be churned up and taken away, perhaps even down to the Great Southern Sea.

The logjam at the convergence of the Wester and the White would be dislodged, obliterated. The evidence of the crimes against the One Forest swept away.

Tiny motes were floating and coursing all around Aenguz. Seeds, tens of thousands of seeds were pouring out and down the falls into the Wester. They would flood the banks and barren-blighted Lands of the Earth and stripped borders of the One Forest. The Vaults of Corundum had been rent by the Dagba Stone.

The mouth of the Galangall would back up. The mounts at the entrance of that river would be drowned. At least for a time.

Down the southern arm of the Wester, at a peninsula of rock near a driftwood crowned cairn, the water would rise. And the barrow would become an island. The driftwood littered shore would be cleared and the root wall of the One Forest covered.

But Aenguz survived.

The swell moved out into the distance toward the sun. A rich mocha flood pushed by a white rush.

He was perched on a height that would surely kill him if he let go. The perilousness of his situation rushed into him like the water that threatened to pull him over.

How would he get to safety?

The water sounded like it bore his name. Was it a kind of gratitude? A warning?

He looked around, and over his right shoulder was Mandavu. The giant was wading along the toothed shore of the pool. A rope was lashed around his waist. It led back to Lokah and Kachota.

Legerohn, Mond, and Stokke were in the line as well braced on a crystal stair. They were soaked through and through. Their mouths moved but he could only hear the giant.

Mandavu fought through the water, stone by stone to reach Aenguz.

Then suddenly, he remembered the Dagba Stone. Lost now somewhere in the torrent below. It would be lost again and not found in time.

And what about his weapon? That was lost too somewhere in the deep renewed headwater of the Wester.

There was a pain at his wrist. He bent his hand and grasped the *mithrite* chain. Selene's ribbon was gone. The unleashed torrent had ripped it away. But it had protected his fragile skin from much of the metal cord's teeth.

He wound the chain in his hand until he felt the tip of the dagger. The keen edge, that to anyone else would be impossibly sharp was as dull as wood to Aenguz. He drew his weapon up and out through the crest of the waterfall.

And there, threaded through the hook and the spike at the head of his weapon was the fossilized cochlear Dagba Stone. Through its own cryptic theurgy, the Dagba Stone had lodged impossibly onto the hardest metal in all the Lands of the Earth as if it was designed to fit there. His *montmorillionite* gleamed with an elemental joy.

～

Here ends

Ruinwaster's Bane

Book One

of

The Annals of the Last Emissary

The story continues in

Book Two

of

The Annals of the Last Emissary

The Earthmight War

GLOSSARY

Aenguz: Warrior of the Sidor Clan. Son of Sairik fallen Ruler of the Akkeidii. Also named the Last Emissary.

Akkeidii: People of the Mashu.

Arkarua: A Ruinwaster.

Azari: Remnant of the One Race. Bearers of the One Sight.

Baierl Clan: Clan of the Akkeidii from the line of Michael Baierl.

Bane of Corundum: Another name for the Well of Sorrows.

Black Earth, the: A hell.

Blasted Flats, the: A land eradicated by Tycho Ruinwaster.

Bremball: A Counsel Lord of Corundum.

Byrgir: Lord of the Baierl Clan.

Cairngorm, the: Southern point of the Lower Mashu. Burial ground for the Akkeidii Heroes of the Last Battle.

Carrowen Celd: The Deepest Hole. Domain of Lord Morgrom.

Channi: Remille's wife.

Chimere: A Moresi.

Chosen Freeholder: Mystics charged with warding the treasures of the Earth.

Cleve, the: The former road between the Upper and Lower Lands.

cog: A primitive river boat.

Counsel Lords: Protectors of the Lands of the Earth.

Corundum: Home of the Counsel Lords.

Creche of Life, the: Another name for the One Forest.

Crystal Citadel: Another name for Corundum.

Cuzzoul: A Stonemage master. Son of Curufin.

Dagba Stone, the: A powerful talisman used to channel the poiesis of creation. Lost in the Last Battle.

Dahlward: Lord of the Deerherds, father of Sairak, grandfather of Aenguz.

Deerherd: A lore wise Akkeidii adept in the ways of the Mashu and a tender of roe deer.

Divider, the: Counsel Lord name for Lord Morgrom.

Divine Oculum: A powerful ocular room in Corundum used to view the Lands of the Earth.

Dormund Treachery, the: A bitter betrayal during a Challenge. Reviled by the Akkeidii.

durann: Akkeidii Stonemage tool used to manipulate stone.

Earthmight: The last fortress built by the Remnant and unified peoples. Also called the One King's Keep.

Erebim: Servants of Lord Morgrom.

Finit Clan: Clan of the Akkeidii from the line of Estevobahn.

First Treacher, the: Moresi name for Lord Morgrom.

Flayer, the: Akkeidii name for Lord Morgrom.

Forhnthulen, the Stairs of: The long stair that leads to Corundum.

Galangall Wash: A bridge city built by the Hyrrokkin for Lord Morgrom.

Gambl Clan: Clan of the Akkeidii from the line of Lerxst.

Ganzir: A vast desert made by Tycho Ruinwaster.

Gildelmun: A rare potent long-lived tree of the Lands.

gingrass: An analeptic herb.

Glaize, the: A persistent mist that occludes Corundum and the Divine Oculum.

Gran Lake: Lake near Straathgard.

Great Southern Sea, the: The great sea to the south.

Grieg's Gate: A man-made headwater that bars entrance to the Upper Mashu.

Grieg Sidor: Hero forefather of the Akkeidii. Also called the Venturer.

Haag's Lake: Lake in the Lower Mashu.

Hallock: Champion of the Gambl Clan.

Hearthless: Shunned Akkeidii forbidden a home.

Hertha: Dahlward-mate. Clan Mother of the Akkeidii and of the Sidor Clan.

Hernus Kriel: Hero of the Akkeidii. Best friend of Grieg Sidor.

hulk: A primitive river barge.

Hyrrokkin: Stone creatures thought lost in the Lands. Builders of the first structures.

Inverlieth: Home of the Moresi.

Jorgen: Squire to Aenguz.

Kachota: Warrior of the Makan Clan. Son of Warrum. Brother of Mandavu.

Kaissene: Land of the Sallow.

Keystone of Creation: Another name for the Dagba Stone.

Kriel Clan: Akkeidii Clan from the line of Hernus Kriel.

Lana: Counsel Lord.

Larau: Slocum's wife.

Last Battle, the: The old battle between Lord Morgrom and the Counsel Lords where Morgrom was thrown down and the Dagba Stone was lost.

Last Emissary, the: Honorific given to Aenguz by Lord Morgrom.

Legerohn: A Moresi leader.

Leono: A Straathgardian fisherman.

Lihkit Vale: Village in the Lower Land.

Llangollen: Seaside village in the Lower Land.

Lokah: Warrior of the Kriel Clan. Son of Ruel. Champion of the Challenge.

Lord Morgrom, the Divider: Counsel Lord name for Lord Morgrom. Enemy of the Lands of the Earth.

Makan Clan: Clan of the Akkeidii from the line of Ryker.

Mandavu: Warrior of the Makan Clan. Champion of the Challenge. Son of Warrum. Older brother of Kachota.

Mashu, the: Mountain home of the Akkeidii.

Mashu, Lower: Lands south of Grieg's Gate.

Mashu, Upper: Lands north of Grieg's Gate.

Mere Gurudev: The Chosen Freeholder of the Ganzir.

Mezekiah: A Ruinwaster.

Mia: Granddaughter of Mono Lord Venrahl.

Millin, the river: A river in the Mashu.

Mimirmere: Pool at Corundum beneath the Divine Oculum.

Mithrite: A rare metal fashioned by the Moresi akin to *montmorillionite*.

Mond: A Moresi. Warder of Legerohn.

Montmorillion lore: Study and knowledge of the properties of *montmorillionite*.

Montmorillionite: Rare metal found only in the Mashu engendered with magical properties.

Moodley: A Deerherd of the Kriel Clan.

Moresi: People of Inverlieth.

morillion: A rare loam that possesses healing properties. Made of *montmorillionite*.

Oasis of Ganzir: A secret place hidden within the Ganzir.

Oblivion: Azari name for Lord Morgrom.

Ochroch: A Hyrrokkin. Stonethrall.

Ondolfur: Warrior and Champion of the Finit Clan.

One Bridge, the: A remnant artifact of the One Race.

One Forest, the: The first great forest of the earth. Also known as the Creche of Life.

One King, the: Thelen, the Ruler of Earthmight.

One Race: The state of all the peoples of the Lands before the Division.

One Sight: Ability of the Azari to all share the same sight.

Ophiactii: A Ruinwaster.

Oso, the: River between Gran Lake and the Wester.

Philamay: Thank you in Moresi tongue.

Pogacar: Step Mark of the Stair Guard.

purna: an immuring salve.

Ragbald: Warrior and Honor Guard of the Sidor Clan.

Rainbow's Creche: Another name for Mimirmere.

Reaver, the: Hyrrokkin name for Lord Morgrom.

Remille: Champion of the Gambl Clan.

Remnant, the: Fractured races left after the dissolution of the One Race.

Ridder: Son of Ragbald. Champion of the Sidor Clan.

Roberge: Son of Lakaadon. Champion of the Baierl Clan. Older brother of Strey.

roona: an herb that aids in wakefulness.

Ruinwasters: Five powerful servants of Lord Morgrom. Banished to the Black Earth.

Rursh Keleg: An ancient road that leads from the City of the Sho-tah to the Stairs of Fohrnthulen.

Saiga: A white herbivorous antelope.

Sairik: Lord of the Sidor Clan, Ruler of the Akkeidii. Polemarch of the Akkeidii Warriors. Son of Dahlward Lord of the Deerherds.

salaage: A Warrior's practice with a *montmorillionite* weapon.

Sallow: The denizens of Kaissene, loyal to Lord Morgrom.

Selene: Sidor maiden betrothed to Aenguz.

Selvin: A Deerherd of the Sidor Clan. Brother of Selene.

Shattered Lands, the: Ruinwaster destroyed lands in the southwest.

Shivic: A Ruinwaster.

Sho-tah: A Remnant people annihilated by Tycho Ruinwaster.

Sho-tah, the City of the: City ruined by Tycho for disobeying Lord Morgrom.

Shudaak: Son of Stellan. Champion of the Finit Clan.

Sidor Clan: Clan of the Akkeidii from the line of Grieg Sidor.

Silvercryst: Common name for *montmorillionite*.

Slocum: Son of Shurn. Champion of the Kriel Clan.

Spine of the Earth, the: The north south mountain range that divides the Upper and Lower Lands of the Earth.

Stonemage: A lore wise Akkeidii who studies the properties of stone and building.

Stokke: A Moresi.

Straathgard: City and region of Men.

Strey: Son of Lakaadon. Champion of the Baierl Clan. Brother of Roberge.

Stroud: Azari of Corundum.

Sunfall Sea: The sea in the west.

Surasanskeld: Old lore used to fuse *montmorillionite* with bone.

Tahnka: Honorific for Legerohn among the Moresi.

Tavinahl: Lord of the Kriel Clan.

Tormont Vale: A village in the Lower Lands.

trullen: The diminished offspring of the Hyrrokkin.

Tsurah: Reptile race loyal to Lord Morgrom.

Tycho: A Ruinwaster.

Tycho's Dune: A slow moving dune east of the Ganzir.

Uran: Stair Mark of the Stair Guard.

Urning: Powerful beings loyal to Lord Morgrom.

Venrahl: Mono Lord of Corundum.

Venturer, the: Honorific for Grieg Sidor.

verrandulum: Artifacts of the One Race.

Vopal: Squire to Ridder.

wadi: A valley or ravine dry except during the rainy season.

wakeel: A trustee, an agent.

Warrior: An Akkeidii with knowledge of *montmorillionite* lore and the ways of battle.

Warrum: The Makan Clan Lord.

Water bridge: An ancient means for relocating water.

Water Gate: Another name for Grieg's Gate.

Well of Sorrows: Shaft where the Dagba Stone is believed to be lost.

Wester, the river: A river in the Lands.

White, the river: A river in the Mashu.

White Deeps, the: The cold north where glaciers grow.

White Earth, the: A heaven.

Woe Sower: Common name for Lord Morgrom used by the peoples of the Lands.

World Stair, the: A remnant artifact of the One Race.

Once in a dream,
I dreamt above a dream.

NOTES

WHEN I WAS YOUNG it was a different time. When I was enrapt with a book, I would send a letter to the publisher and wait for months or years for a reply. Sometimes I only received a stock reply. Sometimes I received a handwritten note.

Today you can reach out to an author and hear back within days. When I reached out to one of my favorite authors via email and actually received a reply, I was stunned. I still have all those notes, letters, and emails.

In the past, one only learned about new books by walking into a bookstore and seeing what was on display. Now the avenues to learn about new books are endless.

Today digital impressions, followers, email lists, and algorithms rule the day. Reaching out to an author in a moment is the norm. And it is always appreciated. One thing that can really help an author is to leave a review on Amazon, Goodreads, etc. If you enjoyed this story, please take a moment to leave a review even if it's just a rating. It may help someone else who wants to read a story like this one.

Thank you to all the readers. I'm grateful that you chose to embark on the venture of the Last Emissary. If you are interested in learning more, I can be found at www.jjasonhicks.com, jjhicks@jjasonhicks.com and @JJasonHicks on twitter, Instagram, Medium, LinkedIn, Facebook, and TikTok.

ACKNOWLEDGMENTS

No BOOK IS AN island. Few dreams come to the light of day by the efforts of a single person. It takes a village, a team, a close-knit group of supporters and allies. It is fair to say that this idea, this book, would not exist in its current form without the aid of so many careful hands, insightful eyes, and generous hearts.

"If there's a book that you want to read but it hasn't been written yet, then you must write it." -Toni Morrison

My deepest thanks to Dana Pittman. Her editorial insights revealed what the story lacked and how to fix it. She helped reveal the buried soul of this book. And to my copy editor Megan Joseph. Her deft hand and encouragement helped apply the final brush strokes to this book. Without my editors, this book would not exist in this form.

Along the long journey of this book, there were others that helped, read, supported, and inspired me throughout my life and the life of this book. There have been many Stevens in my life. Without them, this book would have never been birthed from my mind.

Without Steven Piskula's careful reading of the tattered version of this draft and his targeted insights and hard-earned writing wisdom as well as his careful encouragement, I could never have sustained the necessary drive to continue revising and rewriting to get through to the final manuscript. It's a long way from Mythology 101. Thank you, my friend.

Without Steven Pressfield's encouragement, acknowledgment, and support over the years, I might never have allowed myself to believe that I could complete the task of writing this book. His emails, fiction, non-fiction, videos, blogs, Jabs, and Writing Wednesday posts allowed me to entertain the thought that I could complete such an enterprise and that I could devote my life to writing. Many thanks, Steve.

Without Stephen R. Donaldson, I would not have been inspired to write this book and the ones that followed. Thanks to my brother Michael for introducing me to Thomas Covenant.

Without Stephen King, I would not have cultivated a love of reading. With so many books over so many formative years, once I got past the envy of his prolific production, I could enjoy the tales.

Shawn Coyne's Story Grid book and the conference I attended in 2019 gave me a near-unending stream of writing insights and tips that I refer to, recall, and remember to this day. If ever there is a roadblock or a pause, or confusion, I just recall his professorial insights and I'm right back on track. Thank you, Shawn.

Thanks to my beta-readers, ARC readers, and proofreaders. Without their eyes, I would have overlooked much in the drafting of this book.

Thank you to Jeff Brown for the amazing cover art and cover design. Seeing my world come to life with such a vivid rendering still leaves me in awe.

There are so many YouTubers, BookTubers, and AuthorTubers to thank that I could have a list a mile long. What a great time to be an author where you have so many resources and reviewers and coaches on hand to help you. It makes what authors did before the advent of technology or the internet seem even more impressive.

I always had More(s)i in my story, but because of Jenna Moreci they became more than they originally were. Because of her, the Warriors selected for the Challenge became Champions. I owe a debt of gratitude to the Cyborg Queen and her funny and straight-talking videos. I learned a lot watching them, especially what not to do.

There have been courageous readers and tireless supporters. Kris Hicks, Mike Hicks, Paul Hicks, Tracee Hicks, Chris Wees, Kim Young, Aaron DeBoer, Brian Neidermeier, Jessica Riley, and Jason Riley. No book is an island. And when I came up for air these people gave me the encouragement I needed to keep going. I am grateful for their patience to listen to me while I verbalized my understanding of the writing process.

This book is dedicated to my wife Jennifer Hicks. Without her support, this book simply would not exist.

AUTHOR BIO

J. Jason Hicks studied English Literature, Political Science, and World Religions with a focus on classic literature at the University of Wisconsin Oshkosh. *Ruinwaster's Bane: The Annals of the Last Emissary* is his debut novel. He lives in Tucson, Arizona with his wife and his dog. A one-eyed Boxer named Drake.

www.jjasonhicks.com

jjhicks@jjasonhicks.com

Printed in the USA
CPSIA information can be obtained
at www.ICGtesting.com
LVHW041659091123
763265LV00035B/1112/J

9 781960 481085